Withdrawn from Stock
Dublin City Public Libraries

The 9th Girl

D1513450

Also by Tami Hoag

TAMI HOAG

The
9th
Girl

First published in Great Britain in 2013 by Orion Books,
an imprint of The Orion Publishing Group Ltd
Orion House, 5 Upper Saint Martin's Lane
London WC2H 9EA

An Hachette UK Company

1 3 5 7 9 10 8 6 4 2

Copyright © Indelible Ink, Inc. 2013

The moral right of Tami Hoag to be identified as the author
of this work has been asserted in accordance with
the Copyright, Designs and Patents Act of 1988.

All rights reserved. No part of this publication may be
reproduced, stored in a retrieval system, or transmitted
in any form or by any means, electronic, mechanical,
photocopying, recording, or otherwise, without the
prior permission of both the copyright owner
and the above publisher of this book.

All the characters in this book are fictitious, and any resemblance to
actual persons living or dead is purely coincidental.

A CIP catalogue record for this book is
available from the British Library.

ISBN (Hardback) 978 1 4091 0959 4
ISBN (Export Trade Paperback) 978 1 4091 0960 0
ISBN (Ebook) 978 1 4091 0961 7

Printed in Great Britain by
Clays Ltd, St Ives plc

The Orion Publishing Group's policy is to use papers that
are natural, renewable and recyclable products and made
from wood grown in sustainable forests. The logging and
manufacturing processes are expected to conform to the
environmental regulations of the country of origin.

www.orionbooks.co.uk

With thanks to Susan and Tina for keeping me fed and connected to the real world, if only by a fraying thread. Good friends on the front line of deadline.

And with thanks to Nick Tortora for introducing me to the world of mixed martial arts and for helping to keep me focused and sane (more or less) through the war that is writing a book.

1

New Year's Eve. The worst possible night of the year to be the limo driver of a party bus. Of course, Jamar Jackson had really not found a night or an occasion when it was good to be a limo driver. In the last two years working for his cousin's company, he had come to the conclusion that the vast majority of people hired stretch limos for one reason: so they could be drunk, high, obnoxious, and out of control without fear of being arrested. Getting from one place to the next was secondary.

He drove the Wild Thing—a twenty-passenger white Hummer with zebra-print upholstery. A rolling nightclub awash in purple light, it was tricked out with a state-of-the-art sound system, satellite television, and a fully stocked bar. It cost a month's rent to hire on New Year's Eve, which included a twenty percent gratuity—which was what made hauling these assholes around worth the headache.

Jamar worked hard for his money. His evenings consisted of shrieking girls in various stages of undress as the night wore on and frat boys who, regardless of age, never lost the humor of belching

Leabharlanna Poibli Chathair Baile Átha Cliath

Dublin City Public Libraries

and farting. Without fail, driving party groups always involved at least one woman sobbing, one verbal and/or physical altercation between guests, some kind of sex, and a copious amount of vomit by journey's end. And Jamar handled it all with a smile.

Twenty percent gratuity included was his mantra.

On the upside: These experiences were all grist for the mill. He was a sociology grad student at the University of Minnesota with a master's thesis to write.

His customers for this New Year's Eve were a group of young attorneys and their dates, drunk on champagne and a couple of days' freedom from seventy-hour workweeks. His assignment for the evening was carting them from one party to the next until they all passed out or ended up in the hospital with alcohol poisoning.

Sadly, the night was young by New Year's Eve standards, the booze was flowing, and if he had to listen to Maroon 5's "Moves Like Jagger" one more time, he was going to run this fucking bus into a ditch.

Twenty percent gratuity included . . .

His passengers were loud. They wouldn't stay in their seats. If one of them wasn't sprawled on the floor, it was another of them. Every time Jamar checked the rearview he caught a flash of female anatomy. One girl couldn't keep her top from falling down; another's skirt was so short she was a squirming advertisement for the salon that did her bikini wax.

Jamar tried to keep his eyes on the road, but he was a twenty-five-year-old guy, after all, with a free view of a naked pussy behind him.

They had started the evening at a private party in the tony suburb of Edina, then moved to a party in a hip restaurant in the Uptown district. Now they would make their way to downtown Minneapolis to a hot club.

The streets were busy and dangerous with drivers who were half-drunk and half-lost. Compounding the situation, the temperature was minus seventeen degrees, and the moisture from the car exhaust was condensing and instantly freezing into a thin layer of clear ice that was nearly impossible to see on the pavement. An unwelcome complication on a rotten stretch of road that was pockmarked with potholes big enough to swallow a man whole.

Twenty percent gratuity included . . .

Jamar's nerves were vibrating at a frequency almost as loud as the music. His head was pounding with the beat. He had one eye on the girl in the back, one eye on the road. They were coming to a spaghetti tangle of streets and highways crossing and merging into one another. Hennepin and Lyndale, 55 and 94.

The girl with her top down started making out with Miss Naked Pussy. The hoots and hollers of the partygoers rose to a pitch to rival Adam Levine's voice.

". . . moves like Jagger . . . I got the moves like Jagger . . ."

Jamar was only vaguely aware of the box truck passing on his left and the dark car merging onto the road in front of him. He wasn't thinking about how long it would take to stop the tank he was driving if the need arose. His attention was fractured among too many things.

Then, in a split second, everything changed.

Brake lights blazed red too close in front of him.

Jamar shouted, "Shit!" and hit his brakes in reflex.

The Wild Thing just kept rolling. The car seemed to drop, then bounce, the trunk flying open.

Now his attention was laser focused on what was right in front of him, a tableau from a horror movie illuminated by harsh white xenon headlights. A woman popped up in the trunk of the car like a freak-show jack-in-the-box. Jamar shrieked at the sight as the woman flipped out of the trunk, hit the pavement, and came upright. Directly in front of him.

He would have nightmares for years after. She looked like a freaking zombie—one eye wide open, mouth gaping in a scream; half her face looked melted away. She was covered in blood.

The screams were deafening then as the Wild Thing struck the zombie—Jamar's screams, the screams of the girls behind him, the shouts of the guys. The Hummer went into a skid, sliding sideways on the ice-slick road. Bodies were tumbling inside the vehicle. There was a bang and a crash from the back, then another. The Hummer came to a rocking halt as Jamar's bladder let go and he peed himself.

Twenty percent gratuity included . . .

Happy New Year's fucking Eve.

2

"Happy freakin' New Year," Sam Kovac said with no small amount of disgust.

What a mess. Headlights and portable floodlights illuminated the scene, with road flares and red-and-blue cruiser lights adding a festive element. The television news vans had already swooped in and set up camp. The on-air talent bundled into their various team color-coordinated winter storm coats had staked out their own angles on the wreck.

Fucking vultures. Kovac kept his head down and his hat brim low as he walked toward the scene.

A white Hummer of ridiculous proportions sat sideways across two lanes of road. The back window was busted out, allowing a glimpse of the interior: purple LED lights and zebra-striped upholstery.

Erstwhile holiday revelers milled around the vehicle, overdone and underdressed for the weather. Most of them were either talking or texting on their cell phones. The girls, who had undoubtedly begun the evening looking the height of hip fashion, now looked like cheap hookers on a hard night: hair a mess, makeup smeared, clothes disheveled. They were in short dresses. One was wrapped in a fur coat; another was wrapped in a tuxedo jacket. They all either had been crying or were crying, while their dates tried to look important and serious in the face of the crisis.

A Lexus coupe appeared to have rear-ended the party-mobile, which hadn't worked out for the Lexus. With the front end smashed back almost to the windshield, the car looked like a pug dog on wheels. A third car had hit the Lexus from behind. A Chevy Caprice with a busted-up front end had pulled to the shoulder.

But Kovac hadn't come out in the minus-freezing-ass cold on New Year's Eve to attend to a three-car pileup. He was a homicide cop. His business was murder. How murder figured into this mess, he had no idea. But it was a good bet it was going to take half the damn night to sort it out.

Not that he had anything better to do with his time. He didn't have any hot date to ring in the New Year with. He wasn't going to any parties to watch people get drunk and make fools of themselves for no other reason than having to buy a new calendar.

"Happy New Year, Detective."

Kovac growled at the fresh-faced uniformed officer. "What's happy about it?"

"Uh . . . nothing, I guess."

"I'm assuming there's somebody dead here. Should we be happy about that?"

"No, sir. I'm sorry, sir."

"Jesus, Kojak. Just 'cause you're not getting laid tonight doesn't mean you get to take it out on young Officer Hottie here."

Kovac turned his scowl on his partner as she walked up. Nikki Liska was decked out in her standard subzero outfit—a thick down-filled parka that reached past her knees and a fur-lined Elmer Fudd hat with the earflaps down. She looked ridiculous.

Liska was five foot five by sheer dint of will. Kovac called her Tinks—short for Tinker Bell on steroids. Small but mighty. If she'd been any bigger, she would have taken over the world by now. But bundled up like this she looked like the little brother in *A Christmas Story*, ready to have someone knock her down on the way to school so she could lie helpless on her back like a stranded turtle.

"How do you know I'm not getting laid tonight?" he grumbled.

"You're here, aren't you?" she said. "Neither one of us is ringing in the New Year with an orgasm. And I *did* have a date, thank you very much."

"Yeah, well, I've got news for you," Kovac said. "If that's what you were wearing, you weren't gonna get laid either."

"Shows what you know," Liska shot back. "I'm bare-ass naked under this coat."

Kovac barked a laugh. They'd been partners for a long time. While she could still make him blush, he was never surprised by the shit that came out of her mouth.

The uniform didn't know what to make of either of them. He might have been blushing. Then again, his face might have been frozen.

"So what's the story here, Junior?" Kovac asked.

"The guy driving the Hummer says a zombie jumped out of the trunk of the vehicle ahead of him," the kid said with a perfectly straight face. "He hit his brakes but couldn't stop. The Hummer hit the zombie. The Lexus rear-ended the Hummer. The Caprice rear-ended the Lexus. No serious injuries or fatalities—other than the zombie."

"You had me at 'a zombie jumped out of the trunk,' " Liska said.

"A zombie," Kovac said flatly.

Shaking his head, he walked toward the small knot of people hovering around the body in the middle of the road. The crime scene team was taking photographs. A couple of state troopers were working the accident, taking measurements of the road, of the distances between the vehicles.

Steve Culbertson, the ME's investigator, spotted Kovac and started toward him. He was lean and slightly scruffy, with salt-and-pepper beard stubble and the narrow, shifty eyes of a coyote. He always had the look of a man who might open up one side of his topcoat and try to sell you a hot watch.

"Steve, if I got called out here for a traffic fatality, I'm gonna kick somebody's ass," Kovac said. "It's too fucking cold for this shit. The hair in my nose is frozen."

"Tell me about it. Try to get an accurate temp on a corpse on a night like this."

"I don't want to hear about your social life."

"Very funny."

"So a zombie falls out of the trunk of a car . . . ?"

"I don't have a punch line, if that's what you're looking for," Culbertson said. "But I will quote my favorite movie: This was no boating accident."

Kovac arched a brow. "My vic was attacked by a great white shark?"

Culbertson cast an ironic look at the giant white Hummer. "Hit by one. But I don't think that was the worst of her problems. Have a look."

Kovac had seen more dead bodies than he could count: men, women, children; victims of shootings, stabbings, strangulations, beatings; fresh corpses and bodies that had been left for days in the trunks of cars in the dead of summer. But he had never seen anything quite like this.

"F-f-f-f-uck," he said as the air left his lungs.

Liska was right beside him. "Holy crap. . . . It *is* a zombie."

Half of the female victim's face appeared to have melted. It looked as if the skin and flesh had been burned away, exposing muscle and bone, exposing her teeth where her cheek should have been. The right eye was missing from its socket. The skull had shattered and cracked open like an egg. Brain matter had already frozen in the dark hair and on the pavement.

"The car hit one of these craters we call potholes, and the body bounced out of the trunk. The limo driver says she was upright and facing him when he hit her," Culbertson explained. "So the head hit the pavement and busted open like a rotten melon."

"The back of the head," Kovac said. "What about this face? What caused that?"

"You'll have to ask the boss," Culbertson said. "Looks like some kind of chemical burn to me, or contact with something hot under the car. I don't know, but look at this," he said, pointing a gloved finger at the victim's upper chest. "She didn't get stabbed repeatedly by that Hummer, so my money is on a homicide."

Kovac squatted down for a closer look. The damage to the face was so horrific, it was difficult to get his brain to accept that this was a real human being he was looking at and not some Halloween prop. She lay like a broken doll, limbs at unnatural angles to the body. Young, he thought, looking at her arm and hand—the smooth skin, the blue nail polish. Several of the fingernails were broken. A couple were torn nearly off. There were cuts and scrapes on the knuckles, indicative of defensive wounds. She had fought. Whoever had done this to her, she had fought.

Good for you, honey, he thought. *I hope you did some damage.*

She was naked from the waist down. The left leg was badly broken. She had been stabbed repeatedly in the chest and throat. The top she wore was torn and drenched in blood.

Who hated you this much? Kovac wondered. *Who did you piss off so badly that they would do this to you?*

"Any ID on the body, Steve?" Liska asked.

"Nope."

"Great."

Kovac straightened to his feet, knees and back protesting. Even the fluid in his joints was freezing.

"What time is it?" Liska asked.

He checked his watch. "Eleven fifty-three. Why?"

"I want this year to be over."

They had started the year just a few miles from where they were standing, New Year's Day, on a callout to a dead body, a young woman who had been brutally murdered, her body chucked out of a vehicle into a ditch. No ID. A Jane Doe. Their first of the year. The press had dubbed her "New Year's Doe." It had taken weeks before they were able to match their unidentified body with a missing persons report out of Missouri. The case remained open.

And here they were, twelve months later, standing over the body of a murdered female with no ID. The ninth Jane Doe of the year.

Doe cases generally got names fairly quickly. They often turned out to be transients, people on the fringes of society, people who had minor criminal records and could be ID'd from their fingerprints or were matched to local or regional missing persons reports. Their deaths were related to their high-risk lifestyles. They died of drug overdoses or suicide or because they pissed off the wrong thug. But this year had been different. This year, of their now nine Jane Doe victims, three had fit a very troubling pattern.

Jane Doe 01-11 had turned out to be an eighteen-year-old Kansas girl, Rose Ellen Reiser. A college student, she had been abducted December 29 outside a convenience store in Columbia, Missouri, just off Interstate 70 while on her way back to school in St. Louis.

Jane Doe 04-11—found on the Fourth of July—had eventually been identified as a twenty-three-year-old mother of one from Des

Moines, Iowa, who had gone missing while jogging in a park near Interstate 35 on July first.

A Jane Doe found Labor Day weekend had yet to be identified. The body had been found near the Minnesota State Fairgrounds, making it a case for the St. Paul PD, but the obvious similarities to the two prior cases in Kovac's jurisdiction had earned him a phone call to consult.

He had dubbed the killer Doc Holiday, a name that had stuck not only with the Minneapolis cops but also with detectives in agencies throughout the Midwest where young women had been abducted— or their bodies had been found—always on or around a holiday, always near an interstate highway. Over the months, it had become clear that the Midwest had a serial killer cruising the highways.

"She came out of the trunk of a car," Liska said.

The prevailing theory was that Doc Holiday was a long-haul trucker. The serial killer's dream job. His chamber of horrors ran on wheels. He could snatch a victim in one city and dump her in another with no one questioning his movements. Victims were readily available all along his route.

"So he's a traveling salesman," Kovac said. "I don't care what he's driving."

He cared that he was standing over another young woman who would never have the chance to become an old woman. Whoever this girl was, she would never have a career, get married, have children, get divorced. She would never have the opportunity to be successful or make a shambles of her life, because she didn't have a life anymore.

And no matter if she had been the perfect girl or a perfect bitch, somewhere tonight someone would be missing her, wondering where she was. Somewhere on this New Year's Eve a family believed they would see her again. It would be Kovac's job to tell them the hard truth. If he could manage to figure out who the hell she was.

On the sidelines, the reporters had begun to get restless, wanting details. One of them called out, "Hey, Detective! We heard there was a zombie. Is that true?"

Off to the southwest the sky suddenly exploded with color. Fireworks over the burbs.

Kovac looked at his partner. "Happy freaking New Year."

3

"I couldn't stop. I couldn't stop the damn Hummer," Jamar Jackson said. He had the look of a man who had seen a ghost and knew that it was going to haunt him every night for the rest of his life.

"That thing is like driving the fucking *Titanic*!" he said. "You can't just stop! I hit the brakes. It was too late. She popped out of that trunk and *bam*! I just hit her. I killed her! Oh my God. I killed somebody!"

He cupped his head in his hands, his elbows resting on the table, holding him up. He was sweating like a horse. As cold as it had been at the scene, it was equally hot in the interview room. Something had gone haywire with the heating system, and no one from the maintenance staff was answering their phones on New Year's Day.

Liska had stripped off two layers of clothing and she still felt like she was wearing her parka.

Jackson had jerked loose his bow tie and opened the collar of his tuxedo shirt. It was clear he was replaying the memory of the accident in his mind over and over. Liska tried to picture it herself—driving down the road, the trunk of the car in front flies open, and like a scene from a horror movie, out pops a body.

"What kind of car was it?" she asked.

"I don't know," he said impatiently, as if he didn't want his macabre memory interrupted. "Black."

"Big? Small?"

"Big. Kind of. I don't know."

"American? Foreign?"

"I don't know!" he said, exasperated. "I wasn't paying attention!"

Liska gave him the hard Mom look. "You're a limo driver. You're paid to get your passengers from one place to another in one piece, and you weren't paying attention?"

Jackson threw his hands up in front of him. "Hey! You don't know what was going on behind me! I got drunks, I got fights, I got half-naked women making out with each other—"

"You were distracted."

"Hell yeah! You would be too!"

"As much as the men in my life like to fantasize about it, half-naked women making out isn't my thing," Liska said. "So what *do* you remember seeing, Mr. Jackson? On the road. In front of you."

He heaved a sigh and looked up at the ceiling, as if the scene might play out there like a movie on a screen. "There was a truck on my left."

"What kind of a truck? A pickup truck?" She didn't care about the truck. She wanted her witness zooming in on the details. She wanted him to see the picture as clearly as possible.

"No, like a box truck. And then this car merged into traffic in front of me."

"Two doors? Four doors?"

Jackson shook his head. "I don't know."

"Could you see how many people were in the car?"

"No. I didn't look. I didn't care. It was just a car—until the zombie came out of it."

"Can you describe the zombie for me?" Liska asked with a straight face. If it somehow made Jamar Jackson more comfortable calling the victim a zombie instead of a woman, so be it.

He wasn't happy with the request. "You saw it."

"I know what I saw," she said. "I want to know what you saw before you ran over her. The trunk popped open and . . . ?"

He squeezed his eyes shut as if it pained him to think about it, then popped them wide open to avoid what he saw on the backs of his eyelids.

"It was freaky. She just popped up, and the next thing I knew she was right in front of me. Like something out of *The Walking Dead*." His mouth twisted with distaste at the mental image. "Man, her face was all messed up like it was rotten or melted or something. She was all bloody."

His complexion was looking ashen beneath the sweat. He was breathing through his mouth. Liska leaned over discreetly and inched the wastebasket closer to her chair.

"Did she appear to be conscious? Were her eyes open?"

Jackson grimaced again. Sweat rolled down his temples like rain. "That one eye—it looked right at me! And there was blood coming out the mouth, and I couldn't stop the Hummer, and then I hit her, and— Oh, man, I don't feel so good."

Liska handed him the wastebasket. "I'll give you a moment alone."

She left the interview room to the sound of retching.

"Cleanup on aisle twelve!" she called, walking into the break room.

Kovac was pouring himself a cup of coffee that resembled liquid tar. He had stripped down to his shirtsleeves—now rolled halfway up his forearms—and jerked his tie loose at his throat, revealing a peek of white T-shirt underneath. His thick hair—more gray than brown as he skidded down the downhill side of his forties—looked like he had run his hands through it half a hundred times in the last five hours.

"What did he come up with, besides puke?" he asked.

He looked as tired as she felt, the assorted stress lines and scars digging into his face. He had sort of a poor man's Harrison Ford look: a lean face with asymmetrical features, narrow eyes, and a sardonic mouth. He had recently shaved his old-time cop mustache because she had harped at him for months that it made him look older than he was.

Liska leaned back against the counter and sighed. "Nothing much. He's pretty hung up on the fact that he killed a zombie."

"Technically speaking, I don't think it's possible to kill a zombie," Tippen said. "They're already dead."

Tall, thin, and angular, he sat a little sideways to the table, like he was at a French sidewalk cafe, his long legs crossed, one arm resting casually against the tabletop. His face was long and homely, with dark eyes burning bright with intelligence and dry wit.

"That's not true," Elwood Knutson corrected him from the opposite end of the table. "Zombies are the *un*dead. Which is to say, they were dead but have been reanimated, usually through some kind of black magic. So, technically speaking, they're alive."

Elwood was the size and shape of a circus bear, with the mind of a Rhodes scholar and the sensitivity of a poet. They had all been working cases together for half a dozen years, going back to the Cremator homicides when they worked the task force to catch a serial killer.

"We should all be shocked that you know that much about zombies," Liska said, snagging a doughnut off the tray on the counter. "But we're not."

"They're always shooting zombies in the movies, but they never seem to die," Tippen pointed out. "Which to me implies that they can't be killed because they're already dead."

"You have to kill a zombie by killing its brain," Elwood explained. "It's not that easy."

"You can't shoot it through the heart with a silver bullet?"

"That's werewolves."

"A stake through the heart."

"Vampires."

"Elwood," Kovac interrupted. "Get a fucking life. Go out. See people. Stop watching so much cable television."

"Oh, like you should talk, Sam," Liska scolded. "You live like a hermit."

"We're not talking about me."

Kovac took a drink of the coffee and made a face like someone had just punched him in the gut. "Jesus, how long has this shit been sitting here?"

"Since last year," Tippen said.

"Vampires and werewolves have roles in classic literature," Elwood said.

"And zombies?"

"Are a contemporary pop culture rage. I like to stay current."

"I like to stay on point," Kovac said. "And I don't want to hear any more about fucking zombies. The phones are ringing off the hook with reporters wanting to talk about zombies."

"Zombies are news," Elwood pointed out.

"Zombies aren't real," Kovac said. "We've got a dead girl. That's real. *She* was real. We're not living in a television show." He turned his attention back to Liska. "Did you tell him he probably didn't kill her?"

"No," she said. "Because I think he probably did."

"She has, like, twenty stab wounds in her chest," he pointed out.

"That doesn't mean she died from them. Jackson says the trunk popped open and the victim sat up."

"That could be what he saw," Kovac conceded. "The car hit a pothole, the trunk wasn't latched so it popped open, the body bounced and appeared to sit up. That doesn't mean she was alive."

"She was upright when he hit her," Liska said. "A dead body falls out of a trunk, it hits the ground like a sack of wet trash."

"I think if I fell *alive* out of the trunk of a moving car, I would hit the ground like a sack of wet trash," Elwood said. "Who gets up from that?"

"Depends on how fast the car was going," Tippen said.

"Depends on how bad I want to stay alive," Liska said. "If I'm alive coming out of that trunk, you can bet your ass I'm doing everything I can do to get up and get out of the road."

"Tinks, you would kick down death's door and beat its ass," Kovac said. "But that's you."

"And maybe that's our zombie girl too," Liska argued. "We don't know her. That's for the ME to tell us."

"It's a moot point," Kovac said. "I'm never gonna charge the limo driver with anything. Our vic is dead because of whoever put her in the trunk of that car and whatever that person did to her."

"What did the limo driver say about her face?" Tippen asked.

They had all taken a look at the digital photos Liska had snapped at the scene. Kovac had called in Tip and Elwood because of the possible connection to the Doc Holiday murders. The four of them had formed their own unofficial task force on the two previous cases in their jurisdiction. That enabled them to keep the engine churning on cases that were essentially going cold.

The general rule of thumb in the Homicide division was three concentrated days working a homicide. If the case wasn't solved in three days, it had to take a back burner to newer cases—homicides and assaults—and the detectives had to work the old cases as they could. With four of them doing follow-up, the cases kept moving. Even at a snail's pace, it was better than nothing.

If this Jane Doe case looked enough like the other two murders, plus the one in St. Paul, they might be able to convince the brass of the need for a formal task force. In the meantime, they did what they could on their own.

"He said she looked that way when he hit her," Liska said. "The poor kid is going to see that face in his sleep for years to come."

"But he isn't seeing a license plate?" Kovac asked. "A make and model? A parking sticker? Nothing else."

"He wasn't paying attention. He was more interested in the two half-naked girls making out in the back of the Hummer."

"Where are they?" Tippen asked. "I volunteer to interview them."

Liska broke off a piece of her doughnut and threw it at his head. "You're such a perv!"

He arched a woolly eyebrow. "This is news to you?"

"Topic, people!" Kovac barked. "It's as hot as Dante's fucking inferno in here. I'd like to get out of here sometime before heat-stroke sets in."

"He says there was a box truck ahead of him," Liska said, "on his left, as the car merged into traffic in front of him."

They all perked up at that.

"What kind of a box truck?" Kovac asked.

"I had to psychologically beat him like a rented mule to get that much out of him," Liska said. "And how could that be relevant any-way? The truck was already to his left. The car was only just merg-ing into traffic from the right. And the vic fell out of the car, not the truck. It's the one thing he's very clear on. The vic fell out of the car."

"Would he work with a hypnotist?" Elwood asked. "He's too traumatized now to want to consciously go after those detailed memories. A hypnotist could be the thing."

"I'll ask him," Liska said. "What's the harm?"

"Go for it," Kovac said. "If he can give us a tag number—even a partial—on that car, we could find our whodunit before we even know who he done it to."

Liska took his coffee and washed down the last of her doughnut, shuddering at the bitterness.

"Oh my God! That's horrible!" she said. "Start a fresh pot, for Christ's sake!"

"It'll put hair on your chest, Tinks," Kovac said.

"Great. Something more for Tip to fantasize about," she said, heading for the door.

"And, Tinks?"

She looked back over her shoulder.

"Tell the guy he didn't kill anyone."

4

The residents of Minneapolis were waking to a new year by the time Liska finally went home. Waking, or better yet, sleeping in. She had been up for twenty-four hours. Sleeping in sounded like the greatest luxury in the world. Unfortunately, she probably wasn't going to find out firsthand whether it was or not.

If she could grab a couple of hours before the boys roused themselves, she would be lucky. Kovac was pushing for the autopsy on their Jane Doe to be done ASAP. If he could get an ME to give up New Year's Day and jump their dead body to the head of the line, they would all be standing around the dissection of a corpse instead of a holiday turkey before the day was out.

She pulled into her driveway, enjoying the feeling of being home that was unique to this house. She had purchased it a year and a half ago—a side-by-side duplex in an established older neighborhood near Lake Calhoun. Built in the 1940s, it was solid and substantial. Renovated in 2000, it had all the necessary creature comforts. She and her boys lived on one side. The other side she rented to the twenty-six-year-old sister of a patrol cop she knew.

Liska felt like she had been an adult for a hundred years, but the day she had bought this house, she had felt like she was just becoming a grown-up all over again. It was the first house she had ever purchased on her own. There was something very important in that.

When she and Speed Hatcher had been married, they had done what all young married couples did—bounced from a cheap apartment to a better apartment to their first real home—a bungalow in a nondescript neighborhood a few blocks off Grand Avenue in St. Paul. There had been some happy times in that house, particularly when the boys were small. There had been plenty of not-so-happy times in that house as their marriage had disintegrated, and after the divorce.

She had stayed there for too many years on a handful of sad excuses. She got the house in the divorce. It was the only home her sons knew. It was convenient for their father to visit.

Speed worked Narcotics for the St. Paul PD. His schedule was erratic at best. Nikki had reasoned it would be better if he could drop in to see his sons when he could. If she moved them closer to her job in Minneapolis, he would have to make an effort to visit. Effort was not Speed Hatcher's forte, not even where his boys were concerned.

But he had let them down so many times, Nikki had begun to think it would be better if they lived in the other of the Twin Cities. Easier for her to make excuses for him. Instead of blaming their dad for being absent from their lives, they could blame their mom for moving them away from him. Hell of a compromise.

The move had not gone over well. Uprooting a twelve-year-old and a fourteen-year-old had been nothing short of child abuse by the boys' standards. The adjustment period had been brutal. But R.J.— her youngest—had inherited his father's easy charm and made friends quickly, and Kyle—her studious one—had immersed himself in his new school. A year and a half later, they didn't entirely hate their mother anymore.

They had made this house their own, their family of three. There was no Ghost of Speed Past haunting their holidays here. There were no memories of rare happy family times or too-common arguments that ended with doors slamming.

As predicted, Speed's visits were infrequent, but better to be infrequent with the excuse of distance than infrequent with the excuse of just doesn't give a shit. Nikki accepted that bargain and considered her short commute to work downtown her consolation prize for the rest.

The house was quiet as she let herself in. She stopped in the powder room off the front hall, as was her habit coming home from a homicide. She wanted to see what she looked like, as if the most recent murder might have left some indelible mark on her—a line, a scar. All the years she'd been working homicides, if they had each left a visible scar she would have looked as much like a zombie as her Jane Doe by now.

She checked herself in the mirror. Purple shadows were smudged beneath blue eyes that had been bright with the promise of a night out New Year's Eve. All that remained of her eye shadow was a dark line in the crease of her eyelids. Her pixie-short silver-blond hair had been flattened by her Elmer Fudd hat, then had made a halfhearted effort to bounce back with a few swipes of her hands. She looked a little like she might have stuck her finger in a light socket at some point during the evening, or seen a ghost . . . or a zombie.

The thought took her back to the scene on the highway, to the young woman lying like a discarded bundle of rags, torn and stained and forgotten.

Probably not forgotten, she corrected herself. Assuming the killer had been the one driving the mystery car, he must have had a rude surprise when he realized his victim had managed to somehow get out of the trunk.

While there was probably some valid twist of the laws of physics that might have allowed that body to fall out of a moving vehicle and bounce back upright, Nikki was set on the idea that their Jane Doe had still been alive when the Hummer hit her. It was a terrible thought. It would have been less terrible to believe the victim had already been deceased, but she didn't. That the young woman had been alive when she came out of that trunk was a stubborn notion that had dug its talons in deep and wasn't about to let go.

She sank down on one end of her couch and closed her eyes as her body relaxed. She tried to imagine what that would have been like: stuffed in the trunk of a car, surely thinking her life was over, then seeing light as the trunk latch let go. Hope would have surged, would have urged her to do something to save herself no matter how impossible it seemed. Adrenaline would have given her the strength to sit up. What would have pushed her out of that rolling coffin? Bravery? Fear? In Nikki's experience, those were two halves of the same emotion. You couldn't be brave without knowing fear.

And that moment—when bravery tipped the scale—was what brought tears to her eyes. That was the moment an ordinary human became a hero. She had no idea who that young woman was or what she had done that had somehow, some way, led her to become a victim of a violent crime. The guys in the squad had already started calling her Zombie Doe. But in this it didn't matter who she was. That emotion was universally human: the overriding need to fight for life. And when that fight ended in triumph, it brought the highest high. And when it ended in defeat . . . *it brings me,* Liska thought.

It would be her job, and Kovac's, to put a real name to Zombie Doe, to find her family, to devastate them with the news of what had happened to their daughter, their sister, their niece, their grandchild.

Liska had learned the lesson long ago—that no one dies in a vacuum. Everyone's life touches someone for good or for ill. Almost everyone. The few left over who died unknown and unclaimed were buried by the city and mourned in only the most abstract way by the people who had dealt with their bodies.

The person sleeping on the other two-thirds of her couch began to stir beneath the thick burgundy chenille throw. A leg moved, an arm stretched, a head emerged, big brown eyes blinking.

Marysue Zaytoun sat up with a smile on her lovely face, looking fresh and well rested. "Hi, Nikki. Happy New Year."

"I hope so," Liska said. "It's not off to a good start."

Marysue frowned. "It was a bad date?"

"Murder. I mean an actual murder," Liska said. "Half an hour before 'Auld Lang Syne' I got called to a scene. So much for my big date."

At least she had driven herself to the party, knowing she was on call, knowing there was a better-than-even chance her phone would ring. She kept a change of clothes in the car for just that reason.

"And here I thought you must have gotten lucky," Marysue said.

All Liska had texted her was a cryptic *Going 2 b late. Can U stay?*

"I don't know what I'd do without you, Marysue. Thanks so much for staying with the boys. I owe you. Again."

Marysue touched her fingertips to her dark hair and it fell perfectly in place. There were no red creases on her face from pressing into the pillow. There was no mascara smudged beneath her eyes. She was perfect. And on top of being perfect, she was sweet and kind and generous. An angel in the guise of Officer Bobby Zaytoun's little sister. Liska couldn't have conjured up a more perfect renter unless she could have gotten all of Marysue's fine qualities in the body of George Clooney.

"I'm glad to help. With Kevin out of town, my idea of the perfect New Year's Eve is curling up with a good book anyway. I have no interest in being out on the roads with a bunch of drunken fools."

There was the soft sound of the South in her voice. The Zaytouns hailed from North Carolina. Marysue had followed her brother north. She worked from home as a website designer and manager to pay the bills, and worked in her spare time on designing her own line of clothing. Fashion was her passion. But her personal style transcended what she wore. Marysue could have put on the proverbial burlap sack with the perfect accessory and be hailed as a chic sensation all over town. Her fiancé, Kevin Boyle, was a lucky man.

"So how was your evening?" Liska asked. "What did you guys do?"

"Ate pizza, played video games, watched a movie about aliens invading the planet. Darn near everything blew up by the end of it."

"An R.J. classic."

Guns, bombs, Transformers, aliens, shoot-outs, explosions—that was her youngest. He was a boy bursting at the seams with life. With R.J. everything was on the surface. He wore his heart on his sleeve and his emotions on his face. Thirteen now, he was looking more and more like his father—blue eyes full of mischief, blond hair full of cowlicks, and a crooked grin that could stop a girl's heart. Unlike Speed, he was loyal to a fault.

"What about Kyle? What time did he get home from his party?"

Marysue frowned. "A little after ten. I don't think he had a very good time. He came in and went straight up to his room."

Liska sighed. Kyle was fifteen, quiet, too sensitive, internalizing everything and giving nothing away. He had broken up with his first girlfriend before Nikki had even known he had one. And she might never have known if she hadn't had to dig through the trash for a permission slip R.J. had accidentally thrown away. Only then had she found the torn photograph of Kyle with a pretty, smiling blond-haired girl. When she had tried to broach the subject with him, he had gone within himself and slammed the door shut.

She worried about him in a way she didn't worry about her youngest. When R.J. got in trouble, it was right out there for all the world to see. In fact, he was usually the first one to tell her about it. And R.J.'s trouble was the obvious kind. He threw a baseball and accidentally busted a car window. He got sent to the principal's office for making farting noises with his armpit during class. A bully picked on a friend after school, and he kicked the bully's ass.

Kyle was another matter. Bright and artistic, he had won a scholarship to the Performance Scholastic Institute, a prestigious private school for academically and artistically gifted students Nikki would never have been able to afford to send him to otherwise. His acceptance to PSI had helped prompt her to make the move from St. Paul.

The school had seemed a perfect fit for him the first year. He had welcomed the academic challenge and thrived in his art classes. The girlfriend had happened over the summer. Things had begun to slide ever so slightly downhill from there. His guidance counselor had felt a need to express concern at the fall parent-teacher conference. Kyle's grades had slipped a bit. He had become uncommunicative with school staff and was having trouble getting along with some of the other students. He didn't seem to have many close friends. He hadn't done anything wrong, the counselor stressed. He wasn't in any kind of trouble, and yet . . .

Nikki's worry was that, like the secret girlfriend, she would find out about Kyle's trouble only after the disaster, when the only thing left to do was to sweep up the pieces and put them in the trash.

Marysue pushed the throw aside and got up from the couch. There was barely a wrinkle in her chocolate brown velour tracksuit.

"I'm going to make breakfast," she announced. "How would you like your eggs?"

"I think I'm out of eggs."

"I'm not. Come over and eat something before you crash. You'll worry better with a little protein in you."

"Give me twenty minutes."

As Marysue went out the front door, Nikki trudged up the stairs to the second floor, fantasizing about a hot shower. R.J.'s bedroom door was ajar. He was sprawled sideways across his bed as if he had fallen there, dead, one arm hanging over the side. She slipped into the room and covered him with the Vikings blanket he had gotten for Christmas. She brushed her fingers over the back of his head and smiled. He didn't move, didn't flinch. He slept the sleep of the innocent and unworried. She envied him.

Across the hall, the door to Kyle's room was shut. The door was an amazing original work of art created by her son, a surreal, shadowed landscape in red, black, and white, with an elaborate, life-size Samurai warrior in the foreground, guarding the portal with a wicked sword raised above his head.

Nikki tried to turn the knob. Locked. She stood there for a moment, not sure what to do or think. There were only two reasons to lock a door: to keep one's self in and protected, and to keep one's family out and excluded. Either way, she didn't like it.

She pressed her ear to the door and held her breath, hoping to hear him moving around or snoring. Silence.

She knocked tentatively. "Kyle?"

Nothing.

Her instincts began to stir the pot of motherly emotions. He had been withdrawn lately, too quiet. He had gone to a New Year's Eve pizza party two blocks away and had come home too early and in a bad mood.

She knocked a little harder, spoke a little louder. "Kyle? Are you awake?"

No response.

Now her heart was beginning to beat faster. Recent stories of teen suicides rose in her mind. She berated herself for working too much, not being with the boys 24/7. She cursed their father for his neglect. All in a span of three seconds. She rattled the doorknob again and raised her voice. "Kyle Hatcher, open this door. Now!"

She let anger rise to the surface. It was easier to deal with than the fear that her son might have done something to harm himself. She began to think about kicking in the fucking door.

Kyle called back in a groggy voice. "I'm sleeping!"

Nikki let out a breath of relief. "If you were sleeping, you wouldn't have answered me."

"I'd be sleeping if you weren't pounding on the door."

"Open the door."

"I'm not dressed."

"Then put some pants on and open the door."

"Why can't you just leave me alone?"

"Kyle, open the door, or I'll kick it in. I mean it. And guess whose allowance will pay for the repairs?"

She could hear him stirring then, muttering curse words.

"No swearing!" she snapped.

"You do it!"

"Not when I think you can hear me."

"You're such a hypocrite."

"I'm an adult. Double Standard is my middle name. Open the door."

The door opened a foot and the profile of her firstborn filled the space, blocking her view of the room behind him. She had to look up at him, which seemed completely wrong. He was only five feet seven, which made him small for fifteen, but he was still taller than she was. In plaid pajama bottoms, a T-shirt, and tousled blond hair, he was still more of her little boy than he was the man he was too quickly trying to grow into, but he was on his way.

"Are you okay?" she asked. "Marysue said you came home early last night."

"I'm fine," he muttered.

"What happened to the party?"

"It was boring."

He had yet to make eye contact with her. Suspicion rose inside her.

"Look at me," she said.

He looked at her sideways with his right eye.

"Turn and face me," she ordered. "Now."

Frowning hard, he turned and squinted down at her, his left eye swollen, an unmistakable knuckle abrasion skidding across the crest of the cheekbone beneath it.

The bottom dropped out of Nikki's stomach. "What happened to you?"

"Nothing."

"Kyle—"

"I tripped and fell."

"Into a fist?"

She advanced and he yielded, stepping backward into his room. Nikki followed him in. She didn't look around to see if he had been trying to hide anything. If Kyle wanted something hidden, it was already done. The Library of Congress should have been as orga-nized as her son's bedroom. Anything hidden was well hidden. It would have taken a team of crime scene investigators to dismantle the place in order to find it.

"Sit down," she said.

He sat on the edge of his bed, frowning, squirming, trying to twist away from his mother's hands, the same way he had done when he was five. Nikki grabbed hold of his chin with one hand, and he winced as her thumb pressed into a fresh bruise.

"Ouch!"

"Be still!"

She snapped on the nightstand lamp with her other hand and zeroed her critical gaze in on his face.

"What happened?" she asked again.

"Nothing!"

"Kyle! Goddammit, I know what it looks like when someone has been punched in the face! What happened to you? The last I knew you were going to a party. Just a few friends at the McEvoys', you told me. The science club, you told me. What happened? You got into a fight over the theory of relativity? Did creationists crash the party and start a rumble? I don't understand how you went to a party of science geeks and came home with a black eye."

"It's no big deal!" he said. "Just let it go, will you?"

"I'm calling Mrs. McEvoy—"

"No!"

Nikki stepped back and jammed her hands on her hips. "Then spill it, mister. And you'd better not leave anything out. It's your bad luck your mother is a police detective."

"It sucks," he said, looking down at the floor.

"Well, it can suck for ten minutes or it can suck all day long. Your choice. I'm not leaving this spot until I have an explanation. Where were you when this happened?"

"On the lake," he said. "We went skating. We ran into some kids, that's all."

"You ran into some kids and what?"

"I crashed into a guy and he got pissed and he hit me. That's all."

He was lying. She always knew. He had yet to acquire his father's ease with it, thank God. Hopefully, he never would. Where Speed would look right at her, wide-eyed, and spew a streaming line of bull, Kyle wouldn't make eye contact. He looked off and down to the left, as if he was staring at an imaginary teleprompter feeding him this crock of shit.

Nikki sighed and sat down beside him. She put an arm around him and put her head against his shoulder.

"You make life more complicated than it needs to be."

She could almost hear his thoughts: *You don't know anything. You don't know anything about me.* She'd had those same thoughts herself at fifteen. Life had seemed unbearably complicated and difficult, and no one had understood her, least of all her parents. They could have put bamboo shoots under her fingernails and she would never have told them anything.

She put her right hand gently over Kyle's left, which was pressed hard into his thigh. The knuckles of his right hand were swollen, the middle one split open. He had fought back. Whoever had given him that shiner had gotten something back in return.

"Let's see that eye," she said, getting up.

Tenderly, she pressed her thumb along the brow bone, wondering if she should take him for an X-ray. A blood vessel had burst in the inside corner of his eye, filling the white with blood. While it looked scary, she knew from personal experience it was no cause for true alarm.

"Do you have a headache?"

"I do now," he muttered.

"Don't be sarcastic. I can drag you to the ER and we can waste our day there while they ask you all the same questions in triplicate. Follow my finger with your eyes," she instructed, drawing a line in the air to the left and back to the right. His vision tracked.

"Do you feel nauseous?"

"No."

"Any double vision?"

"No."

"Why did you lock your door?"

" 'Cause," he said stubbornly, then thought better of leaving it at that. "I wanted to be alone. I didn't want R.J. bothering me."

Fair enough, she thought. R.J. could be like a big golden retriever puppy—curious and lovable and annoying all at the same time. He was still too much of a little boy to understand the seriousness of being fifteen.

"Make yourself presentable," she said, moving toward the door. "Marysue is making eggs. I want you to eat something. Then you can have some Tylenol and spend the rest of the day brooding. All right?"

He shrugged and looked away, and her heart ached for him. She would have taken all his hurts away and eaten them for breakfast if she could have.

She went back to him and pressed a kiss to his forehead. "I love you," she said softly. "Nothing is ever as bad as it seems."

A mother's lie, she thought as she left his room, her memory calling up the image of a dead girl lying broken on the road.

Some things were every bit as bad as they seemed.

Some things were even worse.

5

It was midmorning before Kovac dragged his sorry ass home. He lived in a quiet, older neighborhood that had gone a bit shabby over the years. Huge old oak and maple trees lined the boulevards, their roots busting up the sidewalks. Built in the forties and fifties, the houses were square and plain, of no discernable architectural style. These blocks would never be in any danger of restoration by the upwardly mobile. Some of the bigger, uglier houses had been cut up into duplexes and apartments. Most were single-family homes. His neighbors were working-class people and working-class retirees. It was a boring place, which suited him fine.

He trudged up the sidewalk, his eyes going, as always, to his neighbor's yard, which was crowded with a mad mix of Christmas decorations the old fart started putting up every year around Halloween. Santa Claus figures swarmed over the property like commandoes, creeping out of the bushes, climbing on the roof and into the chimney, skulking around the Nativity scene. Giant plywood toy soldiers stood sentry on either side of the manger. All of it was lit up at night with so much juice it had to be visible from space.

Fucking madness. Kovac particularly hated it on a day like this, when he was coming home from scraping a dead girl off the pavement. What the hell was there to be festive about in a world where young women were murdered and chucked out onto the road like garbage?

His brain superimposed the images onto his neighbor's lawn: Rose Ellen Reiser, aka New Year's Doe, lying in front of Frosty the Snowman, her face beaten to a bloody pulp with a hammer; their new Jane Doe flung like a broken rag doll at the feet of the three wise men, half her face burned away by Christ knew what. Zombie Doe.

He went into the house, toed his shoes off at the door, dumped his coat on the sofa, and went straight upstairs. He cranked the shower on as hot as he could stand it, stripped, and just stood under the water for he didn't even know or care how long. He felt grimy and sweaty from the too-hot office, yet his feet seemed not to have thawed out from the hours at the scene in subfreezing temperatures.

From the shower he went straight to bed, falling naked on top of the tangle of sheets. He stared up at the ceiling, willing his mind to go just as blank.

He had been up for thirty-three hours. After Liska had left the office, he had stayed, staring at his computer screen, going through missing persons reports, hunting for any missing women who might fit with his case. He'd spent so much time in the last year looking at missing persons websites, he knew many of the cases by heart. The sad fact was a lot of those cases would never be closed. Young women went missing—many by choice, others not. There weren't a lot of happy endings to be had.

The National Crime Information Center reported more than eighty-five thousand active missing persons records on file. How many lives did those eighty-five-thousand-plus touch? Parents, spouses, siblings, children, friends . . . the cops who worked their cases . . .

He had printed out pages on half a dozen missing women in a five-state area as possibilities. None were from the Twin Cities area. But then, if this case was linked to Doc Holiday, their victim wouldn't be from here. She would have been snatched in Illinois or Missouri or Wisconsin or someplace else. She would have gone missing a couple of days ago. The last two days of her life would have been spent as his captive, being raped and tortured and finally killed.

Kovac couldn't decide which would be worse: if their girl was a victim of Doc Holiday or if someone else had come up with the list of depraved shit that had been done to her.

He'd been a homicide cop for a lot of years. He'd seen firsthand that people's cruelty to one another knew no bounds. The fact that it still disturbed him five layers down under the thick hide the job had grown on him was both a blessing and a curse.

He was still human. He could still feel pain and sadness and despair and disgust. He could still dread holidays and hate coming home to an empty house.

It was always times like this when the darker emotions washed over him. Thirty-three hours without sleep, a brutal homicide, the knowledge that he didn't have enough manpower or resources to devote to solving the case quickly. Christ knew how long it would be before they could get a confirmed ID on their vic, let alone develop a suspect list. Who the hell wouldn't be depressed over that? Who wouldn't look at that poor dead girl and think, *What if that was my kid?*

He'd had too much cause to have thoughts like that in the last year.

When asked, Sam always said he had no children. He had raised no children. He got no cards on Father's Day. He paid no child support. The truth was more complicated than that.

He had a daughter in Seattle—or so he'd been led to believe a couple of lifetimes ago. She had been born here in Minneapolis shortly before the divorce became final. His soon-to-be-ex had already moved on with her life plans. She was in love with someone else, wanted out, wanted to start over, wanted nothing more to do with him. He had signed away his rights and she had headed west.

He had never seen the girl since. He had no idea what she looked like, if she favored him—God help her. He had spent a lot of time telling himself the kid had probably not been his at all, that his ex had stuck it out with him for his insurance coverage. But he had never entirely convinced himself of that. And so, during cases like this one, the thoughts came back to him—that he had a daughter, that he had lost a daughter, that she could have been dead for all he knew and for all he would ever know.

What a fucking mess you are, Kojak.

Twice married, twice divorced, no prospects. Lying in bed alone on New Year's Day, with a dead girl foremost in his thoughts.

The phone rang as if his loneliness had reached across the country and tapped his last near miss on the shoulder. Her name came up on the caller ID: *Carey.* He stared at it as the ringing of the phone raked over raw nerve endings. He let it go to voice mail. What would she have to say that she hadn't said a hundred times already? That she missed him. That she had to take the job with the Department of Justice because . . . excuse, excuse, excuse.

He didn't want to hear it. What good did it do to talk about it? She had made her choice for her own reasons, all of them more important than he was.

He shouldn't have let it bother him as much as he did. She had been through a lot of rough shit. An attempt on her life over a ruling she had made as the judge on a high-profile murder case. Kidnapped by a homicidal lunatic. Kovac still believed her ex-husband had plotted to have her killed, though the attempt had never actually been made, and Kovac had never been able to make the case for conspiracy to commit. All of that, then her father had died, and suddenly there were just too many painful memories.

She had needed a change of scenery. She'd been offered the position with the DOJ. Why wouldn't she take it? Why wouldn't she take her young daughter and go? Start over, start fresh, no ties to the past.

They hadn't been much more than friends, really . . .

She had been gone now nearly a year and a half. When she came back to visit, he wasn't available. When she called, he didn't answer.

When he fell asleep, he still saw her in his dreams.

6

Assistant Chief Medical Examiner Dr. Ulf Möller had volunteered himself for the New Year's Day autopsy of Zombie Doe. He was standing outside the back entrance to the morgue, smoking a cigarette, when Kovac pulled up and parked in the chief's spot.

The morgue was open for business, receiving bodies 24/7/365. An ambulance sat in the delivery bay now, having dropped off its unlucky cargo. There had been no autopsies planned for the day, however. Death never took a holiday, but MEs did. Anyone dead on New Year's Day would be just as dead on January second. But Kovac had pressed for an exception. It was important to ID their Jane Doe as soon as possible, for the sake of any family who might have been looking for her and for the sake of the case. Ulf Möller hadn't hesitated to say yes to Kovac's request, giving up his holiday afternoon with his wife, Eva, and their two daughters.

Tall and lean, Möller had a European elegance about him right down to the way he held his smoke, pinched between his thumb and forefinger. He was wrapped in a handsome black leather trench coat, a plaid cashmere scarf wound artfully around his neck. Despite the cold, he wore no hat. The icy breeze teased the ends of his fine sandy hair, though not a strand strayed out of place. He watched Sam approach with a wry expression.

"I appreciate this, Doc," Kovac said.

Möller sketched a brow ever so slightly upward, a certain kind of amusement lighting his eyes. "How could I resist? It isn't every day I get to autopsy a zombie. Maggie is going to be jealous, I think."

ME humor: every bit as dark and inappropriate as cop humor. Civilians would have been offended to hear it, but it was a necessary vice for people who dealt in death and depravity on a daily basis.

"She got the vampire on Halloween," Kovac reminded him. "And that Santa Claus burglar who died inside that chimney."

"Greedy bitch," Möller said mildly. He took a long pull on the cigarette and exhaled a jet stream of smoke.

Head honcho Maggie Stone, who had performed the autopsy on Rose Reiser a year ago, had gone to Vegas for New Year's with the latest of her slightly shady boyfriends. Möller, who had spent the last New Year's holiday visiting family in Germany, had done the autopsy on the Fourth of July vic—Independence Doe.

"What do you think, Sam? Is this the work of our serial killer?"

Kovac shrugged. "You'll have to tell me. I don't like the coincidences: holiday, dumped on the road, stabbed, disfigured . . . I don't want to think there are a lot of guys running around doing shit like that."

"Any prospects for an ID of the victim?"

"No local missing persons matching her description. At least, not yet. Someone goes missing New Year's Eve, it might take a day or two for anyone to sound the alarm," Kovac said. "I pulled a few sheets for missing females in a five-state area. Whoever she is, I hope to God she has a record and we can ID her from her fingerprints. That face is nothing to work with. Have you had a look at her yet?"

"And start the party without you and your lovely partner?" Möller said. "I wouldn't dream of it. Cigarette?"

Kovac took the offer automatically, as a matter of male bonding. He had officially quit the rotten habit about thirty-two times—had quit entirely when he had been seeing Carey Moore and spending time around her little girl, Lucy.

Intellectually, he knew smoking was a stupid thing to do. And Liska kicked his ass for it every time she caught him doing it. Emotionally, he didn't always care. In his darker moods, he did it deliberately, daring the universe to kill him. Who would give a shit anyway? Today was one of those days.

Möller shared his lighter. They both lit up and stood there in the freezing cold, tarring up their lungs like a couple of fucking idiots. Kovac felt perversely pleased with himself. He reminded himself how much he liked smoking, how soothing the ritual of it was; how a cigarette was like an old friend you called up every time the world kicked you in the teeth, and you went out and got drunk together and felt like shit afterward.

Liska pulled up to the curb then and parked her car in a loading zone. She got out wearing her don't-fuck-with-me face and stomped up to them.

"You're a couple of damned fools, and when you die slow, lingering, horrible deaths, don't come crying to me."

Möller arched a brow. "Lovely to see you, as well, Sergeant Liska. Happy New Year."

Liska gave him the stink eye.

Kovac had the grace to feel guilty. He dropped his smoke and ground it out in the snow that had accumulated on the sidewalk overnight. He picked up the butt and discarded it properly. She could accuse him of being a fool, but at least he had some common courtesy.

Liska shot him her mother's look of utter disgust nevertheless and headed into the building. Kovac looked at Möller and shrugged.

The ME's mouth curved up on one side in amusement. "You make such a lovely couple."

"The hell," Kovac grumbled as they fell in step behind his partner. "She'd eat me alive."

"And not in the good way," Liska tossed back over her shoulder. Typical Tinks. Always with the smart mouth.

Kovac had to admit, the two of them had been partners longer than he had stayed married to either of his wives. He doubted there was much one of them didn't know about the other. Liska delighted in embarrassing him with the details of her dating life. He weighed in routinely on her ex-husband and had learned to read and assess her moods with sharp accuracy.

She was pissed now, but his smoking a cigarette had little to do with it. Quick and tense, her every movement was reminiscent of an angry cat snapping its tail.

"Speed?" he guessed as they hung up their coats and grabbed yellow gowns.

"Isn't answering his phone," she said curtly.

"How is that a problem? It's not as much fun to call him a lazy-ass selfish dick on his voice mail?"

She stood still and looked up at him with grave meaning. "Kyle got into a fight last night."

"Kyle?"

"I know. Right? Kyle doesn't get into fights."

"Does he have an explanation?"

"Sure. It's bullshit. He claims he and his friends went skating on the lake last night, that he crashed into some kid and got into a fight with him."

"You don't believe him."

"It was seventeen below zero last night," she reminded him. "Nobody was skating on Lake Calhoun. The knuckles of his right hand are scraped. He wasn't wearing gloves when he hit whoever he hit. They weren't outside," she concluded. "He's lying to me."

"And you think he'll tell Speed the truth?" Kovac asked. "Speed is more apt to give him pointers. How to Sell a Lie 101 by Speed Hatcher. The asshole ought to do a video series. Maybe he could pay his back child support with the proceeds."

"I don't know what good he would do," she admitted. "I just know I want him to suffer through this too."

Kovac held his tongue and bent over to pull on the yellow paper booties over his shoes. Suffering was not on the Speed Hatcher agenda any more than shouldering his share of the responsibility for parenting two teenage boys.

"I know what you're thinking," Liska said.

"Well, that's going to save on conversation, then."

"I'm worried," she admitted.

"I know."

He put a hand on her shoulder and gave a little squeeze at the rock-hard tension there. "Kyle's a great kid, Tinks. You're doing a great job raising him and R.J. But they're boys. Boys do stupid things. Boys get into scrapes. It's a wonder half of the male population even makes it to maturity."

"That's a fact." She tried without much success to muster her usual smartass smirk.

"Hey, it could be worse," Kovac pointed out. "He could be a zombie."

WATCHING ULF MÖLLER conduct an autopsy was like watching performance art. Classical music played softly in the background, with bone saws and oscillating saws and the clank of surgical instruments against stainless steel overlaying the orchestral score. The white background of the room was like the white of a blank canvas, clean and austere. Möller and his assistant glided around the table like a pair of ballroom dancers in blue surgical gowns, elegant and smooth and perfectly in step with each other.

The autopsy of Zombie Doe would have been a mesmerizing thing to watch if not for the utter horror embodied by the decedent. Or maybe she was the jarring focal point that put the entire picture into perspective. She was a thing from another dimension, all harsh angles and strong colors, dirty and bloody and broken in too many places. Her face was a mask of raw meat and white bone. The dark hair was shaved to the scalp on one side of the skull and a Medusa's mane of twisted, matted snarls on the other.

"I see what you mean," Möller said, glancing from the young woman's face to Kovac. "You'll have your work cut out for you to get an ID."

"Right?" Kovac said. "What are we supposed to do with that? We can't put out a photograph. And what's a sketch artist going to make of it? Can you tell what she must have looked like? Any artist's rendition is going to be pure guesswork."

"A bad sketch is worse than no sketch at all," Liska said.

People cruising the missing and unidentified persons websites looking for loved ones rode a double-edged sword, both wanting and not wanting to find the person they were looking for. Staring at sketches, they would fixate not only on similarities to their missing daughter, sister, friend but also on the differences. Maybe this one was . . . but the nose was too narrow or the mouth was too wide. They remembered their lover's, mother's, brother's crooked smile, but no one died smiling, and sketches were rendered with little emotion on the victim's face so as not to distort the features.

Kovac himself had sat up late at night staring at the computer screen, at those photographs and sketches, trying to put a name to a victim. He had compared their sketch of New Year's Doe (Jane Doe 01-11) to the missing persons photo of Rose Reiser again and again without being able to conclusively say the two were the same girl. His victim's nose had been smashed to a pulp. The sketch artist had given her a generic nose. Rose Reiser's nose in her photograph was short and turned up at the end.

"The witness says her face was messed up like that when she came out of the trunk," Liska said. "Like half her face had melted, he said."

Möller gazed down at the dead girl, frowning. "Acid."

"What kind of acid?" Kovac asked.

"The lab will have to tell you that. Could be one of several. Hydrochloric, ferric, sulfuric, phosphoric. Not hydrofluoric. Hydrofluoric doesn't damage the skin so much. It's better for dissolving bone. It likes calcium. If you want to get rid of a skeleton, hydrofluoric acid is your best choice."

"Why does it creep me out that you know that?" Liska asked.

Möller looked right at her with amusement in his eyes. Behind his mask he was undoubtedly smiling like a cat.

"For the purpose of damaging flesh, I would choose sulfuric acid," he went on. "It's easily had."

"That's battery acid, right?" Kovac asked.

"Or a component of drain cleaner, or rust remover, or liquid fertilizer. It has a long list of uses," Möller said. "It can be purchased at the hardware store in a strong concentration—and this would have been quite concentrated to cause this kind of deep-tissue damage.

"At strength not only does it hydrolyze proteins and lipids, causing the primary chemical burn, it also causes a secondary thermal burn by dehydrating carbohydrates," he said. "And, if combined with concentrated hydrogen peroxide, one creates a substance called a piranha solution, which will dissolve nearly anything, including carbon on glassware."

"Piranha solution?" Kovac said. "Sounds like something out of an old James Bond movie."

"Indeed."

Using his fingers with delicate care, Möller examined what was left of the victim's lips and mouth. One side of the tongue—which had the appearance of raw hamburger—was visible through the hole the acid had burned through the cheek.

"Burns in the mouth . . . ," he said, gently prying the jaws open, "on the tongue—the tongue appears to have been bitten quite badly."

Kovac said nothing but ground his back teeth together. He had once worked the homicide of a hooker whose pimp had poured Drano down her throat. It had been a horrific death. The caustic chemical had seared her esophagus all the way to her stomach, and all the way back up as the woman's body tried to reject it.

Liska asked the question they were all thinking. "Was she alive when that happened?"

"We'll know soon enough," Möller said.

He continued his visual examination, counting the stab wounds to the chest and throat. He made note of the length and depth of each wound. Seventeen in all.

"This knife was smaller than with the other girl I autopsied," he commented. "This looks more like a paring knife or a pocketknife. The wounds are not as wide nor as deep."

The knife wounds to all three of the previous cases attributed to Doc Holiday—Rose Reiser, Independence Doe, and Labor Day Doe—had been deep and vicious, made with intent.

Möller pointed out several lesser marks on the victim's chest. "Hesitation marks, perhaps? Or perhaps the assailant was not so physically powerful after the initial attack."

"Hesitation or torture?" Kovac asked. "The killer didn't hesitate to pour acid on her face. Why be shy to stab her?"

"That, my friend, is for you to discover, yes? If I were to guess—
and of course, it is not my place to do so—I would guess the acid
came after the stabbing," Möller said. "If the intent was to hinder
identification, yes? The worst deed was already done."

"Stabbing is hands-on," Liska said. "It doesn't get much more
personal and real than physically shoving a knife through another
person's flesh."

Möller raised an eyebrow. "You've given this some thought,
have you?"

"More than you'd care to know. As for the acid . . . It's not so
hard to open a bottle and pour out the contents."

"Onto someone's face?"

She shrugged. "If you're pissed enough or sick enough to stab
somebody seventeen times, why not? It's a hell of a lot easier than
dismemberment."

"That's true," Kovac conceded. "All the satisfaction of deperson-
alizing the victim, and none of the hard labor."

Möller's young assistant piped up. "The three of you are freaking
me out."

"You must be new," Liska said. "Wait until we're in here eating egg
salad sandwiches while Doc scrapes the maggots off a severed head."

The assistant tried very hard not to react. The first rule of dealing
with cops, Kovac thought: Show no fear.

Möller continued his examination of the body. The damage done
to their unknown young woman was devastating—the broken
bones, the shattered skull, the stab wounds, the acid burns. Kovac
wanted to know which had been inflicted by the assailant and which
had been a result of falling from the trunk of the car and being
struck by the Hummer limo. Some of those answers were obvious;
others were not.

Doc Holiday's victims had been severely beaten—a lot of blunt-
force trauma to the head with a hammer or something similar. With

this victim having struck her head with some force as she fell to the road, it would be all but impossible to tell if any of the skull or facial fractures had been inflicted manually.

Möller pointed out matching bruising on both arms, both above the elbows and around the wrists. Finger marks, not ligature marks. She had been grabbed hard and held on to, possibly held down.

Doc Holiday's victims had shown similar bruising, but ligature marks as well. His previous torture repertoire had included cigarette burns. This girl had no cigarette burns. There was no obvious evidence of forcible sexual penetration and no semen present, yet the fact that she had been naked from the waist down strongly suggested a sexual component to the crime.

Möller and his assistant turned the body over with great care, mindful of the alignment of broken bones and the delicacy of torn flesh, handling the head like a basket of eggs. The most significant finding on this side of the victim was a small tattoo on the left shoulder, a couple of Chinese characters that meant nothing to anyone present. Liska took a photograph of the mark with her iPhone.

After the initial visual examination, Möller chose to go to the skull, to carefully dismantle the puzzle pieces of shattered bone in order to extract what was left of the brain to be weighed and examined. He then moved on to the torso and, with an artist's hand, drew the scalpel down the body, creating the Y incision: shoulders to sternum, sternum to groin.

Kovac tried unsuccessfully to tune out the sound of the garden loppers snapping the ribs from the breastbone, and the mechanical cranking of the rib spreader opening the chest cavity. After the literally hundreds of autopsies he had observed during his career, those sounds still got to him worse than anything else, except perhaps the smell of a burn victim or a floater. Something about cracking a chest made him see himself on the gurney and start rethinking that occasional cigarette.

Möller lifted out the internal organs one by one, weighed each, inspected each for signs of organic disease and physical injury. The information was logged and recorded.

The assailant's knife had remarkably missed the vital organs and major blood vessels. There had been significant bleeding into the body cavity, but the damage was not so much that she would have died quickly from it.

"So she could have been alive when she came out of that trunk," Liska said.

"It's not likely, but she probably wasn't dead due to the stab wounds," Möller qualified.

"If she didn't bleed out," Kovac said, "what killed her?"

Möller ignored the question. Homicide detectives were to medical examiners what four-year-old children were to overworked mothers.

He opened the victim's esophagus to find chemical burns. He lifted the lungs from her chest and placed them in the hanging scale, shaking his head.

"The lungs are heavy and wet," he said. "Inhalation of acid fumes damages the mucous membranes and causes pulmonary edema—a buildup of fluid."

"She was alive when the bastard poured the acid on her," Kovac said, anger burning through him just as the acid must have burned through this poor girl's flesh.

"Worse than that," Möller said as he continued his work. "She aspirated the acid itself. There is lung tissue here which has basically been digested."

"Jesus Christ," Kovac muttered.

He jammed his hands at his waist and walked away from the table, his own lungs hurting as he tried a few deep breaths. He had learned long ago never to mentally put himself in the victim's place. Therein lay the road to alcoholism. But it was difficult not to imagine the horror this girl had suffered in her final moments—held down, stabbed, acid raining down on her. It was difficult not to imagine her screams as her flesh burned and her panic as she gasped for a breath and sucked the caustic chemical into her airway.

Without a word to anyone, he walked out of the autopsy suite into the hall and just stood there.

He was by all descriptions, including his own, tough, hardened by long years looking at dead bodies and the wretched things people did to other people. He just needed a moment to regroup, to clear the anger from his head, to take the information of this autopsy and compartmentalize it into the relevant fact file in his brain.

He heard the door open behind him. Liska walked around in front of him and leaned back against the wall with her arms crossed. She didn't say anything. They both just stood there, breathing in and out, neither of them feeling the need to fill the silence.

Finally, Kovac heaved a sigh and said, "She probably wasn't conscious by the time the killer poured the acid on her. The stab wounds . . . She'd lost a lot of blood."

"Probably. I hope so."

"We've got the skin and blood under her fingernails. We'll get a DNA profile."

"Maybe he'll be in a database," Liska said.

"Yeah, maybe. We'll hope so," he said, deciding to at least pretend to grab on to that small hope.

At this point, small hope was as much hope as they had.

7

Liska begged off going for a postautopsy drink in favor of going home to her domestic drama. Kovac begged off going home to avoid the fact that he had no domestic life.

The Minneapolis Police Department lived in city hall, a massive Gothic-looking stone monstrosity of a building the color of liver crowned in steep verdigris-green roofs. Built around the turn of the twentieth century, with turrets and a clock tower and a five-story rotunda, it had originally been the county courthouse building. The courts now did business in the flashy, modern Hennepin County government complex on the other side of Fifth Street. The police department and Minneapolis city offices remained in the old municipal building.

Kovac parked in a slot reserved for a deputy chief, knowing there was no danger of any deputy chief interrupting his New Year's Day to come to the office. The halls were empty, his footfalls echoing as he made his way toward the Criminal Investigative Division offices.

Maintenance had yet to solve the mystery of the rogue heating system. He started peeling off clothing as soon as he was in the door—gloves, coat, scarf, hat. He threw the pile on Liska's chair in the cubicle.

"Judas, it's like the gateway to hell in here!" he declared to no one in particular.

A couple of the younger detectives had drawn the short straws to come in on the holiday. They sat three cubicles down watching the Rose Bowl on an iPad. There was no boss present to worry about busting their asses—which was why Kovac didn't hesitate to reach into his bottom desk drawer for the bottle of Glenmorangie he had stashed there. He poured a couple of glugs into a black coffee mug with white printing: HOMICIDE: IT'S WHAT'S FOR BREAKFAST.

The liquor went down like molten gold, smooth and warm, to pool in his belly and begin unraveling his frayed nerves from the inside out. Only in relaxing did he realize the degree of tension his body had been holding on to. He felt like a coiled spring, slowly relaxing. He took what felt like his first deep breath in three hours and exhaled slowly as his gaze wandered the work space he shared with Liska.

The small gray cubby was chock-full of books and binders and messy file folders. Post-it notes were stuck to every surface— reminders to call for lab results, to contact witnesses, to check with prosecutors for court schedules. Cop cartoons that had been printed off the Internet were taped to cabinet doors and pinned to the walls.

He and Liska had been trading gag gifts for years. Her favorite from him—the pen with the fake eyeball on top—stuck up promi- nently from the coffee mug bristling with pens beside her phone. His personal favorite—a very realistic-looking rubber severed human finger—was reaching into the nose hole of human skull that looked down on him from a shelf above his computer.

These were the comforts of his home away from home. Stuff that meant nothing to anyone but him. Stuff that connected him to no one in any meaningful way. Liska had pictures of her kids around her computer area. Kovac had an anonymous human skull with a rubber finger in its nose.

He checked his phone messages more to escape his own melancholy than anything else. He had a dozen messages, a couple from other cops working the Doc Holiday cases in other states, most from esteemed members of the press wanting to know more about the dead zombie. Fucking newsies.

Like most cops, he hated the media. Their usefulness was far outstripped by their ability to annoy, to misinform, to fuck up, and to do outright damage to a case. Their stock-in-trade was human tragedy, the more grotesque, the better. A young woman with no name dying was of no interest to them. Murder her, and they would prick up their ears. Chuck her from a moving vehicle, and they would come running. Call her a zombie, and they would wet themselves getting there.

Their interest in the case would run equal to the life of the shock factor. For that reason he supposed he should have been grateful his victim had been disfigured by having some sick fuck pour acid in her face while she was still breathing. That would hold the public's interest longer than a mere stabbing or shooting.

"Aloha! Welcome to paradise!"

Tippen had dressed in baggy khaki shorts and a loud Hawaiian shirt, black socks, and sandals. His bony knees looked as big as doorknobs on his skinny, hairy white legs. He sauntered toward the cubicle wearing Ray-Bans, an umbrella drink in hand.

"You look like a fucking cartoon," Kovac said.

"Absurdity is the humor of the superior mind," Tippen returned without rancor.

"Yeah, well, you've got that covered. The socks are an especially nice touch. What are you doing here?" Kovac asked. "Are the strip clubs closed for the holiday?"

Tippen leaned a shoulder against the cubicle wall and shoved the sunglasses on top of his head. "You're not the only one without a life, you know. I came in and commandeered a conference room. I thought maybe if we pretend we have a task force on this, the boss will just go along. We'll act like it's been going on for weeks. He'll be too embarrassed to call us on it."

"A pretend task force," Kovac said. "I like it. Do we get to spend pretend money on it?"

"And get imaginary overtime pay too."

"Is there another kind?"

"Not in this economy."

"Ah, well, what the hell would we do with money anyway?" Kovac asked. "Buy shit we don't have time to use 'cause we're always on the job on account of the city can't afford to hire enough cops?"

He poured more Scotch into his coffee mug and cast the pink umbrella in Tippen's drink a dubious look as they walked toward the conference room. "What the hell are you drinking?"

"A mai tai. In keeping with our tropical surroundings."

"That's a chick's drink."

"Don't ask, don't tell."

"If I'm gonna get fired for drinking on the job, I'm going down drinking a man's drink," Kovac said, raising his mug.

"Belching and farting all the way."

"Damn straight."

"You're a man's man, my friend. A credit to our gender. I'm proud to know you. How did the autopsy go?"

Kovac took another sip of the Scotch as he took a seat at the table where Tippen had deposited several cardboard file boxes full of paperwork generated by the Doc Holiday murders. The room was small and windowless and as hot as a freaking sauna.

"Not so well for the victim," he said, rolling up his shirtsleeves. "Turns out, she's dead."

"Of what?"

"Undecided. Möller wants more time to go over the results and get the labs back. We know she probably didn't die from the stab wounds. She was still alive—technically, at least—when her killer poured acid on her face."

"Charming." Tippen perched a hip on the tabletop, settling in. "So Tinks is right? She could have been alive when she came out of that trunk?"

"Not likely. If the knife didn't kill her, she could have died from inhaling the acid. There was lung damage. Can't breathe if your lungs have melted."

"Can't live if half your brain is knocked out of your skull by a Hummer either."

"True enough," Kovac said. "Or she could have died of shock. Or she could have died from ingesting the acid—it burned the hell out of her esophagus. Or maybe she had her head bashed in with a hammer like Doc Holiday did to how many of his victims? And we'll never know for sure because she was then run over by a Hummer, which busted her skull like a rotten melon.

"At this point, I don't even care what killed her," he said. "All I want to know right now is who she is. If we can't get an ID, where the hell do we go with the investigation? We can want to believe Doc Holiday killed her, but what do we *know*? Jack nothing, that's what.

"Could be she had a rotten boyfriend," he said. "Could be she had a rotten father. Could be she pissed off a dealer or a pimp. Could be everyone in this girl's life hated her and had a reason to want her dead. Could be anything. We need a starting place. If we don't know who she is, we can't know why she's a victim."

"No word on the prints?" Tippen asked.

"Nada. She's got about seven teeth left in her head, and Möller pulled a couple of loose ones out of her airway. We might be able to get a match if we can get dental records to compare to," he said. "She had a bunch of body piercings. Five in each ear, a nose ring, a belly ring. A couple others. All the jewelry is missing."

"Doc Holiday took the jewelry from the others."

"But he didn't pour acid on them," Kovac said.

"Maybe he's trying something new, broadening his torture horizons."

"Maybe," he conceded. "But the knife is wrong too. Too small. Seventeen stab wounds and none of them significant enough to kill her. What's that about?"

"What a great terror factor," Tippen said. "He gets to look in their eyes every time he sinks the knife in, over and over and over. All the better if it doesn't kill the victim."

Kovac wasn't convinced. "These tigers don't change that many stripes in one go. Maybe he changes the knife. Or maybe he adds the acid. But both?"

Tippen raised his hands in frustration. "He's ambitious. He's bored. He's got time on his hands. He saw it on *Dexter*. I don't know. Do you want the bad guy *not* to be Doc Holiday?"

"It doesn't matter what I want," Kovac said. "I want world peace. I want not to have acid reflux after eating pizza. Nobody gives a shit what I want. I want the truth. I want to know who this girl is and who killed her."

"And if we press the theory Doc Holiday killed her, then maybe we get our task force, and maybe we get to investigate our other two cases in something other than our spare time, of which we have none," Tippen pointed out. "And maybe we get the media to show some renewed attention in those other cases, and maybe something shakes loose for one of them, if not for all of them."

Kovac sighed and rubbed a hand across his jaw. He needed a shave. "I've got no problem with that part of it. It's the media part I hate."

"The media is the key. If we chum the water for them with our zombie girl, they'll create the public pressure we need with the brass," Tippen said. "We need these cases in the public eye. If people think there's a monster running around the metro area, they'll want action. Nothing captures the public imagination quite like a serial killer."

"You think we should yell 'fire' in a theater?"

Tippen made a face. "No one is going to start a stampede. It's not like Doc Holiday is breaking into homes and dragging young women from their beds," he said. "The threat is a couple of steps removed from most people's comfort zone. But the idea of a killer stalking innocent coeds and young mothers along the roadways still strikes a significant amount of fear. All we need is a good dose of vocal public outrage."

Kovac considered the argument and sighed. "I'm not against it."

The downside would be the glaring spotlight that kind of publicity would bring to the investigation itself. They had a victim with no face and no name. They had their work cut out for them. To run that investigation under a media microscope would not be a pleasant thing. He could already hear the questions: *Why haven't you caught him yet? What did you discover today? Why haven't you identified the victim?* Every moron who had ever watched an episode of *CSI* thought they were a fucking expert in forensic sciences and criminal investigation.

But he also knew the media would lose interest quickly if no answers were forthcoming, and by then he would have gotten what he needed.

"All we need is that initial excitement," Tippen said, reading his mind. "It's not our fault if their headlines dry up."

"That's true."

"Was there any sign of sexual assault?"

"Nothing obvious. No semen present."

"That fits. There was no semen with the others."

"A lot fits," Kovac conceded. "But the others were obvious sexual assaults, this one . . . I don't know."

He sat back in his chair and looked at the wall where Tippen had put up the photographs and sketches of the supposed victims of Doc Holiday—the three dumped in the Twin Cities, and five others whose bodies had been discovered in Iowa, Illinois, Nebraska, and Wisconsin. If they decided Zombie Doe had enough in common with the other cases, she would be the ninth victim. She was already their ninth Jane Doe of the year. She was the ninth girl on two counts.

"She has a tattoo," he said. "Some Chinese gibberish on her shoulder. Tinks took a picture."

"That's something. We can hit the tattoo parlors tomorrow."

"And hope that she's from here. If she's one of Doc's, Christ only knows where she came from."

They both heaved a sigh over that prospect and took a pull on their drinks.

"She had skin and blood under her fingernails," Kovac said.

"Enough for a DNA profile?" Tippen asked. "That would be a hell of a break."

"Yeah. Why would we get that lucky? The guy hasn't put a foot wrong in eight murders. Why would he be so careless with this one?"

"Because that's what happens," Tippen said. "That's what always trips these guys up. They get cocky. They get careless. They think we're too stupid to solve a case, so they get sloppy. They make mistakes."

"He can't manage to kill his vic with a too-short knife and a gallon of acid," Kovac said. "She falls out of his car on the road. She's got his DNA under her fingernails. That's a lot of mistakes for a guy who's gotten away with eight murders."

"And if we say Zombie Doe is his ninth girl, we get our task force," Tippen said, pressing the issue. "We have to leak something, get the ball rolling."

The department had an official press person, but official press releases went through official channels, their content scrutinized and sanitized and overanalyzed by people who had little to do with the actual investigation—especially when it came to high-profile cases. A leak, on the other hand, would be exactly what they wanted it to be, just the right piece of information to hit just the right nerve. The department would be forced to respond to a public now paying attention and demanding answers.

"Who's your best contact?"

"You know I don't play favorites," Kovac said. "I hate all of them equally."

"It should be a woman," Tippen said. "Outrage increases exponentially with the degree of personal threat. Angry women make a lot of noise. I happen to know an angry woman."

Kovac raised an eyebrow. "Just one?

"Very funny. I happen to know the perfect young angry woman to connect us to more angry young women. I'll make a phone call."

"I can't wait," he said with a decided lack of enthusiasm. "Why do I feel like I'm going to live to regret this?"

"Because you're a fatalist," Tippen said, digging his cell phone out of the breast pocket of his aloha shirt. "Which isn't a bad thing. You can't be disappointed if your expectations are low. But in this case I say don't look a gift horse in the mouth, my friend."

Kovac tossed back the last of his Scotch, grimacing not at the liquor but at his distaste for dealing with reporters.

"Here's what I know about horses," he said. "They bite."

8

Liska groaned aloud at the sight of the black Jeep parked in front of her house. Speed. As much as she had wanted to dump her frustration and anxiety regarding Kyle all over her ex, she had wanted to do it over the airwaves and be able to turn the phone off afterward. Neat and clean—at least in the moment. She didn't have the energy to do it in person. She was exhausted, operating on three hours of sleep in the last thirty-three. The last thing she wanted to add to this shit day was a mental sparring match with her ex-husband.

She told herself she should have been glad he had shown up—for the boys' sake. No matter how many times he let them down, he was still their dad, and they loved him. It was important for them to have their father's presence in their lives, even if it was sporadic. But there was always an emotional price to pay after the fact—for the boys and for her.

The television was blaring a football bowl game in the living room as Nikki let herself in. The house was warm and smelled of chili simmering in the Crock-Pot. She wanted to feel the tension melt away, but that wasn't going to happen.

She peeled off the layers of outerwear and wedged her coat in among the boys' things in the tiny hall closet, then ducked into the powder room, disheartened to see she hadn't turned into a Swedish bikini model in the last three minutes. It pissed her off that it mattered to her. She didn't want to care what Speed thought when he looked at her, but she couldn't seem to shake that particular vanity.

Unfortunately, she looked exactly how she felt: older than she wanted to be, worn, tired and jaded by life and by having just watched the autopsy of a young woman whose gruesome death had earned her the nickname Zombie Doe. Möller had estimated the dead girl to be between fourteen and eighteen—roughly the same age as Nikki's own children.

She splashed cold water on her face and rubbed some color into her cheeks with the towel, then finger-combed her hair and muttered, "Fuck it," under her breath.

In the living room Speed and R.J. were playing Nerf football as the television crowd cheered. Speed, ball cap backward on his head, grunted out a play, ran backward in his stocking feet, and fired the bright green football with a rocket arm. R.J. bolted across the width of the room, hurdled an ottoman, and crashed onto the sofa, then leapt up with the ball in hand. Father and son hooted and hollered and did a victory dance that knocked over a lamp.

Nikki said nothing. She would already be considered the bad guy by default in this scenario. No need to dig the hole any deeper over a lamp.

Neither Speed nor R.J. had noticed her yet. She watched them with an old familiar pang of envy in her chest. Hallmark couldn't have conjured up a more adorable father-son picture: the matching football jerseys, the matching backward caps, the matching bad-boy grins as they grabbed hold of each other and wrestled each other to the floor.

R.J. had always been a mini-Speed. Looking at them side by side was like looking at some kind of crazy time-warp photo. At thirteen, R.J.'s body was only just beginning its metamorphosis from boy to adolescent. He was still on the small side. His shoulders were just starting to widen. The baby fat was beginning to melt from his once-cherubic cheeks. Beside him was the grown man he would become: broad shouldered, flat bellied, square jawed, handsome.

These days Speed was sporting a laser-sharp trimmed mustache and goatee that emphasized the angles of his face and gave him a certain sinister edge. Time and life had etched lines beside his too-blue eyes, but instead of aging him, instead of making him look tired—as those same lines did to her—they only served to give him a sexy ruggedness. She hated him for that.

"Uh-oh," Speed said, looking up. "We're busted, sport!"

"Nice to see you too, Speed," she said. "I thought you'd left the country. You haven't been answering your phone."

"Lost it," he said, getting to his feet.

"Again?"

He shrugged, unconcerned with the phone or the lie. He shoved up the sleeves of his jersey, displaying a blue-inked sleeve of tattoos on his left arm. A tat artist's masterpiece, the work of art ran from shoulder to wrist, depicting an epic battle of good and evil, complete with a horned demon and an avenging angel.

Nikki always wondered which character represented Speed. The conclusion she inevitably came to was both. Working undercover narcotics, Speed Hatcher's world was gray with the rot of moral ambiguity. He was both the good guy and the bad guy, depending on the scenario, depending on the point of view. He had always been too comfortable with that dichotomy. What made him so very good at his job made him equally bad at being a husband and a father.

"I smell chili," she said, choosing diplomacy. "Hungry, R.J.? Or have you guys spent the whole afternoon eating junk?"

"Both," R.J. said, tossing the Nerf ball back to his father.

"Where's Kyle?" she asked, turning for the kitchen.

"Who cares?" R.J. crabbed. "He's a jerk."

"He went to a friend's house," Speed said.

Nikki turned back around. "And you let him?"

"Sure. What's the big deal?"

"R.J., please go wash up for dinner," she said pointedly.

Her son rolled his eyes. "Are you guys gonna have a fight already? Jeez, Mom. You just got here."

"We're not having a fight; we're having a discussion," Nikki said. "And not in front of you, so as not to further warp your perception of male-female relationships. Go wash up."

Father and son exchanged a glance and a shrug that clearly said, *Women. What can you do?* R.J. bounded up the stairs.

Nikki put her full attention on her ex, giving him a meaningful look as she stepped across the hall into her small home office. He followed, rolling his shoulders back like a fighter getting loose before the bell. She closed the door behind him.

"Did you truly not get my messages?" she asked. "Kyle was in a fight last night. He's got half a concussion. How could you just let him go?"

"What was I supposed to do? Arrest him?"

She thought her eyes might burst from her head at the sudden rise in her blood pressure. Her jaw hurt from biting back a flood of angry words. "Did you speak to him?"

"About what?"

"Oh my God, I want to hit you in the head with a brick," she said. "I don't know what would be worse—believing you're a flip asshole or believing you really are just that obtuse."

Speed rolled his eyes. "Jesus Christ, Nikki, he's a fifteen-year-old boy. He got in a scrape. It's not the end of the fucking world."

"He *lied* to me about it."

"Did you miss the part where I said he's a fifteen-year-old boy?"

"Kyle does not lie to me. He didn't inherit your comfort with it, thank God," she said. "He lied to me about what happened. I believe he lied to me about where he was when it happened—"

"Have you checked his story out?"

"I've been at an autopsy all afternoon."

"And your vic is going to get more dead while you take the time to make a couple of phone calls?"

Nikki gasped. "Don't you dare give me a hard time about making a phone call! You can't even be bothered to answer when I leave you a message that your son is in trouble. And don't give me that bullshit story about losing your phone. I called every number you have. Why don't you just say you don't give a shit?"

"You overreact to everything, Nikki! A kid gets a fucking hang-nail and you're texting me with the 911! So he got in a scrape. So he got popped. So he hit the kid back. So what?"

"Thank you for reminding me yet again why I'm not still married to you. You don't get this at all, do you?"

"I guess not. Never mind that I was a fifteen-year-old boy once."

"You're still a fifteen-year-old boy," Nikki argued. "That's half the problem."

"And what's the other half?" he asked. "Not you. Not you blowing every fucking thing out of proportion."

"When am I supposed to bring you into the equation, Speed?" she asked. "When are you available for consultation on this? He's having problems at school—a kid who has *never* had problems at school. He's having problems getting along with other kids—a kid who has *never* been in a fight in his life. He's lying to me about where he's going and what he's doing—a kid who has *never* told me a lie. Just when are you willing to get involved here, *Dad*? When am I supposed to call you? When he's jacked an automatic weapon and gone into school with guns ablazing?"

Speed slapped his hands to the sides of his head as if to keep it from popping off his neck. "That is *so* you, Nikki! You jump from A to fucking Armageddon! He's embarrassed to tell you he got his ass kicked, and you've got him planning the next Columbine massacre. Jesus!"

"And you don't find any of this alarming in the least?" she said. "Mr. Drug Enforcement Officer. A fifteen-year-old boy's grades are suddenly slipping. He's having trouble with friends. He's lying to his parents and exhibiting secretive behavior. This doesn't send up a red flag with you at all?"

"Kyle's not using," he said, and though his attitude was dismissive, Nikki thought she might have caught the briefest flash of alarm in the very backs of his blue eyes. "He's too smart a kid for that."

"He's fifteen," Nikki said, happy to throw one of his own lines back at him.

Speed physically took a step back from the argument, resting his hands at his waist, and blew out a sigh. "I'll have a talk with him when he gets home."

"Thank you."

They both stood there, breathing hard, as if they had been wrestling physically as well as verbally. The fight was over. All the hard energy had been burned off. Awkwardness descended. *So strange,* Nikki thought. They'd spent so many years fighting, it didn't make any sense that they still felt awkward in the aftermath.

"You'd know if he was using," Speed said quietly. His kind of reassurance.

"Would I? I don't know, Speed. I don't know the world these kids live in. It changes every day. Used to be they smoked pot or they did speed. Kids with money could afford cocaine. These days it's synthetic grass and bath salts—whatever the hell that is. They mainline heroine, and they make their own meth out of cold medicine. They know more about prescription drugs than most doctors. It scares the hell out of me."

In that moment it was only worse that she was a cop and that she knew things and had seen things other parents only read about in the newspaper, unless they were unlucky enough to have a child mixed up in it.

"I spent the afternoon at the autopsy of a girl Kyle's age," she said. "Someone stabbed her seventeen times and poured acid on her face while she was still alive. How did that happen? How did a girl Kyle's age come to be in a situation like that? What did her mother not know about her life?"

To her horror, tears filled her eyes. She was one tough cookie in every other respect, but not when it came to her boys. In that she was as vulnerable as any mother, fearful of what the world was capable of doing to her children.

"We know how that happens, Nikki," Speed said softly. He put one hand on her shoulder and stroked the other one over the back of her head. "She was a junkie or a hooker or a runaway. Her life put her in harm's way, and some predator took advantage. You've seen it a hundred times. So have I."

Too tired to tell herself not to, she slipped her arms around Speed's waist and pressed her face into his shoulder. He folded his arms around her and held her.

She *had* seen it. She *did* know how it happened. Sometimes. Not all the time. And the question still remained. Even if their ninth girl had been a junkie or a hooker or a runaway, the question still remained: What did her mother not know about her life that might have prevented her death?

"My Life"
by Gray

Me
One
Lone
Alone
Longing
Belonging
Acceptance
Accept
Except
Exception
Exclusion
Conclusion
Alone
One
Me

9

Sonya Porter was one angry young woman. She came into Patrick's bar with narrowed eyes homed in on Tippen like a pair of dark lasers. She came across the room to their booth with all the purpose of a heat-seeking missile and clipped him upside the head with the back of a hand.

Tippen winced. "Ouch! What was that for?"

"I don't remember," she said, clearly annoyed he would ask. "I was pissed off the second I heard the sound of your voice on the phone."

"You were annoyed because you were hungover," Tippen said. "That wasn't my fault."

"Yes, it was," she snapped, then softened a bit. "Well, maybe not this time. But it was your fault that other time, and I never hit you for that."

"So we're even."

She gave him a look of disgust. "Oh, hardly."

Kovac looked from one to the other and back and forth. The

girl—he put her around twenty-two—was a stylized character from a postmodern noir film. Jet-black hair cut in a sleek bob that played up the angles of her face. Dark purple lipstick on Kewpie-doll lips contrasted sharply with the perfect milk white of her skin.

She shrugged out of her heavy trench coat and hung it on a hook at the end of the booth. Bright-colored tattoos peeked out of the V-neck of her sweater. A green-inked vine with a purple morning glory flower crept up one side of her neck. A tiny steel barbell pierced the severe arch of one eyebrow. A matching steel ring went like a fish hook through her plump lower lip.

There was a part of Kovac that wanted to get up and leave this circus sideshow now. He was exhausted and out of what little patience he ever had. He had already dealt with two reporters over the phone, carefully doling out the information he wanted to let go of. Just enough detail, just enough insinuation that their Jane Doe's murder might be tied to others. No, they couldn't quote him. No, he didn't have a name for the victim. And now he had to hope they didn't fuck it up or fuck him over.

Now *this*: a Tippen family reunion.

"Oh, well," Tippen said. "I have something to look forward to."

"Maiming, for instance," the girl said.

Tippen was unconcerned with the threat. "Sonya, this is my colleague Sergeant Sam Kovac. Sam, my niece, Sonya Porter, activist, feminist, anarchist, and freelance journalist."

The girl narrowed her eyes at Kovac as she slid into the booth. "Do you have a problem with any of that?"

"I don't like journalists," he said. "The rest of it is none of my business."

"That's fair enough," she said. "I don't like cops."

"Wow, this is gonna work out for everyone," Kovac said sarcastically.

A waitress pissed off to be working New Year's came over and asked if they wanted anything. The girl ordered a shot and a beer. Kovac ordered his usual burger and fries, a heart attack on a plate. Liska usually ate half of his fries, which he figured took the damage down to a minor stroke.

They had chosen Patrick's for the meeting—and for the greasy food. An Irish-named bar owned by Swedes that catered to cops. Strategically located halfway between the police department and the sheriff's office, the pub was open 365 days a year from lunch 'til the last possible moment allowed by the city—and sometimes later, depending on circumstance.

It was a place for meals, camaraderie, and the drowning of sorrows and stress for people not understood by civilian society. Even on a holiday the place was busy with cops coming off their shift, dogwatch uniforms grabbing dinner before heading out, and the retired and otherwise disenfranchised hanging out because they had nowhere else to go. College football was playing on the big-screen TVs above the bar and pool tables.

"Who do you freelance for?" Kovac asked.

"Whoever. That would be the definition of 'freelance,' wouldn't it?"

"I can do without the attitude."

She shrugged. "I can do without being here. You need me. I don't need you."

Kovac looked at Tippen. "And I figured you for the least charming member of your family."

"Oh, I'm a peach," Tippen said.

"This is about the zombie, right?" the girl said.

Kovac gave her a hard look. "This is about a Jane Doe murder victim. There is no fucking zombie. There's a teenage girl lying dead on a steel table in the morgue with half her face dissolved by acid. She has a name, but we don't know what it is. We can assume she has a family somewhere, but we don't know who they are. How about that?"

Porter stared at him. "The zombie is the angle. You want people to get to the rest of what you just said? Embrace the zombie. We live in a society of self-absorbed, unaware drones desensitized to the suffering of others. You have to hit them in the fucking face to get their attention."

Kovac thought about it. He had to grudgingly admit he liked that she wasn't intimidated by him. "You have a poor outlook on humanity."

"Don't you?"

"I've lived longer than you have. I've earned the right to be bitter. You're not old enough to be bitter."

"Oh, I'm bitter," she assured him. "Bitter and outraged."

"Outraged by what?"

"Pretty much everything except puppies and kittens. The economy, ecology, foreign policy, social policy, women's rights, gay rights. The list goes on. There's a lot to be outraged about, including the lack of outrage exhibited by the average American."

"Well, good for you," Kovac said. "Hang on to that. But tell me, what good are you to me, Miss Outrage? I always think 'freelance' is just another word for unemployed. I need information disseminated."

"Why don't you call a press conference, then?"

"It's delicate."

The brow with the barbell sketched upward. "Ah. 'Sources close to the investigation' delicate?"

"Yeah, like that," he said. "Do you have a problem with that?"

"That depends. Is what you're going to tell me true?"

Kovac sat back, pretending confusion. "You're a reporter, right? What's truth got to do with it?"

"Oh, nothing," she said. "I live to compromise my journalistic integrity the same way you live to beat confessions out of innocent people."

"I've never beaten a confession out of an innocent person."

"And I don't knowingly lie to my readers."

The sulky waitress returned with a tray of drinks and Kovac's dinner. He shook the ketchup bottle as Sonya Porter tossed back her shot. They never took their eyes off each other.

"What readers?" Kovac asked. "Tip tells me you do stuff on the Internet. What does that mean?"

"Online news sources. Twitter. Facebook. My blog."

"And people actually read this stuff?"

She looked at her uncle with an expression that clearly said, *Are you kidding me with this guy?* Tippen shrugged.

"No one under the age of thirty reads an actual newspaper," she said. "Seriously. How old are you?"

Kovac felt like a dinosaur. In the technological revolution, he usually felt like he had chosen the wrong side. He could make a computer do what he needed it to do—which wasn't much—but in the last couple of years, with the meteoric rise of online social media, he felt like he had been run over on the information superhighway and left in the dust. Tinks stayed more current because of her boys, but as far as Kovac was concerned, tweeting came from birds, and a post was something that held up a fence.

"It doesn't matter how old I am," he said. "It matters that my victim is a teenager. And the other victims have been in their teens or early twenties."

She sat up at that. "Other victims? What other victims?"

"We could be dealing with a serial killer," Tippen said. "But the department is going to want to downplay that angle. From a public relations standpoint, a serial killer is a bad way to set the tone for the New Year."

That was a good angle, Kovac thought. Play to her desire to be outraged. She could rage against the establishment, rage against his generation. Whatever would put words on the page—or the screen—worked for him.

"This is the third victim dumped in Minneapolis," he said. "And there was one in St. Paul. None of them were from here. They were abducted in other states and dumped here when their killer was through with them.

"He's dumped bodies in other states too," he said. "This new one makes nine. You want to be outraged about something, be outraged about this: young women being abducted, raped, tortured, disfigured, murdered, and chucked out along the road like a sack of garbage. This girl's face is so destroyed it's anybody's guess what she looked like before this asshole got hold of her."

He paused to take a bite of his dinner while he let Sonya Porter digest the information he'd fed her. Sonya Porter, twenty-young, with her lip ring and her anger; the illustrated girl from a generation that could have been from another planet as far as he was concerned.

"What do you need from me?" she asked.

"I need to reach the people who might have known this girl. Kids she went to school with, hung out with. Siblings, maybe. Anyone. Anyone who might know anything," he said. "And I need this information to go out as far and as wide as possible, because I don't have any idea in hell where this girl came from."

"What have you got to go on?"

"A tattoo." Kovac picked his phone up off the tabletop and brought up the photograph Tinks had taken at the autopsy and texted to him. "Any idea what it means?"

Sonya Porter's expression changed as she spread her thumb and forefinger across the screen to enlarge the picture of the Chinese characters. From interest to confusion to recognition to sadness.

"Yes," she said quietly. "I know what it means."

She put the phone down on the tabletop and pushed up the sleeve of her sweater to reveal the same set of Chinese characters inked into the delicate skin on the inside of her forearm.

"It means acceptance."

10

Kyle sat on his bed with his back against the headboard and his knees pulled up. The light on his nightstand glowed amber, holding at bay the cold black night beyond his window.

The artwork on his walls took on a sinister feel in the dim light. His own renditions of characters from his favorite comic books and graphic novels, *300* and *Batman: The Dark Knight Returns,* loomed large. Leonidas, the Spartan king, fierce and bearded. Xerxes I of Persia, beautiful and evil, with his elaborate body piercings and glowing eyes. Batman and the Joker.

Characters of Kyle's own creation looked down on him as well. Most notably, Ultor, defender and avenger of the downtrodden and the disenfranchised. Ultor, a man of chiseled muscle with an iron jaw and narrowed eyes, was loosely fashioned after Kyle's favorite mixed martial arts fighter, Georges St-Pierre.

With GSP, a man of few words, with swift and terrible punishment in his hands, there was no bullshit, no trash talk, no preening or posing. He was a gentleman, a man of honor. He wasn't the biggest fighter. At five feet ten inches, 170 pounds, he had a compact body cut with lean muscle. He had been a small kid, bullied merci-lessly by older schoolmates. Now, as a world champion fighter with millions of fans, he spoke out against bullying, which made Kyle admire him all the more.

A black belt in Kyokushin karate and Brazilian jiu-jitsu, GSP came, he saw, he conquered with a superior mind, superior skill, and conditioning. And when he won, he was thankful and gracious. Ultor was like that: a man who fought with honor, a man of the people and for the people. He was a man Kyle had created to fill a need in his own life.

He could hear the voices downstairs: his mother's and his dad's. They were talking about him, he supposed, though he couldn't make out any of the words, just the cadence of conversation in the living room below.

He preferred to live under their radar. They didn't understand anything about his life. They were both obsessed with the idea of drugs, which was an insult to him. Like they thought he was stupid enough to do shit like that.

He had smoked pot, but he didn't like it. Everyone smoked pot. His dad did (Kyle had seen the evidence in his dad's apartment, had smelled it) and he was a narc. A narc and a hypocrite. He drank, he smoked, he smoked pot, he had cheated on Mom. Kyle hadn't ex-actly understood about that at the time because he was just a little kid, but he had known it wasn't right. He had heard their argu-ments, listened to his mom cry after the fight, when his dad had left and she thought she was alone.

Speed Hatcher wasn't a good father. He lied. He let them down. He showed up when it suited him and made excuses the rest of the time. He would make it if Kyle or R.J. was in a sporting event, but he had never made it to a single art show Kyle had been a part of. He had never come to see Kyle get an academic award.

He took them to see the Twins and the Vikings and the Timberwolves and the Wild because those were things he liked to do and he looked like a hero. And for sure, those were fun things to do, but Kyle saw it for what it was—part bribery and part self-indulgence. R.J. fell for all that crap because he was still a little kid and because he wanted to, but Kyle didn't.

So it didn't impress Kyle that his dad had come to his room, all serious and wanting to have a talk with him. It hadn't concerned his father all that much when he had first shown up earlier in the day and saw Kyle's face busted up. He had accepted Kyle's excuse with an offhand comment about how he expected the other guy to look worse.

His sudden concern tonight was Mom's doing. She hadn't been satisfied with the story Kyle had told, and she had sent Dad in for the second interrogation. Bad cop, good cop. She thought Kyle might confess something to his father, man-to-man. But his father wasn't the kind of man Kyle admired or wanted to be. No confession would be confidential. His father would go straight to his mother and spill everything. No confession would be forthcoming.

His parents understood nothing about the world he lived in, the pressures he was under. He lived in a world of extremes. He was smart. His teachers and his mom pressured him to perform academically. He was gifted. His art instructors pushed him to become a more commercial, traditional artist, to not "waste his time" on tattoo designs and comic book characters. He was athletic. His dad wanted him to play football, to play hockey, to play baseball, to be a part of a team, to be a guy's guy. Kyle wanted to study Muay Thai kickboxing and Brazilian jiu-jitsu and do his own thing for his own reasons.

Because he was good-looking and talented, socially he was expected to be cool, to be popular, to act a certain way, to like certain kinds of girls—and, more important, to *not* like certain people, to *not* like the kids who were misfits. He didn't care about being cool.

He definitely didn't run with the popular crowd. And because he didn't care about those things, he was generally disliked by the kids who did.

He had thought it would be different when he started going to PSI. Theoretically, Performance Scholastic Institute was the biggest geek school in town. It was the place for brainiacs and kids in the arts—kids who always got picked on and beat up at public school. But it was no different. Every clique hated another clique. There were still cool kids who picked on the kids who didn't fit in.

In fact, in some ways it was worse at PSI because the smarter the kids, the meaner they could be. At least in public school the meanest kids tended to be stupid. The cruelty was less sophisticated.

Kyle had been excited to win his scholarship. He had been excited to be challenged academically and encouraged in his art. But now he wished he could just take his GED and be done with school. He didn't believe he needed an education to succeed as an artist. Talent was all that mattered. And he sure as hell didn't need the rest of the high school bullshit.

He wanted to work on his drawing without anyone pushing their opinions on him. He wanted not to be forced into a mold that didn't fit him. He wanted to be with the people he wanted to know, and not have others judge him or his friends. He dreamed about having his own place to live where he never had to explain himself to anybody, where he could be who he was and live how he wanted.

But he couldn't tell his parents any of that . . . or anything else about his life.

He dug his cell phone out from under his pillow, went to his contacts, and touched a name.

The phone on the other end rang and rang and went to voice mail. Again. Kyle ended the call without leaving a message and went to his text messages instead. The message he had first sent late two nights before, then again and again and again, remained unanswered.

Where r u? R u ok?

He sent it again, just in case.

No answer returned.

The voices downstairs were droning on. Kyle got up and stuck his head out in the hall. R.J.'s door was closed, his television mumbling on the other side. With the coast clear, he went down the hall to the bathroom, locked himself inside, and turned on the shower as hot as he could stand it.

The water stung the abrasions on his face and his knuckles but soothed some of the aches in his body. He examined himself as he dried off. The bruises were starting to come to the surface. At least that was all he had—bruises. No broken bones. No open wounds to try to explain away. The worst of the damage was invisible. The damage done to his heart, to his spirit. The thousand cuts of cruel words.

Why did people have to be so full of hate and ignorance? Why couldn't they just let everyone be who they were?

He glanced over his shoulder at his reflection in the mirror and the two small symbols tattooed on his shoulder. This was what he believed so strongly that he had saved up his own money and had the ideal etched into his flesh with ink: *acceptance*.

11

"Which one of you is the 'source close to the investigation'?"

Captain Ullrich Kasselmann sat behind his desk looking like a banker: well-tailored charcoal suit, crisp white shirt, stylish orange tie knotted just so, every silver hair in place. Only the faintest sheen of perspiration on his forehead suggested he even noticed that the office was as hot as Florida in August.

Kasselmann was a man with a solid build and an immovable, brick-wall quality about him that was a physical manifestation of his character. He'd been the head of the Criminal Investigative Division long enough to have substantiated his initial paranoia regarding his employees.

"Don't look at me," Tinks said irritably. "I don't even know what you're talking about."

Kovac gave her a sideways glance. She looked like maybe she had tried to catch an hour's sleep on a bench at a bus stop—hair more disheveled than usual, dark smudges under bloodshot eyes, pasty complexion.

"The lead story on the early morning news, channels five and eleven," Kasselmann said. "'Zombie Possible Victim of Serial Killer.' You don't know anything about that?"

He turned his laser gaze on Kovac.

"Yeah, right," Kovac said sarcastically. "I have such a close personal relationship with the media."

Kasselmann was poker-faced. "Then who?"

"How should I know?" Kovac asked. "Call Culbertson," he said, readily throwing the ME's investigator under the bus. Culbertson didn't answer to Kasselmann. Nothing would come of it. And frankly, Steve Culbertson loved to play the role of subversive. This could work out for everyone.

"Is it true?" the captain asked.

"Could be. Yes. Definitely could be," Kovac said, resisting the urge to glance again at his partner. Liska had argued against the possibility of Zombie Doe being one of Doc Holiday's victims. She said nothing now.

"New Year's Eve, stabbed repeatedly, sexual overtones, facial disfigurement," he said. "More pieces fit than don't."

"She came out of the trunk of a car," Kasselmann said. "In traffic."

"Looks like the car hit a pothole, the trunk popped open, and the body bounced out," Kovac said. "Then again, Möller says there's a slim chance she might have still been alive at the time. Maybe she escaped. It certainly wasn't anybody's plan for her to get out of that trunk when she did."

"We don't have a plate on the car?"

"The limo driver was distracted. He's coming in today to get hypnotized." He shrugged. "Maybe he'll come up with something."

"But you're not hopeful."

"He had two hot half-naked babes making out with each other in his backseat. What do you think he was looking at?"

Kasselmann heaved a sigh, disapproval set in the chiseled lines of his face. "I've had phone calls from three deputy chiefs already this morning. And I've been called to the chief's office for an urgent meeting in twenty minutes. He's not going to be in a good mood."

"Yeah?" Liska piped up aggressively. "Well, imagine what a good mood he'd be in if this was his daughter lying on a slab in the morgue with her face burned off from the acid her killer tried to force down her throat. He should think about *that*, shouldn't he?"

Kasselmann's silver brows climbed his forehead.

"This is somebody's daughter," she went on emphatically. "Just like Rose Reiser was someone's daughter, and the victim from Iowa—who was not only someone's daughter but someone's *mother*. The chief should maybe think about those things, shouldn't he?"

"You seem to have an ax to grind, Sergeant," Kasselmann said.

"I'm a mother. I'm a woman. Do I need something more than a vagina to be outraged that we're letting a serial killer run around loose destroying the lives of young women because the mayor doesn't want his constituents to think we live in a dangerous place?"

The captain looked pointedly at Kovac.

Kovac spread his hands. "What? You think *I* have some control over her? She's gonna go fifty shades of whoop-ass all over the both of us."

"Rein it in," Kasselmann warned, turning his attention to the offender.

Tinks looked like she might just hurl herself across his desk and bite an ear off him. Kovac stepped a little in front of her, cutting off her direct route.

"I'm not saying we don't want this case solved—or the other two, for that matter," Kasselmann said. "But there are consider- ations to be made in how we go about doing it and how it gets presented to the public. There are protocols to be considered. There are proper channels to go through. The two of you have been at this long enough to know better than to end-around the brass on a high- profile case."

No one pointed out that it hadn't been a high-profile case until now, until the sensational headline.

"Look, boss, the horse is out of the barn," Kovac said. "We've just got to deal with this and go forward. I need manpower. We've got to identify this vic. All I've got to go on at this point is a tattoo. I need people canvassing the local ink shops. I need eyes going over the other cases, looking for some kind of thread."

"You want a task force."

"I don't care what you call it."

"Our hand is being forced now," Kasselmann said. "The public is going to expect a task force. The media is going to be crawling up our asses like cheap underwear. You know how this goes. You went through this with the Cremator cases. You want to do that again?"

"Like I want a colonoscopy," Kovac admitted. "I just want to run my investigation. I want the time and the warm bodies to do it right. Why should anybody be against that?"

Kasselmann pushed to his feet. "Because it costs money. Because a multi-agency task force is a logistical nightmare. Because it draws the wrong kind of attention—"

Liska stepped back into the fray. "And a dead girl with no face doesn't? With all due respect, sir, that is *fucked-up*."

The captain gave her a hard-eyed stare. Liska pushed it right back at him. Kovac held his breath, feeling like he was caught between a she-wolf and an angry bull.

Kasselmann blinked first. He looked at Kovac. "Set up a room. You get Tippen and Elwood for starters. The rest remains to be seen. I have a meeting to get to."

"Yes, sir."

"And I don't want anybody talking to the press about anything. Got it?"

"Got it."

"Redistribute whatever other cases you've got going on that aren't a priority."

"Yes, sir," Kovac said, wondering just which murder on his caseload *wasn't* a priority and how he would explain that to the families involved. Maybe he would foist off some of his assaults on a couple of the younger guys.

He put the matter to the back of his mind and herded Liska out of the captain's office and past the cubicles, steering her into the conference room he and Tippen had set up the night before.

"Do I need to inject coffee into you intravenously?" he asked, shrugging out of his sport coat. "Or would you prefer the hair of the dog? In which case we should leave the building because, despite all evidence to the contrary, I would prefer not to be fired and lose my pension."

"I'm not hungover."

Kovac raised an eyebrow as he rolled up his shirtsleeves. "How long have we known each other?"

"All right," she admitted grudgingly as she slipped out of her wool blazer and hung it on the back of a chair. "I'm a little hungover. And I haven't slept in two days," she confessed, melting into a chair at the long table. "I thought a glass of wine might help."

"A glass?"

"A glass . . . as in *bottle*. Red wine is good for you," she added defensively.

"Yeah, you're the freaking picture of health here. Is this still to do with Kyle?"

She pulled in a long breath and let it back out. "Yes. Speed tried to talk to him last night, but he didn't get anywhere."

Kovac perched a hip on the table, settling in to offer his sage wisdom. "You're not going to know everything that goes on in a teenage boy's life, Tinks. Trust me, you don't want to know."

She gave him a look. "Oh, that's reassuring. Thanks."

"What I mean to say is, he's fifteen. He's not a little boy anymore."

"He's not a man either."

"He's a *guy* now. Guys have their own shit going on that they aren't going to share with their mothers—unless they're weird or gay."

"Spoken like a guy."

"See?" he said. "I wouldn't tell you my shit either."

"You don't have any shit to tell about."

"That's beside the point."

"You don't get it, Sam," she said. "Do you know the stuff kids get into today? Drugs, guns, sex. Every day is like another chapter in *Lord of the Flies*."

"At the pansy-ass private brainiac school," Kovac said. "PSI is not exactly the mean streets. I mean, what are the gangs in that school? The math club versus the science club?" He sat back and held his hands up as if to fend off an attacker. "Ooooooo . . . Look out! They're packing fountain pens and slide rules!"

Liska tried to rally up a sense of humor, but the attempted smile looked more like a result of gas pain.

"Slide rules went out with the dinosaurs, T. rex."

"Whatever."

"I just don't want to see him make a hard mistake," she admitted. A sheen of uncharacteristic tears brightened her eyes. "He's my baby, Sam. I look at him and I see him when he was two, when he was five, when he was ten. I don't want him to grow up. I don't want him to get hurt."

"But we all do, Tinks," Kovac said gently. "That's part of the deal. We grow up. We make mistakes and we learn from them. That's how it works.

"Look at the two of us," he said. "We smoked weed and drank 'til we puked, and had sex, and flunked algebra. Look how we turned out. We're not dead. We're not in prison. We've lived long enough to fuck up a million more times.

"He got in a fight," he said. "No lives were lost. Let it go. You can't keep him on a leash like a dog."

"It's so hard." She put her elbows on the table and rubbed her hands over her face, messing up her makeup.

"Jesus Christ," Kovac grumbled with a phony gruffness meant to cover his actual concern. He dug a clean handkerchief out of his hip pocket and offered it to her. "Now you look like the Joker. Go fix yourself, and put your cop face on. We've got work to do."

Taking the handkerchief, she swept it under each eye and around her mouth, scrubbing off smeared mascara and lipstick. She looked up at the wall with the victim photos, seeing it for the first time and looking like she welcomed the distraction. "What's all this?"

"Tip and I did this last night. We wanted to hit the ground running today."

He moved off the table for a closer look at the photographs.

"You've got a kid with a black eye," he said, tapping a finger beneath the sickening close-up of what was left of the face of Zombie Doe. "Someone out there has a daughter who looks like this. Count yourself lucky and get your head in the game, kiddo."

Tippen stuck his homely head in the door. "Are we a go?"

"One way or another," Kovac said.

The detective walked in, tossed a bag of bagels on the table, and arched a brow at Liska. "Did you spend the night in the drunk tank or is this a new look for you?"

She flipped him off.

"Admitting you have a problem is the first step," he said, then turned to Kovac. "Sonya e-mailed me her first piece. It's going up on her blog this morning as soon as we give it the thumbs-up."

"Who's Sonya?" Liska asked, grabbing an iced coffee from the carrier Elwood brought in with him.

"Tip's niece," Kovac said.

"God help her," Liska muttered. "I always figured you for someone's creepy uncle, Tip."

"She's some kind of cyberjournalist," Kovac explained. "Our liaison to the victim pool."

"She's got a lot of readers," Tippen said. "And contacts. She's hooked in to every online page the sixteen- to twentysomethings read. Web news sites, Facebook, Twitter. And she's reaching out to people she knows in the tattoo business."

"She says the tattoo on our vic is the Chinese symbol for acceptance," Kovac explained to the others as he stood looking at the close-up he had taped to the wall with the rest of the autopsy photos. "She has the same thing on her arm. Apparently, it's something the young people are doing these days to make a statement."

"For kids the victim's age, that's not even legal in this state," Tippen pointed out. "Minors can't get tattoos, even with parental consent."

"Thank God," Liska said, digging a cinnamon-raisin bagel out of the bag. "Kyle wanted a tattoo for his last birthday. I said absolutely not until he runs away and joins the circus."

"It's an artistic form of self-expression," Elwood said. "Tattoos are a road map of the bearer's personal journey."

"The kid who works the counter nights at my local convenience store has a tat of a snake wrapped around his throat," Kovac said. "Apparently, his personal journey took a detour through hell."

"Possibly," Elwood said seriously.

"The girl I work out with at the gym has a leprechaun on her stomach," Liska said. "She's twenty-two and you could bounce quarters off her abs. She thinks it's cute. I wonder how cute she'll think it is after she's had a couple of kids and the thing has morphed into Larry the Cable Guy."

"Not everyone gives their choice as much consideration as they should," Elwood conceded. "Each of my tattoos has a deep personal meaning."

Kovac made a face. "Please don't tell us where they are on your person."

"I want to know how the artist negotiated all the body hair," Tippen said.

Liska wrinkled her nose. "Eeeww."

"I waxed first," Elwood said nobly, making everyone moan in unison.

"Speed has that whole sleeve on one arm," Liska said. "And I get what it means, what it represents for him. The struggle between good and evil; the juxtaposition of himself as the avenging angel or the devil. And, of course, he wants to look badass at the gym. But he's allegedly a grown man, so if he wants to illustrate himself, that's his choice. Kyle is fifteen. Should a fifteen-year-old permanently etch something into his body?"

"That depends on what it is," Elwood said.

"He's into comic books and samurai warriors. When he's an adult and working as an attorney, is he going to thank me for letting him get a giant tattoo of Spider-Man?"

"What's more disturbing is that you'd let your kid become a lawyer," Tippen said. "And you think *I'm* sick?"

Kovac brought them back on topic. "So the question here is: If by law minors can't get a tattoo in this state, and our victim is only fifteen or sixteen, does that mean she came from out of state? Or did she just have a good fake ID? Or are there tattoo artists around town who just don't give a shit what the law says?"

"You're not exactly talking about a group of straight-arrow conformists," Tippen said.

"No," Elwood agreed, "but the majority are very defensive of both their art form and their integrity as businesspeople. The artists I know were glad for the law restricting minors. They want their work to be respected and meaningful, not some idiotic drunk-ass whim."

"Sonya tells us this particular tat is about acceptance and tolerance," Tippen said. "Racial tolerance, religious tolerance, tolerance of sexual preference. It's a statement, part of a social movement. Given the gravity of the meaning, I don't think it's a stretch to imagine there could be an artist or two willing to bend the rules to put it on younger kids in order to further the message."

"How many tattoo parlors are we talking about?" Kovac asked.

"About twenty close in on Minneapolis proper," Elwood said. "Plus St. Paul, plus the outer burbs. And we're not taking into account that artists will freelance outside the studios. There's our likely culprit for tattooing underage kids—some young artist trying to make a few extra bucks on the side. This is a simple, straightforward design requiring minimal skill and minimal equipment."

"Meaning this is going to be a long process," Liska said. "Quicker if we just post a photo of the tattoo and get it to the media and ask if anyone is missing a daughter with this tattoo."

"Assuming all parents know whether or not their kid has an illegal tattoo," Tippen said.

Liska conceded the point. "Okay. Is anyone missing a best friend, a sister, a teammate, a girlfriend . . ."

"And this is where Sonya comes in," Tippen said. "She'll reach that peer group."

"In the meantime, we have to reach out to the schools," Kovac said. "I want lists of absentees from every school we can hit in the metro area. Girls, fourteen to eighteen, just to cover as many bases as possible."

"What kind of manpower are we getting?" Elwood asked.

"Remains to be seen," Kovac said. "Kasselmann is meeting with the brass assholes as we speak. He's not happy, but he'll get over it. Or not. Whatever.

"For now, we're it," he said. "My gut feeling is we won't get a full-on task force, which is fine with me. I don't want to lose time with all the front-end bullshit and red tape of a multi-agency thing. I'm hoping we keep it in-house but pull in a couple of detectives from Sex Crimes or somewhere else.

"In the meantime, we just have to get on it. Hopefully, we'll end up with enough manpower to revisit the first two Doc Holiday cases, but our priority for now is to get an ID on our new girl."

All eyes went to the horror-movie still of Zombie Doe's face taped to the wall as the centerpiece of a macabre montage.

"God help us," Tinks muttered.

"He'd better," Kovac said. "He already missed his chance with her."

12

Gerald Fitzgerald never missed the news if he could help it. It was a Minnesota thing. Minnesotans, from childhood, watch the news daily. He had not realized there was anything unusual in that until he heard Garrison Keillor make jokes about it on *A Prairie Home Companion*. He still didn't get why people thought that was funny.

Some of his earliest memories were of sitting on the living room floor watching Walter Cronkite while his mother banged pots and pans together in the kitchen, making supper. As an adult, the first thing he did upon waking up was turn on the TV to catch the news. Lunch and dinner happened in front of the television, watching the local news. The day officially ended with the ten o'clock news.

The news was the scale of the day, the place to find out if society was in balance or out of whack. People trusted the news, and they trusted the people who delivered the news. News was truth. At least it had been in Cronkite's day.

Nowadays, you couldn't trust the news. Used to be you went to the news to get the facts. Now you had to fact-check everything that came over the airwaves yourself. News personalities seemed to have no compunction lying outright to slant things in the favor of whomever they worked for. Cronkite had to be rolling over in his grave. It was disgraceful.

The headline on the screen caught his attention first.

ZOMBIE MURDER.

He grabbed the remote off the nightstand and jacked up the volume. The perky blonde seemed to look right at him as she spoke.

"Sources close to the investigation of a New Year's Eve homicide in Minneapolis say this murder may be the work of a serial killer law enforcement agencies have dubbed 'Doc Holiday.'

"The partially nude body of an unidentified female fell from the trunk of a vehicle New Year's Eve in the Loring Park area. The gruesome condition of the disfigured corpse led one witness to describe the deceased woman as a *zombie*!"

Film footage showed the New Year's Eve scene. A giant white Hummer sitting crosswise in the road. Emergency vehicles with strobe lights rolling. Uniformed officers walking around.

"No official statement has been made by the Minneapolis Police Department regarding the victim or the possibility of a serial killer in the metro area. The detective in charge of this most recent case would neither confirm nor deny any possible connection to several similar crimes committed over the course of the last year with the bodies of victims being discovered on holidays."

He spotted the detective. Kovac. He knew him. He had met him, had spoken with him. Decent guy, Kovac. A straight shooter, an old-school cop. Appropriately suspicious, thorough. But, like all cops, he was not an original thinker. He put one foot in front of the other and plodded along.

And there was his partner, the little blonde. Liska. She was a pistol. He liked the look of her, but she was too old for his tastes, and he had no doubt that messing with her would be like grabbing a wildcat by the tail. Way too much trouble. He didn't mind a little sporting fight in his girls, but one that could seriously mess him up? No, thanks. Maybe when she was eighteen or nineteen . . .

The blonde giving the news was more his speed—wide-eyed, young, idealistic. He could easily picture her in his control. He could see those wide eyes even wider and filled with terror. He could feel the blood start to heat in his veins. She could be one for Doc Holiday.

Doc Holiday. He liked the name, the play on words.

Growing up, he had been a big fan of Westerns—*Gunsmoke* and *Bonanza* on television, and all the old Western movies. *Gunfight at the O.K. Corral* had always been a favorite when he was a kid. Wyatt Earp and Doc Holliday. He owned the DVDs of the two movies made in the nineties—*Wyatt Earp* and *Tombstone*. He preferred *Tombstone*'s Kurt Russell over Kevin Costner as Wyatt Earp, but he thought Dennis Quaid should have won the freaking Oscar as Doc Holliday in the Costner film. Val Kilmer's portrayal of the dentist/gunslinger had been way too gay for his taste.

Not that the historical Doc Holliday had anything to do with the Doc Holiday who left dead girls on the side of the road.

That was his doing.

Doc Holiday. Gerald Fitzgerald.

He hadn't gotten nearly the publicity he could have for his exploits. He was much more prolific than anyone would ever give him credit for. But that was the trade-off. He could be careful and successful, or careless and caught.

He had no intention of getting caught. Not by anyone. Not ever. He was very skilled. He was very smart. He thought of himself as a professional. He didn't make mistakes. The risks he took were calculated. He always had a plan.

He had one now.

13

"What time did you last eat?" Liska asked.

The forensic artist was a short, doughy, twentysomething young man named Nam Pham, whose actual job was as a computer nerd in the business technology unit.

As in most police departments, there was no salaried position for a forensic artist in the MPD. City budgets didn't allow for that kind of extravagance. There wasn't enough work to warrant a full-time artist here. In fact, there were only a handful of salaried, full-time positions for forensic artists in the entire country. It was standard op—and far cheaper—to make use of someone with artistic talent who was already getting paid for doing something else within the department.

Pham had been a poli sci major and an art minor in college. The department had footed the bill for a couple of seminars in forensic art. He had paid out of pocket for additional training, just to get the opportunity to do the job. He had been doing suspect composite drawings for the last eight or nine months in addition to his regular duties.

He looked at Liska with confusion.

"When did you last eat?" she asked again.

"About an hour ago," he said, apprehension dawning. "Why do you ask?"

Liska didn't answer. She would have worried about the contents of her own stomach this morning, considering the hangover, but she was feeling too mean to get sick, aggravated by the situation of the case. She hated the politics that manipulated a high-profile investigation. There should have been no place for it, and yet they had to play that game just to get what they needed in order to do their jobs. It sucked.

They followed Möller down the hall toward the room where Jane Doe 09-11 lay waiting. Pham glanced around, trying not to look as uncomfortable as he was to be at the county morgue.

"Have you ever seen a dead body?" Liska asked skeptically. Everything about Nam Pham was annoying her now. His hair was too thin. His shirt was too green. He looked clammy.

"Yes," he said defensively.

"And I don't mean your grandmother in a casket."

"Um, then, no."

"Great," she muttered.

"I can work from photographs," Pham said. "I mean, really, I *need* to work from photographs. It takes time to get it right. I need to study the angles. You could have just brought me the photographs. It really isn't necessary for me to see the actual body."

Liska grabbed a packaged gown off the service cart parked in the hall and hit him in the stomach with it like a quarterback handing off a football.

"Put this on, and try not to puke in your mask."

The room Möller took them into was cold and smelled strongly of burned flesh and a terrifying death, a smell that hit like a fist and forced its way down a person's throat. Liska scowled as if she might frighten it away. Nam Pham turned green.

Möller, already in scrubs, getting an early start on the day's autopsies, shrugged and apologized as he waited for them to gown up.

"A house fire in Whittier," he said, waving a hand at the charred remains of what had once been a human being, now lying on a gurney like some strange, grotesque, twisted driftwood sculpture. "Someone cooking meth for New Year's supper."

"Meth cooked the cook," Liska remarked. "That's a crispy critter if ever I've seen one. Man, I'd rather roll around in week-old, maggot-infested roadkill than smell that smell. I couldn't have your job, Doc."

"What smell is that, Sergeant?" Möller asked. ME humor. "Barbecue?"

Nam Pham pressed his mask to his mouth and muffled a gag.

"Any leads yet on our Jane Doe?" Möller asked, moving on toward another door.

"Nothing," Liska said. "If she's going to be missed by someone, I would think that someone would be pretty worried by today. We can only hope if she has loved ones, they live in the area.

"We've got to get this sketch done and out there on the Internet, on TV, in the newspapers," she said.

Möller led the way into a cold-storage room where several bodies lay covered on steel tables. He looked at Pham.

"Have you done reconstruction work, Mr. Pham?"

"I took a course," Pham said weakly, his eyes fixed on the draped human form the ME stood beside.

Möller arched a brow as he picked up the corner of the sheet. "You're about to take another."

Even the green drained from Nam Pham's complexion as he got his first look at their Jane Doe.

Liska counted half under her breath. "Three . . . two . . . one . . ."

Pham's knees started to buckle. He yanked down his mask, turned, and grabbed on to a laundry cart and threw up into it.

Möller sighed. Liska rolled her eyes.

"I think perhaps your artist is a bit overfaced," Möller said. "No pun intended."

Liska stepped over and cuffed Pham hard on the shoulder. "Suck it up, nerd boy. You're all I've got. And you're all she's got, too."

She curled a hand into the collar of his shirt and pulled him back to the table like a recalcitrant third grader. "Do you understand now why I insisted you come here and see her in the flesh?"

"To make me puke?" he said miserably. He was staring just to the left of the victim's head, concentrating on *not* seeing her.

"This isn't about you. It's about her. Look at her," Liska ordered, yanking on his collar like she was pulling on the leash of a dog. "Look at her!"

Pham took a breath as if he were about to put his head underwater and looked straight at the disfigured mess that was their victim.

"If I just showed you a photograph of this girl's face, what would you see?" Liska asked. "You'd see a monster. You'd see a character from *The Walking Dead*. You'd see something that your brain would tell you wasn't real.

"But she *is* real. This girl *is* real," she said. "She's not a zombie. She's not a movie prop. This was a living, breathing young woman. You need to get that. She had a life and someone took it away from her.

"I need you to give it back to her, Nam," she said. "I need a drawing of a real live girl. Do you understand me?"

"How?" he asked, shrugging away from her. "How am I supposed to do that? Half her face is missing! She doesn't even have a nose!"

Liska had made the same argument to Kovac. A bad sketch could be worse than no sketch at all. But they had so little to go on, they had to grab on to something, to start somewhere.

"You'll have to concentrate on what she does have, not what's missing," she said. "Get the jawline from the good side, get the one good eye and make two. Get the hair right. She had piercings. Draw them with jewelry in place."

"If I give you a drawing and it doesn't resemble what the victim looked like in real life, won't that be doing more harm than good?" Pham asked. "Her family won't recognize her."

"I have to trust that you're gifted, Nam. I have to hope that someone recognizes her haircut or the arch of her eyebrow," Liska said. "I have to hope that someone will find enough similarities in the features, add that to the tattoo on her shoulder, and come up with a name."

"No results with her fingerprints?" Möller asked.

Liska shook her head.

"The whole face needs to be reconstructed," Pham argued. "What I come up with is going to be a guess. You need to reconstruct her skull."

"That can be done," Möller said. "I can disarticulate the head from the body. We can soak the skull in acid to clean the flesh from the bone. Of course, there is a considerable amount of damage to the skull itself, and the flesh is all that's keeping it together in places. But then it's like a jigsaw puzzle. We glue it back together."

"And when we find her family, I get to explain why we decapitated their loved one and dissolved what was left of her face in acid," Liska said.

"If no one can identify her, there is no family which needs an explanation," Möller pointed out.

Liska tried playing that line through her mind in an imaginary conversation with Captain Kasselmann. Even in her imagination he wasn't receptive.

"You need a forensic sculptor," Nam Pham said.

"Yeah?" Liska said. "Well, I don't have one. I have you. And I need a drawing. Today."

NAM PHAM TOOK his own photographs of Jane Doe. Liska had to give him credit. As squeamish as he was, and as horrific as Jane Doe's face was, he stood in there and took pictures from every possible angle. And Möller, as busy a man as he was, assisted, positioning the battered skull, arranging the dead girl's hair with the gentle hand of a man who had daughters of his own.

This was what it would take, she knew. This was what they would have to do. They had to become this girl's family. They didn't know her name or the circumstances of her life or her death, but they had to become her family. They had to be the first line to keep her connected to the world of the living, or else she simply ceased to exist and the universe closed the tiny void left by her light going out, and it would be as if she never mattered. No one should ever die as if his or her life never mattered. Until they found a family to mourn her, the people dealing with her case would be her family.

When Liska had first come into Homicide, Kovac had drilled into her that the person they worked for wasn't their immediate boss, wasn't their chief, wasn't the collective population of the city of Minneapolis. The person they worked for was the victim. They had to become the voice for the voiceless, the avengers for those who couldn't avenge themselves. That truth was no truer than when their victim had no name.

Avenger sounded so much more dramatic and grandiose than *cop*. Avenger was a word to describe a comic book hero, not a civil servant. Like the character Kyle had created for his comic book stories, Ultor. Avengers had names like Ultor, not Sam or

Nikki. They looked like gladiatorial gods and wielded super-human powers.

Liska would have settled for the power to see the past, to see who this girl had been and what had happened to her. But she had no such power. She would have to use the tools she had, the most prominent being tenacity and determination. She would have to leave the comic book heroes to her son.

14

R U OK?

Kyle typed the words into his phone, then stared hard at the recipient of his text message. She sat two tables down in the next row, facing him, pretending to read her history book. Brittany Lawler: blond, pretty, popular, with big blue eyes that were like lakes on a cloudless summer day.

They were in the library. No talking allowed. No phones either, but everyone brought them anyway, turned them to silent mode and spent the study hour texting or on Facebook or Twitter. The librarians didn't care as long as there wasn't any noise.

He could tell by the way her eyebrows pulled together that she had gotten his message. She frowned. She knew exactly where he was sitting, but she didn't look his way.

I C U, he typed and sent.

She frowned harder. Her thumbs worked the keyboard.

His phone vibrated in his hand.

Quit stalking me

Not stalking, he typed. *Caring*

Quit caring then
Trying 2 help
Don't need ur help
O right. Cuz u have such good friends. Not.

She held up her phone so he could see it, turned it off, and put it facedown on the table. She picked up her history book and made a show of pretending to read it.

Kyle sighed and turned his attention back to his sketch pad. His fictional world made so much more sense to him. His alter ego, Ultor, was decisive and in control. He saw a problem; he took care of the problem. He identified a victim and became that person's champion. Ultor was wanted, needed, appreciated. Only the bad guys fought with him—and they always lost. There was always a struggle, a fight, and Ultor did not always come out unscathed, but he always came out of the fight victorious. He was a hero and people loved him for it.

In real life—in high school, at least—people didn't always want to be helped. Real life was more complicated.

Kyle worked his pencil over the paper, patiently adding detail to the scene. Ultor was muscular and angular, with broad shoulders and narrow hips. His arms and legs were sculpted. His belly was flat and cut, the six-pack showing through the skintight T-shirt he wore. His brow was low, his eyes narrow, his jaw wide and shadowed.

In this scene Ultor was putting himself between the girl he was protecting and the villain's henchman. One arm reached back, putting the victim behind him. One arm stretched forward, directing the forceful beam of energy from the palm of his hand into the face of the attacker. Ultor was the center of the scene, the source of power. Everything else was pushed away from him by that power. Through the strength of the lines of Ultor's body, Kyle had captured that sense of power and the tension that resulted from that power.

He was pleased with the look of the drawing. He paused for a moment to study it closely, and it dawned on him what it really said about his hero: that through his strength he protected the weak and fended off evil, but in doing so he isolated himself. Ultimately, Ultor was alone in his act of heroism.

The thought gave Kyle an empty feeling in the pit of his stomach. Was that the price of heroism? By definition a hero went above and beyond what an ordinary person would do. In doing so the hero separated himself from others in order to save them. He set himself apart. And while he might gain the admiration and adoration of those he saved, at the same time he distinguished himself as being different from them.

Kyle knew what that felt like without being a hero. He didn't fit in. Unlike Brittany, he didn't want to fit in. The clique she so desperately clung to was all about popularity, appearance, affectation. As lonely as it was to be an outsider, Kyle knew he would feel so much more alone and empty trying to exist within that phony social structure. Brittany was finding that out firsthand, and yet she didn't want any part of him reaching out to her. She treated him like he was the enemy, while it was her so-called friends turning on her.

He refocused on his drawing, his eye going to the girl Ultor was attempting to save. She was pretty, blond. If he were to color this, she would have eyes the blue of lakes on a cloudless summer day.

With a couple of deft strokes of the pencil he changed her expression from one of relief at being saved to something more like resentment. Leaving Ultor standing truly alone, a hero to an ideal.

The bell rang. Kyle stuffed his phone in the pouch of his hooded sweatshirt, closed his sketch pad, and gathered his things. Brittany fumbled with her phone, dropped it on the floor, spilled half the stuff out of her purse. Her cheeks flushed red as she scrambled to grab everything up and get out of the library. Kyle waited and held the door open for her like a gentleman. She didn't thank him.

"What was it Christina tweeted about you again?" he asked as they started down the hall.

Brittany refused to look at him. "She was joking."

"Yeah. Lesbian slut. That's funny," he said flatly.

"You don't understand."

"I understand with a friend like that you don't need an enemy."

She huffed a sigh and rolled her eyes. "Kyle, just butt out. You're not helping."

"I thought you didn't need help," Kyle said. "You don't want *my* help because I'm a freak. I'm a loser because I don't think it's funny to bully people and call girls whores on Twitter. You'd rather have friends who treat you like shit. That's fucked-up, Britt."

She hugged her books and her purse tight to her chest, her shoulders hunched with tension as they negotiated the mob in the hall. "Why can't you just leave me alone?"

"Because I know you're not like Christina. You're so much better than her and the rest of them. You deserve better."

She heaved a sigh as they turned with a flow of other students and started up the stairs like salmon bucking up a stream. She didn't answer him. Kyle wasn't sure if she didn't believe she deserved better or if she didn't believe she wasn't like Christina Warner.

Christina was the bitch queen of the popular crowd. Girls wanted to be like her, wanted to be around her, wanted to be included in her inner circle of friends. She was the president of the sophomore class and belonged to all the right clubs. Teachers loved her. The people she liked saw her as successful and clever, always stylish. The people she didn't like saw a different side of her.

"Have you heard from Gray?" he asked as they turned at the top of the stairs and started down the sophomore hall. Brittany stopped at her locker and focused on dialing her combination.

"No. Why would I hear from her? She hates me. That's the last thing she said to me before she left. That she hated me and couldn't wait to get out of here and never see anyone from here again."

"Yeah, well, who could blame her?" Kyle said, leaning a shoulder against the next locker.

Christina Warner's laugh drifted down the hall. Kyle could see them coming: Christina; her BFF, Jessie Cook; and her guard dog / boyfriend, Aaron Fogelman. Fogelman had a fat lip that gave Kyle a feeling of great satisfaction to see since he had made that happen.

Fogelman was over six feet tall and already beefy, like he was on steroids or had been held back five years or something. Despite the fact that he was a good enough student to attend PSI—or that his parents were rich enough to buy his way in—he struck Kyle as being as dumb as an ox. All the girls thought he was good-looking, but his eyes were a little too small and mean, and his mouth was always a little bit open. He was certainly stupid when it came to Christina. He followed her around like a big dog, willing to do whatever she told him. Kyle had given him the nickname the Henchman, though he didn't call him that out loud. Calling people names was against his personal principles.

Brittany heard them coming too. She huffed another impatient sigh and gave Kyle a nasty look from the corner of her eye. "Would you just leave me alone?"

"You worried they'll think you're consorting with the enemy again?" he asked. "What's Christina gonna put on Twitter this time? Last week you were a lesbian slut. Now you'll just be a regular slut?"

She narrowed her eyes, trying her best to look mean. "There's a reason people don't like you, Kyle."

"Yeah," he said. "Because I tell the truth."

"Hey, Brittany," Aaron Fogelman said. "Is this runt bothering you?"

Kyle pushed away from the locker and stood with his feet shoulder-width apart, his books held low in front of him with both hands. He could be quick to drop them straight to the floor and move forward out of a fighting stance. Fogelman had taken the first swing of their last fight, but because Kyle tried always to be aware and ready, as Bruce Lee had taught, he had been able to move quickly, and Fogelman's knuckles had only grazed his cheekbone.

"You're calling me a runt, and I kicked your ass," Kyle said. "What does that make you, Fogelman?"

"You didn't kick my ass, Hatcher," Fogelman said, irritated. "You must have a concussion."

"From what?"

The truth was his body still hurt. Fogelman had fists the size of bricks, and he used them with what they called in the fight world "bad intentions." He didn't hit just to connect; he hit to hurt, to do damage. But Kyle would never show that Aaron Fogelman had hurt him. Fogelman might have been able to break him physically, but Kyle would always beat him when it came to gameness and psychological warfare.

Christina Warner held up her phone and took a picture of Kyle's battered face. "This is what a loser looks like," she said, tapping the keyboard. "Hashtag 'Loser' at XtinaW."

She flipped her long white-blond hair back and gave Brittany a look, her perfect red lips turning down at the corners, her dark eyes filled with disapproval. "What are you doing with him, Brittany?"

"I'm not *with* him," Brittany protested. "He won't leave me alone."

"You're like a booger on a finger, Hatcher," Fogelman said.

"I guess you'd know about that," Kyle said.

Fogelman's ears started turning red. It pissed him off no end that Kyle was more quick-witted than he was. He went for the cheap insult. "Why are you following a girl, anyway? Everyone knows you're gay."

Kyle narrowed his eyes, resisting the urge to punch Fogelman in the mouth, which was what he wanted to do. Not because he was a homophobe but because Fogelman was one, and thought that made him superior. Kyle thought of his hero, Georges St-Pierre, and what GSP said about dealing with bullies. Stand up straight; look your bully in the eye; do not retaliate with violence; be confident and tell the truth.

"Name-calling is the last resort of an ignorant mind," he said.

Fogelman took a step in close, looming over Kyle, his expression dark. Kyle held his ground, never taking his eyes from the other boy's. His heart started to beat a little harder. His ribs hurt as he tried to draw a deep breath, reminding him of the weight of this kid's punches.

But instead of hitting him, Fogelman grabbed for his books, snatching hold of his sketch pad and quickly stepping back. A big grin spread across his stupid-looking face. Christina Warner laughed lightly, like she thought he was delightfully cute.

"What do you have in here, runt?" Fogelman asked.

Kyle stepped toward him and swiped at the sketch pad. Fogelman held it up out of his reach.

"Give it back," Kyle ordered.

"Pictures of your boyfriend?"

"Fuck you, Aaron, that's my work. Give it back."

He grabbed at the pad again, and again Fogelman lifted it out of his reach. Changing strategies, he stepped back and rested his hands on his hips, waiting. He looked off to the left, down the hall. Mrs. Arness stepped out of her classroom, glanced their way, disinterested, and went back inside.

Fogelman opened the sketch pad and laughed out loud at the first page, a series of three drawings of Ultor showing different degrees of energy through movement.

"Is this supposed to be you?" Fogelman asked, holding the pad so Christina could see it.

She laughed. "Oh my God! That is *so* gay!"

"You think you're a superhero or something, runt?" Fogelman asked.

Kyle stepped toward him, reaching out. "Give it back."

"Too bad you're not ripped like this, dude; maybe you could take it away from me."

"Maybe I could anyway," Kyle said.

Fogelman turned away from him and called out to a couple of his buddies down the hall.

"Hey, look what the runt thinks he looks like!"

More laughter. Kyle felt his face flushing red. His blood was roaring in his ears.

"It's missing something," one of Fogelman's friends said, grabbing the pad.

Kyle tried to push his way past Fogelman. Fogelman blocked him. Kyle stepped right, pivoted around, and tried to lunge forward, only to be blocked by another body, and another body. By the time he got through the knot of people, Fogelman had taken the pad back and was holding it up for all to see. Someone had taken a pencil and drawn a giant erect penis onto each version of Ultor, making it look like the first one was having anal sex with the second one, who was having anal sex with the third one, who was masturbating.

"Give it back!" he snapped at Fogelman. To his horror, his voice cracked, drawing more laughter from the bigger guys. Anger spiked through him. He moved toward Aaron Fogelman with purpose.

"Give it back!"

Fogelman laughed, still holding the sketch pad up out of reach. "Or what?"

"Or this," Kyle said.

He hooked his right leg around Fogelman's left and drove his shoulder hard into the bigger kid's solar plexus. The breath left Fogelman in a gust, and he tripped backward and fell like a giant redwood. Kyle went down on top of him, kneeing him in the groin, then the stomach, as he scrambled his way up Fogelman's body, reaching for the sketch pad, now on the floor.

As he grabbed for it, a pair of polished dress shoes came into view. Kyle's stomach dropped as he looked up to see Principal Rodgers glaring down at him.

Rodgers bent over and picked up the sketchbook, scowling at the pornographic drawing. "Mr. Hatcher, Mr. Fogelman. I will see you both in my office. Now."

Fogelman groaned and rolled onto his side, cupping his balls with his hands. Kyle scrambled to his feet, shooting a glare at Brittany, who looked on with wide eyes, her books clutched to her chest.

"Nice friends you've got, Britt," he said. "I can see why you'd rather hang with them."

15

"Are you nervous, Jamar?" Liska asked. "There's really no reason for you to be."

"I've never been hypnotized before," Jackson admitted, his eyes darting from Liska to the other woman in the room.

"It's nothing to be worried about," she said. "I promise."

The other detective was Valerie Edgar, who worked Sex Crimes. She was a nice-looking woman in a next-door-neighbor kind of way—simple, shoulder-length brunette hair; a friendly, open face; a nonthreatening, feminine quality. Hypnosis was something she had studied and become very good at in addition to her training as a detective, in order to help victims and unlock the memories of witnesses. Her demeanor was comforting and reassuring.

Jamar Jackson, however, did not seem comforted or reassured. The sweat on his forehead gleamed under the fluorescent lighting in the interview room. He wiped it off with his hand and shoved up the sleeves of his sweater.

"Man, it's hot in here," he complained, shifting on his chair. "Why is it so hot in here?"

"I'm sorry," Liska said. "There's some problem with the heating system. They can't seem to get it sorted out."

"Eight freaking degrees below zero outside and it's like the damn jungle in here," Jackson said, then quickly caught himself. "Pardon my language."

"I hear you," Liska said. "It's like a sauna. We're all dying here. If they don't get this fixed today, I'm coming to work in a bathing suit tomorrow. Can I get you something to drink, Jamar? Water? A can of pop?"

Jackson looked suspicious, like he figured they would try to slip him something.

Kovac watched through the one-way glass and rubbed at the tension in the back of his neck. Tippen stood beside him, eating a red Twizzler.

"Jesus," Kovac muttered, "you'd think he killed the girl with his bare hands. I've never seen a witness so freaked out."

"He probably thinks she's going to put him under and make him cluck like a chicken," Tippen said.

Jackson tried unsuccessfully to look cool about the whole thing. "Naw, I'm good. Thanks." He looked at Edgar, forcing a smile, like he wanted her to think he was joking. "You're not gonna make me cluck like a chicken or anything like that, right?" He tried to laugh a little.

Valerie Edgar smiled warmly, sharing the joke. "No. I promise. All that happens here is I help you relax so you can easily access your memories. It's a good thing. You'll feel calm and safe, with none of the tension you had during the event itself. You're in complete control the whole time."

"Will I be out? Like unconscious?"

"No, not at all. I want you just to take a deep breath now and exhale slowly through your mouth."

She took him through that exercise for a good five minutes before asking him to close his eyes. He squeezed his eyelids shut like a five-year-old child pretending to take a nap. Edgar continued with the breathing exercise, her voice going softer and softer.

In another five minutes, Jackson cracked open one eye. "Am I out? Is this it?"

Kovac swore and tipped his head back, looking at the ceiling. "This is a fucking disaster."

"Just wait," Tippen said. "Valerie is good. I've watched her hypnotize a rape victim who was so terrified she couldn't bring herself to close her eyes. She'll get him."

Again Valerie Edgar smiled gently. "You feel fine, don't you? You're in complete control."

"Yeah," Jackson said, relieved. "I'm good. It's all good."

"This is all there is to it. Relax, close your eyes; breathe deeply and slowly."

Kovac could see the tension leave Jamar Jackson's body. The kid relaxed. His breathing deepened. Impressive.

Edgar asked him a couple of easy questions first, as he settled into that mysterious state of unconscious consciousness, gradually leading him to the heart of the matter: those crucial few moments before and during the incident on New Year's Eve.

Jackson recalled vivid details about the goings-on in the back of his limo, right down to the color of the pubic hair on the girl with no panties (not a natural blonde). Details of what had been going on in front of his Hummer were sketchier.

The box truck to his left had been white with orange and black lettering. He didn't remember what it said. Probably a U-Haul truck, Kovac thought. There had to be hundreds of them based in the Twin Cities, to say nothing of trucks coming into Minneapolis from anywhere else.

The body of Rose Reiser—New Year's Doe—had been discovered by a guy driving a box truck. But they had thoroughly searched the truck, and the driver had been completely cooperative with the investigation. He had been ruled out as a suspect. This box truck was probably no more significant to the Zombie Doe investigation than that one had been to the investigation a year past.

The detail Jamar Jackson was very clear about was the image of the girl coming out of the trunk of the dark car in front of him. That image had seemingly blinded him to all else. Even in his relaxed hypnotic state, he had nothing to say about the make or model of the vehicle, and no memory of the license plate.

"Probably a Minnesota plate," Tippen suggested. "Something unusual would have stood out."

"Great," Kovac said. "That narrows it down to what? A million vehicles? Two million?"

"Probably only thirty or forty thousand dark sedans."

"I'll put you right on that, then."

The door opened and Elwood walked in with a handful of papers.

"Sixty-seven girls between the ages of fourteen and eighteen absent from metro-area schools today," he said. "We can pare the list down pretty quickly. Two people on the phone. A couple of hours or so, if all goes well."

"Let's get on that, then," Kovac said. "Kasselmann wrangled us two uniforms to help out. You and Tip get with them and cut the call time in half, then hit the streets with any follow-up. Maybe by then we'll have the sketch."

Liska came in looking unhappy. "I was hoping for him to remember at least a partial tag number on the car," she said with a big sigh. "Valerie says we can try again in a day or two. Now that Jamar knows we're not going to make him put his underpants on his head and bark like a dog, he'll be more relaxed next time. Something might come to the surface for him."

"Yeah," Kovac said without hope. "Like if that chick in the backseat maybe had a pussy piercing. That's where his head was at."

"We can't pick our witnesses, Kojak," she said. "And by the way, that's where your head would have been too."

"My head's there now," Tippen remarked.

Liska gave him the stink eye. "You're disgusting."

"I'm honest."

"You're honestly disgusting."

"You have a talent for overstating the obvious, Tinks," Elwood said.

Kovac held up his hands. "Can we all agree Tippen is a pig and get on with our day? I want out of this building before I get a freaking heat rash."

"Where are we going?" Liska asked as they headed back to their cubicle.

"We're meeting Tip's niece at a tattoo parlor," he said, grabbing his heavy coat off the rack. He made no move to put it on. The idea of stepping out into below-zero weather was, for once, almost appealing. "Will the artist have the sketch done by the end of the day?"

"He said he would, but he's afraid of me, so he could just be buying time to flee the state. He didn't want to do it at all," she said as they left the CID offices. It was only marginally cooler in the hall. "He said the same thing I did: A bad sketch could be worse than no sketch at all."

"I get that," Kovac said, "except this girl has a few extra distinguishing characteristics. How many young women are running around with multiple piercings, half their head shaved, and a Chinese tattoo?"

"Spoken like a man who doesn't have teenagers," Liska said. "That probably describes a quarter of the kids Kyle knows—male *and* female. I'm lucky he hasn't had something pierced by now."

"Maybe he has. It's just somewhere you can't see it."

"I hate you sometimes."

Kovac was immune to the comment. "I'm driving."

"Great. Then there's a good chance I won't live long enough to find out my son has a Prince Albert."

"Do me a favor," he said as they stepped out into the ball-numbing cold. "If you find out your son had his dick pierced, don't tell me."

"I won't have to tell you. You'll get the call out to the homicide."

THE HELM OF AWE SOCIAL CLUB was barely large enough for the name to fit across the front awning. Crammed between a coffee-house and a funky vintage clothing store, it was located on a run-down side street near the University of Minnesota's West Bank campus. The buildings were brick, two and three stories high; shops and hole-in-the-wall restaurants with apartments overhead, probably mostly student housing.

The street was a mess—half-plowed, rutted, dirty cars parked at screwy angles. How any vehicle survived a winter in Minneapolis intact and dent-free had to be a miracle. Kovac wedged the sedan into a loading zone, pointing the wrong way on the far side of the street, and they trudged across the ruts, both of them cursing the conditions as snow went into their shoes and up their pants legs.

A bell rang as they opened the door of the shop and stepped inside. The walls of the place were glossy Chinese red, the floors old checkerboard linoleum. The place smelled as clean as a hospital. Photographs lined one wall—close-ups of elaborate tattoos, shots of customers posing with tattoo artists. Kovac recognized a couple of professional athletes. Other subjects looked like they might have been members of rock bands. A few looked like suburban grandmas, smiling happily as they displayed their body art.

Sonya Porter was shooting the shit at the front counter with an enormous bald guy. He turned away from them to reach for something on a shelf. His hairless dome was tatted out with a terrifying black-and-gray face of a Chinese foo dog. The thick folds of flesh in the back of his neck undulated as he moved his head, animating the creature.

He turned around and glared at them with narrow, vaguely Asian eyes, his face no less frightening than his tattoo. A thick, wiry, white-blond Fu Manchu mustache bracketed his downturned mouth, making him look like an angry walrus. The shop's namesake, a Viking helm of awe tattoo, was inked into his forehead like a third eye. Black disks the size of dimes stretched his earlobes. The overall impression was of a Viking sumo wrestler.

Liska leaned into Kovac's shoulder and murmured, "I'll bet he has a Prince Albert."

"He could be your next boyfriend, Tinks," Kovac muttered back.

Sonya, perched on a tall stool, sat up at attention as they crossed the narrow room. She wore purple-and-white cat-eye glasses and had deep blue streaks through her shiny dark hair that caught the light like a blackbird's wing. Her lipstick was royal blue.

"It's Sam the Man," she announced. "You're late."

"Sorry," he said without real apology. "I've just been sitting around on my ass eating doughnuts and running a homicide investigation."

He pointed a finger at Liska—"My partner, Sergeant Liska"—and tipped his head in Sonya's direction—"Sonya Porter, Tippen's niece."

Liska nodded. "My condolences."

Sonya Porter chuckled, a dark, slightly sultry sound. "I hold my own."

"So does he, but when he says that, he's talking about something else entirely."

The girl laughed out loud at that, delighted. "I like you!"

Kovac turned to the big man. "Sam Kovac. Homicide."

"This is Pooch," Sonya Porter said. "This is his place."

"Pooch Halvorsen." He reached out an elaborately tattooed hand the size of a catcher's mitt. Kovac met it and shook it, wondering if the lettering on the sausage-link fingers had begun as prison tats. *You R* on the right hand, *NEXT* on the left. His fingernails were impeccably manicured. "Sonya tells me you have a murder victim with an acceptance tattoo."

"That's what she tells me too," Kovac said. "I'm taking her word for it. I don't read Chinese."

"I do," Pooch Halvorsen said. "The odd symbol, at least. People come in here all the time wanting this or that in Chinese. I run it all past my grandma on my mother's side. She's from Hong Kong."

"I always wondered about that," Liska said. "How do these people really know what they're putting on their bodies if they don't know Chinese? It could say *I'm a moron* for all they know."

"Research," Halvorsen said. "You're going to wear a tattoo for the rest of your life, you'd damn well better take the time to know what it really says."

"So, for sure the tattoo on our victim says *acceptance*?" Liska asked.

"Absolutely. I started that here." He pulled down one side of the V-neck of his black T-shirt to show the same symbols incorporated into the complicated design on his chest. "I wanted to make a statement and see how many people would take it up as their own. Spread the message."

"Pooch did mine," Sonya said, pushing up the sleeve of her purple sweater to show Liska.

"I've done a couple hundred of these, at least," the artist said proudly. "It's big with the college crowd. People want to think this younger generation is completely egocentric, but that's not so. Acceptance is an important message for a lot of them. Acceptance of race, gender, religion, sexual preference."

"What about teenagers?" Kovac asked.

Halvorsen pointed to a big sign on the wall behind him:

YOU MUST BE 18 TO GET A TATTOO.

PHOTO ID REQUIRED.

NO EXCEPTIONS.

"Let's say a kid was really determined," Liska said.

The big man shrugged. "Nothing is foolproof to a really deter-mined fool. Somebody wants something badly enough, they'll find someone willing to do it for a price."

"Do you happen to know any of those *someones*?"

"I hear things," he conceded. "Young artists just starting out. Guys who are hard up for money do stuff on the side. People who have no business owning machines think they can learn by doing on their friends.

"There's a boom in the business now," he explained. "Everyone wants ink. Demand will find supply. It's basic economics. When I started out, there were a handful of shops in the Twin Cities. Now these places sprout up like mushrooms—and die just as quick. You've got to know what you're doing to run a business in this economy. People get into it because they think it'll be fun. They think it'll make them cool to run a tattoo shop the same way people think it'll make them cool if they own a bar."

The buzz of tattoo machines and muffled conversations coming from the back of the shop gave credence to his claim of a booming business. A narrow hall on one side of the space led back to hidden rooms where the magic happened.

"You didn't do the tattoo on our victim?" Kovac asked.

"No. That didn't happen in my shop. Sonya showed me the pic-ture. That's none of my people."

"Any idea whose work it might be?"

He shook his head. "There's not enough to it to show a particular style. You get into real art, I can recognize whose work it is."

Sonya tugged down the scoop neck of her sweater, revealing a full-color heart with elaborate wings reaching across the width of her chest edged with a subtle leopard print. In the center of the heart was an ornately detailed gold-colored padlock with the words *Try Harder* delicately drawn in an arch above the keyhole. The shading of the ink was masterfully done, the outlining impeccable. The longer Kovac looked at the tattoo, the more he saw.

"This is Pooch," she said. "Everyone who knows tattoos in this town knows Pooch did this."

Halvorsen nodded, proud. "My foo dog is the work of a friend of mine from Florida. He specializes in traditional Chinese and Japanese art. Everyone in the business knows Shane's work.

"But it takes years and a true artist to develop a distinctive signature look," he said. "Most people—even really good technicians—never do."

"And not the person who did our dead girl's tattoo," Kovac said.

"No. That's an amateurish job. The outlines aren't as sharp as they should be. There's no artistry, no shading. Any newbie could have done that."

"And do you know if this symbol is being used in other parts of the country?" Liska asked.

"Absolutely. It's everywhere now. Half a dozen of us started doing it at the same time—East Coast, West Coast, middle America."

"So our victim could have come from anywhere," Kovac said.

Liska's phone rang, and she dug it out of her pocket, frowning at it as she excused herself and stepped toward the door.

Pooch Halvorsen spread his hands. "I can't help you there. But I'll sniff around, ask some questions, see if I can get a lead on anyone here in town."

"We'd appreciate that," Kovac said. He sighed, not sure what he had been hoping for. Zombie Doe's photograph on the Helm of Awe Social Club's wall of fame, perhaps.

He turned to Sonya. "You'll get together with Tip later and go over any kind of response you might have gotten to your story, right?"

Even as he asked, his eyes darted to Liska, who was in conversation, her expression tense. Jaw set, she jammed the phone back in her coat pocket and looked up at him.

"I have to go," she said. "Now. I need to commit an infanticide."

16

As with any good interrogation, the suspects had been separated and taken to different rooms so as not to be able to get their stories straight. The downside of that was that Liska was not in charge of this investigation and had access to only one side of the story. That did not sit well. She was coming into the situation with no background, and she wasn't going to be able to hear both sides of the story to decide which parts of the individual tales to piece together into what was probably the truth.

If the culprit had been her younger son, R.J. would have readily spilled his guts, openly and honestly portraying his own culpability in the incident. Kyle sat sullen and silent, avoiding eye contact.

"You need to tell me what this about, Kyle," Nikki said firmly, pacing at the end of the table with her arms crossed tight over her chest. "Principal Rodgers is going to come in here and I'm not going to be able to help you if I don't have a clear picture of what happened."

"It was nothing," he said, staring at the tabletop. "Guys were just horsing around."

" 'Just horsing around' doesn't end up in a fight."

"It wasn't a fight," he said. "There was no fight."

"You realize how serious this is, don't you?" she asked. "This school has a zero-tolerance policy for fighting. That means you can be expelled."

"I wasn't fighting!" he insisted, finally looking at her. "Jeez, could you believe me for a change?"

"How can I believe you if you won't tell me what happened? I have to piece this together from what other people tell me, Kyle. I can't read your mind. I wasn't there. I don't know what happened."

Quick tears filled her son's blue eyes and he looked down at the tabletop again, trying to stare a hole through it. His face was red with the effort to wrestle the emotions back into their box.

As exasperated as she was, Nikki wanted to go to him and put her arms around him as she had done when he was a little boy. It physically hurt to see him in emotional pain. But she knew her touch would not be welcome, not here, not now when he was trying so hard to be a man and take whatever fate was about to deal out to him.

Sighing, trying to release some of her own tension, she pulled a chair out and sat down, close enough to him that their knees touched beneath the table. Maybe if they were at the same eye level, he would confide in her. Maybe if she wasn't physically asserting her position of authority, he wouldn't feel so defensive. Advanced Interrogation Skills 2.0.

"So what's with this Fogelman kid?" she asked. "You have some beef with him?"

He tipped his head, tilting his chin toward her but looking the other way. "He's a jerk."

"In what way?"

"In every way."

"Did you hit him?"

"No."

"Did you knock him down?"

Hesitation. He was about to twist the truth into something he thought would be more acceptable. "I banged into him and he tripped and fell, and I fell on top of him."

"Kyle . . . ," Nikki said. "Who do you think you're talking to? Not the mother who writes the checks for your jiu-jitsu lessons. You took him down."

He didn't deny it. "He had my sketchbook. I was just trying to get it back. He's bigger than me. I couldn't reach."

"He took your sketchbook," Nikki said. Now the picture started to come together. "You wanted it back."

"It's my work," he said, his face gravely serious.

"I know."

She also knew it wasn't *just* his schoolwork. Kyle's drawings were to him no different than a writer's journal, or a teenage girl's diary. *He* was in those drawings—his feelings, his struggles. He might have been stingy with his words, but his art told his story eloquently. To Kyle, having his sketchbook taken, pawed over, passed around, made fun of, was a personal assault.

At conference time the guidance counselor had told her Kyle was having difficulties getting along with some of the students. He hadn't offered anything in the way of explanation, no specific incidents, just hearsay. And Kyle had brushed the topic off again and again.

"Is this the same kid you got in the fight with New Year's Eve?"

"I wasn't in a fight."

"Right. You banged into his fist with your face and accidentally scraped your knuckles across his teeth."

Silence.

"Why don't you get along with this guy?" she asked.

"Because he's an asshole."

She didn't chide him for his language. He would have welcomed the diversion, and honestly, she could think of worse things than her fifteen-year-old son using the same bad language she used on a daily basis. This was not a conversation about manners and etiquette.

"Why is he an asshole?" she asked. "And don't say because he stole your sketchbook. I think it's safe to assume he's been an asshole for a while. Why don't you get along with him?"

"Because he does stuff like this all the time."

"To you?"

"To lots of kids."

Now they were getting to the heart of it. Aaron Fogelman was a bully.

Bullies had been Kyle's big hot button for most of his life. He had always been small for his age, which made him a natural target for bigger kids. But he had also always been tough and athletic, which meant anyone planning on trying to intimidate him physically had their work cut out for them. Because he knew what it was like to get picked on, he often took the role of champion for weaker kids who were targets.

That theme played out through his comic book characters. His hero, Ultor, was the champion of the weak and the misfits. And Aaron Fogelman had snatched his sketchbook full of drawings of Ultor.

Perfect storm.

"I don't care if they kick me out," he said glumly, scratching his thumbnail at some imagined speck on the polished tabletop. "I hate it here anyway."

"You don't hate it here," Nikki said quietly. "You hate what you're going through."

"What's the difference? I don't want to be here. I wish I could go back to my old school."

"You can't run away from a situation because you don't get along with someone."

"You did," he said, shooting her a nasty look. "With Dad. That's why we moved here."

Nikki felt as if she'd had the wind knocked out of her. She did her best to hide it, to absorb the blow. He had unerringly hit her in her most vulnerable spot.

"Now who's the bully?" she asked. "You said that just to hurt me. That would be the definition of a bully, wouldn't it?"

She saw the tears rise again in his eyes even as he tried to hide them by putting his head down on the table and covering up. It wasn't in his nature to be cruel. It went against his grain to lash out like that. His conscience would now eat him up for it.

"Have you told Principal Rodgers this Fogelman kid is a bully?" she asked.

The Big Sigh, which in this case clearly translated to *no*.

"Then how is he supposed to know?" she asked. "How is he supposed to do anything about it?"

"He won't anyway," Kyle said.

"The school has an antibullying policy."

He looked up at her and rolled his eyes at that, like he couldn't believe she was stupid enough to think that would make a difference.

"His dad donated all the new computers in the library," he said.

Voices in the hall caught their attention. Nikki stood up, ready to go to battle for her child.

After a quick perfunctory knock on the door, Principal Rodgers came in looking appropriately grave, Kyle's sketchbook in hand.

"Mrs. Hatcher," he said by way of greeting.

"Liska," Nikki corrected him, the chip on her shoulder coming up. "My last name is Liska. No missus."

Rodgers didn't want to be bothered apologizing. A man used to dealing with wealthy, pompous parents, he had a chip of his own. He took the seat at the head of the table like a king ready to suffer through the tedious complaints of his subjects. He was a distinguished African-American man in his late forties, always meticulously groomed and wearing an impeccable suit. Nikki felt rumpled and sweaty in comparison. She resisted the urge to comb her hair with her fingers.

"I've listened to Kyle's explanation and to Mr. Fogelman's," he began. "I'm not satisfied that anyone is telling me the complete truth."

"Brittany was standing right there," Kyle said. "She saw the whole thing. She'll tell you."

"She told me she didn't really know what started the problem," Rodgers said.

Kyle looked shocked and, beneath that, hurt.

"Mr. Fogelman said it was all just a joke," Rodgers said.

Mr. Fogelman, Nikki thought, annoyed, like this other kid somehow deserved a title.

Kyle said nothing. He wouldn't argue because to make the circumstances seem more serious would then cast a worse light on his actions. Neither would he pretend to make light of what had happened, because it so went against who he was. Nikki could feel his frustration.

"This isn't the first time you and Mr. Fogelman have run afoul of each other, is it, Kyle?" Rodgers asked.

Again, Kyle said nothing.

"I know you're well aware of our policy on violence here at PSI."

"It's my understanding," Nikki said, "that *Mr. Fogelman* took my son's sketchbook and wouldn't give it back to him."

She remained on her feet and took it as an insult that Rodgers had sat down. Now everything about the man was irritating her—the tidiness of his cuticles, the way he pursed his lower lip, the fussy double Windsor knot in his pretentious prep school striped tie.

"There's no excuse for attacking another student, Mrs. Liska."

"I haven't seen any evidence of an attack," Nikki said. "Is Mr. Fogelman claiming Kyle attacked him?"

"Not in so many words. He said your son can't take a joke."

"Oh? This is joke to him?" she asked, moving forward, pointing at the sketch pad on the table. "Kyle is in this school on a scholarship due in large part to his talent as an artist. That book is not a joke to him."

"Nevertheless, Mrs. Liska, violence is not tolerated here."

"I believe it's been established there was no violence done here," she said, advancing another step. "No one was attacked. It was just a joke. You said so yourself. Just boys being boys. And apparently stealing isn't an issue with you—"

"No one *stole* anything—" Rodgers started defensively.

"And no one was *attacked*," Nikki countered, staring him down. She was close enough to him now that he had to raise his chin to look up at her. He didn't like it, but neither would he give up his seat.

Instead, he backed off the subject, turning his attention to the sketchbook. "Then there's the rather disturbing business of the subject matter of your son's art."

He opened the cover to three poses of Ultor with huge, badly drawn penises connecting one Ultor to the next, to the next.

"Your son was showing this around," the principal said.

"I was not!" Kyle protested.

"And when Mr. Fogelman took it from him, the trouble started."

"That's a lie!" Kyle said, his voice cracking.

"I don't know about you, Mrs. Liska, but I find this extremely offensive."

Like he thought she probably sat around looking at gay porn as a matter of course and found it perfectly acceptable if her son wanted to draw pictures of overly muscular men having anal sex.

Kyle turned to her. "I didn't do that, Mom! You know I wouldn't do that!"

"I know," she reassured him.

Rodgers gave her a patronizing look. "Mrs. Liska, I'm sure no mother wants to think her son would draw something like this—"

"My son *did not* draw that," she said firmly.

"Mrs.—"

"*Principal* Rodgers," she said, biting the words off, her temper fraying. "If you're going to insist on everyone having a title, you may call me *Sergeant* Liska, but you will definitely stop calling me *Mrs.* And please stop talking to me like I'm some meek little housewife.

"I'm a homicide detective," she said. "I know exactly what people are capable of. And I know my son. I also know my son's dedication to his art.

"Look closely at this," she said, leaning over the table, tapping a finger on the drawing. "If you think for a minute an artist who would put that much painstaking detail into every line of his drawing would then ruin his work with badly rendered penises, you don't know anything about artists. If my son was going to draw pornographic images of men having sex, I assure you, the penises would be anatomically correct and proportional."

Rodgers was looking at her like she had just walked out of his worst nightmare. He had no idea what to say.

"That means someone else defaced Kyle's work," she said. "I don't find that funny. I find it aggressive and offensive behavior in a school that makes so much of its high standards. If other kids took my son's sketchbook, defaced his work, and wouldn't give it back to him, tormenting him to the point he felt the need to take drastic action, Mr. Rodgers, I think you need to look more deeply into the real root of the problem."

He didn't like being chastised. His expression was as tight and pinched as a sphincter. He closed the cover of the sketchbook and slid it away from him.

"Because the facts of this incident aren't entirely clear," he said, "I'm giving you a warning this time, Kyle. But a notation will be made in your file, and I will not be lenient if there's a next time."

"And Aaron Fogelman will receive the same note in his file," Nikki said. Not a question. A statement.

Rodgers didn't quite make eye contact. He took a beat too long to answer. "Yes. A notation will be made."

They were dismissed like a pair of servants. Nikki thought the top of her head might blow off from the pressure of the anger steaming inside her. She tried not to let it show as they walked out of the school and across the parking lot. She had a momma bear's ferocity when it came to defending her offspring. At the same time, she didn't want Kyle to think she condoned how he had handled the situation with the Fogelman boy—even though she wanted to track the bigger kid down and beat the shit out of him herself.

The contradictory emotions buzzed around inside her mind like angry bees and gave her an instant headache. At times like this she cursed Speed more than usual. They were supposed to both shoulder the burden of difficult parenting moments. As usual, she got to do all the heavy lifting. When he finally cruised into the picture days from now, he would probably give Kyle an *attaboy* for getting the better of Aaron Fogelman.

She looked at her son walking beside her with his hands stuffed into his coat pockets and his shoulders hunched up to his ears against the biting cold, his backpack hanging heavy over one shoulder. Now was when she was supposed to come up with something profound and motherly to say, but she couldn't think of what that might be. And if she was conflicted, how must he feel?

They got in the car in silence and she started the engine and cranked up the heater. She looked over at her son and sighed.

"I hated being fifteen," she confessed. "I didn't feel like I fit in anywhere. Every day I felt like I was holding my breath, waiting for someone to see through me and then everyone would turn on me.

Then I finally figured out the best thing about high school: It doesn't last forever. And when it's over, none of what seemed so important about it matters at all."

Kyle said nothing, but she knew what he was thinking. He was thinking he was just a sophomore and graduation was a tiny light at the end of a long tunnel full of the daily horrors of being a kid who was a little too sensitive and cared a little too much.

She thought of their Jane Doe, the same age as Kyle, with her piercings and her half-shaved head and her tattoo declaring acceptance of all people, and wondered if she had been that kid too—on the outside, trying to figure out who she wanted to be. She hadn't lived long enough to find out.

"I love you," Nikki said softly as she put the car in gear and headed it toward the gate. "And I promise you, you won't die of high school."

17

"What would you be doing tonight if we weren't doing this?" Elwood asked.

Elwood had commandeered the car keys, citing a desire to survive the night. Kovac hadn't put up much of a protest. He sat in the passenger seat feeling drained as they cruised the rutted, frozen streets of one neighborhood and then another, knocking on doors in search of teenage girls who had been absent from school that day. If he were home, he would probably be falling asleep on the couch, drooling on the cushions while the Travel Channel played in the background, showing all the exotic places he had never been and would probably never see.

"Oh, I'd be working out for a couple of hours, bench-pressing Buicks before a gourmet dinner and an evening of competitive ballroom dancing and crazy hot sex with my supermodel girlfriend," he said. "You?"

"Bikram yoga."

"Oh, Jesus," Kovac said, cringing. "I could have lived my whole life without that image in my head."

Now it was there in vivid color: Elwood looking like a Sasquatch in a Speedo, contorting his massive body into unnatural positions.

"It's very therapeutic," Elwood said. "The heat opens the pores and allows the body to eliminate toxins through sweat."

"Oh, Christ. Thanks for the Smell-O-Vision. Pull over. I'm gonna puke now."

"You should try it, Sam. Yoga would do you a world of good."

"Yoga would put me in the hospital," he returned. "I'll settle for a lead on this case and a decent night's sleep."

Tippen had gone off with his niece to look through whatever the hell young people were doing and commenting about on the Internet, looking to see if Sonya had gotten any interesting responses to the story she had posted. Kovac had taken his place on the KOD patrol with Elwood, knocking on doors of families whose teenage daughters had been absent from school. A needle-in-the-haystack exercise that came with a side order of twisted emotions.

They wanted to find their victim's identity, which meant going up to the homes of families and hoping they were missing a child, and being weirdly disappointed if they weren't able to shatter some parent's life.

It always sucked when the victim was a kid. There were never any winners in a murder investigation, but it especially sucked when the victim was young. And if they didn't find the unlucky relatives tonight, Kovac would go home, nuke some horrible plastic plate of frozen whatever, and eat it in front of the computer while he trolled the websites that featured thousands of people gone missing from around the country. Misery everywhere. Despair from one side of the country to the other.

They were in a nice old neighborhood on the west side of Lake Harriet. Large, sturdy homes in the styles popular in the 1940s and 1950s interspersed with more modern McMansion replacements. Big trees that shaded the yards and boulevards half the year stood as naked, bony sentinels for the long winter months. Now, with the sun long gone, their black trunks stood out against the backdrop of snow; their limbs disappeared into the night sky like desperate fingers clawing for the stars.

The house they were looking for was a Tudor-style with a steeply pitched roof and multicolored Christmas lights in the shrubbery. The Christmas tree was lit up and on display in the front window.

Happy holidays. Is your daughter missing? We may have found her murdered corpse. . . .

The house was the last on a block that dead-ended onto parkland, situated on the lot in a way that gave an enviable sense of privacy. Elwood pulled in the narrow driveway behind a black Lexus sedan.

"Which school is this one from?" Kovac asked.

"Performance Scholastic Institute."

"Tinks's kid goes there."

"Academic and artistic excellence," Elwood said. "Their motto."

They left the relative warmth of the car and trudged up the sidewalk to ring the doorbell.

The woman who answered the door had the stereotypical suburban soccer mom look—blond bob, big brown eyes, a pleasant smile, a holiday-themed sweater over a white turtleneck. She opened the door as if it had never occurred to her not to let strangers into her home, though she seemed to think better of it as soon as she looked at them and didn't recognize them.

"Mrs. Gray?" Kovac asked, holding up his ID. "I'm Sergeant Kovac. This is Sergeant Knutson. Sorry to disturb your evening, ma'am."

She looked worried now. "What's this about?"

"Do you have a daughter named Penelope?"

"Yes," she said, guarded, a little defensive. "What's she done?"

Not: Is she all right? "What's she done?"

"Is she home tonight?" Kovac asked. "She was reported absent from school today."

"They send the police out for that now?" Julia Gray asked with a nervous laugh.

Kovac smiled a little, sharing the joke with her. "Is your daughter home this evening?"

"No. No, she's not. What is this about?"

"Do you know where she is?"

"You're making me very nervous, Sergeant."

"I'm sorry, ma'am. We don't want to alarm you—"

"Well, you *are* alarming me," she said. "Penny is staying with a friend."

"Have you spoken to her today?"

"No, I haven't."

"Could we step inside?" Kovac asked. "I don't know about you, ma'am, but I know my heating bill is big enough without me leaving the door wide open when it's fifteen below."

She didn't seem happy about it, but she stepped back from the door nonetheless. Kovac and Elwood stepped into a lovely small foyer. The house smelled of cleaning products, pine trees, cinnamon, and coffee. The staircase to their left curved up and around to the second floor. To the right was the living room where the Christmas tree stood—a formal room with tidy furniture and bookcases flanking a small brick fireplace. The hall they stood in led to the back of the house. Lights from other rooms spilled into the dark passageway. Faint voices might have been company or a television somewhere in the back.

"Have you heard from your daughter in the last day or so?" Kovac asked. The chandelier overhead washed out Julia Gray's face, making her look tired. She had a bruise emerging on her left cheekbone, wearing its way through the makeup she had probably put on that morning. An elastic brace wrapped her right hand and wrist like a fingerless glove.

"Of course," she said. "She sent me a text today."

"But you haven't spoken to her?" Elwood asked.

"Julia?" a man's voice called. "Is everything all right?"

The owner of the voice came into the hall, walking toward them, drying his hands on a red kitchen towel. He was tall and soap opera handsome, with sandy hair shot through with a distinguished touch of gray. He wore charcoal slacks and a camel-tan cashmere sweater over a button-down shirt. He looked like he had stepped out of an ad for an upscale menswear store.

Julia Gray turned toward him. "These men are from the police department. They're asking about Penny."

His brow furrowed. "What's she done?"

"Nothing that we know of, sir," Elwood said. "We don't want to alarm you, but we're trying to identify a young lady whose body was discovered New Year's Eve."

Julia Gray looked stricken. She pressed the hand in the brace to her chest as if to keep her heart from leaping out.

"Oh, dear God," the man said. "That's terrible."

"Are you Penelope's father?" Kovac asked.

"No, no. I'm Dr. Michael Warner."

"Michael and I are engaged. We just got engaged," Julia Gray announced with the nervous awkwardness people often had giving personal details to strangers—or to the police, at any rate. She absently and automatically fingered the diamond ring on her left hand. "Penny's father and I are divorced."

"If we could get your daughter's phone number," Kovac said, "and the name and address of the person she's staying with. That would be helpful."

Julia Gray smiled with a mix of nervousness and confusion.

"She's fine," she said, more to convince herself than them. "I told you. She texted me."

"How do you know it was her?" Kovac asked.

"What?"

"The text. How do you know it was your daughter who sent the text?"

"Who else would it be? Her name came up on my screen. It was Penny."

"The message came from your daughter's phone," Elwood pointed out. "That doesn't necessarily mean your daughter sent the message."

"Do you have a photograph of your daughter, Mrs. Gray?" Kovac asked.

"This is ridiculous," Julia Gray muttered. "My daughter isn't missing."

"Why don't you call her?" Elwood suggested. "That would clear everything up."

Julia Gray heaved a sigh and turned to a hall table to dig awkwardly through her purse with her uninjured left hand. She pulled out her phone, fumbled to punch in a number, and pressed the phone to her ear while she stepped into the living room to retrieve a five-by-seven framed photo off a shelf on the wall. She handed the frame to Elwood as she spoke into the phone.

"Penny, it's Mom. Could you please call me back? Soon. It's really important."

"It went to voice mail," she said unnecessarily. Her breathing had quickened, belying the façade of calm she was trying to project. "My daughter is sixteen. Have you ever had a sixteen-year-old daughter in your life, Sergeant?"

"No, ma'am," Kovac said.

"When girls turn sixteen they believe they know everything," she explained, a strong thread of frustration running through her tone.

She looked down at the phone as she tapped out a text message with her thumbs. "And they don't appreciate the reminder that they still have to answer to their mothers."

"Penny is a difficult girl," Michael Warner offered, as if anybody had asked him anything.

Kovac ignored him, his attention on the school photograph Julia Gray had given Elwood. The girl in the picture looked younger than sixteen. Her hair was a nondescript shade of brown, just past shoulder length and parted down the middle. There were no crazy piercings. She didn't look like the kind of girl who would get an illegal tattoo.

She looked a little sad, a little lost, a little pissed off.

She didn't look much like Zombie Doe.

Of course, they had yet to get the artist's rendition of what their dead girl might have looked like if her head hadn't been bashed in like a rotten Halloween pumpkin. The artist wasn't as afraid of Kovac as he was of Liska, and Liska had gone off to deal with her own teenager.

"When did you last actually speak to your daughter, Mrs. Gray?" Elwood asked.

She sighed impatiently. "Penny hasn't spoken to me in several days. We had a disagreement, and her way of punishing me is silence. But she usually answers her text messages, even if only to say yes or no to a direct question."

"She might be more inclined to answer a call from the police," Michael Warner suggested to her.

"This is so embarrassing," Julia Gray muttered, staring at her silent telephone, willing something to appear on the screen.

"If we can just get her number and the address for where she's staying, we'll make sure she calls you," Elwood said. The diplomat. He took his little spiral notebook and pen out of his coat pocket and offered it to her.

Embarrassment flushed her cheeks as she awkwardly wielded the pen with her injured hand.

"I don't know the exact address," she confessed. "She's staying with a friend from school. The last name is Lawyer—no—Lawler. They live nearby. Just a few blocks over. Washburn and Forty-Sixth? Forty-Fifth? I'm just not sure of the exact address. I've met the girl's mother," she hastened to add. "She's a very nice woman. I think she's an accountant. Or her husband is."

She looked up, unable to resist the urge to see how her lousy, fumbling explanation was being received. Kovac just looked at her, his eyes flat, his face expressionless.

"This isn't making me look like a very good mother," she said, forcing a nervous smile. "If you had teenagers, you would under-stand."

Her hands were trembling as she gave the notebook back.

"What happened to your wrist?" Elwood asked.

"Oh," she said, looking at her hand as if it had just sprouted from the end of her sweater sleeve. "Oh, I fell. I sprained it. I slipped on the ice and fell. It's a hazard of my profession," she said with a nervous laugh.

"What do you do?" Kovac asked.

"I'm a pharmaceutical rep. I have to negotiate a lot of nasty parking lots this time of year. Snow, ice, high heels, dragging my case behind me."

"You might want to rethink the high heels," Kovac said.

Julia Gray nodded, trying to smile.

"I'm sure Penny is fine," she said again, her thoughts quickly back on the daughter she hadn't seen in several days. Suddenly, a routine mother-daughter spat was looming large in her mind. An innocent stay-over with a schoolmate was taking on sinister overtones.

"I'm sure she is," Elwood said kindly. "We're just checking out all possibilities."

"This isn't about that story on the news?" Michael Warner asked, frowning with concern. "The girl on the freeway?"

"Thank you for your time," Kovac said, deliberately not answering the question, a longtime cop habit. It was ingrained in him to give nothing away. But a part of it this time was both the compassion to keep a parent from thinking the worst, and the perverse twist of that: letting them wonder. In the case of Julia Gray, he felt she deserved a bit of both.

"We'll let you folks get back to your evening," he said. "Please let us know if you hear from your daughter."

They left the house with Julia Gray and Michael Warner looking uncertain in the foyer.

"If you had a sixteen-year-old daughter in this day and age," Elwood said, "wouldn't you be a little more insistent about knowing who her friends are and where she might be?"

"If I had a sixteen-year-old daughter," Kovac said as they walked back to the car, "I'd have her microchipped with GPS."

18

"Mom, can Alex come over and play with the Wii?"

Liska's youngest placed the last of the dinner dishes on the counter above the dishwasher and looked up at her with bright, hopeful eyes, the hint of mischief playing at the corners of his mouth.

"Are you done with your homework?"

He nodded enthusiastically, smelling the victory. His gaze darted quickly to the clock on the microwave.

"Did you ask Kyle if he wants to play?" Nikki asked.

R.J. rolled his eyes. "He went upstairs to feel sorry for himself."

"Maybe he'll come down later," she said, knowing R.J. could not have cared less. It was her own futile, wishful thinking. Kyle hadn't said ten words since they'd gotten home.

Marysue had come to the rescue with spaghetti Bolognese and her usual sunny disposition. She and R.J. had chatted about their days, while Nikki had spent the meal twirling her pasta and watching her eldest stare at his plate.

R.J. shrugged. "Whatever."

Nikki frowned. "You know, your brother is going through a rough time right now. You could be a little nicer to him."

"He's a dork," R.J. said bluntly. "He's a dork, and he likes being a dork, and that's why he doesn't have any friends who aren't dorks."

"He's your brother," Nikki said sternly. "And I don't care if he's a dork. You stick up for your brother. Family sticks together."

"He's the one who shuts his door," R.J. pointed out, snagging a fresh chocolate chip cookie off the plate on the island. He took a bite. "He doesn't want to hang out with me."

"Why would he hang out with someone who calls him a dork?" Nikki countered. "And don't talk with your mouth full."

He swallowed and glanced at the clock again. "Can Alex come over?"

Nikki sighed. "Yes, Alex can come over if his mom says it's okay. And he goes home at ten on the dot. It's a school night."

Grinning, R.J. backed toward the hallway. His thank-you came a split second before the doorbell rang, and he bolted.

"And that would be Alex," Nikki said.

She turned with a sigh toward Marysue. "I hope being with my family won't make you sterile."

Marysue smiled kindly, seeming much too wise for twenty-six. "I love your boys. You know that. They're good boys, Nikki. You've got a lot on your plate right now, that's all."

"Yeah, well, I've had a lot on my plate for fifteen years. That doesn't seem to be getting any better. And their lives are only getting more complicated too."

She went to the coffeemaker, popped a pod in, and hit the button to start the thing hissing and spitting into the lopsided Christmas mug R.J. had made for her—with Marysue's help—at a local pottery store. She would pour a generous shot of Irish cream liqueur into the coffee and have it with one of the cookies Marysue had made that afternoon.

There was a painful truth: Marysue was a better mother, and she had yet to give birth to anyone.

"I feel like suddenly I don't know anything about Kyle's life," Nikki admitted, and with the admission she recognized a small knot of cold fear in her chest. How had this happened? How could she not know her own child?

"He was my little boy, climbing trees and scraping his knees and building a cardboard dinosaur for the science fair," she said. "Suddenly, he's a teenager, and everything about his life is a secret. He had a girlfriend over the summer. I didn't have any idea! Now he's getting picked on at school. He's getting into fights. And I just realized I don't even know who his friends are anymore, let alone his enemies."

She poured the Baileys into her coffee and climbed onto a stool at the island. Marysue slid the plate of cookies toward her and took the other seat.

"How did this happen?" Nikki asked. "Have I just not been paying attention? He's always been such an easy kid, self-sufficient, never in trouble. Did I really just forget about him? I don't get it.

"I grew up thinking how great it would be when I had my own family," she said, catching a glimpse of her younger self in her mind's eye—innocent and full of romantic notions of love and of having a life untainted by her parents' mistakes and disappointments.

"All the wonderful things we'd do together," she went on. "All the time I'd spend with my kids—hours and hours of playing games and reading stories and going places and watching the wonder in their little faces as they learned the new things that I'd teach them."

She saw it all play through her head like a silly dream sequence in some stupid, sappy movie. How incredibly naïve.

"The reality is I spend most of my time trying to earn a living to keep a roof over their heads, to keep clothes on their backs and shoes on their feet," she said, the weight of that reality pressing down on her shoulders. "I feel lucky when we get to grab a meal together. Our conversations are five minutes here and ten minutes there, usually in the car on the way to some activity I won't get to see all the way through because I'll get a callout to a crime scene. We live our lives like hamsters running in wheels."

She took a sip of her coffee and stared at the mug R.J. had made, her heart aching with love as she took in all the lumps and bumps and imperfections, the childish printing: TO MOM ♥R.J.

"Sometimes I think, what if I had a different profession?" she said. "What if I had some normal kind of a job? But would it be any different? Is it really any different for anyone—for any *single* mom?

"So . . . what? I should find the perfect husband, right?" she said. "And when am I supposed to do that? Where am I supposed to find him? A fender bender in a parking lot? He bumps his cart into mine at the supermarket? That never happens. My life is not a Lifetime movie or a Harlequin romance. Statistically, I probably have a greater chance of being killed by a terrorist than getting remarried. I don't even *want* to get remarried.

"And what are the odds the boys would like anyone I brought home, anyway?" she asked. "Pretty much zip. They're loyal to their father—even Kyle, who thinks he hates his dad, doesn't *really* hate him. He's disappointed by him. That's not hate. Once you cross the line to hate, disappointment is irrelevant; it's a given. If you hate someone, you're only too happy to have them disappoint you. It just proves your point.

"He wouldn't bond with another man at this late date, anyway," she went on. "He's fifteen. He's already looking at the light at the end of the tunnel. Three more years and he's off to college and leading his own life. And that's it. I had my shot, and it was over in the blink of an eye."

She sighed, exhausted, and looked at Marysue—young and fresh-faced with her big brown eyes and her rosebud mouth. Just looking at her made Nikki feel old. She forced a wry smile.

"So you've got that to look forward to, Marysue," she said. "What do you think?"

"I think you drink too much caffeine," Marysue said without hesitation.

Their laughter broke the tension, at least for a moment.

"Well, you've probably got that right," Nikki said. She took another long drink of her coffee anyway, savoring the smoky sweetness of the liqueur laced through it. "Thanks for letting me dump all that on you."

"It's okay," Marysue said with a soft smile.

"I've got a victim," Nikki said quietly. "A girl around Kyle's age. We don't know who she is. We haven't found her family. No one has come looking for her. And I want to be outraged by that. I want to say, how can someone be missing a daughter and not even know she's gone? Then I look at my own son. I have him right here with me, and I don't even know who he is."

A sense of deep, quiet desperation closed around her and squeezed. The air hissed out of her lungs, and she put her face in her hands and pressed her fingers against her closed eyes in an effort to keep the tears at bay.

Marysue Zaytoun put an arm around her shoulders.

KYLE HAD ESCAPED to his room at the first opportunity after supper. His mom had been relentless in trying to dig details out of him about his problems at school and his problems with Aaron Fogelman. That was one of the things that sucked about having a mom who was a police detective. She interrogated people for a living. But he was used to it. He had grown up learning how not to give anything away. Like a counterpuncher in a fight or a jiu-jitsu player rolling with a skillful opponent, his best offense was his defense.

His greatest fear was that his mother would pull the ultra-trump card and call Aaron Fogelman's parents in an attempt to get to the bottom of things. He couldn't think of anything worse or more embarrassing. He would rather have taken a beating by Fogelman and his goon friends every day for a month. Of course, that was exactly what would happen if his mother called Fogelman's mother.

He could only imagine the things his enemies would say about him then, the names they would call him, the rumors they would spread.

He dug his phone out of the pocket of his hoodie and brought up his secret Twitter account.

He had a Facebook page and a Twitter account that were readily accessible on the computer in the family room. But they were basically dummy accounts. His "friends" were the pages of mixed martial arts fighters he followed and bands he liked, not kids from school.

There was no such thing as absolute privacy in this house. The rule was that he and R.J. had to share time on the computer, and Mom had access to anything and everything on it. She policed their pages regularly. R.J. was constantly getting in trouble for friending people he didn't know and liking pages Mom disapproved of. She never said anything about Kyle's stuff.

He had set up separate accounts on his phone using an alias. Nobody on Twitter knew @PSIArtGeek was really him. There were a million art geeks at PSI. They all followed one another automatically. The profile photo he used was the PSI mascot, an angry-looking comic owl. The stuff he tweeted was generic—mostly re-tweets of stupid memes and cartoons and art. He used the account mainly to lurk, to see what other kids were talking about. The tweets he followed were full of vicious shit from the likes of Aaron Fogelman and Christina Warner and their minions.

Beneath all the unintelligent commentary about pop culture and what everyone had for dinner, the Twitterverse was a turbulent sea of vicious accusation, unsubstantiated rumor, and outright lies. The false facelessness of it gave people the freedom to strike out in ways they might never have dared in person. Even the meek became assassins on Twitter, drunk on the counterfeit confidence of imagined anonymity.

Fogelman and his toadies were all over it tonight with their usual unimaginative cracks about Kyle being a queer, being a faggot, deserving a beat-down, and promising to give him one. Christina Warner was in the mix too, supporting her lackey's take on what had gone down in the hall, while at the same time riding Brittany about being seen with him.

@XtinaW: Watch out @lilBritt people will think ur in luv w/ psycho stalker boy! Don't wanna b Mrs Loser

Kyle didn't care what Christina thought about him. It was the tweet that followed hers that hurt.

@lilBritt: Not me!!! hate u stalker boy. get a boyfriend loser! LOL!

He didn't want to believe she hated him. He didn't believe it. She was better than that. At least, she had been BC—before Christina.

Brittany's family had moved to Minneapolis in the spring, just as school was ending. The Brittany Kyle had met in his English class had been sweet and a little shy. He had signed up for a summer writer's workshop—even though he sucked at writing—just to get to know her better.

They had become friends with the possibility of, the hint of, something more. At least he had thought so. They had hung out together after the workshop classes, sitting around Lake Calhoun talking about stuff—him and Britt and Gray and a couple of kids who went to other schools. They talked about poetry and art and self-expression and accepting people for who they were.

Kyle didn't really know Gray. He suspected nobody really knew her. She was intense, deep, wrapped up in internal drama. Acceptance was her thing. Why couldn't people just accept other people? Why was it everyone thought they had to change to be more like someone else? Why were people so threatened by someone who wanted to live their own life in their own way?

The tattoo had been Gray's idea, but they had all done it—Brittany too.

But then school had started again, and Brittany found herself drawn into Christina Warner's orbit.

Kyle saw Christina as an evil queen in a fairy tale and Brittany as the pure, innocent heroine being dragged away by the powerful undertow of Christina's dark spell. And as Christina pulled her in deeper, Brittany let go of who she had been over the summer.

Kyle wanted her to break free. He supposed that cast him in the role of hero by default. He didn't really see himself that way. He was no Ultor. He wished he were. He wished he had Ultor's strength and the powerful energy currents Ultor could send from his hands to battle his enemies. But Ultor was fantasy, and high school was the real world. And maybe the truth was that the real Brittany was the one who called him a loser and told him to get a boyfriend, and the Brittany who got the Chinese symbol of acceptance inked on her body was the fake.

If he was writing that into the story line of his comic book, he would make it so the tattoo burned every time Brittany did something that went against the philosophy behind it.

Agitated by the thought, Kyle went to his small desk and opened his sketchbook, frowning at the ruined drawing of his superhero. All the painstaking time and effort he had put into the three views of Ultor, the deliberate care he had taken to express different levels of strength simply with the lines and shading, all ruined by a pack of juvenile morons who thought degrading other people somehow built them up.

He stared at the drawing, trying to detach from it emotionally, trying to see it as something other than an attack on him. What would his personal hero do in his place? It was hard to imagine the UFC champion fighter Georges St-Pierre being in this situation, but Kyle knew GSP had faced his own bullies as a kid.

He would have tried to find a way to turn the situation against his enemies, Kyle decided. On his website St-Pierre gave the standard advice adults gave to kids, telling them to turn to an adult for help. But Kyle figured the adult GSP would have done what he did when he was fighting in the octagon. He would have found a way to take his enemy's power and defeat him with it.

That was exactly what he would have done.

Kyle sat down and dug an eraser out of a drawer as the idea took hold of him. He rubbed away, erasing not the ridiculous giant penises that had been added by Fogelman's idiot buddies but the carefully rendered profiles of Ultor's face. He beheaded his superhero, then went to work with a pencil, a kind of giddy joy rising in his chest as he worked.

In contrast to the realistic, anatomically perfect bodies of the three Ultors, the new faces he drew were comic caricatures, oversize heads with exaggerated features. Kyle started chuckling as the faces came to life—as he took the power away from his enemies and turned it into something else.

When he was finished, he was no longer looking at three images of Ultor. He was looking at two of Aaron Fogelman's stooges—Thing One and Thing Two—and Fogelman, grinning like an idiot. The lead idiot at the head of the idiot threesome sex train.

Kyle admired his masterpiece, grinning, then laughing, feeling light and happy for the first time in days.

This was sweet. This was awesome. This was going to make Aaron Fogelman flip his shit.

He grabbed his phone and snapped a picture of the drawing. And before he could really think about what he was doing and what the fallout would be, he posted it to Twitter via @PSIArtGeek

The shit was about to hit the fan.

19

Brittany sat on her bed in her pretty yellow bedroom, her iPad on her lap, her iPod playing on the nightstand, feeling like a fraud and a bitch and someone who didn't belong in a pretty princess bedroom.

When her family had moved to Minneapolis from Duluth, her mother had thought the transition would be easier if they didn't change everything about their lives at the same time. Brittany had agreed. She didn't like change. She hadn't wanted to move and leave her friends. It did make her feel better to at least have all her familiar things surrounding her in her bedroom.

They had painted the walls the exact same shade of yellow as her old bedroom. She had her same ornate white iron bed with the quilts her grandmother had made. The same white wicker-framed mirror hung over the white painted dresser with the collection of old perfume bottles on top.

It was the frilly room of a sweet little girl. Brittany felt like she didn't deserve to be there tonight.

Tonight she wanted to rewind the calendar to before the move to

Minneapolis. She wanted to go back to Duluth and the kids she had known her whole life. Here she felt like she was swimming with the sharks in deep water.

She didn't really think she was smart enough or talented enough to be in PSI. She was a good student, but she had to work at it. She liked to write short stories and poetry and songs, but it didn't come easily to her, and she never thought what she wrote was very good. Socially, she felt like a hick among the city kids. Even though Duluth wasn't exactly a small town, it was a world away from Minneapolis.

Brittany didn't like being an outsider. She wanted to fit in. She wanted to blend in. To be yourself, to go your own way, to express yourself like Gray did, sounded exciting and admirable, but Brittany wasn't brave enough to stand out. She didn't want to be a rebel. She wanted to be accepted. She wanted to be popular. There was nothing wrong with that.

Gray acted like wanting people to like you was a sign of weakness, but Brittany didn't see it that way at all—and she didn't believe Gray really saw it that way either. Gray wanted to be accepted too. Her poetry was all about feeling like an outsider but wanting to belong. It had been Gray's idea to get the acceptance tattoo.

To want to be a part of the group was a natural thing, Brittany thought. It felt good to belong with other people. It felt . . . safe. She had always been one of the popular kids—not the leader, not the trendsetter, just . . . a belonger, she thought, knowing that wasn't a real word. It should have been. It expressed what she meant exactly. She just wanted to belong.

That was ironic, she supposed. She wanted to be accepted. She had gotten the tattoo along with Gray and Kyle. She had gotten the tattoo that stood for acceptance so she would be accepted by kids who wanted to stand apart. Now she wanted to be accepted by a group of kids who singled out other kids to be ostracized.

She lived in fear of Christina seeing her tattoo, and she was glad every day that she had put the tattoo on her hip, where she could easily cover it up. She wished she hadn't gotten it at all. In the first place, getting it had hurt really badly. Then she'd been terrified trying to hide it from her mom. More important, she felt like such a phony and fake wearing a symbol of acceptance. Sometimes she imagined the inked marks burning every time she said something or did something that went against the philosophy behind the tattoo.

She felt that way now after tweeting what she had about Kyle. She felt wrong and bad, and a little sick in her stomach. She didn't like saying mean things. She felt bad for calling him a loser, and she knew he wasn't gay—not that it should have mattered to anyone if he was.

Acceptance. She wanted to scratch at the tattoo. She had pledged acceptance of people's choices, including sexual preference. She knew gay kids. Gray claimed to be bisexual, which kind of made Brittany uncomfortable because it seemed so . . . darkly . . . brave? Fearless? Creepy? She wasn't sure what word was the right word.

She knew she was the kind of person who was afraid to leave the straightest, most well-lit road of life. It had taken courage for her to befriend a girl like Gray. She didn't think Gray fully appreciated that. Not that it mattered now. They would probably never be friends again after what had happened at the Rock & Bowl.

And the emotional merry-go-round came back to guilt while Beyoncé sang in the background.

The group of kids she hung out with now used the word *gay* as the worst kind of insult, and Brittany pretended to go along with them. The girl with the acceptance tattoo. And what had she just tweeted about Kyle? *Get a boyfriend.*

Christina had told her talking trash about Kyle was the best way to get rid of him. If he wouldn't leave her alone, then she had to send a message. He wasn't the kind of guy she needed to be hanging out with—according to Christina. He was weird. He didn't try to get along with anyone—except other outcasts. He spent all his time reading comic books and drawing his stupid superheroes.

And if he really liked her, Brittany reasoned, he wouldn't have put her in the position he had that afternoon. He would have left her alone like she asked him to. He was all Mr. Antibully, but what was he doing to her by hanging around when she asked him not to and pressuring her about the people she wanted to be friends with? He was a bully too, in his own way.

It was his own fault Aaron and Christina and practically everyone else didn't like him, she thought angrily. It wasn't her fault everyone got on Twitter and Facebook and talked shit about him. He practically invited them to. But even as she thought that, another wave of guilt swept through her. She could see the accusation and disappointment and betrayal on his face as he had glared at her in the hall today.

Nice friends you've got, Britt. I can see why you'd rather hang with them.

She felt like she had betrayed him, and then she felt angry with him for making her feel that way.

On the nightstand beside her, her phone made the little *ding!* that announced a new text message.

Xtina: R U OK?

Brittany ignored it. She didn't want to interact with anyone—especially not Christina. No more than she wanted to interact with Kyle. She felt like the two of them were fighting over her like she was a rag doll, one pulling her this way, one the other.

Kyle made out like Christina was an evil witch, which wasn't true. Christina could be a diva, but she could also be kind and generous, and she was fiercely protective of her friends. She had taken it upon herself to help Brittany survive the first brutal weeks of chemistry and helped her get on the yearbook committee. Christina saw Kyle and Gray as the bad influences. They were the ones trying to separate her from her friends and cut her off from things she wanted to do.

Gray and Christina's relationship was complicated by the fact that Christina's father was dating Gray's mom. Gray felt threatened by the relationship. She felt like Christina was the daughter her mother would have liked. She resented Christina, resented the way she looked and the way she dressed. She resented Christina's popularity.

Brittany found herself caught in the middle between them—and a little bit used by both of them.

Tired of thinking about it, Brittany looked down at her iPad and tried to distract herself, browsing through the pages and apps she checked every night. She didn't want to think anymore about Kyle Hatcher or Gray or Christina or anything. She touched the icon for an online magazine called *TeenCities*. She had used this magazine as her guide since moving to the Twin Cities. It was full of fun articles about things to do and places kids her age could go all over the metro area. There were always great articles about fashion and celebrities and the local music scene.

Those were the pages that interested Brittany, especially after the kind of day she'd had. She didn't have any interest in the more serious news articles. She didn't want to read about bulimia or cutting or dire warnings about the latest street drugs. She certainly had no interest in reading a column about cyberbullies.

She sometimes read Sonya Porter's blog about current issues. She thought the writer had a great hip style that was easy and conversational with a wry sense of humor. Her pieces read as if the writing had been effortless—a quality Brittany longed for in her own writing. And Sonya Porter's profile picture fit perfectly with that image— hip and cool, the perfect chic blend of sophistication and youth.

Brittany wished she could have been half as cool as Sonya Porter. Fat chance of that. She wasn't even brave enough to get her belly button pierced. She would never be bold enough to be as cool as Sonya Porter.

She touched the screen to go to Porter's blog, hoping for one of her lighter pieces. But the piece couldn't have been any heavier or more depressing. The article was about young women being murdered in horrible ways, their bodies dumped along roadways.

That was the last thing Brittany wanted to look at tonight. She was depressed enough already. She didn't want to know some girl her own age had been found dead on New Year's Eve.

Downstairs the doorbell rang. Brittany paid no attention. Her mother was having her book group in tonight. The bell had rung half a dozen times already. The voices of the women rose and fell like a distant wave of conversation and laughter.

She scrolled through the virtual pages of her magazine, unable to find anything that held her attention for more than a few lines. Her mind kept going back to Kyle and the things she had said about him, and the way she knew that would hurt him when he read it. And of course he would read it. He lurked on Twitter and Facebook all the time, reading all the nasty, mean things kids wrote about other kids so he could feel morally superior.

When the knock came on her bedroom door, she jumped, startled.

"Britt?" her mother asked. "Can I come in?"

Brittany set her iPad aside and went to the door, expecting her mother to ask her to turn her music down. But when she opened the door her mother was not alone. Two men in suits and heavy coats stood behind her.

"Honey, these men are police detectives," her mom said, looking worried. "They're looking for Gray."

"Gray?" Brittany looked from one man to the other. Police? One was older; one was bigger. They both scared her with their serious expressions. "Why? Is she in trouble?"

The older cop showed her his ID and badge. He was lean and

hard-looking, with a lot of gray shot through his thick hair. His eyes seemed to burn right into her.

"Brittany, I'm Sergeant Kovac. This is Sergeant Knutson. Penny Gray's mom told us she was staying with you," he said.

"She was here for a couple of days," she said. "Then she left."

"Where did she go?"

Brittany shook her head. "I don't know. I thought she went home."

Police. In her bedroom. Asking about Gray. A chill ran down her back.

"When did you last see her?"

"Um, the night before New Year's Eve."

"Have you heard from her in the last day or so?" the cop Kovac asked.

Her heart beat faster. The way he stared at her made her feel like she was some kind of criminal. It was unnerving. She hadn't done anything wrong, but she was still afraid. Her palms were sweating.

"No," she said.

"Do you have any idea where she might be?"

"No."

"She didn't tell you where she was going?"

"No."

He looked at his partner and gave a sharp sigh.

"Britt," her mother said, "if you know where Gray is, you have to tell these men."

"I don't know where she is!" Brittany snapped. "We went to a party and she got mad and left; that's all. I don't know where she went. I thought she went home."

"Where was the party?" Kovac asked.

Brittany bit her lip and tried not to look at her mom. She was going to be in such trouble.

"Brittany . . . ," her mother said in that tone of voice that warned of worse to come.

"This is important, Brittany," Kovac said. "I can't speak for your mom, but personally, I'd cut you some slack on the party if you had something to share about your friend Gray. She's missing. She could be in some serious trouble. We need to locate her."

This is so weird. This can't be happening, she thought. Police in her bedroom asking about Gray. Gray missing? Gray wasn't missing. She was just being Gray.

"Brittany Anne Lawler," her mom said, enunciating every syllable.

"We went to the Rock & Bowl," Brittany confessed.

Her mom gasped. "Brittany! You told me you were going to Christina's house!"

"We were! But then everybody went to the Rock & Bowl first—"

"You know I don't like you going to that place!"

Brittany rolled her eyes and huffed a sigh. "Mom. Everybody goes there!"

"It's in a terrible neighborhood!"

"No, it isn't! It's practically right by the Mall of America."

"The mall has to have its own police force for a reason," her mother said.

"How did she leave?" Kovac asked.

Brittany looked at him. "What do you mean?"

"How did Gray leave? Did she call a cab? Did she take a bus? Did she leave with someone?"

"She has a car," Brittany said. "She just left."

Her mother looked as though she wanted to strangle her. Her eyes were practically bulging from her head. "You told me Aaron's father was picking you up."

She glanced at the cops, embarrassment and anger turning her cheeks red. "My husband and I were at a dinner party," she said, almost like an apology, like the detectives would think she was a bad mom because her daughter had gone to the stupid Rock & Bowl.

She turned back to Brittany. "And you know I don't want you riding in a car with her. She just got her license!"

"I don't see what the big deal is," Brittany argued. "She had to pass a test to get it. She's just as good a driver as anyone else."

"Oh my God," her mother muttered, looking up at the ceiling.

"What time was it when you last saw Miss Gray?" the big cop asked.

Brittany shrugged. "I don't know. Nine thirty? Ten, maybe. Maybe ten thirty. I don't remember."

"Brittany . . . ," her mother said.

"She's not missing," Brittany insisted. "Gray gets pissed off. Sometimes she just goes somewhere for a couple of days. She always comes back."

"This isn't the first time she's gone missing?" Kovac asked.

"She's not missing," Brittany said stubbornly.

It seemed important to say that, to believe it.

"She gets mad. She goes and stays with whoever."

"Can you give us names?"

"I don't know them. She has friends outside our school. Musicians, poets, older kids. They're not people I hang out with."

A chill went through her suddenly as her gaze swept over her iPad lying on her bed. Sonya Porter's article on *TeenCities* . . . A girl found dead on New Year's Eve . . . Two police detectives were standing in her bedroom asking questions about Gray . . .

A sickening sense of dread swirled in her stomach.

"She hasn't called you?" Kovac asked. "No text messages?"

"No posts on Facebook?" the big one asked. "Twitter?"

Tears rose in Brittany's eyes. "You're scaring me. Stop it."

Kovac didn't apologize. He just kept looking at her with those hard eyes. "Do you have any pictures of Gray, Brittany?"

Her hands were trembling as she picked up the iPad off the bed and touched the icon to call up her photographs. The pictures swam in the tears that welled up on the edge of her eyelashes.

She told herself nothing was wrong. It was stupid to be ready to cry. There was no reason to cry. Just because there were police detectives in her bedroom . . . Just because they didn't know where Gray was . . . Just because some stupid reporter wrote about something bad that happened . . . It didn't mean there was any reason for her to cry.

Three tears spilled down her cheeks as she touched one of the photos and it filled the screen. Herself and Gray posing like movie stars, lips pursed as they pretended to blow kisses at the camera.

"Nothing happened to her," she said, sounding more afraid than defiant.

The picture was from summer, from when they were in the writer's workshop. Gray said she wanted to speak like Dorothy Parker and write like Sylvia Plath. Side by side they looked like some kind of day-and-night comparison. Brittany with her blond hair and fresh face. Gray with her multiple piercings, her thick dark hair swept to one side. She stood facing away from the camera, looking back over her shoulder.

The police detectives stared at the photograph, giving nothing away with their stone faces and hard eyes. Kovac reached out a finger and touched the screen, touched Gray's bare shoulder just below her tattoo and murmured the word: "Acceptance."

Brittany knew right then, even though they didn't say it, that something terrible had happened. And even though she was standing in her bedroom with adults all around her, she had never felt so alone in her life. For the first time she thought she understood that sense of isolation Gray had talked about in her poems.

She had never felt so lost.

20

"What do you mean, she isn't there?"

Julia Gray looked at them with an expression Kovac had seen many, many times in his years of delivering bad news. It was a deliberate kind of confusion layered over apprehension, layered over a sickening sense of primal fear.

They stood in the small foyer of the Gray home again, the scent of Christmas tree and spice candles perfuming the air. Kovac and Elwood, sweating inside their heavy coats; Julia Gray and her gentleman friend, Michael Warner, looking vulnerable, the way civilians do when confronted by cops. Like rabbits facing wolves.

Warner was in shirtsleeves now, a fine blue button-down oxford with his initials monogrammed on the pocket. He had stripped off the cashmere sweater and tied it around his neck—a look that always irritated Kovac. What the fuck was up with a guy like that? What kind of message was he trying to send? To Kovac, a sweater tied around the neck said "gay." Not that he gave a shit. It was just an observation. But then there were these metro guys—or whatever the hell the fashionable people called them now. Sweater around the neck, manicures and facials. Mixed messages. He just never quite trusted a guy who sent mixed messages. Have a girlfriend or have a boyfriend. Pick a side.

"According to your daughter's friend, they went to a place called the Rock and Bowl. There was some kind of argument. Your daughter got mad and left," Kovac said.

"And went where?" Julia Gray asked stupidly. She probably wasn't a stupid woman. She just wanted him to have an easy answer. She wanted him to tell her where her daughter was—alive and well, of course, not on a slab in the Hennepin County morgue.

Kovac sighed and scratched his ear. "Mrs. Gray, it might be better if we could all sit down and talk. Do you mind if we do that?"

Of course she minded. Of course she didn't want them making themselves at home. She didn't want them there at all. She hugged her arms tight across her chest and looked around the foyer as if looking for permission from some unseen audience to ask them to just leave so she could go back to pretending nothing was wrong.

"Julia, they're right," Michael Warner said quietly. He put a hand on her shoulder as if to anchor her. "Let's all sit down and try to figure this out."

"Oh my God, this is—is—just so—," she muttered, shaking her head, agitated as Warner herded her toward a seat at the dining room table. "I can't believe she's doing this."

Kovac arched a brow at Elwood, who shrugged. It didn't seem to be sinking in to Julia Gray that they were considering the possibility her daughter might be a victim of a brutal homicide or that, at best, her daughter had disappeared. This unpleasantness was something her daughter was doing to her, purposely making her look bad.

"She texted me," she said, turning back into the foyer. She grabbed her phone off the hall table and brought up the message on the screen. "She texted me back an hour ago. She's fine. She's just off in one of her snits."

She shoved the phone at Kovac. The message read: *Y cant u leave me alone?*

It meant nothing more than that whoever had Penelope Gray's phone was smart enough to answer a text message.

"What kind of phone does your daughter have?" Elwood asked.

"An iPhone. The latest one. I got it for her for her birthday." She shook her head. "It's crazy the things these kids have to have. iPhones, iPads, iPods . . ."

"Do you know if the phone has a tracking app enabled?"

"I don't know what that is. I'm not very good with technology."

"If the software is enabled and the phone is turned on, we would be able to locate the device," Elwood explained. "We'd need to access her Apple ID account, which means jumping through some legal hoops—unless you have her password."

She laughed without humor. "No. I don't have access to much of anything in my daughter's life."

The immediate implications of that truth pressed down on her, and tears flooded her eyes. She pressed a hand across her mouth.

Michael Warner corralled her with a long arm and steered her back into the dining room. "Julia, let's sit. We'll think out loud. We'll figure this out."

"Have you called any of your daughter's friends?" Elwood asked.

She closed her eyes for a moment as she sank down onto a chair at the dining room table, as if against the pain of a monumental headache. "My daughter doesn't share her friends with me."

"Girls this age are asserting their independence," Michael Warner said. "Particularly where their mothers are concerned."

Kovac gave him a who-asked-you look.

"I'm a psychiatrist," Warner said by way of explanation. "I work with a lot of girls Penny's age. And I have a daughter myself. Between the flux of hormones and the changing brain chemistry, girls this age are volatile in the best of cases."

"And this isn't the best of cases?" Kovac asked.

"Her father and I divorced when Penny was twelve," Julia Gray said, her attention on her phone again as she searched her contacts for a number. "The four years since have been . . . difficult, to put it mildly."

She put the phone to her ear and listened to it ring on the other end.

"She's a bright, talented girl," Warner said. "But she doesn't apply herself, she doesn't try to fit in, she's defiant—"

"Tim? It's—" She checked herself, her brows knitting with frustration. She sighed, waiting for the voice mail message to play through. "It's me. Is Penny with you? Have you seen or heard from her? Please call me back as soon as you get this."

She clicked the call off and put the phone down on the table with a little more force than was necessary.

"Has your daughter ever been in trouble with the law?" Kovac asked, thinking if the girl's prints were on file they could eliminate her as a possible victim. Their Jane Doe's prints had not been in the system.

Even as he thought it, he could see Brittany Lawler's photograph in his mind's eye and the tattoo on Penelope Gray's shoulder.

Pooch Halvorsen said a lot of kids had that tattoo. . . .

"No, thank God."

"Does she have a boyfriend?"

"Not that I know of."

Elwood got out his little spiral notebook and pen. "What kind of car does your daughter drive, Mrs. Gray?"

"It's a black Toyota something—"

"Camry," Michael Warner supplied. "An oh-four."

"Is it registered in her name?"

"No. In mine," Julia said. "Michael bought it for Penny's sixteenth birthday, but it made more sense to register it to me—for the insurance, you know."

Kovac reached inside his coat and pulled out the photograph Brittany Lawler had printed out for him from her iPad and put it on the table.

"This seems to be a more recent photograph than the one you showed us earlier," he said.

Julia Gray got a sour look, narrowing her eyes. "She did all that this summer," she said bitterly. "The piercings, the tattoo. I can't stand the sight of it."

"Penny feels the need to make self-destructive statements," Michael Warner said. "It's a manifestation of her inner pain. She feels emotionally isolated by her father's abandonment. It's normal, really."

"If it's so normal, why doesn't Christina have holes in her face?" Julia asked him, the hint of bitterness in her voice old and worn. They'd been over this ground before.

"I didn't abandon Christina," he said. "Her mother's death brought us closer together. Your split from Tim drove a wedge between you and Penny. It's a completely different set of circumstances."

"It's my fault," Julia said.

"Tim left you. The blame lies with him."

"Not as Penny sees it," she said. "I drove him away. That's what she believes. It's all my fault her father took up with his twenty-six-year-old receptionist."

"Does Penny have any tattoos other than this one?" Kovac asked, tapping a finger on the grainy print.

"I don't think so," she said. "I can't imagine that she would hide them from me. She knows how much I hate them. It shouldn't even be legal for a girl her age to get a tattoo."

"It's not," Elwood said.

"Her latest act of defiance was shaving off half of her hair," she said.

The statement struck Kovac like an electrical shock. He glanced at Elwood from the corner of his eye.

Tinks said girls shaved their heads now. They pierced everything. They got tattoos. How many did all three and then went missing?

"She claims it's a statement about her sexuality," Julia Gray went on bitterly. "This is her new thing—claiming she's bisexual. I could have strangled her. She looks like she escaped from a concentration camp!"

"I'm going to suggest you file a missing persons report, Mrs. Gray," Kovac said calmly. "That way we can get your daughter's information into the system immediately."

They could get out an AMBER Alert, giving them maximum media coverage. Even if Penelope Gray turned out to be Zombie Doe, it would take time to confirm that, and they wouldn't have to release the information immediately. In the meantime, media spotlighting the case of a missing girl would make people aware, get people talking, get them looking for Penny Gray's car. Maybe someone would remember having seen her.

"Oh my God," Julia Gray murmured, pressing her hand to her forehead as if feeling for a fever. She grabbed the phone again as the screen lit up and a *ping* sounded, heralding the arrival of a text. Tears filled her eyes and her face turned mottled shades of red that clashed with her Christmas sweater. "Tim hasn't heard from her."

"You don't think it's her, though," Michael Warner said to Kovac. "Your victim. You don't think it's Penny. If you think we should file a missing persons report . . ."

Kovac looked at him, Dr. Sweater Around His Neck, and wondered if Michael Warner had ever seen a corpse that had fallen out of the trunk of a moving car or the face of a young woman who had been disfigured with acid. Probably not. That kind of privilege was reserved for guys like himself . . . and the parents of murdered children.

"It's not my place to draw conclusions," he said.

"But you've seen Penny's photograph," Warner pressed. "And you've seen the victim. Either it's her or it isn't."

"It's not that simple, Dr. Warner," Kovac said. "I'm going to leave it at that. No need for all of us to have the same nightmares tonight."

Warner frowned at the implication. "This is going to require dental X-rays?"

"X-rays," Kovac qualified.

"Has Penny ever broken a bone?" Elwood asked.

Now the color began to drain from Julia Gray's face as she looked from one of them to the other. "Oh my God," she whispered as realization began to dawn that this could go the wrong way for her—and for her daughter. "She . . . she . . ."

She didn't want to finish the sentence. If she finished the sentence, then it was out there and there was no taking it back and pretending it might not be true. They were asking her this question for a reason, for a real reason, a serious reason. And they were telling her that if her daughter was dead, she was also unrecognizable, that she had been brutalized in the most horrible way imaginable. Julia Gray didn't want to know that.

She started to cry. First just a few tears in a slow trickle; then a dam burst somewhere inside her, and the emotion came in a flash flood of tears and snot and spittle and panic, like something inside of her head had exploded.

"Sh-sh-she b-b-b-ro-ke h-h-her wrist! Oh my God!"

Dr. Sweater Around His Neck looked at her with the same horror with which any man first regarded a sobbing woman.

Kovac got to his feet and sighed, weary to the bone. "We'll need to see those X-rays."

The sound that came from Julia Gray was terrible and primal, like a wounded animal. That's what they all were, in truth, anyway, Kovac thought. Strip away the Christmas lights and the nice house, the stylish clothes and the trappings of society, they were all just animals trying to survive in a cruel world.

Julia Gray was just a mother now, frightened for the offspring she had given life and been charged to keep safe. Before the cops had shown up on her doorstep, she had been struggling but still in possession of the hope that she could turn things around with her child. If her child was dead, then failure was a done deal. There would be no second chances.

Kovac and Elwood moved off to one side of the room while Michael Warner tried to comfort and calm Julia Gray. Kovac pulled his phone out and texted Liska with the address of the Gray house and *pick me up asap*. Elwood would go back to the office and get the paperwork rolling.

"Mrs. Gray," he said after the worst of her hysteria had passed. "We'll need to have a look in your daughter's bedroom."

Michael Warner helped her up from her chair and held on to her as they went slowly up the stairs, as if she had suddenly become physically frail beneath the weight of the stress.

In contrast to Brittany Lawler's sunny yellow bedroom, Penny Gray's bedroom was somber and dark, the walls and ceiling a charcoal blue-gray that absorbed the light instead of reflecting it back into the room. The posters on the walls were of grim and angry young people. Singers and actors, Kovac supposed, though he'd never heard of any of them. They all looked like their moods could be greatly improved by a decent meal and a smack upside the head.

Someone had painted the acceptance tattoo on the wall above the bed in silver paint with the words *Be Who You Are* beneath it. The bed itself was a tangle of sheets and pillows. There was a chair nearby stacked with clothes, and a dresser cluttered with all the stuff girls found essential—jewelry and makeup, hairbrushes and perfume bottles. A bookcase was filled to overflowing with books and magazines and notebooks. Old stuffed toys and odd keepsakes—the things girls collected.

The thing he didn't see in Penny Gray's bedroom that had been in abundance in Brittany Lawler's room: photographs of her with her friends. There were none—not in the bookcase or on the dresser or on the walls.

Kovac had long ago acquired the skill of reading people from the things they surrounded themselves with, the things they placed importance on, the things they *didn't* have, the things they kept hidden. As he poked around the bedroom of the girl her friend called Gray, he put these pieces together with what he had seen in her photograph and the things people had said about her.

Her mother called her Penny—a name that called to mind something shiny and bright. She called herself Gray—the color of gloom and ambiguity. Her bedroom was an obvious reflection of that self—a difficult, conflicted girl who seemed to work at alienating herself while preaching a message of acceptance.

The thought crept into his mind as he looked around that somewhere on the far side of the country he had a daughter. He wondered what her room might look like, what it might say about her, and he thought about how he would have to gather together the pieces of information about her by looking at her stuff because he knew absolutely nothing about who she was.

These thoughts sifted around in the lower reaches of his mind as he looked through Penny Gray's room and formulated his thoughts about who Penny Gray was. Julia Gray and Michael Warner watched from the doorway.

"Is there something in particular you're looking for?" Warner asked.

"Does your daughter keep a calendar or a diary, Mrs. Gray?" Elwood asked.

"I don't know. She keeps everything in her phone and on her laptop."

"Is her laptop here someplace?"

"I doubt it. She always has it with her. She thinks she's going to be a writer. A poet. Who reads poetry anymore?"

"I do," Elwood admitted.

Kovac glanced over the things on Penny Gray's desk—schoolbooks, a dog-eared paperback novel about vampires, some completely indecipherable math homework. Not that long ago the girl's computer would have been an immovable box, and files would have been stored on floppy disks that he could have taken and given over to a geek to figure out. Now everything was portable and files got saved to a cloud in the ether someplace.

On the upside, technology would allow them to track her telephone—provided it was turned on. They would be able to narrow down a location based on the towers the signal was pinging off. As soon as they got the missing persons report filed and the AMBER Alert up and a warrant to get the information from the phone company . . .

"Is her phone in her name?" he asked. "Or do you have a family plan?"

"We have a family plan."

Elwood looked at him. "That makes life a little easier," he said quietly.

They had run into walls in the past trying to get information from the cell phone service providers of missing individuals. The phone companies were more concerned about being sued over violations of privacy laws than about hindering a police investigation.

"I still want a warrant," Kovac murmured. "Dot all the i's and cross all the t's. I don't want a hairsbreadth of room for some oily lawyer to slide through if it comes to that."

He glanced at his watch. Half past exhaustion, with a long night to go.

"Is this some of your daughter's poetry?" Elwood asked, pointing to the wall above the small cluttered desk, where printed pages and small drawings and pictures cut out of magazines had been taped into a patchwork collage of teenage angst and self-expression.

"I guess so," Julia Gray said.

She didn't know her daughter's writing. She didn't know her daughter's friends. She didn't know where her daughter went, didn't know why she made the choices she made. It struck Kovac that this woman didn't know much more about her daughter than he knew about his. Even living in the same house, they were living worlds apart.

The title of one of the poems caught his eye. He pulled his reading glasses out of his coat pocket and stepped closer, a deep sense of sadness settling inside him as he read the words.

He thought about the girl Julia Gray had portrayed through her words and her attitude this evening: defiant, disrespectful, disappointing in every way. He thought about the girl who had written this poem, the girl with the acceptance tattoo: a kid trying to express herself, trying to figure out who she was and who she wanted to be, feeling misunderstood, like every teenage kid did. He thought about the girl whose body he had knelt over on the cold and frozen road New Year's Eve: used, abused, discarded. Taken. Lost. Gone.

It was his job as a detective to be the one person in the world who accepted her for exactly who she had been. It wasn't his place to judge her, and in judging her close off his mind to possibilities in the investigation. It was his job to see her for who she was and to see every avenue that opened to him from that place of acceptance.

Somehow, he doubted that was what Penny Gray had had in mind when she had gotten that tattoo or when she had written this poem.

"Lost"

Looking for me
I am
Who do they see?
Not I
I want to be
Myself
They want me to be
Gone
I'm lost

21

"The Rock and Bowl?" Liska asked.

Kovac looked at her from the passenger's side as he buckled his seat belt. "You know it?"

"I've been there with the boys."

She had been there more than once—to a couple of birthday parties and to an outing with R.J.'s hockey team. It was the kind of place that drove her crazy as a mother who happened to be a cop—or a cop who happened to be a mother. The place was too big with too many different things going on, catering to too many different kinds of people. It was a bowling alley / arcade / pizza place à la Chuck E. Cheese, with a second-story dance floor that overlooked the lanes. The crowd was a mix of families, kids, teenagers, single young adults. It was the kind of place where she always worried about pedophiles and low-level drug dealers slipping shit to kids in the midst of the chaos.

"And this girl goes to PSI," she said flatly, wondering vaguely if any of this was really happening. Maybe she was asleep and dreaming. Maybe these last couple of days had all just been part of the same long, strange nightmare. God knew she felt that tired. Maybe she was asleep and dreaming she was exhausted and that her life was a mess.

"I'd say what are the odds," Kovac said, "but the odds are no different she'd go to that school than any other. Everybody comes from somewhere."

"You really think this is our girl?" Liska asked, pulling away from the curb, leaving behind the pretty Tudor-style house with its cheery Christmas tree in the front window.

"Too many pieces match up," he said. "The tattoo, the piercings, the hair, the fact that she's missing. This girl broke her wrist last April. The mother will get us a release for the X-rays for comparison."

He looked hard at her. "Do you know these people?"

"No," she admitted, hating the way that answer made her feel.

She should have known every kid who went to school with her son. She should have known their parents too. She should have served on committees with this girl's mother. They should have been in a book club together. Never mind that there were more than a hundred kids in Kyle's class, and probably no one's mother knew all of them. Never mind that she did her part working with PSI's drug awareness program. None of that seemed like enough now.

"This girl is sixteen," Kovac said. "Her friends call her Gray. She's artsy, writes poetry. Sounds like someone Kyle might know."

Liska huffed a sigh as she turned the corner, heading toward 35W. "Maybe she is. Maybe she's his girlfriend. I obviously know nothing about what goes on in his life. I just occasionally show up to drive him someplace and feed him the odd meal."

"You're not the only mother that has a job, Tinks."

"No," she said. "But I'm the only mother my sons have."

"Even if you were June fucking Cleaver, you wouldn't know everything that goes on in their lives."

"That's not the point."

"The point is you're a control freak."

"And you're not?"

"We're not talking about me," he said. "Did Kyle get kicked out of school today?"

"No."

"Is anyone pressing charges against him?"

"No."

"Were lives lost today?"

"No."

"Then get your head where it belongs," he said. "Here. Now. Unless you win the lottery or land yourself a millionaire husband, you're going to be a working mother."

"Yeah, well, maybe I need to rethink what that means," she said, merging onto the freeway, heading south. It sounded ominous. It scared her a little to have said it out loud. She felt like Pandora cracking open the box. She was afraid to even steal a glance at her partner. She could feel his reaction from across the car.

"What's that supposed to mean?" he asked. It was more of a dare, really. His tone was almost intimidating, as if maybe he could bully her into taking back what she was thinking.

She took a deep breath. "It means there's a big difference between being a mom who works nine to five at a desk and a mom who gets called out at all hours of the night and pulls—how many hours have we been on this? I've had half a night's sleep in three days. Marysue spends more time with my kids than I do."

"You're a cop," Kovac said, bemused by this whole strange turn her brain seemed to be taking. Being a cop was the absolute fabric of his being. He didn't know anything else—didn't want to know anything else. "That's how it is. You're a homicide detective."

"That's what I'm saying. I choose to work Homicide. That's my choice. There are other options. I could go to Forgery/Fraud. I could go to Internal Affairs—"

"IA," he said. "You. Right. Why don't you aim for the stars," he said sarcastically. "Join the graffiti squad. Better yet, become a department chaplain."

"Don't be such an ass," she snapped. "I'm serious, Sam. I choose to work a job with crazy hours."

"You're damn good at it."

"I love it," she confessed. "I love my job. But I love my kids more. If I have to pick one over the other, that shouldn't be a hard choice."

And yet, she had never made it in all these years.

"You don't have to pick," he said stubbornly. "Every once in awhile we get a case like this one, and yes, the hours suck, but—"

"Every once in a while?" she said, incredulous. "What's our caseload right now? How many active open cases do we have going? Murders *and* assaults."

He didn't answer, conceding defeat on the point. They seemed always overworked and understaffed. He complained about it all the time, constantly lobbying Kasselmann to fight with the brass for more detectives.

"Maybe you should apply for Kasselmann's job," he said, only half-sarcastic.

"The brass would never let me go straight from investigation to running Homicide," she said. "That's too big a plum. Every wannabe chief is champing at the bit to cycle through Homicide. They'd stick me somewhere else first, somewhere boring and awful. I'd be an underling to some dickhead in the pencil-counting division."

"You're serious," Kovac said. "You're seriously thinking about this."

She signaled a lane change, checked the rearview, refrained from looking over at him. She didn't answer him.

"Jesus, Tinks."

This wasn't the first time in her career she'd thought about making a change. She had thought about it, but only vaguely. There had always been a good argument to stay put when she had first made her way into the division. She'd been on a good track, increasing her pay grade, building seniority. Homicide was the place to get noticed. Theoretically, it made a good launching pad to bigger things.

But she had never really wanted to launch. She liked what she did. She liked the people she worked with. They were a unit, a family. She couldn't imagine going to work and not having Kovac right there, her anchor, her foil. They had been partners for years. He had practically raised her as a detective. They had gone from student and teacher to colleagues and equals. Their relationship was a marriage without the sex. The thought of leaving that brought on a whole wave of unpleasant emotions.

Eyes on the neon Rock & Bowl sign, she exited the freeway.

"Well, you're not leaving me tonight," Kovac grumbled. "And you're not leaving me tomorrow or the next day."

"No."

"So get your head in the game. We've got a girl missing. We've got a girl dead. We've got a killer running around loose. If this is Doc Holiday, he could be out trolling while you're sitting there mulling over your career choices. He's already made his career. His career is torturing and killing young women. In the big scheme of badness, he's way ahead of you."

That was Kovac—crankiness as a defense mechanism. He was right, anyway.

"Thanks for the pep talk," she said as she pulled into a loading zone in front of the sprawling building.

"You know I'm always here to kick you in the ass when you need it."

She turned the car off and looked across at him. "Sometimes I would prefer a hug, you know."

The corner of his mouth lifted in his trademark sardonic smile.

"I don't trust you not to pop me in the kisser afterward," he admitted. "Sucker punch me for all the shit I give you."

"That could happen. I'd like to hit somebody for something."

He sighed and unbuckled his seat belt. "Oh, for the days when you could club the shit out of a suspect for looking at you the wrong way."

She rolled her eyes. "You're so full of it. You never did any such thing."

"No," he confessed. "But I saw it in a movie once. It looked like fun."

They got out of the car, and Liska looked around, seeing the place as if she'd never been there before. She looked at the proximity to the freeway and the big gas plaza just down the frontage road.

The consensus was that Doc Holiday traveled the highways of the Midwest, possibly as a trucker. His victims had all disappeared from locations along major roadways. Rose Reiser, New Year's Doe, had disappeared literally from the doorstep of a convenience store along a major highway in Columbia, Missouri. Her car had been found parked nearby—moved and hidden by her killer.

Kovac read her mind. "I've already got every unit in the vicinity looking for her car. We'll hit the gas station after we leave here, and get the security tapes."

They walked the length of the Rock & Bowl's poorly lit parking area, their eyes scanning the cars, looking for Penny Gray's Toyota, hoping against hope to catch an easy break. The parking lot ran down the side of the building going away from the frontage road and possible witnesses there. It was bordered by a chain-link fence with a parking lot of huge, heavy road equipment on the other side. Giant, hulking machines that stood like abandoned dinosaur carcasses with snow blown up around them.

A small knot of the Rock & Bowl patrons stood near a side exit toward the back of the building, braving the cold to have a smoke.

Their voices rose and fell. The sound of music went from muffled to clear and back as the door opened and closed.

The place was busy despite its being a weeknight. The colleges were still on break even if most of the high schools had gone back to business already. No one paid any real attention to Kovac and Liska as they walked past and kept going, all the way to the dark, narrow street that ran behind the Rock & Bowl property. The businesses on that street were places that closed early—a body shop, a glass shop, a tire store. There would be no one lingering on the sidewalk back there, no one glancing out a window this time of night.

"No witnesses handy back here," Kovac said. "A good escape route."

"So where's her car?" Liska asked. "If someone grabbed her out here and took her, where's her car?"

"He could have followed her away from here. Or she might have stopped for gas or had car trouble or went to a Starbucks and he nabbed her there."

Liska looked down the dark, deserted street, unease drawing a bony finger along the back of her neck at the thought of being a woman alone, unsuspecting, unaware that a predator was following her away from the safety of a busy place.

That was something her male counterparts would never truly get—that sense of absolute vulnerability when a woman realizes the potential for danger from a man with bad intentions. She always harbored the secret hope that victims like their ninth girl never saw it coming, that it was over before they could know what terrible thing fate held for them. Of course she knew that was almost never the case.

For an animal like Doc Holiday, the kill itself was almost secondary to what preceded it. For a sexual sadist, inflicting pain and instilling terror were like foreplay. He relished the chase, the cat-and-mouse game, the rush of holding the switch on life or death. His highest high was seeing that look of abject horror in the eyes of his victim as she fully grasped the sure knowledge that he had all the power to do with her whatever his sick heart desired—and the sure knowledge that what he desired was her pain . . . and her life.

The idea of a sixteen-year-old girl being put in that position made Liska feel physically ill.

The idea that she could be instrumental in bringing down the animal that perpetrated that kind of crime was what kept her on the job. What they did mattered. They'd come to the party too late for the victim at hand, but if they did their job well, they took a killer off the street before he could claim another life, and another, and another.

"Let's go see if there's a camera on this parking lot," Kovac said, starting back toward the building. "Maybe we'll get lucky."

Liska forced a laugh. "Well, that would be something. The last time I got lucky, gas was a buck fifty."

THE MANAGER OF the Rock & Bowl was a small, nervous guy in his early thirties with thinning hair and round brown eyes. He took the news of having detectives in his business like a mouse facing a pair of hungry cats.

"We haven't had any trouble here," he said, leading the way down a hall away from the noise of the bowling alley. "We run a clean family business. I don't want people thinking this isn't a safe place. We've never had an incident. I mean, the odd scuffle. Nothing crazy."

"Anything happen the night of the thirtieth?" Kovac asked.

"I was off that night. Nobody called me. You don't think this girl was snatched from here, do you?" he asked, throwing a worried look back over his shoulder. "I mean, somebody would have seen something, right? We can't have people thinking something like that would happen here. That's terrible."

"We're trying to piece together what might have happened," Liska said. "We need to establish a timeline. This was the last place she was seen by the friend she was staying with, so this is where we start. We don't know what happened after she left here."

"Last seen at the Rock & Bowl," the manager said. "That's great. That'll look good on the news."

"Do you have any cameras on the parking lot?" Kovac asked.

They went into the cramped and cluttered office. The manager turned and faced them like he was facing a firing squad. "Ordinarily we do. I'm really sorry to say this, but that camera went down right after Christmas. It developed moisture behind the lens, which then, of course, froze. The thing is shot. The security company is supposed to come change it out, but with the holidays and all . . . it hasn't happened yet."

"Well, why should this be easy?" Kovac muttered. "Have you had any cars towed out of here in the last few days? We're looking for a black Toyota Camry."

The manager shook his head. "We've had a few dead batteries with the cold and all, but they all left under their own steam. Nothing a good jump start didn't fix."

"How many cameras do you have inside?" Liska asked.

"One in the entrance, one in the bowling alley, one in the arcade, one on the dance floor."

"Are they digital or do they record to tape?"

"Tape. It's an old system. Like I said, we run a nice business. We don't have a lot of trouble here. There hasn't been any need to worry about upgrading the security system."

"We'll need to see everything from the night of the thirtieth," Kovac said. "And if you don't mind, I'd like to look at them right here, right now."

"Don't you need a warrant or something?" the manager asked.

Kovac gave him a hard look. "Are you fucking kidding me? We have a missing sixteen-year-old girl, last seen at the Rock & Bowl, and you're gonna tell me I need to go downtown, write an affidavit, find a judge, and waste hours while this girl is being tortured or Christ knows what?"

"No! No, no, no," the manager said hastily, holding his hands up in front of him as if he might need to fend off an attack. "I just, um, watch too much television."

"It's okay," Liska intervened. "People coming here have no legal expectation of privacy. The tapes belong to the Rock & Bowl. You can do whatever you want with them."

"Good. That's great. Have at it," he said, going to a cupboard and pulling out VHS tape cassettes. "Make yourselves at home. Whatever you need."

"We need a minor miracle," Kovac said. "But I'll settle for a cup of coffee if you have any."

The manager scurried away and they settled in front of an ancient thirteen-inch television with a built-in VCR. The quality of the tapes was grainy and bad. They had probably been taped over many times. The cameras were wall mounted and stationary, giving only one view of the area they covered. The people who moved through the outer reaches of the frame were blurry and ghostlike. Those closer to the camera were washed-out and distorted.

"This is shit," Liska complained. Her eyes had begun to burn from staring at the small screen. When she looked away from it, she continued to see black and white pixels like a swarm of gnats on the surface of her eyes. "I wouldn't recognize my own kid looking at this."

As she said it, Kovac went on point, his eyes narrowing as he looked at the screen. "Really?" he said. "Because there he is."

"What?"

Liska grabbed the remote, froze the picture, backed it up, ran it forward again. She repeated the process twice, hoping against hope that the picture would change, that the angle was bad, that she wasn't seeing what she thought she was seeing.

The figures on the screen scurried backward, walked forward, scurried back, walked ahead. The view was a wedge of space in the entrance of the building, people coming in, going out, stopping at the front counter to purchase tokens. And there was Kyle, walking toward the door, his head slightly bent, his hands jammed in the pockets of his father's old letterman's jacket.

"That's your boy, Tinks," Kovac said.

She stopped the tape and ran it backward again and punched the Play button. A moment before Kyle came into the picture, another figure moved through the area, heading for the door. A white female with half a head of dark hair.

Liska felt the bottom drop out of her stomach.

"And that's our girl."

22

Fitz sat in his car watching the parking lot of the apartment building across the street, eating a ham sandwich and listening to a call-in radio show about alien abductions. Living in the moment, he came to two conclusions simultaneously: There is nothing quite as tasty as Miracle Whip on a ham sandwich, and the world is just chock-full of lunatics.

The caller was going on at length about the aliens sticking a probe up his ass like they were digging for buried treasure. What the hell? If there were beings out there in the universe with the brainpower to build these elaborate spaceships, what could they possibly want from the intestinal tract of a moron?

Well, it passed the time to listen to this craziness. He had to stay awake because there was always a very good chance that the next caller would be even crazier than the last. He didn't want to miss anything, and he didn't want to fall asleep. Dana Nolan would be coming out of her apartment soon.

The female callers always talked about the aliens strapping them down on examination tables and experimenting on them sexually.

That he could get into. He cast himself in the role of the Alien in those fantasies. He knew what it felt like to stand over a helpless woman. The sense of omnipotence that filled him was intoxicating. To look into the terrified eyes of a victim, knowing that everything about her life—and death—was his choice to make was like no other power in the world.

A woman in that position—naked, immobilized, helpless, exposed—was completely at his mercy. A woman in that position realized his power. A woman in that position never mocked him, never scorned him. In that scenario he was God and the devil all in one—which made him more powerful than either entity individually.

A woman in that position didn't care that he was short or that he had a potbelly. She didn't care that he was losing his hair or that he looked more like a cartoon hobo than a matinee idol.

A woman in that position cared only that he had the power to give pain or take it away, to give life or take it away.

A woman in that position had to accept him. In every sense of the word.

Fitz knew exactly what he was, and he knew exactly why, and he was good with it. He had arranged his life to suit his hobbies. He traveled the highways and back roads of America, buying and reselling antiques and junk. His trails were his hunting grounds. He was a lucky man. He would never be the kind of loser who called a radio show in the middle of the night to make up shit about aliens sticking a probe up his ass.

Dana Nolan came out of her apartment building at 3:07 A.M. The people who worked the early news programs on local television had terrible hours—and terrible pay, he imagined. The apartment building she lived in was as basic and unimaginative as possible—a square, blond brick box in a row of square, blond brick boxes built in the seventies. There was no kind of doorman or security.

Fitz had followed her home from the TV station earlier in the day and scoped it all out. He then had gone home, done some work on a couple of antique motorcycles he had found on a pick in Illinois, then took a nap. Around two A.M. he stuck hand warmers in his boots and coat pockets and drove here in his nondescript panel van to watch and wait.

This wasn't his usual MO. He preferred to hunt on the road, snatch a victim of opportunity, and keep moving. He had his routine down to a smooth science. But he had a point to prove now. He had decided to up his game, to show people exactly who they were dealing with.

The parking lot for the apartment buildings was not well lit. There was no one around at this time of night. This was a quiet middle-income neighborhood. People here worked hard and went to bed early. They got up early and watched their cute neighbor girl on the news.

Dana Nolan was twenty-four (according to the station's website and her own Facebook page), still with a breath of that fresh-from-college scent on her. Pretty and petite, no doubt preoccupied with her first big job at a television station, she walked out of her building in the middle of every night and crossed this lonely parking lot by herself.

Tonight she had her arms full—a purse that kept slipping off her shoulder, a suit bag, a tote bag. She juggled the stuff as she fumbled with her car keys. She was paying no attention to her surroundings.

Fitz watched her get into her cute little green Mini Cooper. He waited for her to get the car started and negotiate her way out of her parking spot and into the street. When she was about a block away, he started the van and drove out after her.

The Alien was on the prowl tonight.

He hung back, running with no lights. The streetlights were bright enough. He didn't want her to notice headlights coming behind her, didn't want her looking over her shoulder.

He followed her out of her neighborhood and onto 494, where

Leabharlanna Poibli Chathair Baile Átha Cliath

Dublin City Public Libraries

he popped his lights on and felt free to run a little closer up behind her. He dropped back a few lengths again when she signaled for her exit and left the freeway. The television station was only a couple of blocks away now. But at the bottom of the off ramp, Dana Nolan signaled to go left instead of right.

Fitz couldn't help but smile to himself as he let her drive on ahead of him. She turned into the parking lot of a Holiday gas station / convenience store. The name made him laugh out loud. Holiday—just like the news people liked to call him. Doc Holiday. Perfect.

He drove past, then doubled back around.

The place was well lit and busier than anyone might have expected at that hour. A big bearded guy in a snowmobile suit was pumping gas into a four-by-four truck with a snowplow on the front. Two cars other than Dana Nolan's Mini were parked near the building.

Fitz pulled in two spaces down from the girl and went inside. The clerk, a tall, gaunt African guy, gave him a cautious look. Somali, Fitz figured. His skin was absolutely black, making the whites of his eyes stand out shockingly bright in his long, narrow face.

Fitz smiled broadly and banged his gloved hands together a couple of times.

"Holy smokes, it's cold out there!" he said. "Why do we live here, right?"

The Somali guy didn't feel compelled to answer, though he had probably asked himself the same question a thousand times every winter since his arrival in Minnesota. A lot of the local Lutheran churches were keen to rescue people from whatever shithole God had originally thrown them into—the Hmongs from Cambodia in the eighties; the Somalis in the nineties. The irony was laughable—plucking people out of some of the hottest fucking hellholes on earth and plunking them down in Minnesota, where they had to be freezing their asses off six months out of the year.

Dana Nolan was busy getting her coffee and doctoring it with artificial creamer and chemical sweeteners.

"That stuff'll kill you!" Fitz said cheerfully, grabbing a cup and pouring himself some French roast from one of the pots on the counter.

The girl glanced at him with a sweet smile and a laugh. She squinted like that actress, Renée Zellweger, her eyes all but disappearing into slits above her cold-rouged cheeks.

"Oh, I know," she said. "It's so bad for us, but I can't start my day without it."

"I hear you," he said, tearing open a pink packet and dumping the contents into the nasty, oily blackness of the convenience store coffee. "Some mornings I think I should just get coffee injected straight into my veins."

"Me too! I say that all the time!"

"Hey . . . ," he said, giving her the perfect friendly, quizzical look—a little surprise, a little uncertainty, a little smile. He raised a finger. "You look like— You're not—"

She was pleased with the prospect that he might recognize her. This was part of why she had gone into broadcast news—to get that rush of self-importance at being recognized in public places.

"You're that girl from the news!" he exclaimed with delight. "I'm right! Am I right?"

She beamed, eyes disappearing again. "That's me!"

"Dana. Right? Wait 'til I tell the missus!" he said. "We watch you every morning! You know, I work nights for the DOT. I'm just getting home and my wife is just getting up. She teaches third grade at St. Ann's. We have some breakfast together and watch the news."

"That's so nice to hear!" she said. "We start so early, sometimes I wonder if there's anyone out there awake to see us."

"Oh, believe me, we're watching."

"I'd better get going, then," she said, moving a step toward the counter. "I don't want to be late."

"It was great meeting you, Dana," Fitz said, grinning. "Just wait 'til I tell the missus!"

She laughed and beamed, the picture of sweet, innocent youth. "Nice meeting you too!"

He stuck out a gloved hand. "Frank Fitzpatrick," he said. "Call me Fitz."

She shook his hand, her grip a little hesitant, meek. She would be easy to dominate.

"Nice meeting you, Fitz," she said. She gave a little wave as she moved toward the counter. He waved back, smiling widely.

And that is how it's done, he thought, watching her pay the Somali guy for her coffee, then hurry back out into the cold. *Identify the potential victim. Engage the potential victim in a nonthreatening manner on neutral ground. Establish a cordial connection, thereby causing the potential victim to lower her defenses.*

The next time he encountered Dana Nolan, she would recognize him as that nice man from the Holiday station, the friendly guy who watched her on the news while having breakfast with his wife. He wasn't anyone she needed to be afraid of.

And that assumption would be the worst mistake she would ever make in her young life.

He picked a couple of doughnuts out of the bakery case and took them and his coffee up to the counter to pay. The Somali guy rang him up and took his money without joy.

"You have a nice day, sir," Fitz said enthusiastically. "Stay warm!"

And he went back out into the frigid early morning, got in his van, and drove home to eat his doughnuts and watch Dana Nolan on the news . . . and fantasize about how he was going to kill her.

23

He was sound asleep and dreaming. In the dream he was fighting. Left, right, front kick, spinning back fist. He was breathing hard, sweating, his muscles straining. He couldn't see his opponent, just a black shape that was bigger than he was, stronger than he was, and seemed to be all around him at once. He spun and kicked and threw his fists.

Then something had hold of his wrists and he couldn't pull away. He came awake with a start and a gasp.

"Kyle!" His mom's voice. "Kyle, wake up! You're having a dream."

Kyle sat up, pulling back from her, pulling his hands free. The anxiety of the dream was still on him. He felt like he was drowning in it.

"What are you doing?" he demanded, focusing on her face. She sat on the edge of the bed. The light on the nightstand was on. Her expression frightened him. Too serious. Worried. It was the middle of the night.

"What's wrong?" he asked, a chill running over him. "Did something happen to Dad?"

His father worked undercover narcotics. It was a dangerous job. He'd been hurt before. Kyle had always secretly feared that his dad could be killed and he would die thinking Kyle hated him. Panic and guilt rose inside him.

"No, no," his mother said. "Your dad is fine."

"What are you doing? You scared the shit out of me!" he said, his voice cracking.

"Kyle, I need to ask you some questions," she said.

For the first time, he became aware of another person in his room, by the door. His mother's partner, Sam Kovac, looking grave. Kyle looked from one of them to the other and back.

"What's going on?"

"Kyle, do you know a girl named Penelope Gray?" his mother asked.

"Penelope?" He said the name like he had never heard it before. Who the hell named their kid Penelope? He didn't know anyone named Penelope.

"Gray," Sam Kovac said, coming farther into the room. "Her friends call her Gray."

"Gray?" None of this was making any sense. Maybe he was still asleep and dreaming a dream within a dream.

"She goes to your school," his mother said. "Dark hair—half-shaved, lots of piercings."

"Gray," he said. "Yeah. I know her. Why? Why would you wake me up to ask me that? What's going on?"

Sam pulled the chair away from the desk and sat down.

"Kyle," Kovac said. "Gray is missing."

"Missing?" He felt stupid parroting everything back at them like he was some kind of retard. But none of this made any sense to him. They were questioning him like he was a suspect or something.

"No one has seen her since the night before New Year's Eve," his mom said.

"I haven't seen her."

"Have you heard from her?" Kovac asked. "A phone call? A text? Anything?"

"No."

"What were you doing at the Rock and Bowl?" his mother asked in her cop voice. Kyle drew a breath to answer and she held up a finger in warning. "Don't even think about lying to me. I saw you on the security video. This is a serious situation, Kyle. I don't recall you asking my permission to go there. I would remember that. You know why? Because there is no way in hell I would have said yes."

"I didn't ask," Kyle said defensively. "Because you weren't here. You're *never* here."

His mother jumped to her feet looking like he had slapped her and knocked her off the bed.

"You have a cell phone," she said, her voice trembling a little. "You know to call me before you go somewhere. I expect you to be responsible, Kyle. How did you get there?"

"What difference does it make?" he asked belligerently. He was busted and now he had to listen to his mother berate him like he was a little kid. He was almost sixteen. He wanted to be treated with some adult respect, but at the same time he knew breaking the rules didn't earn him that respect.

"I asked you a question."

"I got a ride with a friend."

"What friend?"

"What does it matter?!" he shouted.

"You told me you were going to a movie that night."

"So we changed plans. So what?"

"What's going on?" R.J. asked, wandering into the room in his pajamas. His hair stuck up all around his head like he'd stuck his finger in a light socket.

"Nothing," Mom said, steering him by the shoulders back into the hall.

"Then why is everybody yelling?"

Kovac leaned forward in the desk chair, resting his forearms on his thighs. "Kyle," he said quietly. "Your mom's upset because she worries about you. She's seen a lot of shit go down. She knows the kind of bad things that happen off of one bad decision.

"We're investigating a homicide right now, and I can guarantee you that victim didn't start her evening out thinking that she would end up murdered. You know what I'm saying? Nobody thinks that's gonna happen to them, but it does. We see it all the time. So don't be too hard on your mom, okay?"

Kyle looked down and scratched at the leg of his sweatpants just to avoid Kovac's eyes. Now he felt guilty. He loved his mom. He knew she had it tough, working and trying to raise him and R.J. more or less on her own. Most of the time he tried not to make her life harder.

"So," Kovac said, moving on. "I don't give a shit how you came to be at the Rock and Bowl. I need to know, did you see Gray there? Did you speak to her?"

"Yeah, I saw her."

"Did you notice if anyone was bothering her, following her?"

"No."

"The friend she was staying with said Gray got pissed off and left. Do you know anything about that?"

Kyle shrugged. "She doesn't get along with a lot of people."

"Why is that?"

" 'Cause she's not into phony bullshit jerks."

His mother came back into the room, closing the door behind her. "What kind of girl is she?"

"I don't know. She's . . . different."

What was he supposed to say? That she was wild? That she was a slut? He didn't think either one of those things was true. He didn't believe in putting labels on people, except dickheads like Aaron Fogelman.

"Is she into drugs?" Kovac asked.

"No," Kyle said, frustration rising inside him. "I don't know! Maybe she smokes a little. Why do you guys always think kids are into drugs? Not everybody is into drugs!"

"Did she have an argument with somebody that night?" Kovac asked calmly.

"I guess."

"With who? What about?"

"Christina Warner," he said. "They got into it."

"Over what?" Kovac asked.

"Gray writes poetry. Christina was making fun of one of her poems, making fun of Gray. People were laughing. Gray got pissed off and she left."

"Did you follow her outside?" Kovac asked.

"Yeah, but she was already driving out."

"You didn't speak to her."

"No."

"Did you see which way she went?"

"Toward the gas station."

"Did anybody follow her?"

"Not that I saw," Kyle said.

He watched them exchange a look, speaking without speaking. Kovac had said they were investigating a homicide. The victim was a female. Gray was missing.

"You don't think she's dead, do you?" he asked. "Gray gets pissed off, she goes and stays with one of her weird friends. She does that all the time."

"Do you know any of those friends?" his mom asked.

Kyle shook his head. "They're like musicians and poets and coffeehouse people. I don't know them. They're older. Gray's not dead, is she?"

"We don't know," his mom said. "Right now, we don't know."

"You think she is," Kyle said. He felt the bottom drop out of his stomach like he'd just gone over a big hill on his bike. He'd never known anyone who was killed. That just seemed crazy, impossible. Kids his age didn't get killed except in car crashes and stuff like that, or kids who were in gangs. He didn't know anybody like that.

"Kyle, are you friends with Gray on Facebook?" Kovac asked.

"Yeah."

"Can we go on the computer and have a look?"

They went downstairs to the family room and Kyle sat down at the desk and brought the computer to life. He logged on to his Facebook page. He felt self-conscious having his mom and Kovac looking at it. His profile picture was a photograph of the door to his bedroom, the Samurai warrior he had painted. What came up in his news feed were posts from pages he followed, pages about mixed martial arts and Brazilian jiu-jitsu, tattoos and comic books. He clicked on the search line and typed in *GrayMatter*.

Gray's page came up. Her profile picture was a drawing Kyle had done for her: herself as a comic book character. He had drawn her as angry and sharp featured with bold, dark lines and large, snapping black eyes. She had only seventeen friends. She liked twenty-two pages. Her last post was four days past—the last day Kyle had seen her. It was a poem.

"Liar"

Two-faced liar
Pants on fire
You fool everyone
But not me.

I know what you are
You're nobody's star
I'm gonna rat you out
Wait and see.
Fine and upstanding
You're very demanding
Your standard is high
I know.
But wait 'til they see you
The liar, the real you
You're gonna fall down
So low.
I'm gonna take you down
You know.

24

Three hours of sleep. A shower. A shave. A cup of bad coffee from 7-Eleven. Days like this, cases like this, a voice in the back of his head grumbled, *You're getting too goddamn old for this.*

Kovac ignored it because at the same time that voice was grumbling, his adrenal glands were pumping out a rush of intoxicating fuel to keep him focused and moving forward. This was his purpose in life. This was his calling: a case with a sense of urgency attached. In that he was like a hound on a scent. Tunnel vision shut out the extraneous world. The wheels in his head spun like the workings of a Swiss watch.

He loved what he did. He didn't love why he had to do it, but he couldn't imagine doing anything else.

He thought about Tinks and what she had said about changing jobs. He couldn't imagine doing that. Over his career he had put in time in different departments, but nothing suited him like Homicide.

Eventually he would have to retire, but the idea of that secretly struck fear in him. Like every cop he knew, he bitched about the job and joked around about retiring. He knew to the day how long before he got his thirty years in. But the reality of it was something he didn't want to face. Most cops he knew took their twenty years and got out. He had already passed that milestone. What would he do with himself when his career was over? He couldn't see it. He didn't want to.

He went through his checklist in his head as he parked his car in the structure that had been named for a murdered cop a couple of decades past. He had already sent a young detective to Liska's house to gather as much information as possible from Penelope Gray's Facebook page. It made more sense to him to do it there, where they already had access to the page, than to waste time going through the process of setting everything up from scratch in the office.

He wanted as much information as possible about the girl's Facebook friends—names, contact info, what connected them to Gray. He wanted their posts looked at with an eye for anything angry, violent, disturbing. Had any of them threatened Gray? Were they into anything that might have led to the girl's death?

He wanted to know who was the liar she had written about in her last Facebook post. The obvious assumption was another kid her own age, a schoolmate, someone in her social circle. But he knew better than to assume. She could have been talking about an adult, a teacher, someone in a position of authority, someone who would have been ruined by a revelation. Had her threat to expose that person been enough to motivate a killer? Possibly.

They needed to talk to the other kids who had been in that group at the Rock & Bowl, find out what exactly had set the girl off that night. They had to get Penelope Gray's cell phone records ASAP. They had to get her medical records, get the films of her once-broken wrist to Möller at the morgue to see if they would match up with their victim. They would do a DNA test for absolute proof, but DNA tests took time, and time was a luxury they didn't have.

The CID office was already bustling with the extra detectives

Kasselmann had assigned to the case, answering phones, taking down tips, tracking down leads.

Kasselmann appeared in the door of his office, looking like a Wall Street executive in a crisp navy-blue suit, every silver hair on his head perfectly in place. He hailed Kovac like he was taxicab.

"You think this Gray girl is your victim?" he asked, taking his seat behind the desk.

Kovac slouched into a chair. "I think so. There's too much that matches up. We have to get her old X-rays from her doctor this morning and get them to Möller to compare a healed fracture, but I'd put money on it."

"Why wasn't she reported missing?"

"The mother thought she was staying with a friend, and the friend assumed she had gone home. And apparently the girl will up and take off for days at a time, so no one was really alarmed not to hear from her. Then the mother got a couple of text messages supposedly from the girl. She didn't think she had a reason to be concerned. We're tracking down the girl's friends off her Facebook page. And we'll get her cell phone records this morning."

"What's the family situation?"

"Strained. It's pretty clear the mother finds the daughter a major problem and a disappointment. The girl resents the mom. There was some serious rebellion going on. The father is out of the picture for the most part. Mom is dating a shrink, and the shrink's daughter and this girl don't get along. They had an argument at the Rock & Bowl on the night in question. Our girl left the club in a huff and was never seen again."

"You're getting a lot of media attention with the AMBER Alert for a girl you think is in cold storage at the morgue."

Kovac shrugged. "I don't know for a fact. In the meantime, maybe we stir up someone who saw something. Maybe we locate the girl's car."

"I'll make a statement for the press later this morning," Kassel-mann said. "I'd like the mother to be there. She can make an appeal."

"I'll put Elwood on that," Kovac said. "I want her to come in anyway. We need a more detailed timeline about who was where, when."

"An added bonus to the AMBER Alert: I think I'll get the green light from upstairs to add a couple more warm bodies to your team," Kasselmann said.

"Great. I'll take them."

"The state patrol has a chopper in the air. BCA has offered assistance."

"And I'd like to bring in John Quinn to have a look at the case. See if he thinks this is Doc Holiday's handiwork."

Quinn had been one of the FBI's top profilers, brought in by money and political influence to assess the Cremator murders several years past. He had since retired from the bureau and settled in the Minneapolis suburbs to work in the private sector and raise a family.

"I'll see what I can do about that," Kasselmann said.

Kovac pushed to his feet. "You'd better. He'll be here at nine."

Ignoring his captain's mutterings, Kovac left the office and went to the room they had set up as command central for the case. The new photograph of Penelope Gray had been added to the montage on the wall, along with the sketch artist's rendering. It wasn't an exact match, but it wasn't bad considering what he'd had to work from.

Kovac stared at the picture he'd gotten from Brittany Lawler. He had enlarged the photo and cropped the Lawler girl out. The girl her friends called Gray looked at him coyly from over her shoulder. She had been portrayed by people who knew her as an angry girl, but she wasn't angry in the photo. She looked bright and mischievous. Her dark eyes had a spark in them.

Kovac wondered if she meant to make a statement with the half-shaved head and the piercings. Or was all that a disguise, intended to distract the eye from the essence of her—the sensitive, misunderstood poet? Probably a bit of both.

In the best scenarios, kids that age were a bundle of insecurities. They were children who thought they wanted to be adults but at the same time were afraid to let go of teddy bears and dolls. They thought they wanted to be individuals, yet they clung to their peer group, desperate for acceptance. Penelope Gray looked like the poster girl for contradictions.

Liska and Tippen came into the room, Tippen with a venti iced coffee, wearing a silk necktie with a palm tree painted on it. Liska clutched a cup of coffee to her chest as if hoping to will the caffeine directly into her veins.

"Jesus Christ," she grumbled, "when are they going to get this fucking furnace situation under control? It's like the ninth circle of hell in here."

"I'm starting to like it," Tippen said. "It's kind of like visiting my parents in Boca Raton. They set their thermostat at ninth circle of hell."

Kovac studied his partner as he rolled up his shirtsleeves. "Jeeze, Tinks, you look like a heroine addict."

She narrowed her bloodshot eyes. "Thanks. That makes me feel so much better about myself. You need to make a motivational video and sell it on the Internet."

"Did you get any sleep?"

"I'll sleep when I'm dead."

"Yeah, well, you're looking like that could be sooner rather than later."

"Shut up," she snapped. "What's next?"

"We need to talk to the kids who were at the Rock and Bowl. Maybe that can happen right at the school," he suggested. "Faster and easier than trying to drag them down here."

Tippen raised his eyebrows. "Privileged darlings at a fancy private school? Parents with lawyers on retainer? I don't think any part of that is going to be easy."

"Let's get on it right away, then," Kovac said. "Tinks, you must have an in with the principal at PSI."

She rolled her eyes. "Yeah, right. He's a pompous ass who can never get my name straight and believes my son is a violent thug who draws gay pornography. I'll have him wrapped around my little finger."

"Just be your usual charming self, then," Tippen suggested. "Put his balls on the table and smash them with your tactical baton."

"If only . . ."

"I'll go with you," Kovac said. "Make sure you don't get called up on brutality charges."

"You spoil all my fun," she said, pouting.

"Later I'll let you roll a junkie, just for kicks."

"There's no sport in that."

"If you want a sport, take up cage fighting," he said. "You can beat the shit out of people and get paid for it."

"Sounds good to me."

"In the meantime, I'll get Quinn set up to look over what we have with an eye toward Doc Holiday; then you and I can hit the bricks. Tip, I want you to go have a chat with Penelope Gray's father. See what he's all about."

He turned and looked at the horrific autopsy photos.

"Somebody in this girl's life hated her enough to do this. Let's find out if it was personal."

"It's absolutely out of the question," Principal Rodgers stated. His tone had the ring of finality, like a steel door slamming shut. "I won't have my students interrogated."

They stood in his office, where everything was perfectly in place, perfectly polished—including Rodgers himself. The blotter on the desk was pristine white. Papers were stacked in perfect alignment, books on the bookshelves arranged by size. All this tidiness made Liska wonder if the man actually did any real work.

She glanced at her partner. Kovac had on his poker face, but she could feel his irritation. She raised her eyebrows at him as if to say, *See what a dick this guy is?*

"We're not looking to interrogate anyone," Kovac said. He picked up a paperweight off the desk, a solid glass ball with some trite motivational phrase etched on it, and tossed it back and forth from one hand to the other. Rodgers snatched it away from him and put it back exactly where it had been. "We just need to talk to them about what they might have seen, noticed, heard that night and the days leading up to that night. We're trying to put together a picture of the events that led up to Penelope Gray's disappearance."

"We need to establish a timeline, Mr. Rodgers," Liska said. "We know these kids were all at the Rock and Bowl the night Penny Gray went missing. It's essential that we speak to them."

"I can't have you question my students without parental consent."

Kovac stepped over to the credenza and gave the globe there a lazy spin. Rodgers put a hand on it to stop it.

"Please don't touch my things, Detective."

"Sorry."

Kovac went around the front of the desk and plucked up a family photograph in a silver frame. "Do you have kids, Mr. Rodgers?"

Rodgers leaned across the desk and pulled the picture away from him. "I have a niece and a nephew," he said, rubbing at Kovac's fingerprints with a small cloth meant for cleaning eyeglasses.

"I think you would feel differently if one of them were missing," Kovac said.

"That would be different," Rodgers said. "That would be strictly a personal reaction. I can't do that here. I have a job to do. I have an obligation to my students and to their parents."

"Penny Gray is your student too," Liska said. "Do you have any concern for her, for her family?"

Rodgers gave her a look like she was a turd on his rug. "Of course I do. I won't have you question my dedication to these young people, Mrs. Liska."

"Really? Tell me about Penelope Gray, then," she challenged. "Who are her friends? Who are her enemies? Does she have a boyfriend? What are her interests? Does she have a teacher or an upperclassman mentoring her? Was she having difficulties with anyone in the days before the holiday vacation started?"

"I have over five hundred students here," he said defensively. "You can't expect me to know all the small details of their personal lives."

"No, but so far you don't seem to know *any* details of her life," Kovac said. "Do you even know what this girl looks like, Mr. Rodgers?"

"She has dark hair and recently shaved part of it off," he said. "She has multiple piercings—which are against our appearance code here at PSI."

"You know how she annoys you," Liska said. "You know how she doesn't fit your profile of the perfect PSI student."

"That's unfair."

"I would say so."

"It's unfair to me," Rodgers specified. "Miss Gray works at standing out in a negative way. If she was an outstanding student or an outstanding leader, those would be the things I would remember her for."

"If she was like Christina Warner, for instance," Kovac suggested.

"Christina is an exemplary student."

"We understand the two girls didn't get along."

"Christina's father brought that to my attention," Rodgers said.

"Penelope is jealous of Christina and resentful of Dr. Warner's relationship with her mother. He wanted me to be aware of the situation and take it into account if Miss Gray began exhibiting disruptive behavior."

"Did she?" Kovac asked.

"Nothing over and above the average for Miss Gray."

"I've been told that a particular clique of kids bullied Penny Gray," Liska said. "That they made fun of her poetry and taunted her about the way she looked and about her sexuality."

"That seems like an exaggeration," Rodgers said.

"But you're not out in the middle of it, are you?" Kovac said, picking up a fat black Mont Blanc pen from beside the spotless blotter. "Something you see from a distance as 'kids will be kids,' the kids might see something else entirely. We need to talk to them."

Rodgers stared at the pen as Kovac twirled it around his fingers, visibly fighting the urge to grab it away from him.

"I can't make promises, but I'll try to arrange something for this afternoon. There's a protocol to be observed here, Detective," Rodgers said. "I have to contact the parents and consult them. I would recommend they be present at any kind of questioning. They may want to consult their attorneys—"

"And while all this protocol is going on, Penny Gray is missing and possibly in the hands of a madman," Liska said.

She didn't believe that. She believed the girl was dead in the morgue, but she wanted Rodgers to think otherwise. She wanted to make him feel guilty and responsible.

"I think Julia Gray will take a very different view of your stalling tactics, Mr. Rodgers," she said. "Her daughter is missing. You should probably think about her consulting *her* attorney. If this was *my* son missing, I would be on the air with every TV station in the metro area, calling you out. How would *that* look for PSI?"

"My hands are tied, Mrs. Liska," Rodgers said primly. "I'll get back to you as soon as I've contacted the parents."

Kovac set the pen back down on the desk, just far enough out of the principal's reach that he had to lean across the desk to retrieve it and put it back just so beside the blotter.

"Frankly," Rodgers said, looking at Liska, "I don't think it's appropriate for you to be one of the people questioning these children, considering the situation with your son."

"What situation is that?" Liska asked.

"Your son is involved with Miss Gray."

"They know each other. I don't consider that a situation."

"And there's this latest outrage concerning the other students on your list." He glanced at Kovac, pausing for drama.

"What outrage?" Liska asked.

Rodgers heaved a put-upon sigh. "I was going to call you this morning."

"Well, I'm here. So let's do this now."

Rodgers glanced at Kovac again.

"It's okay," Kovac said. "I'm her father. It's all in the family."

Rodgers pursed his lips in disapproval. He picked up his smart phone from its charging stand. "This was brought to my attention first thing this morning by Aaron Fogelman's father."

He punched some buttons and brought up a picture, then thrust the phone at Liska. "This was posted on Twitter last night. I don't know who posted it, but there's no doubt in my mind who did the artwork."

She looked at the picture and felt a flush of heat rush through her. It was Kyle's drawing of the three Ultors, the one that had been ruined by the kids he didn't get along with. The heads of the Ultors had been changed out for caricatures. One she recognized instantly as Aaron Fogelman, grinning like a fool as he fondled himself.

"Are you going to deny your son did that?" Rodgers said.

"You're going to assume that he did," she countered.

There was no question that it was Kyle's work. Still, she was going to defend him against this jerk. The Fighting Liska/Hatcher Family motto: Go down swinging.

"That's not Kyle's Twitter account," she said.

"Mrs. Liska—"

"*Sergeant* Liska."

"I find this drawing very disturbing," Rodgers said. "I don't know anything about Twitter, but I believe your son made this drawing. I'm suspending him for the remainder of the week, at least. I've already spoken to him. He's in the conference room across the hall waiting for you."

Anger and frustration flooded through her. Anger and frustration with Rodgers. Anger and frustration with her son. The pressure of it roared in her ears until she couldn't hear.

Kovac stepped between her and the principal and gently moved her backward toward the door.

"Take the car," he murmured, pressing the keys at her. "Take Kyle and go home. Ground him or beat him or chain him in the basement. I don't care which. I need you downtown."

She took the keys and left the room, feeling embarrassed and helpless and exhausted. To her horror, tears burned her eyes. She felt like a failure on multiple levels.

As she walked into the conference room Kyle looked up at her from the far side of the table. She thought his expression was probably a mirror of her own. He was upset and angry and fighting tears.

"Get your things," she said. "We're going home, where you will be grounded for the rest of your life."

25

Kasselmann was the king of the press statement. He had the perfect look: as solid as a bull, as serious as a heart attack, handsomely groomed. He had the perfect authoritative voice. He was articulate and concise.

Kovac watched the live news feed on the television in the conference room. He had no desire to be questioned by the media. Reporters asked stupid questions, and they asked them over and over. He was more than happy to let Kasselmann take that spotlight.

Julia Gray stood beside the captain, looking stunned. She was as pale as a ghost, and the bruise on her cheek stood out despite her efforts to hide it with a clever hairstyle. When it was her turn to make her appeal for the return of her daughter, it seemed for an uncomfortable moment that she wasn't going to say anything. She looked down at the podium, locked inside her own mind.

Kovac wondered if the good Dr. Warner had prescribed something for her nerves. Probably—and rightly so. Having dealt with more child abductions and disappearances than he cared to count, Kovac knew the terrible strain it put on the parents. They labored under a heavy burden of anxiety, fear, anger, uncertainty, and guilt. What could they have done to prevent this? Why couldn't their child have been more careful, less headstrong? What was happening to their kid? Was she or he alive, dead, frightened, in pain?

Beside him in front of the television, John Quinn stood with his arms crossed and his brow set in concentration as he watched Julia Gray finally rouse herself to make the standard appeal for the return of her daughter or the revelation of any information that might shed light on her disappearance.

When they made the movie of Quinn's life, George Clooney would be first in line to play him. He had that look about him—dark hair peppered with distinguished gray, dark eyes, strong jaw. He was the guy other guys wanted to be and the man every woman drooled over. He used those attributes to his advantage when he could but didn't rely on them to carry him. He had a keen intellect, and he knew his subject as well as or better than anyone else in the business.

"What happened to her face?" he asked, not taking his eyes from the screen.

"She says she took a fall on the ice," Elwood said. "Sprained her wrist too."

"What does she do for living?"

"She's a rep for a pharmaceutical company."

"Where's the husband?"

"They've been divorced for four years. He's an odontologist. He remarried a younger woman who worked in his office."

"Mom's in a relationship with a shrink," Kovac said.

"What's he like?"

"Like a shrink. Dr. Know It All and Let Me Explain It to You Like You're a Moron. Wears his sweaters tied around his neck," Kovac added with disdain.

"I googled him," Elwood said. "Turns out he's fairly well-known in the metro area."

Kovac scowled. "I've never heard of him."

"Because you're out of touch with the world around you," Elwood pointed out. "He has a radio show on one of the local AM stations for parents dealing with teenagers. Two hours every Saturday morning. And he does a five-minute guest spot on the channel twelve morning show every Monday."

"Oh, great," Kovac grumbled. "A celebrity in his own mind. I'm liking him more and more."

"What's he like with the mother?" Quinn asked.

"He tried to be supportive last night," Elwood said. "He came with her this morning."

On-screen, Julia Gray had collapsed against Kasselmann, crying. Kasselmann held her upright and put an end to the press conference with another appeal for anyone with information to contact the department. The news feed cut back to the studio and perky Dana Nolan for a rehash of everything that had just gone on.

"So, John, you've already looked at everything we have on the Doc Holiday cases," Kovac said, going to the coffee machine and pouring himself a cup of something that looked like used motor oil. "Now you've had a chance to look at our Zombie case. What's your impression?"

Quinn jammed his hands on his hips and looked at the photos of the body that had been taped to the wall.

"It depends on where Doc is at in his career," he said. "Based on the known cases we attribute to him, he's dumped more bodies in the Twin Cities area than anywhere else—as far as we know. If we count this girl, he's dumped four bodies here in a year's time. To me, that says he's comfortable here, he knows the area. Could be he lives here and he's getting lazy. Dumping victims in his backyard, so to speak, allows him to easily revisit the spots and relive the fun. But it's also risky.

"The other victims dumped here came from outside the state. If

Zombie Doe and Penelope Gray are the same girl, then he both grabbed her here and dumped her here. That says he's getting careless and he's possibly escalating."

He turned and faced them, looking grim.

"Some of these guys implode at the end of their careers," he explained. "They start doing things they don't normally do, varying from the pattern they've perfected.

"The classic example of this was Bundy. After years of following the same pattern, being careful enough to elude capture, to hide his victims' remains, he went to Florida and went on a spree. In one night he attacked multiple victims in a sorority house, left them to be found instead of getting rid of their bodies, left potential witnesses behind, then went into another house and attacked another woman. A couple of days later he snatched a girl much younger than his usual victim. He was like a shark on a feeding frenzy."

"Why do you think that happened?" Elwood asked.

"We don't really know why some of these guys self-destruct like that," Quinn said. "One theory is they build up a sense of invincibility that grows and grows until it crosses a line into mania. Another theory is they start feeling less and less control over their aberrant desires, that this scares them and they want someone to stop them."

"Doc seems to enjoy the game too much for a conscience to stop him," Kovac said.

"I would agree," Quinn said. "But you never know. We can never truly get inside the heads of these guys. There were people in my field who believed Bundy took his act to Florida at the end because he knew he stood the greatest chance of being executed if he was caught there. Yet once he was convicted, he did everything in his power to stall and appeal and prevent the state from putting him in the electric chair. He played mind games with law enforcement right up to the end and enjoyed every minute of it."

"Doc Holiday could be one of those guys, spiraling out of control," Elwood said.

Quinn nodded. "He could be. There are definitely deviations from his usual pattern if this girl is one of his. The acid is something new. The nature of the stab wounds is different. The knife was different, less efficient."

"Tippen suggested he could have been playing with the victim, creating more terror over a prolonged time period by using a smaller knife," Kovac said.

Quinn considered the idea, raising his brows and tipping his head. "That's possible. Or it's not Doc at all, and we're looking at an inexperienced killer who grabbed a weapon of opportunity, not realizing it wasn't enough to get the job done easily.

"It's just as easy to look at this and say it's a mess created by an amateur. The knife didn't get the job done, so your unsub tried to bludgeon her; thought she was dead and poured the acid on her face to obscure her identity, but she was still alive."

"Great," Kovac said. "So it could be Doc, or it could be anybody. Thanks for narrowing that down for us, John."

Quinn shrugged. "It's an inexact science."

"Let's say it is Doc Holiday," Elwood said. "What would you suggest? Do we press that angle and try to draw him out?"

"The fact that he leaves his victims to be found says he clearly wants credit for his work," Quinn said. "I would expect him to keep a scrapbook with a collection of articles about his murders. But he hasn't tried to contact the authorities or the media up until now, right?"

"Nothing," Kovac said.

"You'd probably get a rise out of him if you *didn't* talk about him, if nobody mentioned him on the news or in the paper, but it's too late for that."

"I had to play that card to get manpower," Kovac said.

"Everything's a trade-off," Quinn conceded. "You could push the idea that he's getting sloppy, that you're closing in on him, that it's only a matter of time—"

"But I can't back it up."

"And you might push him into making a grand gesture," Quinn warned. "You piss this guy off and he could make you pay—by making an innocent victim pay."

Kovac picked up the remote and turned Dana Nolan the perky news girl off midsentence.

"That's not a risk I'm willing to take."

He grabbed a VHS tape cassette off the stand beside the TV and put it in the VCR.

"This is the last known sighting of Penelope Gray," he said, hitting the Play button. "She left the Rock and Bowl at nine twenty-seven P.M. after having words with Christina Warner—the shrink's daughter—and this is her at the convenience store that's down the block from the Rock and Bowl a few minutes later. She comes into the store, buys a six-pack of beer with what we can assume is a fake ID."

The girl walked toward the door, toward the camera, then stopped and spoke to someone who had to be standing outside the door—and outside the camera range. There was no audio. There was no way of knowing what she was saying or what her tone of voice might have been. There was no way of knowing what the other person was saying to her.

The girl took a couple of steps backward into the store, turning her head and looking in the direction of the counter, where several people waited in line to pay for purchases. One of the other customers glanced in her direction, disinterested, and turned back. Then Penelope Gray walked out of the store into the night.

Kovac froze the frame.

"Is there a camera outside the store?" Quinn asked.

"On the gas pumps, not pointed at the building."

He rewound the tape and played the last bit again, feeling haunted by the image of Penny Gray walking out of sight. Walking toward a friend? A stranger? A killer?

Tippen came into the room holding up a sheaf of papers. "The Gray family cell phone records."

Kovac snatched them with one hand and pulled his reading glasses out of his shirt pocket with the other. "Have you looked this over?"

"No. Hot off the press," Tippen said. "I just got back from seeing Dr. Timothy Gray, root canal specialist to the beautiful, well-off mouths of Edina."

"His daughter is missing, probably dead, and he's at work?" Elwood said.

"The odontology show must go on."

"We can assume dad and daughter aren't close?" Quinn said.

"Dr. Gray says he used to be close to his daughter but that the girl just couldn't understand the complex malfunctions of his marriage to her mother," Tippen explained. "Like his need to do the nasty with the twentysomething receptionist named Brandi-with-an-*i*, for instance."

"Poor kid," Kovac muttered. "Dad betrays her and her mom for a piece of ass. She blames Mom for not being enough of a hot dish to hang on to her father. Mom resents the girl for reacting badly to having her family torn apart. The girl is collateral damage from both sides."

"It's the American way," Tippen declared. "Destructive entitlement family-style. Dad wants what he wants. Screw everybody else. His involvement with his daughter is reduced to writing tuition checks and being annoyed by the fact that she won't leave him to enjoy his shiny new family in peace. He seems more irritated than worried that she's missing."

"A recurring theme among the Gray parents," Elwood commented.

"He said Penny has disappeared before. She's headstrong and belligerent and is probably somewhere relishing the grief she's causing."

"Yeah, like the morgue," Kovac said. "When did he last hear from her?"

"Christmas Day while he was enjoying a Rocky Mountain High holiday at his second home in Aspen. She sent him a text, a poem."

"Did he still have it in his phone?"

"Yes. He says he keeps them all 'just in case.'"

Quinn frowned. "In case of what?"

"The young Mrs. Dr. Gray is afraid of Penelope," Tippen explained. "According to Dr. Gray, his wife is afraid Penny might try to do something to hurt her or their three-year-old daughter."

"Does the girl have a history of violence?" Quinn asked.

"Apparently there was a drunken altercation at the grand opening of Dr. Gray's new office eight or nine months ago," Tippen said. "The spewing of obscenities, a slap, a little hair pulling. Nothing much as catfights go, but it frightened the wife and embarrassed the good doctor. He's still pissed off."

He pulled his phone out of a pocket and called up a text message. "This is her last text to her father:

```
Have a Holly Jolly Christmas
with your happy family
Don't think about the child you left
Your home, your wife, and me.
You live the life you want to
Have everything you need
That's all that really matters
You're all about the greed.
So happy, happy Christmas
my father great and true
```

From the daughter who means nothing
in the greater scheme to you."

"Wow," Kovac said. "She should write for Hallmark. They could have a whole new line of greeting cards for bitter people."

"I'd buy them," Tippen said. "But the bottom line for us here is that our derelict dad was out of state when Penny Gray went missing. He's off the hook—at least directly. He did, however, have some ironic unflattering things to say about his ex-wife."

Kovac arched a brow. "Doesn't every guy?"

"Specific to how she's raising their daughter. He claims if she was more maternal and less self-absorbed and angry, the girl would be more well-adjusted and not hate everyone so much."

"Kind of like how if he was more paternal and less of a dick, the girl would have a brighter outlook on relationships?" Kovac suggested.

"That train of thought somehow escaped him. He says the girl has no respect for the mother as a parent or as a woman or as anything. They fight constantly, and she especially hates her mother's choice in men."

"The girl doesn't like the boyfriend?" Kovac asked, then shrugged. "I don't like the boyfriend either."

"Too bad she isn't your daughter, then."

"Yeah. She'd hate me too."

"She's a teenage girl," Tippen said. "They hate everybody. Except rock stars and Channing Tatum."

"Who's Channing Tatum?"

Tippen gave him a look. "Do you have even a passing acquaintance with popular culture?"

Kovac scowled. "Hell no. Why would I?"

"This is why you're single."

"That's not why I'm single," Kovac said irritably. "I'm single because I spend all my time with you assholes.

"What's going on with your niece?" he asked. "Is she getting any feedback from her Internet stuff?"

"A lot of comments," Tippen said. "Whether or not any of them lead anywhere is another matter. I've got a couple of the guys borrowed from Sex Crimes tracking down the more interesting ones."

Kovac blew out a sigh. "This thing is going in so many directions, I feel like I'm wrestling a fucking octopus."

"You need to know what happened after she walked out of that store," Quinn said. "Right now, that's your key moment. Who was she talking to? Did she leave with them? Did they follow her? Somebody had to see something."

Kovac nodded. "We'll get this video to the TV stations and stress the need for any kind of information at all. If someone remembers seeing her that night, I want to talk to that person whether they think they have information or not.

"In the meantime, Elwood," he said, starting for the door, "let's you and I go talk to the mother and see what lovely things she has to say about her ex."

26

Julia Gray was pacing the narrow width of the interview room, her arms crossed as if holding herself together. Her head snapped in Kovac's direction as he walked in. Under the harsh fluorescent lights, she looked haggard and ten years older than she had the night before. The bruise on her cheek had darkened.

Michael Warner sat at the small, round white table, composed, though he had already shed his coat and pushed up the sleeves of his black sweater. His forehead glistened with a fine mist of sweat. He rose and shook hands with Kovac.

"Detective Kovac."

"Dr. Warner. Mrs. Gray."

"Have you heard anything?" she asked. "Captain Kasselmann said leads are coming in. People have called in to say they've seen Penny. Is that true?"

Elwood pulled a chair out for her. "Have a seat, Mrs. Gray. We'll go over everything."

She glanced at Michael Warner as if looking for his permission. Kovac sat down, perched his reading glasses on his nose, and looked down at the cell phone records he had stuck in a file folder and carried in with him. Elwood took the remaining seat, dwarfing the table like a bear at a child's tea party, ready to jot notes on a yellow legal pad. Julia Gray fidgeted in her seat. "Why is it so warm in here?"

"Apologies for that, ma'am," Elwood said. "There's something going on with the heating system."

"It's really uncomfortable," she complained, yet she continued to keep her arms crossed tight around her.

Michael Warner leaned over and placed a hand on her shoulder. "Try to relax, Julia. Deep breaths."

"We've had a number of calls to the AMBER Alert hotline," Elwood said. "Every potential lead will be checked out. That said, we have yet to locate your daughter's vehicle, and the last substantiated sighting of her was at a Holiday gas station the evening of the thirtieth."

Kovac lifted his head. "May I see your cell phone, Mrs. Gray? I'd like to just take a look at your daughter's text messages to you, see if there might be some bit of information that could be helpful to us."

She hefted her purse onto the table. It was half the size of a gunnysack, with designer logos stamped all over it. She held it open with her injured right hand and dug for the phone with the left.

"Are you right- or left-handed, Mrs. Gray?" Kovac asked.

She glanced up at him. "I'm right-handed. Why?"

"I broke my right hand once. I couldn't write, couldn't type, couldn't turn a doorknob. What a pain in the rear."

"Yes, it is," she said absently, looking into the purse. "I don't have it. My phone. I must have left it in the car."

Kovac flicked a glance at Elwood. What mother of a missing child absentmindedly left her phone in the car? Even if it was likely the girl was dead, until they had confirmation, a mother had to hold out hope, however slim.

"You haven't had any text messages from your daughter's number since we spoke last night?"

"No."

"The phone seems to have been turned off," Elwood said. "Or the battery died. I've been in contact with Apple. Your daughter did install the Find My iPhone app, but in that model the app only works if the phone is turned on."

"So you can't locate it," Michael Warner said.

"No," Kovac said, looking at the phone records. "But we can narrow down the vicinity the phone was in when it was being used. For instance, on the night she went missing, calls pinged off a tower near the Rock and Bowl. Since that night the phone has been in two areas. One hits off a tower on Pleasant Avenue South, west of 35W and north of Highway 62. The other is an AT&T tower located at 3910 Stephens Avenue just east of your own neighborhood, Mrs. Gray."

She looked confused. "I'm not sure what we're supposed to make of that."

Kovac moved on, letting her wonder. "When was the last time you actually saw Penny, Mrs. Gray?"

"The twenty-eighth. Dinnertime. I had just gotten home from work."

"You said the two of you had words. What about?"

She glanced at Warner as she pulled in a breath and sighed sharply. "She was angry. She was hurt. She didn't hear from her father on Christmas, and she'd been stewing on that for two days. She was angry with me for—for—*everything*. For losing her father, for not being who she wants me to be, for my relationship with Michael."

"Penny doesn't approve of your relationship?" Elwood asked.

"Penny wouldn't approve of any relationship her mother has," Michael Warner said. "Unless Julia and her ex-husband got back together—and not even then. What she wants is a fantasy. She wants things to be the way her memory has painted the relationship between her parents when she was a little girl."

"Are you treating Penny, Dr. Warner?" Kovac asked.

"Not any longer. I was her therapist for a time. That's how Julia and I met. Of course, we didn't become involved until after I stopped seeing Penny as a patient," he hastened to add.

"Is that why you stopped seeing her?"

"No, no," he said, shaking his head. "After evaluating Penny and having a number of sessions with her, I determined she would be better served by a female therapist. Because of the situation with her father, she feels a strong need to try to manipulate men. That makes the therapist's job ten times more difficult."

"So who does she see now?"

"No one," Julia said. "I sent her to the woman Michael recommended, and she would go and spend the entire time not talking or making eye contact. I'm not interested in paying for that, and she wasn't interested in going. There was no point."

And once again Julia Gray had taken the path of least resistance where her daughter was concerned. Even when Penny Gray had been physically present in her mother's life, she had been lost.

"So Penny picked a fight with you that night?" he asked.

"Yes."

"Did she ever get physically violent with you?"

"No! Of course not!" she said a little too emphatically. "Why would you ask me that?"

"Your ex-husband mentioned an incident where your daughter attacked his wife," Elwood said.

She rolled her eyes. "That was blown all out of proportion."

"You were there?"

"No, of course I wasn't there," she snapped. "Tim's office manager told me about it. I've known her for years. She said Brandi overreacted. She's such a drama queen. I've never understood how Tim doesn't see right through her. Everyone else does."

"So you and your daughter argued, but there was no physical fight," Kovac said.

"No!" She went to throw her hands up in frustration and stopped midgesture, looking at the brace on her hand and wrist, realization dawning. "I *told* you. I slipped and fell on the ice."

"Where did that happen, Mrs. Gray?" Elwood asked.

"It happened in a parking lot in St. Louis Park," she said, clearly irritated. "I was leaving an appointment at Four Seasons Women's Clinic."

"At least you got quick medical attention," he said.

"I didn't go back into the clinic. I was embarrassed, and I didn't think I was hurt that badly. Besides, what were a bunch of gynecologists going to do for my wrist? I had it checked out at an urgent care later."

"What day was that?"

"That same day. The twenty-eighth."

"That was some bad day," Kovac commented. "And at the end of the argument that evening Penny left the house?"

"Yes," she said. Tears rose in her eyes. She forced herself to sit up straight and hold on to her dignity. "She said she hated me, couldn't stand to be around me, and that she would go be with people who didn't make her want to puke."

The poor long-suffering mother.

"And where did she go?" Kovac asked.

Frustration tightened the lines around her mouth. "I don't know *exactly*. I didn't hear from her until the next day. I know she ended up staying with her friend Bethany."

"Brittany," Elwood corrected her. "Brittany Lawler."

She closed her eyes and pinched the bridge of her nose as if against the pain of a headache, very aware of the fact that she was once again striking out in the Mother of the Year contest.

She scowled at Kovac. "Why are we even talking about this? We know where she was last seen. What difference does it make where she was before that?"

Kovac ignored the question. "Where were you on the evening of the thirtieth, Mrs. Gray?"

"Michael and I went to a concert at the Orpheum and had a late dinner after."

"At what restaurant?" Elwood asked, scribbling down the details.

Michael Warner leaned forward, looking grave. "I don't like the direction this is taking, Detective. You can't possibly think Julia had something to do with whatever happened to Penny."

Kovac smiled blandly. "It's important that we get as clear a picture as possible of the time leading up to Penny's disappearance. An investigation is like a game of chess. We need to know where all the pieces were before our bad guy—whoever that may be—made his big move. We need to see not only the big picture but all the small details."

"What time did you get home?" Elwood asked.

"I've seen this happen on television!" Julia Gray said, alarmed. "A child goes missing and the police waste valuable time harassing the parents. I didn't do anything to my daughter! How could you even think such a thing?"

"We don't know you, Mrs. Gray," Elwood said reasonably. "We can't make assumptions about anyone in your daughter's life. We're not accusing you of anything, but it's essential that we remain open to all possibilities."

"Should Julia have an attorney here?" Warner asked.

"This isn't an interrogation, Dr. Warner," Kovac said. "No one is under arrest. We're just trying to get as much information as possible to help guide us in the right direction."

"I didn't see my daughter after she left the house on the twenty-eighth," Julia Gray said tersely.

"And what time did you get home on the thirtieth?" Elwood asked.

"Twelve thirty or so."

"And you, Dr. Warner?"

"Shortly after that."

"Was your daughter home by then?"

"No. Christina got home around one."

"Did she say anything about what went on at the Rock and Bowl?" Kovac asked.

"She said she spent the evening out with her friends."

"She didn't say anything about Penny Gray?"

"No."

"Even though, according to kids who were there, Christina and Penny had an argument that ended with Penny leaving."

"As you've heard, an argument that ends with Penny leaving isn't exactly newsworthy," Warner said. "Penny is an intrinsically un-happy girl, Detective. She's unhappy with her life. She's unhappy with herself. She's unhappy with her mother and about her mother's relationship with me. She's jealous of Christina. She's jealous of my relationship with my daughter because she doesn't have a relation-ship with her own father. I've tried to fill that void for her in small ways, and she resents me for it."

"I've been told the dislike between the girls runs both ways," Kovac said. "According to a witness at the Rock and Bowl, Chris-tina was picking on Penny that night, making fun of her poetry—something that was also not an isolated incident."

Warner sighed. "I'm not going to try to paint my daughter as a perfect angel, Detective. But you can talk to Christina's teachers, to her friends. She's an excellent student. She's a leader in her class. She mentors younger girls.

"She has tried to be friends with Penny. Penny isn't interested. That Christina occasionally fights back when Penny lashes out at her is only normal."

"Girls will be girls."

"Essentially, yes. Yet when I told Christina last night about Penny being missing, the first thing she wanted to do was help in some way."

"That's admirable," Elwood said. "Hopefully, she'll be able to help. We'll be speaking with the kids later today. Maybe they'll be able to shed some light. People don't always realize what they know. Sometimes a seemingly insignificant detail can mean everything."

"Your daughter's poetry, for example," Kovac said to Julia Gray. "Her last Facebook post was a poem. It certainly seems to be directed at someone in particular."

He pulled a printed copy of the poem entitled "Liar" out of the file folder and slid it across the table to a neutral spot between Julia Gray and Michael Warner. He sat back in his chair and watched them read it with his eyelids at half-mast, as if he might doze off.

Julia Gray looked frustrated by her inability to penetrate her daughter's work—or her world—in any way. Michael Warner read it without expression.

"Any idea who she might be talking about?" Kovac asked.

"Her father, obviously," Warner said. "She was lashing out at him. He has all but cut her out of his life. She was especially feeling the sting of that over the holidays."

"But what's the lie?" Kovac asked. "It's been four years since your husband left you and Penny, Mrs. Gray. It's no secret he was cheating on you, that he left you for a younger woman. Considering your daughter's penchant for public displays of drama, I can't imagine anyone didn't know how she felt about it all. So what's the lie? What's the secret? Who's the star she means to bring down?"

Michael Warner slid the sheet of paper back toward him and said, "We can only hope we get a chance to ask her."

"And for the record, Mrs. Gray," Elwood said, "where were you New Year's Eve?"

"We went out for drinks," she said, tearing up. Michael Warner put an arm around her shoulders to offer comfort while she covered her mouth with her injured hand.

Kovac imagined her remembering the revelry of the evening, dressed to the nines, ringing in the New Year while her daughter was lying dead in the road, a spectacle under the harsh portable lights, TV news cameras angling to get a shot of the carnage.

Every mother's nightmare.

He hoped.

27

"You are *not* to leave this house. Do you understand me?" Nikki said. "I don't care if it's on fire. You are *not* to leave this house."

Kyle didn't look at her. He hung his head and said yes in a barely audible voice.

They had ridden home in absolute, oppressive silence. She couldn't trust herself to speak. She couldn't stand to have music on the radio or DJs trying to fill everyone with phony hilarity. The sound of the blinker was intolerable. Kyle slouched down in the passenger's seat, trying to make himself invisible.

The house was equally silent save for the hum of the refrigerator in the kitchen. The quiet seemed to press in on her eardrums. Every small sound—her purse touching the dining table as she set it down, Kyle unzipping his hoodie—seemed magnified ten times.

He sat down at the table looking despondent. She refused to feel badly for him.

"I can't talk to you about this now," she said. "I am so angry and so disappointed in you, I can't talk about it."

He hung his head. "Are you going to tell Dad?"

"Why would I bother to involve your father?" she snapped. "He's as juvenile as you seem to be. He'll probably think it's funny. It's *not* funny. It is *so* not funny.

"You could lose your scholarship over this. You could be expelled. You can sit here all day and think about that, and what that means. No television. No Internet. And if I find out you've been on Facebook or tweeting on your *secret* account, I will take your phone and smash it with a hammer right before your eyes.

"I have to go now," she said, "because I have to have a job so I can provide for you and your brother, and feed you, and clothe you, and buy you things—all of which you seem to have no appreciation for whatsoever."

He was trying to hide the fact that he was crying. She had to fight like a tigress against the urge to go to him and put her arms around him. She loved him so much it hurt like being stabbed in the heart with an ice pick.

She felt like she was going to explode into a million glass shards as she went back out into the cold and got in the piece-of-crap car from the department pool. It smelled of cold Mexican takeout food. She left the windows cracked as she drove.

Alone, she couldn't help but let some of her own tears fall. She was exhausted, both from the case and from all the drama with Kyle. At times like this she found that terrible, insidious worn-out wish sneaking in the back door. The one where she imagined someone stronger than she felt offering to take some of the burden away and let her rest in a safe place. It was a cruel dream, one she never expected to be fulfilled. But it crept in the back door just the same.

She drove to the medical plaza where Penny Gray had been treated for her broken wrist and picked up the X-rays that were waiting at the front desk, then headed downtown to the ME's offices.

She was informed at the front desk that Möller was in the middle of an autopsy.

"Which suite is he in?" she asked.

The receptionist blinked at her. "You can wait in his office. He's in the middle of an autopsy."

"Yeah, I got that the first time you said it." She held up the large manila envelope with Penelope Gray's name on it. "I need him to look at these X-rays now. I don't care if he's knee-deep in decomposing corpses. Which room is he in?"

The young woman looked alarmed, torn between fear and duty.

"Look, sweetheart," Nikki said brusquely. "You can call Dr. Möller and interrupt him or you can tell me which room he's in and I'll interrupt him myself. I need to know if his Jane Doe is my missing child case. I have a mother hanging in limbo."

Still uncertain, the young woman swallowed and said, "He's in two."

She was already picking up the phone to call the suite and cover her ass as Nikki turned and headed down the hall.

The smell hit her in the face like a baseball bat as she went into the autopsy suite.

"Holy Mother of God!" she exclaimed, reeling. Her stomach flipped over like a beached fish, and her head swam.

Möller looked up at her, his eyes sparkling above his mask. "Ah, welcome, Sergeant Liska! You don't like our ambience today? So sorry. The piquant bouquet of our latest customer isn't for the more delicate nose, I'm afraid."

Liska clamped her nose shut with thumb and forefinger and tried to breathe through her mouth. Her eyes watered as if she had just sliced open an onion. "What the hell is that?"

"A dissatisfied client from a funeral home in north Minneapolis. One of several. Apparently, they ran out of storage while waiting for the weather to cooperate for burials," he explained. "And ran out of embalming fluid, it would seem, as well. Seven corpses stacked in a closet like cordwood."

"I'm gonna puke," she said, then promptly turned toward the nearest receptacle and unloaded her breakfast into a laundry bin.

Unfazed, Möller went on about his business, waiting for her to recover.

"Okay," she said, still breathing hard through her mouth. "That guy isn't going to get any deader. I've got the X-rays to match to our Jane Doe. Can we go somewhere with a lower gag factor and have a look?"

"Of course," Möller said pleasantly, stepping back from the table. "If you had allowed the girl at the desk to call ahead, I would have met you in the hallway."

He stripped off his gloves, mask, and gown and threw them in the laundry bin, then washed his hands in one of the big stainless steel sinks.

Liska didn't wait for him, bursting out of the room and sucking in fresh air by the lungful. Möller stepped into the hall and offered her a wrapped peppermint, which she took in exchange for the X-rays.

They went into his office and he clipped the pictures of Penny Gray's broken wrist to a light box. He had already mounted the matching X-rays from the Jane Doe autopsy. He stood looking at the images, frowning and silent.

"What do you think?" she asked. "Are our pictures the healed version of that?"

"Yes," Möller said. "How did this allegedly happen?" he asked, pointing to Gray's known X-rays.

"The mother said the girl fell off a bike. Why?"

"No," he said. "You fall from a bicycle, you reach out to break your fall like so," he said, stretching out one arm, his hand flexed back. "Your hand strikes the ground, the break happens here." He cut his other hand across the wrist. This is not what happened to this girl."

Liska looked at the fracture, the steep angle of it.

"This," Möller said, "is a spiral fracture. A spiral fracture is caused by a twisting motion."

He turned toward her, grabbed hold of her wrist, and slowly twisted.

"That, my friend—," he began.

Liska finished the sentence for him. "Is abuse."

28

Have u heard about Gray?

Brittany looked at her phone. Kyle. Why couldn't he just leave her alone? That was her first thought. Her second thought was that in her heart of hearts she actually kind of wished she could see him and talk to him. He was always so sure of what to do, of what was right. She didn't always agree with him, but she wished she had some of his strength right now.

She glanced around to see if anyone was watching her, then texted him back. *She's missing. Cops here now. Where r u?*

They sat at a big, glossy wood table in a room in the principal's offices. Christina and Aaron and the other kids who had been at the Rock & Bowl that night—Jessie and Emily, Eric and Michael; the core of the clique. The police wanted to talk to them.

"How did they even know we were there?" Aaron asked.

Brittany was silent, dreading having everyone's attention on her. Would they be angry? Would they hate her? She hadn't asked for the police to come to her house.

She felt Christina's dark eyes on her with extra intensity. She had to tell them. They would find out anyway.

"They came to my house last night," she said. "Gray's mom told them she was staying with me."

Emily's eyes got big. "The police came to your house? Oh my God."

"This is what happens," Christina said with firm disapproval. "This is what you get for letting her come to your house, Britt. She's always in trouble. She *is* trouble. I've told you that a hundred times!"

"I know, I know," Brittany said. "But her mom kicked her out. She needed a place to stay—"

"Let her go stay with one of her weird poet friends. She's not your responsibility, Britt. You don't owe her anything."

Brittany said nothing. Everything with Christina was cut-and-dried and bent to fit, but Brittany never seemed to see things so clearly. She had been friends with Gray before she was friends with Christina. Even though she didn't really get Gray, she felt like she *did* owe her a certain amount of, if not loyalty, then kindness, at least.

She felt badly for Gray. Her father had cut her out of his life. Her mother was a selfish bitch who would have been just as happy if Gray disappeared forever. That was so sad. Brittany had great parents. They didn't always see eye to eye on things, but she knew her mom and dad loved her. They would never in a million years throw her out of the house, throw her away like she was a broken doll or a piece of trash.

"Maybe she had her own reasons for wanting Gray to sleep over," Jessie said sarcastically. "A little girlie action, Britt?"

Brittany looked at her, seeing the nasty little gleam in her eyes. Jessie considered Christina her BFF and was easily made jealous. If anyone had lesbian tendencies, it was Jessie, but Brittany didn't have the nerve to say so.

"Maybe I'm just a nice person," she said. "Maybe if your mom kicked you out, you would like somebody to be nice to you too."

"Leave her alone, Jess," Christina snapped, conveniently forgetting that she had made the same kind of nasty comments before that night at the Rock & Bowl. All was forgiven now.

"What did you tell the cops?" Aaron asked.

"That we went to the Rock and Bowl and that Gray got pissed off and left."

"And you told them that we were all there," he said. "Thanks, Britt."

"What difference would it make if I did?" she asked defensively. "What difference does it make who was there? Gray left. That's all that matters."

"Did you tell them that douchebag Hatcher was there?"

"I didn't tell them anything about anyone!" Brittany insisted. "Stop trying to make me feel like I did something wrong! They're the *police*, Aaron. You think they wouldn't find out whatever they wanted to find out?"

He narrowed his eyes in suspicion. "Was one of them Hatcher's mom?"

"No."

"Then how come *he's* not sitting here?"

"How would I know?"

"He's your boyfriend."

"He is not! How can he be my boyfriend? You're the one who keeps saying he's gay."

"Aaron, stop it," Christina snapped. "This isn't Britt's fault. Kyle probably told them we were all there. Who knows what he might have said."

"Fucking loser runt," Aaron muttered, staring down at his fists on the tabletop. He had a tendency to pout, his full lower lip jutting slightly forward, his eyes narrowing to slits.

When Brittany had first seen Aaron Fogelman, like every other girl in school, she had thought he was hot. He was tall and athletic and good-looking in a young Channing Tatum kind of a way. She had fantasized about him being interested in her, but that hadn't lasted long. First of all, he was Christina's boyfriend. But as she'd gotten to know him, the hot looks had faded behind the fact that he was spoiled and sulky and not very nice to a lot of people.

She hated the way he treated Kyle—the bullying, the nasty gay references—even if Kyle did sometimes ask for it. As she looked at him now she could hear Kyle's voice: *Nice friends you've got there, Britt. . . .*

Her phone vibrated in her hand. She held it down in her lap and tried to read the text surreptitiously.

@home. Suspended.

"Did you see what he put on Twitter?" Eric Owen asked the room in general. He was snickering when he brought the picture up on his phone and held it so everyone could look. He laughed even though one of the cartoon figures was clearly himself.

Aaron swore half under his breath, reached over, and snatched the phone out of his buddy's hand.

"Hey!"

"It's not funny, dickhead!" Aaron declared.

It wasn't funny when Kyle did it to Aaron, but it had been hilarious when Aaron had done it to Kyle. Brittany wished she had the courage to say it, but she didn't.

"Where do you think Gray is?" Christina asked her.

"I don't know."

"You haven't heard from her?"

"No, but why would I?" Brittany asked. "She thinks I set her up."

"You did," Jessie Cook said smugly.

Brittany looked down again at Kyle's text—*@home. Suspended.*—and thought, *Wish I was there.*

She wanted to deny Jessie's charge, but what good would it do her? She wanted to believe she hadn't known Christina was going to retaliate that night. Nobody had told her in so many words. Christina had texted her, knowing full well Gray was with her, and told her to come to the Rock & Bowl. Brittany had convinced Gray to go.

Now she felt ashamed of herself for being a part of it, for not being brave enough to say something that night.

"She had it coming," Emily Peters said.

That was true. Gray had invited the trouble—as she always did. She had written a nasty poem about Christina called "Queen of the Class" and read it out loud at PSI's monthly Artist's Open Mike Night right before Christmas break had started. Brittany could see it in her head like a scene from a movie: Gray standing at the microphone wearing a look that always meant trouble—half-mean, half-excited—as she began to read.


```
Queen of the Class


Princess of sass
Boss of the cool elite.
Mermaid hair
Down to there
Never has tasted defeat.
Believes she's adored
Everyone is so bored
Pretending to worship her shit.
Each one and all
Can't wait for her fall
Just wishing she'd take a big hit.
But life as a rule
Is exceedingly cruel
```

To the queens of phony glory.
They all fall down
And break the crown
And that be the end of their story.
The ones they look down on
The ones that they frown on
Are only too happy to say, Fool
We knew all the time
That this was your prime
Bitch, you peaked in high school.

Gray had been so pleased with herself. She loved making people uncomfortable when she believed they deserved it. No one had been able to make eye contact with Christina. They all knew the poem was about her. Christina's face had turned to stone.

"You know they think she's that dead girl that fell out of that car New Year's Eve," Aaron said. "The zombie."

Brittany frowned at him. "Don't say that."

"It's true. Emily, you said you read about it on *TeenCities*."

Emily nodded. "In Sonya Porter's blog. It was all about how there's this serial killer out there killing young women and doing terrible things to them."

"That doesn't mean it's Gray," Christina said.

"You know," Jessie said, "the way they described that dead girl on the news, it kind of sounded like Gray. God, how weird would that be—to know someone who was murdered by some sick psycho?"

She seemed almost excited at the prospect.

"If it is Gray, the killer got her after she left the Rock and Bowl," Brittany said. "And she left the Rock and Bowl because of us."

"That doesn't mean it's our fault," Christina argued. "It's not our fault there's some maniac running around killing people. All I wanted was to pay her back for what she did to me. I didn't wish for her to be kidnapped and tortured by some sicko! God, Britt, is that what you think?"

"No!" Brittany said. "But if that's what happened to her, I'm going to feel guilty, aren't you?"

"I'm going to feel terrible," Christina said, "but I'm not going to feel responsible. I didn't kill her."

Emily chewed at a fingernail, looking worried. "What do you think the cops will ask us?"

"What did they ask you, Britt?" Christina asked.

She squirmed on her chair. "They just wanted to know where Gray went. Had I heard from her. Did she leave with anyone. That's all."

"You told them she got mad and left," Christina said, leaning closer, lowering her voice. "Did you tell them why she flipped out?"

"No."

"They didn't ask?"

"No."

She leaned a little closer and swept a big curtain of gorgeous blond waves back over her shoulder. "You didn't tell them what she said to me, did you?"

"No!" Brittany whispered. "Why would I do that? I wouldn't do that."

"You were the only one who heard her say it," Christina whispered back. "And it's a lie, anyway, but you know how mean people can be."

She said it with a straight face, as if she had never been mean to anybody, her big brown eyes blinking with innocence.

"You won't say anything, will you?"

Brittany shook her head. "No."

Like the police would give a rip about the petty sniping of teenage girls.

Christina reached over and gave her hand a quick squeeze. "You're such a good friend, Britt."

Gray probably didn't think so, Brittany thought.

"You know," Aaron said, "Hatcher left right after Gray did that night. He's the one the cops should be talking to."

"I WANT TO smack this little prick upside the head."

"That would be wrong," Tippen said with a bored sigh. "Satisfying, but wrong."

They stood in the room adjacent to the one the kids sat in, watching them, listening to their discussion via closed-circuit TV. Kids had no expectation of privacy in school. They were literally spied on all day long, in classrooms, in the halls, in the cafeteria, in this conference room waiting to be interviewed by the police.

Kovac studied one kid and then the next, taking in their body language, their facial expressions. Brittany Lawler looked the least happy of the group. She wanted to get up and leave. She squirmed in her seat, leaning away from the girl next to her—Christina Warner.

Christina leaned toward her with a look of concern, put a hand on her shoulder, and murmured something the microphone didn't pick up. Reassurance. Comfort. Something like that.

Christina was clearly the leader of the pack. Pretty, stylish, aware of her sexuality, bossy. The others looked to her. She was well aware of her position and her power.

It wasn't hard to imagine there would be tensions between her and a girl like Penny Gray, the perennial outsider. They were opposites, light and dark, manipulative and reactive. Because of the relationship between their parents, they were essentially being pitted against each other for the favor of Julia Gray. Julia Gray, who seemed to have nothing but disapproval and disappointment for her only child. Kovac could easily imagine her saying, *Why can't you be more like Christina?*

He turned to Tippen. "Let's do this. The two stooges first," he said, pointing to Aaron Fogelman's wingmen. "Then those two girls. We'll make the Fogelman kid wait a while after his pals, see if we can't drum up a little more paranoia in that one. Then we'll take the Warner girl, then Brittany Lawler again. We'll leave her 'til last. Let the others wonder why."

"Dr. Warner is already getting impatient," Tippen said.

"Good. Let him stew."

The parents had been assembled by Principal Rodgers in his office, Michael Warner among them. They would be allowed to sit in on the interviews with their individual children. At least none of them had brought an attorney along.

Thankful for small blessings, Kovac took one of the Fogelman kid's buddies and Tippen took the other. Neither had much of anything to say. They claimed not to really know Penelope Gray. They claimed to be playing skee ball in the arcade when the argument between Gray and Christina Warner went down. The parents were predictably defensive, doing what parents do: getting between trouble and their kids.

The interviews with the two girls, Emily Peters and Jessica Cook, went much the same.

Kovac took the Cook girl, whose mother was big and square and looked like she might fight for the WWE when she wasn't masquerading as a bank vice president in a sweater and pearls. Momma Bear sat with her meaty arms crossed over her chest and a sour look on her face. The girl had that slightly pinched quality to her expression that spelled a potential for belligerence.

Kovac sat down at the table across from them and began the verbal dance.

"So, Jessica, did you see Gray that night at the Rock and Bowl?"

She rolled her eyes. "You know I did. Otherwise I wouldn't be here, would I?"

"Let's cut to the chase, then. What went down between Gray and Christina?"

"Gray got pissed off and called Christina a"—she glanced at her mother—"bad name, and she left."

"Did anybody follow her out?"

"Yeah. Kyle Hatcher."

"Anybody else?"

She huffed a sigh. "I really wasn't watching. I don't like Gray. I don't care what she does."

"She's missing," Kovac said bluntly. "She might be dead."

"I don't know what you want me to say," she said with just enough whine to set his teeth on edge. "I didn't see anything!"

Momma Bear reared her ugly head. "What does any of this have to do with my daughter? Jessica isn't responsible for what that Gray girl does. Apparently, no one is."

"We're just trying to put together a complete picture here, Mrs. Cook. Any detail, no matter how insignificant it may seem, could be helpful to the investigation." He turned his attention back to the girl.

She tipped her head to one side, bored, scratching idly at the arm of her chair with a shiny red fingernail. "I didn't see anything."

"That's great, Jessica," Kovac said sarcastically. He put his elbows on the table and leaned toward her. "Tell me something. If it was you missing instead of Gray, how would you feel about your friends not trying to help out?"

She gave him a cold look. "She's not my friend. This is stupid, anyway. Gray left. None of us killed her."

Momma Bear sat forward. "Are you trying to intimidate my daughter?"

"No," Kovac said. "I'm trying to make her have a conscience."

Mrs. Cook got to her feet with all the menace of an animal about to charge. "If Jessica says she didn't see anything, she didn't see anything. We're done here. If you have anything more, Detective, you can speak to our attorney."

Kovac followed them into the hall and watched the mother herd the daughter toward the office doors. Tippen came out of the room where they had been watching the video monitor.

"That went well."

Kovac rolled his eyes. "I'm just happy Momma didn't knock me down and hurt me. How did yours go?"

"She wasn't right there when the fight happened. She was in the bathroom or getting a drink or looking the other way. But it was probably Gray's fault because she's just like that."

"Nice."

"Contemporary teenagers. It's *Lord of the Flies* in designer labels."

"How are the other three holding up?" Kovac asked.

They went back into their viewing room. Brittany still looked unhappy, staring down at her phone in her lap. Aaron Fogelman had gotten up to pace, his hands jammed at his waist.

"Why is it taking so fucking long?" the boy asked. "What could they possibly be talking about that's taking so long?"

Christina got up and went to him, stopping in front of him and slipping her arms around his waist. Young love.

"Will you relax?" she said.

"What if this goes in our records?" he whined. "Questioned by the police because of that bitch? My dad's gonna have my ass over this! He wants me to get into Northwestern!"

"Oh my God," Christina said, letting go of him so he could pace some more. "You're such a drama king!"

"Oh, it's fine for you," he said. "Daddy's girl. Your father thinks you shit gold."

"I can see why all the girls go for him," Kovac said. "Silver-tongued charmer."

"Angry white boy," Tippen said. "Raging against the oppression of the bourgeois life in the mean streets of suburbia."

"He needs his ass kicked," Kovac declared.

He went to the room the students were in, opened the door, and nodded to Aaron Fogelman, his face a stony mask. The kid tried to put on a tough front, but the bravado was short-sheeted over the insecurity and his fear of a blemish on his permanent record. The last thing he did before leaving the room was glance back at Christina Warner.

His father, Wynn Fogelman, joined them in the conference room. Kovac took in the immaculate expensive suit, the power tie, the slicked-back hair, the way he carried himself, and thought, *Wealthy self-important asshole,* an assessment proven true the instant Fogelman opened his mouth.

"I hope you realize, Detective, my son's future is something I do not take lightly. I won't have the Fogelman name—mine or Aaron's—tied in any way to this missing girl."

Kovac motioned the two of them to sit on one side of the table. "I'm not interested in your name, Mr. Fogelman. I don't know who you are. I don't care who you are. I'm here because one of your son's classmates has gone missing, and I know that he was among the last people to see her before whatever happened to her happened to her. If he can shed some light on what happened that night, great. If he can't, he can't."

"He doesn't know anything about what happened to this girl," his father said. "From what I understand, she's a behavior problem, and it isn't all that unusual for her to disappear."

Kovac just looked at him for a moment, chewing a little with his back teeth. He wanted to tell Wynn Fogelman that Penelope Gray was a sixteen-year-old girl, not a nuisance to be defined by a label. But even her own mother didn't seem to quite get that.

He was just as guilty of it, truth to tell. He had a moment to assess the people he met in the course of his work. He had to read them, rank them, and label them instantly. Everyone did it. He took umbrage only with regard to the victims he adopted in his role of defender/avenger. No different from these parents trying to protect their kids, he supposed.

He looked at the boy, sullen and slouched in his seat with his arms crossed over his chest. "Who busted that lip for you?"

The kid reached up and touched the swollen spot, as if he'd forgotten he had it. "No one. I tripped and fell."

"Into a pile of knuckles," Kovac said. "Nice.

"Aaron, how well do you know Penny Gray?" he asked.

The boy lifted a shoulder but looked down at the tabletop. "Not very."

He mumbled when he talked. He didn't make eye contact with Kovac, but beyond that, he didn't look at his father. He knew he was in trouble. The old man didn't appreciate being taken out of his Very Important Job to come to school and talk with the police. Junior was supposed to be a chip off the old block, successful at everything, yet here he was . . .

"You have classes with her," Kovac said. He slipped his reading glasses on and opened a file folder on the table in front of him. "Drama, English, something called Visual Media. You're spending a lot of your day with her, you have mutual acquaintances—you must know her a little."

"She's weird. She's a weird, angry bitc—person," he said, shooting his father a glance from the corner of his eye. "Nobody likes her."

"Your friend Brittany likes her," Kovac pointed out.

"That's Brittany," he grumbled. "She likes everybody."

"What a poor quality that is," Kovac said sarcastically. "And Gray and Christina are halfway to being sisters, right? With Christina's dad and Gray's mom getting together. And you're tight with Christina. . . ."

"Is there a point to this?" Wynn Fogelman asked sharply.

Kovac ignored him. "What went down between those two at the Rock and Bowl? I'm hearing Christina started something, making fun of one of Gray's poems."

The one-shoulder shrug. "I don't know."

"You were right there, Aaron. I have a witness who puts you right in the middle of it," Kovac lied.

The boy jumped up in his chair, all shock and righteous indignation. "Fucking Hatcher!"

"Aaron!" the father barked.

"And we have security tape," Kovac went on.

Of course, he didn't. The video was of terrible quality and showed only part of the room from an angle that made it virtually impossible to tell what the hell was going on, and completely impossible to pick out individuals who weren't in the camera's direct path. But Aaron Fogelman didn't know that.

"I didn't do anything!" the boy protested. "She went after Christina! I just got between them! I didn't hit her! Did Hatcher say I hit her? I didn't! It maybe just looked that way. I didn't!"

Kovac sat back and digested that. He looked at Wynn Fogelman, who was glaring at his son.

"No," Kovac said. "I'm sure your father taught you better than to hit a girl."

The elder Fogelman turned on him. "You can't use any of this against my son."

"Not in a court of law," Kovac qualified. "Your son isn't under arrest. He isn't even under suspicion of anything, Mr. Fogelman. Luckily for our overcrowded prison system, being a dick isn't against the law."

Fogelman bristled. "You can change your tone with me, Detective."

"Why would I?" Kovac asked. "I don't care what you think

about me. You will probably find this hard to believe, but this situation isn't about you."

"What is it about, then?" Fogelman asked, his face stone-cold with suppressed fury.

"The truth," Kovac said calmly. "That's all. I want to know every possible reason a sixteen-year-old girl came to be in a position where a predator might have taken advantage of her."

"You don't even know that she's missing," Mr. Fogelman said.

"Oh, I know she's missing," Kovac said. "And by the end of the day I'm probably going to be sure that she's dead and lying on a steel table in the morgue."

"Aaron certainly had no part in any of that!"

"He was part of the little ambush that prompted Penny Gray to leave the Rock and Bowl on her own that night, Mr. Fogelman. And then she disappeared. So see? You can't say Junior here didn't have anything to do with that. You throw a rock in a pond, you don't have control of where the ripples go."

Wynn Fogelman stood up, trying not to look flustered. "I think we should go now, Aaron."

"Kyle Hatcher followed her out," Aaron said, happy to throw the blame on someone else.

"Kyle Hatcher doesn't have a vehicle," Kovac returned.

"He came with her," the boy threw back. "Why wouldn't he leave with her too?"

Kovac refused to react. "What time did *you* leave the Rock and Bowl that night, Aaron?"

Fogelman Sr. put a hand on his son's shoulder. "Aaron. We're leaving. Now."

The boy looked from his father to Kovac, not sure which authority figure to obey. "Later. After them."

"And where did you go?"

"Home," his father said firmly. "He came home."

"Well, then," Kovac said to the elder Fogelman. "You're a hell of a lot luckier than Penny Gray's mother, aren't you?"

He watched the Fogelmans exit the room—father, ramrod straight, chin up; son, looking at the ground, shoulders slouched, hands in the pockets of his hoodie. He followed them to the hall and watched them walk out as Tippen joined him.

"Which do you think would be worse?" Tippen asked. "Knowing you're a son of a bitch or knowing you fathered one?"

"Toss-up," Kovac said as his phone vibrated in his pocket. He pulled it out and looked at the screen. Liska.

"Do I need to help you bury the body?" he asked by way of greeting.

"No. But I'm touched to know that you would."

"Well, in the last hour I've come to a greater understanding of why tigers eat their young."

"That insight might come in handier than you think," she said. "Penny Gray is dead."

29

Liska marched into the lovely offices of Dr. Bob Iverson, her heart thumping with purpose. The receptionist behind the elegant cherrywood counter looked up at her, recognizing her from before, but uncertain about the expression Liska knew she wore now. The bland, polite smile she had given the woman when she picked up the X-rays had been replaced by something harder and darker.

"Did we forget something?" the woman asked quietly.

"I would say so. I need to speak with Dr. Iverson."

"He's seeing patients all afternoon. I'm afraid he won't be available to speak to you until after four P.M.," she said with a practiced look of apol...

Liska pulled her ID out and thrust her badge at the woman. "This is police business in relation to an urgent missing persons situation. Dr. Iverson will see me now."

The staff on the other side of the counter all turned and looked at Liska with wide eyes, like a small herd of gazelles suddenly aware of a lioness in their midst.

The receptionist turned to a nurse in purple scrubs. "Angie, would you please tell Dr. Iverson—"

The nurse scurried back toward the exam rooms before she could finish the sentence.

Liska glanced off to the side, to the waiting area with its mood lighting and big-screen television quietly playing a travel show depicting someplace tropical. A mix of patients sat in the leather armchairs in varying stages of misery, coughing and sniffling. Several were looking at her. Others were absorbed in their magazines and cell phones.

The door to the exam area opened and the purple-suited nurse stuck her head out.

"The doctor will see you now," she said softly.

Liska followed her down the hall and into the doctor's private office. Iverson, a big, good-looking man in his fifties, had already taken his position behind his impressive desk. He rose from his seat and offered his hand.

"Bob Iverson."

"Sergeant Liska, Homicide," she said, holding her ID out in place of the handshake.

"Homicide?" he said, his brow furrowing. "Are we talking about the same case? Penny Gray? I spoke with her mother, Julia, this morning. I thought this was a missing person case."

"It was." Liska put the envelope with Penny Gray's X-rays on the immaculate desktop.

"I don't like the sound of that," he said. "Please have a seat, Sergeant."

Liska perched on the edge of a chair, back straight. The doctor lowered himself into his cushy executive's chair, his hands on the desktop as if physically bracing himself for bad news.

"Are you telling me Penny Gray is dead?" he asked.

"I'm not at liberty to tell you anything, Dr. Iverson. I need you to answer some questions for me regarding your treatment of Penny back in April of last year."

Iverson frowned. "I'm sure you're aware of patient privacy laws, Sergeant."

"As I am sure you are aware of the laws regarding physicians' needs to report child abuse to the proper authorities."

"Penny isn't abused!" he scoffed.

"Really? Because I had the assistant chief medical examiner look at these X-rays that were taken here in your office last April, and he tells me this injury is a spiral fracture, a torsion fracture resulting from a twisting of the limb. This is a common injury in cases of physical abuse. But neither the police department nor Family Services has a report on record regarding Penelope Gray."

"Because Penny was not abused," he insisted. "She took a nasty fall, twisting her arm as she came off the bike. There was no reason for me to report the incident. I've known Julia Gray for years. She's a lovely woman."

"Are you Penny's regular physician?" Liska asked.

"No. She's just at the age to switch over from her pediatrician."

"Do you have a pediatrician as part of this practice?"

"Yes."

"And is that pediatrician Penny Gray's doctor?"

"You'll have to ask her mother that question."

"According to the date on these X-rays, this incident happened on a Saturday. Most people have accidents on a weekend, they go to an ER," Liska said. "They don't call their family practitioner."

"This is a concierge practice," Iverson explained. "As you may have noticed when you came in the building, we have an urgent care facility, we have our own lab facilities. We are one-stop shopping for our clients. There was no need for Julia to take Penny to an ER on a spring weekend where they would have sat for hours before being seen."

"And you personally dropped what you were doing on a Saturday and came in and saw the girl when presumably she could have been taken care of by the on-call doc in your urgent care clinic?"

"Yes," he said with a defensive edge to his voice. "As I said, I've known Julia for years. Of course I would come in when she called me."

"And you believed the story about the bicycle."

"Why wouldn't I?"

"If you're such good friends with Mrs. Gray, then you're probably aware she and her daughter have a difficult relationship."

"I don't see what that has to do with falling off a bicycle."

"And when you saw the nature of Penny's injury, this didn't raise any questions in your mind?"

"No."

"Seriously? How many spiral fractures do you see in the course of your week, Dr. Iverson?" she asked. "How many fractures do you see at all? You're not an orthopedist, are you?"

"No."

"Yet you felt perfectly comfortable treating an unusual type of fracture."

"I worked in emergency medicine early in my career," he said. "I've treated every kind of fracture there is. Penny's break was clean enough to set and cast. It didn't require a specialist."

"That was very lucky for Penny, considering the nature of the injury," Liska said.

"Yes, it was lucky. Sometimes we get lucky."

"She's not lucky now."

"It's inconceivable that Julia has done something to her daughter," he said.

"Tell me, Dr. Iverson, if you hadn't known Julia Gray, if this had been a stranger and her daughter coming to you with that same injury . . . ?"

Iverson shrugged and sighed impatiently. "The point is moot. I *do* know Julia. I assume you've met her. Does she strike you as the kind of woman who would be physically violent with anyone?"

"I've been in this business for a long time, Doctor," Liska said. "I learned my first week on the job not to judge a book by its cover. But let's say for the sake of argument Julia Gray didn't break her daughter's arm. Let's say Penny's father did it, or Julia's boyfriend—"

"Michael? That's absurd!"

"Or one of Penny's boyfriends, or one of the sketchy people she runs with, or someone she encountered that day."

"She in no way indicated she had been attacked," Iverson said.

Liska nodded and rose, picking up the envelope with the X-rays back off the table. "Victims don't want to be victims, Doctor— especially victims of abuse. They often see it as . . . embarrassing . . . shameful . . . They blame themselves. They don't want to admit that someone in their life values them so little or hates them so much. Or they think they won't be believed because maybe their abuser seems above reproach. Which is why we have mandatory reporting laws. I'd be expecting a phone call about that if I were you."

30

Christina Warner looked up at Kovac with big, liquid, dark eyes, her expression soft and innocent. Her long white-blond hair was like something from a mermaid fantasy—tumbling waves framing her face and falling around her shoulders and down her back. Her complexion was peaches and cream, like an airbrushed photograph, complemented by the baby pink cashmere turtleneck sweater she wore.

"I want to do whatever I can to help find Gray," she said.

"Why is that, Christina?" Kovac asked bluntly. "The way I understand it, the two of you don't get along."

The big eyes blinked. She had expected him to be impressed with her generosity of spirit, but she adjusted to his reaction with ease.

"Well . . . we don't," she admitted. "But that doesn't mean I want something bad to happen to her."

"Why don't the two of you get along?"

"She's jealous," she said simply. "I'm popular and she's not. I have friends and she doesn't. I get along with my dad; she and her mom fight all the time."

"It sucks to be her," Kovac surmised. "How do you get along with Mrs. Gray?"

"Great," she said, smiling—a genuine reaction. "Julia is super-nice. We have fun together."

"You think maybe Penny resents that too—that you get along with her mom and she doesn't?"

"For sure."

"Right. 'Cause how's that supposed to work when your dad and Mrs. Gray get married? Everyone gets along with everyone—except Penny, who gets along with nobody."

"Obviously, we have some work to do in that area," Michael Warner said. "But there's no timetable. Julia and I haven't set a date. We're hoping Penny will come around in time."

He sat close beside his daughter with a hand resting reassuringly on her back.

"She makes me angry, but I feel sorry for her, really," Christina said.

"It doesn't sound to me like you were feeling sorry for her that night at the Rock and Bowl," Kovac said. "I've had several people tell me you were making fun of Gray and her poetry and that you and she got into it."

She bowed her head and looked up at him from under impossibly long dark lashes, contrite. "Of course I feel bad about that now. I didn't know she was going to disappear or whatever. I was just so mad at her—"

"Over what?"

"Some stuff she said about me in one of her stupid poems. She read it in front of half the school, practically. It was embarrassing and hurtful and mean."

"Penny is a talented writer," Michael Warner intervened. "She's very good at using words to hurt people, to anger people. Words are her weapons."

"Well," Kovac said, watching him carefully, "she's not big and strong enough to break somebody's arm, after all."

Warner narrowed his eyes. "What's that supposed to mean?"

"Everybody feels a need to strike out at some point in their life," Kovac said. "We get angry, we feel helpless, we feel bullied. It's a basic instinct to lash out at the one who hurt us. Right, Doc?"

"Figuratively speaking, I suppose, yes. But—"

"Were you around last spring when Penny broke her arm?"

"She took a bad fall off her bike," Warner said. "Yes, I do remember it. She was my patient at the time."

Kovac sighed and rubbed a hand across his jaw. "I know about the whole patient confidentiality thing and all, but did she ever indicate to you that maybe that really isn't what happened?"

"No. Why?"

"How about to you, Christina? Did you ever hear her say anything about that? Was there any gossip about that? Was Gray maybe hanging out with a rough crowd? A bad boyfriend? Anything like that?"

He watched the girl process the question. "She hangs out with some sketchy people outside of school—or so she says. I've never actually seen her with a boyfriend."

"Do you think someone attacked her?" Michael Warner asked.

"What about a girlfriend?" Kovac asked. "I'm hearing she had decided she was bisexual."

Christina rolled her eyes. "That's her latest thing. She's through with men. Now she's a lesbian or whatever. *Be who you are.* She's always saying that."

"You don't believe that's who she is? Or you don't like what that means?"

"If that's who she is, then why doesn't she just go hang out with the gay and lesbian kids?" she asked. "Why does she have to throw it in our faces all the time? One minute she's coming on to guys, the next minute she likes girls—"

"What guys was she coming on to? Eric? Jacob? Your guy, Aaron?"

"He's not interested in her," she said firmly. "He can't stand her, actually."

"I don't know," Kovac said. "I was sixteen once. If a girl is coming on to them, sixteen-year-old boys will overlook a lot."

She forced a little laugh and tried to look confident. "Believe me, Aaron isn't interested in Gray, and Gray isn't interested in Aaron."

"Was she interested in you, Christina?"

Michael Warner took exception. "Is this really an appropriate line of questioning?"

"What's appropriate?" Kovac asked, lifting his hands. "Anything that has the potential to help the investigation. No one has to like it. Gray claims to be bisexual, then I have to pursue that angle."

He turned back to Christina. She tried to look offended.

"No!"

"Jessica? Emily? Brittany?"

"No!" she said. She was getting flustered, cheeks blushing beneath the perfect makeup. "I don't even know if she really is into girls. She's probably just saying it to get a reaction. She just likes to mess with people. She's just so, so—"

"Antagonistic." Her father supplied the word. "And manipulative. That's a good point, Christina." He looked to Kovac again. "Penny feels a need to draw attention to herself. She gets the attention, then antagonizes the people giving it to her until they push her away. It's a self-fulfilling prophecy. She believes she is unlovable, so she goes around continually trying to prove that point by alienating people."

"So you wouldn't be surprised if someone broke her wrist," Kovac said.

"That's not what happened," Warner insisted.

"Were you there? Did you see her fall off the bike?"

"No, but I'm sure it was an accident. Julia said—"

"It might have been," Kovac conceded. "Stuff happens in the heat of the moment, right, Christina? Gray lashed out at you, you lashed out at her—all in the heat of the moment. That's what people do. They react. Sometimes it gets out of hand."

"I didn't break her wrist!" she said, alarmed that he might be accusing her. "I didn't do anything to her!"

"No, sweetheart," Kovac said, smiling like a kind distant uncle. "I don't think you broke her wrist, but I have reason to believe somebody did. And I mean to find out who. You say you want to help, so if you hear anything, if you think you might know someone who knows someone who knows something about it, you need to call me."

He held out one of his business cards for her. She took it and looked at it. Her fingernails were perfectly lacquered with glittering rose-pink polish.

"That night at the Rock and Bowl," Kovac said. "I heard things got a little physical, that Aaron got a little rough with Gray. Is that something he does? Smack girls around?"

"No! He was only protecting me!" she said dramatically. "Gray attacked me! She hit me and she scratched me!"

She pulled down the high neck of her sweater to reveal a trio of red marks on her skin.

"Aaron was in trouble here the other day for getting physical with another student," Kovac said.

"That wasn't his fault!"

"That's not how I heard it."

"Kyle Hatcher knocked *him* down," she said. "And kicked him too. And Kyle punched Aaron in the mouth that night at the Rock and Bowl too. *He's* the violent one."

Michael Warner leaned forward. "You can't seriously be considering any of these kids had something to do with what's happened to Gray? There's a serial killer running around loose! You should be out trying to find him, not accusing children, not accusing Julia!"

Kovac gave him a benign smile. "I'm paid to be suspicious of everyone, Dr. Warner. Don't take it personally."

"And in the meantime, there's a maniac running around the city abducting young women."

"We're on that."

"Really?" Warner asked. "How many unsolved homicides are being attributed to this man? Eight? Nine? Isn't that what I read? Penny could be the ninth girl this animal has hurt, and you're here questioning kids? You're questioning her mother? This is absurd!"

"If the tables were turned and your daughter was the one missing, would you want us to leave stones unturned?" Kovac asked.

"I would want you not to waste precious time," Michael Warner said, standing up. "And I'm not letting you waste any more of mine. Come on, Christina. We're going home."

"ALL THIS ANIMOSITY and rejection is going to fuck with my self-esteem," Kovac said as he watched them go. He rolled his shoulders back to loosen the knots and twisted his head to one side against the kink developing in his neck.

"I checked in with Elwood," Tippen said. "Still no luck finding the girl's car. He's tracking down her Facebook friends. Nothing is panning out so far. He's spoken to a couple of them. They claim they barely knew the girl."

"Why should we be surprised? The people who knew her her whole life don't seem to have a clue who she really was."

"Sometimes those are the people who know us the least," Tippen observed. "They have all that time to build us into who they want us to be in their heads so we can disappoint them over and over. Just ask my mother."

"Or any woman you've ever dated," Kovac said. "So far, this girl was nothing but an irritation and a disappointment to everyone she knew. Miss Acceptance."

"Life is full of little ironies."

"Yeah. I hate that," he said with a sigh. "Go talk to the girl's teachers. I'll see what more I can squeeze out of Brittany Lawler. We can both be thankful we're not Tinks. She's on her way to tell Julia Gray her daughter is dead."

LISKA PULLED ONTO Julia Gray's block to the too-familiar sight of TV news vans with satellite antennae raised and video cameramen roaming the street, looking for interesting angles and shots of curious neighbors. She had to slow the car to a crawl and open the window to hold up her ID—her pass to the end of the block and the Gray house.

The way the house was situated on the lot gave it a privacy that was a blessing and a curse. A blessing to Julia Gray, holed up inside, a curse to investigators. It was almost impossible to see the driveway or garage door from any other house in the neighborhood. Potential witnesses would probably have little to tell them about any vehicles parked at the Gray home on the night in question.

She pulled in the driveway beside a patrol car and behind Julia Gray's black Lexus and sat for a moment, recalling Jamar Jackson's scant description of the vehicle Penny Gray's body had fallen from New Year's Eve. A dark sedan. No make. No model.

Julia Gray drove a dark sedan. Penny Gray drove a dark sedan. Probably more than half of Minnesotans drove darker-colored vehicles. They were easier to see against the white backdrop of winter. White cars—popular everywhere south of the Northland—were undesirable here and were involved in a higher percentage of accidents during the winter.

Still . . . no coincidence was a good coincidence as far as Liska was concerned.

She got out and went to the patrol car, holding her ID up for the uniformed officer behind the wheel. He ran the window down.

"How's it been?" she asked, glancing to the street. Reporters were coming like hungry animals to food. She recognized several. The short guy from channel eleven, the perky blond girl from the early morning news, Dana Nolan.

"Quiet," the officer said. "Once we chased the riffraff off the property." He glanced in his rearview mirror and made a sound of disapproval. He flicked a switch on the dash, picked up the mike, and barked an order that blasted over the speakers into the street. "Stay back, folks! This is private property. Stay back!"

He shook his head and glanced up at Liska. "Fucking vultures."

"Is anyone in the house with Mrs. Gray?"

"I don't think so. I haven't seen anyone come or go since the boyfriend dropped her off. What's the news?"

"Bad."

"Damn. I've got a daughter myself," he said. "I don't even want to imagine. I don't envy you being the messenger, Sarge."

"Better giving that news than getting it," Liska said.

She went to the front door, rang the bell, and waited. And waited. And waited.

Maybe Julia Gray was sedated and asleep, she thought. Then again, what mother could sleep awaiting news of a missing child?

Kovac had told her Julia Gray had left her phone in her car while she'd been at the station half the morning, even though she had claimed to have gotten a text message from her daughter just the night before.

She rang the bell again, her mind racing as she waited. Who scraped up their kid from a bike accident and didn't go straight to an ER? A drug rep with long-standing relationships in the medical community? Maybe.

She rang the bell a third time, her nerves starting to itch. What kind of emotion choked a mother whose child went missing, whose last words to that child had been delivered in anger? As angry as she was with Kyle, she still felt guilty for being so hard on him that morning. To see him fight tears at her caustic recriminations was like pouring acid on her soul. If those had been her last words to him, Nikki would never have been able to live with herself.

Maybe Julia Gray wouldn't be able to either. Maybe she would take too many pills. Maybe she would slit her wrists.

As she began to think about getting one of the uniforms to kick in the door, it cracked open and Penny Gray's mother peered out at her with red-rimmed eyes.

Liska showed her ID. "Mrs. Gray? I'm Sergeant Liska. May I come in?"

Julia Gray stepped back from the door. She looked like she hadn't eaten or slept in a week. Her blond hair was pulled back into a messy ponytail. She wore yoga pants and a sweatshirt. Her hands were red and chapped, fingernail polish ruined. The brace on her injured right hand was soaking wet. She rubbed one hand and then the other with a limp white cotton towel.

"I'm sorry," Julia Gray said. "I was in the kitchen. I'm trying to keep busy. I don't know what to do."

"I'm sure it's hard. I have two boys. I don't know what I would do."

Julia Gray just stared at her. Nikki could see the question in her eyes—*Do you have news about my daughter?*—and she could see the fear of asking that question too. If she asked, she might get an answer she didn't want to hear.

"Can we sit down, Mrs. Gray?"

Julia Gray's swollen eyes widened in alarm. "No," she said, shaking her head. "No, I don't think so. You should probably just go."

Bad news was always preceded by *Can we sit down?* Or *We need to talk.* If they didn't sit down, then she could go on thinking maybe her daughter would still be coming home. If they sat down, the bad news would come out, and there would be no escaping it.

"I have to ask you a couple of questions," Nikki said, putting off the inevitable. Once she made the announcement, she would lose her opportunity to get the answers. "About when Penny broke her arm."

"She fell off her bike."

"Were you there when it happened?"

"No. She called me. She had her appointment with Michael that morning. She rode her bike over there. It's not far. It was one of the first nice spring days. She was on her way home. And . . . and she fell. She was cutting through the park. She called me, and I called Michael. He was closer."

"Why didn't you take her to the emergency room?" Nikki asked.

She looked confused by the question. "We called Bob Iverson. His practice is nearby."

"But it was a Saturday. He doesn't normally work Saturday, does he?"

"No. But I know him. Michael knows him too. He came in." Her eyes narrowed; confusion tugged across her brow. "I don't understand why you're asking me about this. He gave you the X-rays, didn't he?"

"Yes," Nikki said. "It just seems a little unusual—the circumstances. And the fracture was an unusual fracture. The ME told me it's the kind of break that happens from a twisting motion rather than a fall."

"Well, she fell," she insisted. Then she went very still as the letters ME penetrated. Her injured hand came up to massage her throat, as if she was suddenly having trouble swallowing. "What else did he have to say?"

Nikki sighed. "Please, Mrs. Gray," she murmured, trying to direct her toward the living room with its still-decorated Christmas tree. "Let's sit down."

Julia Gray stiffened. "No."

There was never any good way to do this, and it never got any easier no matter how many parents she had to disappoint. "The medical examiner has reviewed all the distinguishing marks and characteristics, along with the X-rays of your daughter's wrist, and compared them with the young woman—"

"No!" Julia Gray said again, more emphatically this time. Not as if in denial, but as if she was getting angry because Nikki clearly wasn't listening to her.

"There's really no question, Mrs. Gray," she said firmly. "Your daughter is deceased. I'm so sorry for your loss."

Penny Gray's mother looked frantically around the foyer, looking for help or some hidden escape route. Nikki could feel the electric energy coming off her in waves. She began to tremble visibly, first her hands, then her shoulders, her whole body stiffening like she was going into a seizure. Her face was as white as chalk.

Nikki put a hand on her shoulder. "Please, sit down, Mrs. Gray."

Julia Gray jerked back, eyes wild with pain. "Don't touch me! Get out! Get out of my house!"

"Mrs. Gray, please try to calm down—"

"Don't tell me to calm down!" she shouted. "Get out of my house! Get out! Get out! Get out!"

Like an animal blind with fear and pain, she bolted forward, swinging wildly with her injured hand, striking Nikki hard on the left eyebrow, slicing open the skin.

As blood ran down into her field of vision, Nikki threw her hands up too late to ward off the attack. She stumbled backward into the door, banging the back of her head against it.

"Get out! Get out! Get out!" Julia screamed over and over, incoherent, half sobbing, arms flailing like a toddler in a tantrum.

As she swung one arm down, Nikki caught her by the wrist. She pulled the woman's arm down between them and turned, stepping to the side and reversing their positions, putting Julia Gray's back against the door, and pinning her there with a shoulder to the woman's sternum.

Penny Gray's mother struggled for just a moment, then went limp, the adrenaline-fueled strength draining from her like water down a drain.

"Oh my God, oh my God, oh my God," she mumbled, dissolving into tears. "I can't believe this is happening! How can this be happening to me?"

"I'm sorry," Nikki murmured, lessening the pressure, letting Julia Gray's weight come more against her. She put her arms around the woman and just stood there, holding her—one mother offering comfort to another.

She wanted to tell Julia Gray that she would be all right, that eventually things would be okay, but it was a stupid thing to say, a completely empty, ridiculous promise to make. She knew that no matter what else happened in the coming days, no matter which way this case went, no matter who was responsible for the death of her daughter, Julia Gray would not be all right, and things would never be the same for her again.

31

"Dana Nolan, on special assignment, coming to you live from outside the residence of missing Minneapolis teenager Penelope Gray. Sources inside the Hennepin County Medical Examiner's office are confirming that the New Year's Eve murder victim known as Zombie Doe has been identified as the missing Performance Scholastic Institute student. An AMBER Alert was issued last night for the missing teen, whose mother made a public appeal for her return this morning along with Minneapolis Homicide captain Ullrich Kasselmann.

"No official statement has yet been made by the Minneapolis Police Department either confirming or denying the identification of Zombie Doe. Speculation has run rampant that Zombie Doe may in fact be yet another victim of the serial killer law enforcement has dubbed Doc Holiday, due to his penchant for committing his crimes on or around holidays."

"Doug Irwin here, Dana." The guy from the newsroom broke in. "There seems to be some activity going on there. Can you fill us in on what's been happening in the past few minutes?"

"Yes, Doug. One of the homicide detectives working the case was just seen arriving here at the residence and going into the home, presumably to convey some information to Julia Gray. I'll be coming to you live for *NewsWatch* with any breaking information as things develop. Until then, back to you at the studio, Doug."

Fitz smiled, almost like a proud uncle. He felt a connection to Dana Nolan that truly did border on familial. He had handpicked her, after all, like one of his flea market finds. She was a little diamond just waiting for polish and the perfect setting.

He was so pleased he had chosen her, especially now that she was getting an extra opportunity to make a name for herself by covering this case. There was a wonderful poetry in that. He had chosen her because of her initial reporting of the story of Zombie Doe, the alleged "ninth victim." Fate was allowing her to rise to the attention of the audience because of the ninth victim. And her greatest fame would ultimately come in being a victim. What a beautiful irony. It filled him with pride to be the architect of this story.

She stood there in front of the camera, so wide-eyed and earnest, her cheeks rosy with the cold. So young. So . . . wholesome. She didn't understand what tragedy was. She didn't know what it meant to feel real pain or experience true loss. She observed others and tried to guess what that must be like. Or she tried to relate her own small version of personal catastrophe to these incidents. Maybe she had lost a kitten as a little girl. Maybe an elderly grandparent had died.

She had so much to learn about genuine suffering.

And he would be the one to teach it to her.

Soon.

32

"When I told you to take up cage fighting, I was being sarcastic," Kovac said, looking at his partner.

Her left brow was a red, swollen ledge. A couple of small stitches closed the cut Julia Gray had opened.

Liska made a face. "I guess I need to start joining Kyle at his kickboxing lessons."

"Muay Thai," Tippen said, striking a martial arts pose. "The deadly art of eight limbs."

"Tinks is deadly enough with four," Kovac said. "And that's not counting her tongue."

"Fuck you, Kojak."

"And there it is."

They had gathered again in the conference room. Someone had picked up Chinese takeout, and the boxes littered the long table. Kovac found the beef with broccoli and helped himself. He couldn't remember the last time he'd eaten a real meal.

He looked at his partner. "So she just wigged out on you?"

"She was ready to snap when I got there. She saw bad news coming, and she didn't want to hear it."

"All her chickens are coming home to roost under a big media spotlight," Kovac said. "Her daughter is missing. Her daughter is an embarrassment. Her daughter makes her look like a bad mother. Now her daughter is dead."

"That's not entirely fair," Liska said. "You've never given birth. You can't know what it's like. You get this perfect little being, and then life happens, and suddenly you feel like you don't have any control anymore. And you screw up and they screw up, but they're still your kid. I don't ever want to know what Julia Gray is feeling now. I'm sure she's reliving every mistake she ever made."

"No more do-overs," Kovac said, wondering how much of a mess he would have made raising his kid if he'd gotten the chance. It was probably better not knowing.

He looked to one of his borrowed uniform cops, a burly kid named Adams. "What do the neighbors have to say?"

"We canvassed the neighborhood twice—first thing this morning and at the end of the day. Nobody saw anything out of the ordinary. Even the closest neighbors don't have a clear view of the Grays' driveway because of the way the house is situated. One close neighbor has a security camera on their garage that might catch some coming and going, but they're out of town. The security company needs a release from the owners to give us access to the video. They're working on that.

"Also, one of the neighbors had a New Year's Eve party with a lot of cars parked on the street. That was the thing everyone remembered. No one could really recall the night before that."

"Elwood, what about the girl's Facebook friends?"

"I tracked down a few who live in the area. It seems they didn't really know her that well. They said she came and hung out at a couple of coffeehouses they all frequent. They liked her poetry, but she's a lot younger than most of them."

"So she was building up those relationships that she didn't really have to the kids at school to make it look like she was cool somewhere, if not with them," Liska said.

Elwood nodded. "That's how it looks. A couple of them let her sleep at their places when she was on the outs with her mother. But they've got alibis for New Year's Eve."

"I would rather come back in my next life as a sewer rat than have to be a teenager again," she muttered.

Kovac set his plate aside and sighed. "And we've got no legit sightings of the girl's car?"

"Do you know how many black Toyota Camrys there are in the Twin Cities?" one of the young detectives asked. "To say nothing of other makes that resemble the Toyota Camry. The majority of people don't seem to know one car from another. We've got every agency available checking the tips. It's not a needle in a haystack. It's a needle in a pile of needles."

The lack of progress was tiring. They were expending tremendous amounts of energy and manpower with no reward. As much as Kovac had wanted the opportunity to renew efforts on the rest of the Doc Holiday cases, the effort was spreading them too thin. He had detectives reviewing the old cases with new eyes, but now he would have preferred to have more attention on the case at hand. A cold case wouldn't get any colder, but the window of opportunity on a fresh homicide was small.

The phrase *be careful what you ask for* kept playing through his head.

The blessing and the curse of the previous Doc Holiday cases had been in the fact that the victims were from other places, other states. Difficult to investigate, and yet without a great deal of complication from the victims' family lives—at least on his end of the investigation.

If Doc had snatched Penny Gray, he could have done them all a favor by dumping her in Iowa.

Kasselmann stepped into the room—still looking crisp and together, wanting an update.

Calling on the energy induced by sodium and MSG, Kovac roused himself to go up to the whiteboard and conduct a proper review of what they had, what they didn't have, what they wanted, and what they needed to do.

Bottom line: They had a whole lot of nothing that added up to a strong suspect.

The captain frowned and sighed. "Come see me in my office before you go, Sam."

His frown deepened as he looked at Liska. "What happened to you?"

"The victim's mother decided to kill the messenger," she said.

"The Gray woman did that to you?"

"She's stronger than she looks."

"How about that?" Kovac asked when Kasselmann and most of the others had cleared out.

"How about what?" Liska busied herself clearing away the food cartons and paper plates.

"Julia Gray giving you that eye. You'll be lucky if you don't have a shiner tomorrow."

"I'd probably lose it too, if I was in her place."

"She hit you with her right hand?" he asked. "The one in the brace?"

"Yeah," she said. "She wasn't thinking clearly. Or maybe she wanted to feel physical pain too. You know? I'd rather hit my thumb with a hammer than feel emotional pain because of one of my kids."

"Remind me to follow you home, then, and remove all the hammers from your house."

She gave him the finger.

Kovac turned to Tippen and Elwood. "I don't buy her story about falling on the ice. It's too coincidental."

Liska dumped the last of the trash in the garbage can. "I don't buy the story about the girl falling off the bike, and the whole thing about the mom calling her doctor friend on a Saturday. Dr. Concierge setting a weird fracture instead of sending the kid to a specialist. That's a malpractice suit waiting to happen. Why would he risk that?"

"What was the mother's explanation?" Tippen asked.

"That the girl was on her way home from her therapy session with Michael Warner. She cut through some park, had an accident."

"No witnesses," Elwood said.

Liska shrugged.

Kovac scowled. "That's funny. I asked Michael Warner about it. He didn't say anything about having seen the girl the day that happened."

"Julia made it sound like taking the girl to the doctor she used was a joint decision," Liska said.

"That was back in the spring, right?" Elwood said. "She also told us a lot of her daughter's rebellion developed over the summer."

"If the girl didn't fall off a bike, then what happened?" Tippen asked. "Some kind of precipitating stressor that set off the rebellion?

"I spoke with Penny Gray's adviser at school," he said. "She told me the girl's writing had taken an angrier tone this school year. She said the girl had always been an outsider, had trouble relating to other kids, but she used to be more shy than aggressive."

Kovac got up and went to the board, looking at the timeline they had started. He picked up a marker and extended the line far to the left, then added the date of the alleged bike accident. He made a notation about the changes in the girl's appearance over the summer, and the date of the violent incident with the father's new wife at the open house. He made note of Julia Gray's alleged fall that had injured her wrist.

He stood back and looked at what he'd written. A suspicious injury. A dramatic change in appearance. Escalating violent outbursts. He thought about the comment Christina Warner had made regarding Penny Gray's change in sexual preference—that she said she was through with men . . . a girl who hadn't had a significant boyfriend as far as anyone knew.

"You know what this looks like," he said.

"That our precipitating stressor could be sexual abuse," Tippen offered.

"What do we know about Dr. Feel Good?"

"That he is a man above reproach," Elwood said.

"That makes him a bastard, for sure," Kovac muttered.

"He's got nothing but accolades in the press. Awards out the wazoo for community service and so on."

"That makes him a man with a lot to lose," Kovac said. "Big reputation. Big ego. Big ambition. Dig deeper on him. And I want another talk with him—preferably with Julia Gray present. We'll twist those screws good and hard."

A knock sounded on the door, and Sonya Porter stuck her head in, small oval rhinestone-crusted glasses framing her eyes.

"Welcome to the nuthouse, Sonya," Kovac said, waving her in. "Come have a seat. I don't think you've met Elwood. Elwood Knutson, this is Sonya Porter—Tip's niece."

Elwood got up and made a little bow. "I'm so sorry."

Tippen made a disgruntled face. "Why is no one sorry for me? She's mean!"

Sonya batted her eyelashes at Elwood as she shrugged out of her coat. She wore a peacock-blue sweater with a keyhole cutout in the chest, exposing a tantalizing glimpse of her tattoo.

"Do you have anything for us, Sonya?" Kovac asked. "Anything coming in from the blogosphere or the Twitterverse or whatever the hell it is? A confession would be nice, but I'd settle for an eyewitness."

"I can't make your job that easy," she said, taking the empty seat next to Elwood. He held the chair out for her. "A lot of sensational rumors about the zombie. Some unpleasant comments about your victim."

"Such as?"

"She was a whore. She was a lesbian. She was a lesbian whore," she said dispassionately. "Everybody hated her, and nobody cares if she's dead."

"Charming generation you've got there," Kovac mumbled.

"Kids have opinions," she said. "They're not shy about sharing them on social media."

"No," Tippen said. "It's more like a shark feeding frenzy. Rapacious animosity hidden behind the faceless mask of anonymity. Cyberbullying is rampant. The physical disconnect from the victim gives the bully the false sense of freedom to say whatever they want."

"Their computer isn't going to punch them in the face for typing something hateful," Liska said.

"Just because people have the right to freely express themselves doesn't guarantee they'll have something nice to say," Sonya said. "Ultimately, a lot of people just suck. With social media we get to see instantly who those people are."

"That's my niece," Tippen said. "Always looking for the silver lining."

"There is no silver lining," she returned. "Just the reflection of abject disappointment."

"I prefer to shine a light in the darkness," Elwood said nobly. Sonya looked up at him with her head cocked to one side like a curious little bird.

"I'm with Sonya," Kovac said. "People suck. Shine your light on that, Elwood. Get with Sonya and figure out who the cyberbullies are."

"I was also thinking we might be able to put together a clearer picture about what was going on in Penny Gray's emotional life by looking more closely at her poetry," Elwood suggested. "Poetry is a fingerprint of the soul."

Tippen picked up a file folder off the table. "The girl's adviser gave me access to all the work Penny Gray has turned in this school year. She sent me the whole file electronically. I printed out the poems. There are also some video pieces of her performing."

"If she's into visual media, she'll be on YouTube and Vimeo," Sonya said.

Elwood took the folder from Tippen and opened it. Kovac watched him frown as he looked over the first of the poems of Penny Gray.

"Share with the class, please, Elwood."

The big man cleared his throat and read the poem aloud, the words of a girl who believed no one wanted to hear her. She could never have imagined that she would find her audience among the people trying to solve her murder.

"Silence"

Silence is golden, I hear people say
But words rot inside you
Your heart will decay
They don't want your trouble, they don't
want to care
You're just inconvenient
They don't want you there.
I've learned to stay silent on matters like
this
Absolve them of burden
Give ignorant bliss.
And still I'm more bother than I ever was
worth
I'm nothing but trouble
Since the day of my birth.

33

"Are you okay to drive?" Kovac asked.

They walked toward the parking ramp, flurries coming down like fine powdered sugar. It was later than she wanted it to be. Again. Her head was pounding. She was cold and tired and weighed down by the heaviness of the case and everything else in her life. She felt as if she were made of lead.

"I'm fine," she said. She could feel him looking at her.

"Seriously? You don't have a concussion?"

"No. It's just a cut. I got hit by a girl, not Mike Tyson."

"You're a girl," he pointed out. "I don't want you coldcocking me."

"Yeah, well . . . What did Kasselmann want?" She had watched him go into the boss's office after their session in the war room had ended. He had come out with a dark expression on his face.

"Nothing important." He shrugged it off but then said, "I'm coming home with you."

She looked up at him, surprised. "What? Why? I'm fine."

His mouth twisted a little in that way that told her he was figuratively chewing on something he didn't like.

"I have to confiscate your hammers, remember?"

She waited for the other shoe to drop.

"I need to speak to Kyle again," he said. "I don't think we have the whole picture of what went on at the Rock and Bowl."

Nikki narrowed her eyes in suspicion. "You're leaving something out."

"You're reading something in," he countered. "I just want to clarify a few details, that's all. A couple of the kids today made comments I want to follow up on."

"You know those are the kids Kyle doesn't get along with."

"I know."

"That Fogelman kid," she said, her protective instincts rising. "He's a spoiled, entitled little shit."

"I know."

"Did he say Kyle did something?" she asked.

Kovac looked annoyed. "Will you relax?"

"No," she said, stopping in her tracks. "I won't. Tell me what's going on."

Kovac turned around and sighed. "Don't flip out on me."

"You might as well say 'Flip out now.' What the hell is going on?"

"Kasselmann called me in to let me know the Fogelman kid's father is connected and that he made some noise to an assistant chief that maybe Kyle is getting preferential treatment because he wasn't included in the group I questioned this afternoon."

"Fuck him!" Nikki snapped. "And fuck Kasselmann too! Why didn't he call *me* into his office? Why didn't he speak to *me*?"

"I can't imagine," Kovac said sarcastically. "Fear of death? Conflict of interest? Take your pick. I told the boss there's not a problem. I explained the situation. Everything is cool for now. I'm just dotting the i's and crossing the t's. So let's just get on with it."

Despite Kovac's assurances, she worried all the way home. It was becoming her default state of being—worrying about the boys, that she was missing out on their lives, that she wasn't giving them what they needed; worrying about Kyle in particular, that he would lose his scholarship, be expelled from PSI, get so deep into something that by the time she found out about it, it would be too late to stop something bad from happening.

Marysue sat at the dining table, addressing wedding invitations while R.J. grudgingly did his math homework. Nikki bent over and kissed the top of her son's tousled head. The usual pleasantries were exchanged, the cursory "How was your day?" small talk that seemed so ridiculous when she was knee-deep in a murder investigation. Kovac joined in, as much a part of the surrealism as anyone.

The samurai warrior greeted them at the door to Kyle's room. Liska looked the fierce image in the eye and tapped her knuckles against the door.

"Kyle? It's Mom. I need to talk to you. Sam needs to talk to you."

No sound came from the room, no TV, no music. She held her breath and listened, resisting the urge to knock again too quickly. She could hear him moving around. He opened the door and looked from one of them to the other without saying anything. He looked tired and sad. The bruise on his cheek was dark purple against his pale skin.

"Hey, Kyle," Kovac said. "Sorry I have to bother you again, but I need to ask you a couple more questions about the other night at the Rock and Bowl."

"Gray's dead, isn't she?" he said flatly.

Kovac nodded. "It looks that way. I'm sorry."

Kyle moved back into his room and sat down on his desk chair, bent over with his forearms resting on his thighs and his head down.

"How did you hear?" Nikki asked, struggling against the urge to touch him.

"Someone texted me."

She didn't scold him for being on his phone. What had seemed so important that morning seemed petty and foolish now. Whatever he had done, whatever trouble he had gotten himself into, at least he was alive.

Kovac sat down on the foot of the bed and, consciously or not, mirrored Kyle's pose.

He began with a sigh. "I've talked to everyone who was there that night Gray went missing. There are a couple of holes and discrepancies I think you can help me out with, Kyle. But here's the deal: no more fucking around, okay? I ask you a straight question, you give me a straight answer, no bullshit. You don't shade the truth and you don't leave things out. Man-to-man time, okay?"

"Nothing you say will be used against you by me," Nikki said, drawing a glance from her son.

"Kyle, did you ride to the Rock and Bowl with Gray and Brittany that night?"

He nodded.

"Tell me what happened between Gray and Christina."

"Christina had made up this stupid poem about liars and lesbians and how Gray is a walking freak show and shit like that. Gray got pissed and said some things back."

"What did she say?"

"Like how Christina is such a stupid bitch because she thinks everybody loves her, and nobody loves her at all because she's a fake, egotistical c-u-n-t." He glanced up. "Sorry, Mom. Sam said not to leave anything out."

"It's okay."

"She said something like you think you're living this Barbie doll dream life with your perfect everything," he went on. "And you think your dad's a fucking Ken doll. Stuff like that."

"And at some point things got physical between them?" Kovac said.

Kyle nodded. "Yeah. Gray kind of leaned in and said something I couldn't hear, and Christina went ape shit and lunged at her."

Kovac sat up straighter. "Christina lunged at Gray?"

"Yeah."

"You're sure?"

"Yeah. I mean, Gray fought back, but Christina started it. Then Aaron Fogelman got between them and he punched Gray about here," he said, bringing his fist against his upper left chest.

"And then?"

"And then I got between them. I mean, you can't hit a girl!" Kyle said, offended by the very idea. "I shoved him back; then he took a swing at me," he said, pantomiming the bigger kid's knuckles grazing his cheekbone. "And then I popped him in the mouth and busted his lip," he said, reenacting his overhand right.

"And where was security during all of this?" Nikki asked, unable to bite her tongue any longer.

Kyle shrugged. "It happened really fast. And then I turned around and Gray had left, and by the time I got to the front door, she was driving out."

"Did you see the others leave?" Kovac asked.

"No."

"How did you get home?" Nikki asked.

"There's a bus stop a couple of blocks down."

"And you didn't talk to Gray or hear from her after that?"

He shook his head. "I texted her a bunch of times, but she never answered. I even tried to call her, but it went straight to voice mail." He thought about it for minute, the terrible realization dawning. "I guess she was already dead, huh?"

Kovac sighed. "She might have been, yeah."

"Britt said a serial killer got her. Is that for real?" he asked, incredulous. "That's crazy! That's crazy movie shit!"

"We don't know what happened," Nikki said. "That's a possibility."

"I don't get it," Kyle said, emotion straining his voice. "Why does somebody do that? That's so insane! She never hurt anybody. All she ever wanted was to be . . . was for people to just accept her. Why did somebody have to do that to her?"

Nikki stroked a hand over his bowed head and gently pulled him to lean against her. Looking down, her gaze fixed on his bruised cheek. Her mind went back over what he had said.

Penny Gray had gone missing the night of the thirtieth. Kyle's altercation with Aaron Fogelman had happened on the thirtieth. Yet, she hadn't noticed the damage to her son until New Year's Day. How was that even possible?

She thought back, sorting through the blur of work hours and overtime. They had caught a homicide the night of the thirtieth, a domestic dispute that had turned deadly. The whole thing had been complicated and had dragged on, and she hadn't gotten home until late. The boys had been in bed by the time she got home. They had still been asleep when she left for work the next morning, the morning of New Year's Eve, and in bed by the time she got home from the callout to Zombie Doe's scene.

She had lost an entire day without even realizing it. Her son had been hurt a full day before she had even noticed.

She thought about Julia Gray, who hadn't known her own daughter was missing. How irresponsible that sounded. How uncaring. What a rotten mother.

She thought of Penny Gray and the possibility that she had been snatched off the street while her mother was too busy out with her boyfriend to know where her daughter was.

In her mind's eye she watched the video from the Holiday station play out across her memory. Penny Gray—a kid the same age as Kyle—alone, headed for the door, seeing someone out of camera range, hesitating, turning back, then walking out into the night to never be seen alive again.

Leaving Kyle to his thoughts, she walked Sam back downstairs. Marysue and R.J. had fallen asleep on opposite ends of the couch. The television whispered to itself.

Nikki was silent as they stood in the hall at the front door and she listened to Kovac run through his thoughts on Kyle's chronology of events, what he wanted to clarify, who they needed to talk to. He wanted to go back over all the video from the Rock & Bowl, from the Holiday station. He wanted to speak again to Christina Warner, but he knew Michael Warner wouldn't allow it. He wanted to know what Penny Gray had said that had flipped Christina's switch.

It was all just noise in the background. She felt as if she were hearing him from far away. A weird numbness ran through her like some kind of IV lidocaine.

Kovac finally hooked a knuckle under her chin and picked her head up. She expected to see irritation, but that wasn't it at all. She saw concern and caring.

"Hey," he said softly. "I'm sorry this is hitting where you live, Tinks."

Pain shivered through the numbness. "It's hard," she whispered.

"I know," he said. "Let me give you that hug you asked for."

And she put her head against his chest and let him hold her for a long, quiet time.

AFTER SAM HAD GONE, Nikki went back up the stairs to knock once more on Kyle's door.

He tucked his phone under his pillow as she let herself into his room. He sat on his bed, backed up against the headboard, looking forlorn. Nikki sat down on the edge of the bed.

"I'm so sorry about your friend," she said softly.

"We weren't really friends," he said. "Gray didn't really have friends like other people. She was kind of . . . alone . . . inside her-self."

Like you, Nikki thought. Locked up inside himself, careful not to let anybody in too far.

"I knew her," he said. "We hung out sometimes. She was cool in a lot of ways."

"Yeah? Like how?"

"With her poetry, and wanting people to just be who they are and let other people do their own thing."

That would appeal to Kyle, she thought. He had always marched to his own drummer, even when he was small. He had always been sensitive to the feelings of other kids, had always spent much time in thought and contemplation.

He reached under his pillow and pulled out his phone. He tapped on the screen and navigated his way to what he wanted.

"She was always making videos with her phone," he said. "She shot this one during the writer's workshop and sent it to me."

He touched Play and showed Nikki the screen. "We had to inter-view each other about what made us want to be writers."

The camera focused first on Gray as she introduced herself and explained the purpose of the interview. Then she turned the camera on Kyle while he answered the question. He fidgeted and looked away and scowled, never liking to have his picture taken or to have the moment captured on a video. Gray came back on the screen while she answered. She spoke about how it made her feel to write a poem—like she was opening a window to her soul and letting the feelings escape. Sometimes they were good feelings, and sometimes they weren't. Sometimes it felt as if she opened a vein and bled the words out.

Nikki watched with a sad heart, wishing she could have known this girl, wishing some adult in Penny Gray's life would have cared enough to help her, to listen to her troubles and try to understand. She remembered herself at that age, feeling lost and misunderstood. It was hard to be sixteen, when every little thing seemed a matter of life and death, and the future was too far away to believe none of the immediate crises would mean much at all. She hadn't gotten that kind of understanding from her own mother, and neither had Penny Gray.

She handed the phone back to Kyle as the video ended. "You know, I'm proud of you for sticking up for her the way you did that night at the Rock and Bowl."

He shrugged one shoulder, looking down. "It's not right to hit a girl. None of that was right."

"The other girl, Brittany, do you know her very well?"

"I thought I did." He sighed. "People are disappointing."

"They can be. It's not always easy to do the right thing. Sometimes it's not so easy to know what the right thing is. Sometimes we just do the best that we can."

He shook his head a little. "Sometimes people just do what's easy or what other people want them to. For all the wrong reasons."

She couldn't argue.

"I wish I could have stopped Gray that night," he said, his eyes filling with tears. "If I could have caught her before she drove out, maybe she'd still be alive."

Nikki put a hand on his forearm and squeezed. "You can't think that way, Kyle. A lot of things happened that night. That was just the last one that you know of.

"It's like in a football game when the kicker misses that last-second field goal and everybody wants to blame him for losing the game. But there were a thousand things that happened before that moment that could have changed everything. Nobody thinks about those moments. A missed catch, a bad tackle, a penalty that shouldn't have happened. All of those things were equally crucial. They just weren't the last thing that happened.

"So maybe, yes, if you had caught Gray before she left, if you had gotten in the car with her, maybe she'd be alive today—or maybe you'd both be gone. But there are a lot of other maybes. Maybe if the girls hadn't gotten into a fight. Maybe if your friend Brittany had made a better choice. Maybe, maybe, maybe.

"There are so many maybes," she said. "Maybe if we could have solved this killer's first murder or second. Maybe if he had turned left instead of right at an intersection he never would have met your friend. It's not just about what you did or didn't do, or what I did or didn't do, or even what Gray did or didn't do.

"We try to make sense of things that can't be made sense of. All we can do is the best that we can. The rest is out of our hands. And if our best wasn't good enough, we try harder the next time."

"Gray doesn't get a next time," he said quietly.

"No. But all we can do now is try our best to catch her killer."

"When you said you texted Gray and tried to call her. Was that the night she went missing or after that too?" Nikki asked.

"After too," he said. He dug his phone out and checked the text messages he had sent to the girl. "I tried to text her this morning. I kept thinking she just went off somewhere to be alone. I thought maybe if I kept bugging her, she would answer."

Nikki absorbed that and put it away in her head, too tired to think it might be significant. All she could think was that she was raising one hell of a good human being and that it was a pure damn miracle considering how little time she spent doing it.

"I love you so much," she said, hugging him.

Kyle hugged her back. "I love you too, Mom. I'm really sorry about this morning."

"Me too," she said, squeezing him tighter. "We'll both do better tomorrow, right?"

That was the thought she carried with her to bed. That they would all do better tomorrow. And hopefully that would mean finding Penny Gray's killer.

34

How f'd up was that 2day? Cops! :0

Brittany sat on her bed, tucked up against the headboard, her legs curled beneath her, unconsciously making herself small. She looked at the text from Christina, not wanting to answer. She'd had a stomachache ever since the afternoon, ever since she had to talk again with the police.

She couldn't believe any of this was really happening. How could someone she knew get murdered? How could she be involved in something so sick and twisted and crazy? All she'd done was try to be friends with a girl she felt sorry for. She was a good person. She tried to do the right thing. Usually. It was just that sometimes that was so much harder than it should have been.

She couldn't stop feeling responsible for what had happened to Gray. It was her fault they had gone to the Rock & Bowl that night. She should have just told Christina no. Or better yet, she should have just ignored Christina's text messages.

She was so stupid, always answering her texts like somebody was watching her and would know that she hadn't turned her phone off or left it in her purse or something. How pathetic was she? So desperate to be liked by Christina that she jumped every time Christina looked her way. Why couldn't she be stronger? Why couldn't she be more like Kyle?

Kyle didn't care that the cool kids didn't like him. Or if he cared, he cared more about his integrity and being true to himself. He had pushed her to do the same, but she wasn't like Kyle. She wasn't strong. She wasn't brave. The idea of not being liked, not being popular, was terrifying to her. And look where that had gotten her.

Her phone vibrated again in her hand. Another message from Christina.

Where R U? R U OK?

Even as she told herself not to, her thumbs moved over the keyboard.

OK.

Can U Blieve it? A serial killer! It could've been any of us!

No, it couldn't, Brittany thought, angry. It couldn't have been any of them. They had been with each other. Only Gray had gone off alone. Because of the rest of them. Nothing like that would ever happen to Christina Warner because she was always the center of attention, always surrounded by the people who feared and adored her.

No. It would happen to Gray, who had nobody to prevent it and nobody to care afterward. Gray, who counted Brittany as a friend. One of her only friends. They weren't close the way Brittany had been close with other friends in her life. They didn't confide secrets in each other the way best friends usually did. And yet Gray had chosen to come to her after the last fight with her mother.

And look what I did to her.

Brittany looked over by the big chair in the corner of her room where Gray's duffel bag sat on the floor, half-hidden by a menagerie of stuffed animals. She should take it back to Gray's mom, she supposed. The idea of facing Gray's mother made her feel sick.

Hello, Mrs. Gray. I'm Brittany. I'm the reason your daughter is dead. Here's her stuff.

Her phone vibrated again. She wanted to throw it across the room, but she didn't. Gray would have. No. Gray would have typed *FUCK U* and then thrown it across the room. Brittany looked at the message.

What did they ask U? what did U tell them?

I told them you're a bitch, Brittany thought. *I told them you're mean. I told them it's my fault Gray got killed because it was my fault she was there.* Of course she hadn't told them any such thing. She had told the detective the same thing everyone had told the detective. What difference did it make, anyway? Gray had gone out into the night alone, never to be seen again. That was all that mattered.

She looked down at her phone and typed *Nothing.*

Her stomach cramped like a fist. *You make me sick,* she thought, though she wasn't sure if the thought was directed at Christina or herself.

All Christina was worried about was how this made her look. It had to be Gray's fault that Christina had made up that horrible poem. Gray had to be the bad one for starting the fight between them. It had to be Gray who lunged at Christina because God forbid anyone thought Christina would lose her cool and do something like that. But she had.

It was Christina who had started everything that night. It was Christina who had planned the whole thing, Christina who had humiliated Gray, Christina who had flipped out and thrown herself at Gray.

It was Christina who had told everybody to say that Gray attacked her. She didn't want to look bad. She didn't want to get in trouble. She didn't want her precious creepy father to think the sun didn't rise and set on her. And if Gray was dead anyway, what did it matter that they made her look bad? She *was* bad.

At least she wasn't a hypocrite, Brittany thought, *like you, Christina. Like me.*

The phone buzzed again.

Did U tell what she said?

Did I tell them Gray said you're a phony and a fake, and everything she said about your phony fake Barbie doll life? That people don't really like you, that they hate you behind your back but they're too afraid to say it?

Did I tell them the truth?

She texted back: *No.*

Brittany wanted to scream. She pictured herself like Gray had been that night—in Christina's face, shouting at her. *It's not about you, Christina! No one cares how this makes you look. No one cares if Gray had sex with your boyfriend or father or you or anyone else.*

Her phone buzzed in her hand yet again.

UR the best Britt. I <3 U.

Me 2 U, she typed. Then she turned her phone off, went into the bathroom, and threw up.

35

Fitz had grown up the child of a single mother who had spent all her free time in the local American Legion tavern, shooting pool and tequila and picking up men. In contrast to her lifestyle, she had enrolled Fitz in the Cub Scouts and then the Boy Scouts.

Of course, he had seen that for what it was: a conduit to men who didn't hang out at the American Legion. Still, he had applied himself to the role of Scout, taking advantage of the opportunity to learn interesting things, like how to tie knots, how to use a knife and an ax, and, most important, to always be prepared.

He took his time getting ready, making certain everything was in place, that he was forgetting nothing. He had to be especially diligent in his planning and execution because he was deviating from his normal way of doing things. This was when mistakes could be made if he wasn't careful.

He would be using his small van. He never used the small van. When he worked on the road, he used the box truck, which was set up for the purpose. He went through the van methodically, checking his tie-downs, arranging the blanket, making sure the duct tape was where he needed it to be.

He double-checked the small gear bag on the passenger's seat. Hand tools, knife, plastic zip ties. Good to go.

The adrenaline was beginning to flow. He couldn't rest. He couldn't sit down. He was like a shark, moving constantly, as he visualized what would happen tonight. He could feel the cold air on his face, freezing his nose hair. He could see Dana Nolan's face—the split second of confusion, then the spark of recognition, then the flash of fear and panic.

He could the feel the rush of power, the sexual excitement. He went through the scenario over and over in his head.

This too was different for him. He had always trolled for victims, capitalizing on opportunity. The adrenaline rush was quick and explosive. This excitement of anticipation was almost too much to stand.

He checked his watch.

Go time.

Careful to stay just under the speed limit and to obey all traffic laws, he drove to Dana Nolan's apartment complex. He made sure not to arrive too early. He backed the van into the parking spot beside her car and settled in to wait under the harsh glow of the security light.

Every second seemed like a minute. He tried to listen to the radio. Music annoyed him. People talking annoyed him. He worked on taking slow, deep breaths, concentrating on trying to lower his heart rate. He had once read that Shaolin monks could use their minds to slow their heart rates to practically nothing.

He checked his watch.

He tried the radio again. Hits from the eighties. Hits from the nineties. Hits from today. NPR. Delilah.

He was a sucker for Delilah. He found it kind of comforting that no matter where he traveled, he could always get Delilah's syndicated show on the radio. It was like traveling with a friend.

She had a soothing voice. There was something sweet about all her corny love talk. He didn't believe in any of it—not for himself, at least. An argument could be made that falling for the idea of true love made people weak and ultimately miserable. Still, he listened to Delilah.

She was talking about love being an action rather than an emotion when Dana Nolan emerged from her apartment building.

Fitz took the small bottle of chloroform out of his coat pocket and poured some on a washcloth as he watched her come toward him. He stuck the washcloth in his pocket and got out of the van, keeping his head down, and opened the hood as if he was having engine trouble. As she got within earshot, he groaned: "Oh, man! Not again!"

He stepped back from the vehicle and flopped his arms helplessly at his sides.

"I can't believe this!"

He could see her in his peripheral vision. She had slowed down but was still coming toward him. He heaved a big sigh and shook his head at his phony misfortune as he turned in her direction and began to trudge toward the buildings, hands in his coat pockets, shoulders hunched against the cold.

"Dead battery!" he said.

She was going to walk right past him; she had quickened her step, anxious about meeting someone in the parking lot at this time of night.

Fitz slowed down. "Miss, you couldn't help me out with a jump start, could you? I've got cables. My wife is going to kill me."

She glanced at him, slowed her step. She looked a little annoyed, a little uncertain. Then there it was—the spark of recognition.

"Oh, hey!" he said, feigning surprise. "What the heck? You're Dana! Oh my God! Remember me? Fitz. From the Holiday station."

She relaxed a little, stopped moving. "Oh, yeah."

They were just a few steps from the van.

"What are the odds of this?" Fitz asked, chuckling. He moved back toward the van. "I hate to impose, Dana, but if you could just give me a jump—"

She hesitated. "Oh, gee, I'm really sorry," she said. "I have to get to work."

"It'll just take a second," Fitz said, opening the sliding side door of the van. He leaned inside as if to get the jumper cables.

"Hey, I saw you on the news this afternoon," he said. "You're covering that missing girl case. That's something, huh? Did she turn out to be that dead girl? The zombie?"

"It looks that way," she said, coming a little closer.

Even if she didn't want to help him, she had to come closer to get to the driver's side door of her car. She was only a few feet away.

"That's terrible," Fitz said. "Some lunatic going around abducting young women. What's the world coming to?"

In the next second he turned and lunged at her, and that familiar panic flashed in her eyes. She tried to turn away. He grabbed her ponytail in his left hand and shoved her backward into the side of her car, pinning her there. She tried to draw breath to scream, and he shoved the chloroform washcloth over her mouth and nose.

The struggle was over in seconds. He had only to turn with her in his arms and shove her inside the van. He went in after her and slid the door shut behind him.

Duct tape across the mouth.

Zip tie the hands together.

Tie her up. Tie her down.

Cover her over with the blanket.

He got out and closed the hood of the van, then squatted down beside Dana Nolan's car to glance over the things she had dropped during the struggle: purse, makeup bag, tote bag with papers spilling out of it. He pulled one of the papers out and smiled to himself. It was a flier with a photograph of a young woman. HAVE YOU SEEN THIS GIRL? A missing persons flier for Penelope Gray.

Struck by inspiration, Fitz fished a fat marker out of a side pocket on the tote bag, wrote a note on the flier, and tucked the page beneath a windshield wiper on the Mini Cooper. Then he got behind the wheel of his van and calmly drove slowly out of the parking lot. In his rearview mirror he could see other fliers from Dana Nolan's tote bag taking flight as the cold wind kicked up a gust.

He smiled and turned up the radio and sang along.

36

Three hours of sleep. A shower. A shave. A small bucket of coffee from 7-Eleven. A couple of doughnuts to perpetuate the stereotype. Back to the job.

Kovac stood in front of the whiteboard, taking in the timeline and the notes. He played the possibilities through his head. Doc Holiday. Michael Warner. A friend. An enemy. A stranger. The kids who didn't like her. The mother she rebelled against. Who would have thought a sixteen-year-old girl could have so many people in her life who might want her dead?

He made additional notations on the board: Kyle's version of events at the Rock & Bowl, the fact that Christina had started the physical altercation with Gray, that Aaron Fogelman had struck the girl, and the fact that both Christina and Aaron Fogelman had blamed Gray for starting it. Kovac knew which version he believed.

It probably didn't matter. Two living kids putting the blame on a dead kid to make themselves look better. So what? But it bothered him, just the same.

Christina Warner and Penny Gray were enemies. Whatever the

Gray girl had said to Christina had provoked a violent reaction. Now Penny Gray was dead, and Christina Warner and her boyfriend were both lying to the cops. Not a big lie. A lie of perspective. A reinterpretation of history. It wouldn't have mattered except that after Penny Gray left that place she disappeared. She had an altercation with a known enemy, and then she disappeared.

Not like Kovac wasn't used to getting lied to. Everyone lied to the cops—not just guilty people. Innocent people who didn't want to get involved lied to the cops. People afraid of getting other people in trouble lied to the cops. People afraid of retaliation lied to the cops. Kids and adults and blue-haired old ladies lied to the cops about all kinds of things for all kinds of reasons. Bald-faced lies and white lies, twisted truths and sins of omission.

Videotape, however, always told the truth. He put a cassette in the VCR and watched Penny Gray leave the Rock & Bowl over and over—with Kyle leaving shortly after her. He never saw the other kids leave. He played the tape backward and forward, and he never saw them leave. Which meant they had to have gone out the side exit, which meant he couldn't pinpoint the time they left.

The Lawler girl was the weak link in the chain of students. She wasn't very happy with her so-called friends and the circumstances in which they found themselves. She had been vague and evasive at different points in his interview with her that afternoon. She didn't remember who started what. She was looking the other way when the scuffle broke out.

She had turned her head and looked away from him when she said it.

"You're a poor liar, Brittany," he'd said calmly.

Big tears had flooded her blue eyes, but she hadn't changed her tale.

Brittany had ridden to the Rock & Bowl with Gray. Gray had been staying with her. They were friends enough that Brittany's house was where Penny Gray had sought sanctuary after the fight with her mother. And yet Brittany had convinced Gray to drive them to the Rock & Bowl, where Christina Warner and her minions lay in wait.

None of that was sitting well with Brittany now, which meant she had a conscience. A conscience Kovac could exploit.

He watched the security video from the Holiday station again. Penny Gray buying beer and walking out, hesitating as she started out of the building, almost turning and going back into the light and safety of the busy store. Who had she seen standing just out of reach of the camera? A stranger? An enemy? Doc Holiday? The kids she had just fought with?

He rewound the tape to five minutes before Penny Gray came into the store. People came in, bought things, left. Women, kids, men. Ordinary people. Odd people. A couple of rough-looking customers.

One man caught his eye, not for being suspicious in his behavior, but for seeming vaguely familiar—a short guy, stocky, thinning dark hair, a close-cropped beard and mustache. He got something from the automotive supply aisle, chatted up the customer ahead of him in line, walked out. Kovac couldn't place him. He encountered so many people on a daily basis, everybody started looking familiar.

Several minutes later on the video, Penny Gray walked into the store. Kovac let the tape run on past her leaving. People came, people went. Five minutes after the Gray girl left the picture, Aaron Fogelman walked into the station with his buddy Tweedle Dumb. Fogelman bought cigarettes. The cohort shoplifted a bunch of candy bars. They walked back out of the store, carefree.

Where was Penny Gray at that point in time? Gone? Snatched by Doc Holiday? In the trunk of Aaron Fogelman's car?

Kovac got up from his chair, went to the timeline, made a

note. He stood back, ran his tongue over his teeth, and tried to rub the grit out of his eyes with the heels of his hands. It was nearly five A.M.

In need of a break to reboot his brain, he turned the VCR off and changed the channel on the TV. He would run through the local stations and see what was being said about the case. In the back of his mind he considered what might happen if Dr. Michael Warner's name "somehow" got attached to the case in the media.

A lawsuit and the loss of his job and his pension, probably.

The guy had never had a criminal complaint made against him. Elwood would call any organizations and ethics boards Warner had to answer to in his professional life, but he'd found nothing against the man yet.

Warner had said the reason he had stopped seeing Penny Gray as a patient had been her issues with men and her constant attempts to manipulate him. He had dumped her, not the other way around. If he had been abusing the girl, it seemed that she would have been the one to quit the situation and raise hell.

Then again, just who was she supposed to raise hell to? Her mother? The mother who found her irritating and aggravating? The mother who was now engaged to Michael Warner?

Elwood had taped copies of Penny Gray's poems to the wall at the far end of the room. Kovac browsed over them now, his eye catching on one titled "Unloved."

```
I'm a bother
I'm a burden
I'm a liar
Close the curtain
Don't wanna see it
Don't believe it
Shut your mouth
```

```
She can't conceive it
I'm not the dream
I'm just a nightmare
I'm in the way
Life's just so unfair
I should come first
But I'm called worst
Just a problem
She can't solve
Unloved
```

Just who was Penny Gray supposed to turn to if her therapist abused her and her mother didn't want to hear it? People didn't like her. Warner had said so himself, the girl drew people in only so she could alienate them. How much of that did anyone tolerate before they just stopped listening?

Or had Warner bought the girl's silence with a car? People sold out for less. It seemed pretty damned generous to buy your girl-friend's daughter a car for her birthday. Then again, a mobile teen-ager was out of the way. Warner's decision might have been strategic to getting more alone time with Julia.

Kovac turned back to the TV and changed the channel again. So far, he'd heard virtually identical reports on the case from three of the local stations. On the fourth he expected to see perky little Dana Nolan—the girl he crabbed at every morning when he woke up and turned on his television.

As much as the news media irritated him, he had never been able to shake the habit of beginning and ending his day with the news. He usually chose Dana Nolan in the morning just because she was so fucking chipper and optimistic. Her happy mood antagonized him into setting his personal dial at "curmudgeon" before he even got out of bed.

But it wasn't Dana Nolan's angelic face that greeted him as he changed to her station. A slightly older woman with thick maroon hair and a worried expression had taken Dana's seat at the desk. She seemed flustered and distracted.

Even as Kovac began to form the thought that something wasn't right, a photograph of Dana Nolan filled one corner of the television screen. He turned up the sound.

"Breaking news: Foul play is suspected in the apparent disappearance of *NewsWatch 3*'s own Dana Nolan," the woman reported. "Police were dispatched to Dana Nolan's Minneapolis apartment just an hour ago when Dana failed to show up for work and failed to respond to numerous phone calls and text messages."

Kovac could see the fear and panic building in the woman. Her eyes gleamed with tears. Her voice tightened and trembled as she spoke.

"Personal belongings found in the parking lot of the apartment building near Ms. Nolan's abandoned vehicle seem to indicate she may have been taken against her will."

The screen filled with the image of the missing reporter.

"Her most recent assignment has been covering the disappearance of Minneapolis teenager Penelope Gray, and the possible connection between the discovery of the murder victim known as Zombie Doe and the serial killer law enforcement agencies throughout the Midwest have come to call Doc Holiday. Anyone having any information as to the whereabouts of Dana Nolan is asked to call the number posted on the screen.

"Please, *please*," the woman implored, her tenuous hold on her emotions quickly eroding. "If anyone watching has any information *at all*, *please* call this number as soon as possible.

"Dana, if you're somehow seeing this broadcast, please know that we're all looking for you and praying for you to come home safe."

The station went to commercial as the reporter broke down sobbing.

Kovac swore, grabbed his coat, and bolted for the door.

"WHY THE *FUCK* WASN'T I called the minute this came in?" Kovac snapped at the young detective who had caught the call. "I was right down the fucking hall!"

They stood in the parking lot of Dana Nolan's apartment complex. The early morning darkness had been banished by portable lights from the crime scene unit, and from the half dozen news vans that had circled the scene like wagons in an old Western movie.

The detective—Dickson—barely looked old enough to have a job. Kovac had come out of the womb older than this kid. Still, the young detective tried to put up a tough front.

"Since when do we have to clear our calls through you? It's not even your shift."

"Oh. It's not my shift?" Kovac thought his head might explode. Acutely aware of the cameras and microphones trained on them, he leaned in close. "It's a fucking abduction, you fucking moron! I've got half the fucking department working an abduction/ homicide that's all over the goddamn news, and you think you don't have to bother telling me? The fucking janitor would know enough to tell me! You're a fucking idiot! And where's your partner? He's a fucking idiot too."

One of the uniforms who had responded to the initial call intervened, wedging himself between the two detectives.

"Sarge, the newsies are getting restless. They're asking for a statement."

"They want a statement?" Kovac asked, feigning shock. "It's a clusterfuck. That's my statement. They want a statement, they can pull one out of my ass. I just got here. I don't even know yet what young Dickhead here has managed to fuck up in my absence."

Dickson waved him off. "Fuck you, Kojak."

Kovac turned and looked at the center of their crime scene: a dark green Mini, parked near the security light. Dana Nolan had parked exactly where young women were supposed to park their cars for safety—under a pool of light where they would be able to see danger coming.

Nothing good ever happened in a parking lot after midnight. It was unlikely there had been any witnesses. This was a quiet residential neighborhood. Dana Nolan's belongings still lay on the ground where she had dropped them. She probably had seen danger coming. There just hadn't been a damn thing she could do about it.

Kovac walked over to the car and squatted down for a closer look at Dana Nolan's abandoned belongings. A purse. A makeup bag. A tote bag with papers spilling out of it. He picked one of the papers out and frowned as he looked at it—the missing girl poster of Penny Gray.

He stood up and looked at Nolan's car, at the piece of paper tucked under the windshield wiper. A sick feeling began to stir like a snake waking in his belly.

Careful to touch just the edges of the page, he took it from under the blade and looked at it.

HAVE YOU SEEN THIS GIRL?

Penny Gray looked at him over her shoulder. The photo he had gotten from Brittany Lawler.

At the bottom of the page scrawled in black magic marker were two words and a smiley face.

HAPPY HOLIDAY.

☺

37

"That's not his MO," Liska said.

"It is now."

John Quinn stared at the photocopy of the note left on Dana Nolan's windshield, frowning darkly. He needed a shave. Kovac had called him from the scene and asked to meet him downtown. Quinn had thrown on jeans and a sweater and drove in from his cozy home in the suburbs to join the madness.

Kovac didn't want the press seeing Quinn at the scene. Or, more to the point, he didn't want Quinn being seen on the news. Speculation would come quickly as it was. He didn't want to pour fuel on the fire. Doc Holiday was sure to be watching the news. He hadn't chosen Dana Nolan by accident. Kovac wanted as much control as possible over what went out over the airwaves. If Quinn thought it would be useful to include his name, that was what would happen. If he thought it was better to stay out of the spotlight, then so be it.

"I guess it's safe to say he's liking the attention," Kovac said.

"Loving it," Quinn replied.

They sat in the war room, surrounded by everything to do with

Penny Gray's case. They were going to need another room dedicated to Dana Nolan. They would have to reassign the manpower to divide their efforts between the two cases. Penny Gray was dead. To the best of their knowledge, Dana Nolan was still alive. There was a chance they were dealing with the same perp. If so, then one effort benefited both cases. They would have to shift the manpower to benefit the victim who was potentially still alive.

Quinn sat back against the table and crossed his arms over his chest. "He's taking it to a whole new level. With the others it was enough to dump the victim and then read about it in the paper. Now he's getting cocky. The media has given him a name. He wants to be a star."

"This is why I didn't want to challenge him," Kovac said. "I was afraid he would take me up on it."

"What do we do now? Do we acknowledge him?" Kasselmann asked. He looked harried for the first time in all of this. "Do we keep the note to ourselves? If we let the media run with this, they'll have the public in a panic. I can't have that, and I guarantee that's not going to fly upstairs."

"It's going to be bad enough as it is," Liska said. "First we've got a dead zombie, then a missing girl, now this. One of their own snatched out from under our noses. The news media is going to connect the dots and come up with Doc Holiday anyway. They already have. They don't need to see the note for that."

"If you don't acknowledge him, he's going to get frustrated," Quinn said. "Frustrated could be good."

"Not for Dana Nolan," Liska pointed out.

"Dana Nolan is dead," Quinn said bluntly. "I don't mean to be a pessimist here, but that's a foregone conclusion. Unless you can find her within the next twenty-four hours or so, she's dead. He kidnapped her to kill her. That's what he'll do. That's where the payout is for him. The buildup is just foreplay.

"He might drag it out longer this time because he has a stage," he said. "That's the best you can hope for."

"That's a hell of a thing to be optimistic about," Kovac muttered. "If we're lucky, he'll spend more time torturing her before he stabs her to death and beats her head in with a hammer."

"It's more time to look for her," Quinn said.

"Yeah. If we had a freaking clue where to look." Kovac turned to his boss. "I've got a small army canvassing Dana Nolan's neighborhood. They're knocking on every door that has a sight line to that parking lot and the street."

"And you haven't found anything to go on from the previous cases?" Kasselmann asked.

Kovac shook his head. "Nothing. I've got guys double-checking, triple-checking, quadruple-checking everything from each of those cases—every report, every statement. They're calling the families of the victims. They're reinterviewing the people who reported finding the bodies. Nothing."

"He's smart, he's careful, he's experienced," Quinn said. "But he just changed the way he does things. That's when these guys make mistakes. He's always hunted victims of opportunity, but he singled this girl out. He knew where she lives. He knew her schedule."

"He stalked her," Kovac concluded. "He singled her out because of the coverage of the Penny Gray case."

"This is his big moment to show the world he's smarter than everybody."

"So far," Kasselmann said, "he is."

"We've got to trace Dana Nolan's every move over the last few days," Kovac said. "If he was stalking her, someone might have seen him."

"He might have even interacted with her in the days leading up to this," Quinn said. "He was able to get right up to her in an otherwise abandoned parking lot. He's either a master of the blitz attack or she didn't feel threatened. And the only way she didn't feel threatened in this circumstance was if he was somehow familiar to her."

"So he's probably not a scary-looking guy," Liska said.

"Probably not. Probably average size or smaller," Quinn said. "He's probably friendly, smiling, familiar. He could be using a ploy, like he needs help with something or he needs directions, or something like that.

"I got that feeling looking at a couple of his older cases. The Rose Reiser case, in particular. She disappeared walking out of a convenience store, and no one saw anything, which means she didn't struggle. He had to have gotten right up to her without causing alarm. Then he probably used a stun gun or some other quick way of subduing the victim."

Kovac looked up at the wall and the photos of Penny Gray and thought about the video of her walking out of the Holiday station down the street from the Rock & Bowl.

"The Holiday station," he said. "If he's the one who snatched Penny Gray, that location probably wasn't a coincidence either. It was probably this sick bastard's idea of a joke. Doc Holiday snatches his victims from the Holiday stations of Minneapolis."

"*If* he was the one who snatched Penny Gray," Liska said. "I'm still not convinced she's his ninth girl. And neither are you, Sam. We've got too many other red flags flying."

Kasselmann looked like he needed an antacid tablet. "That's all we need: two homicidal sadists. Who else are you looking at, Sam?"

"The girl had a complicated life," Kovac admitted. "She wasn't exactly Miss Congeniality. And she might have had a secret someone felt was worth killing her for."

"We can't drop that angle just because serial killers are more exciting in the news," Liska said. She looked to Quinn and Kasselmann. "We think she might have been sexually abused by the mother's fiancé. There's some pretty strong indicators if you look at the timeline and the changes in the girl's behavior over the last eight months or so. We have to look hard at him. She also had a run-in with his daughter and her boyfriend the night she went missing."

"It's a freaking shell game," Kovac admitted. "And every time we stop and lift a shell, there's a different killer under it."

Kasselmann frowned hard. "Dana Nolan has to be the priority now."

Liska sighed and looked away. "Great. Everybody else in Penny Gray's life abused and abandoned her. Now we get to do it too."

"Penny Gray is dead, Sergeant," Kasselmann said.

"I understand that. I don't have to like it. I feel an obligation to my victim, and to her mother. How am I supposed to tell Julia Gray that her daughter's death isn't as relevant today as it was yesterday? How would you feel if that was your child?"

"Maybe you're too close to the situation," Kasselmann said with a fine edge of steel in his voice.

"Yeah," Tinks returned. "You're probably right. If the department isn't going to give a shit about these people, then it's probably best to assign a detective who doesn't care about them either."

Kovac intervened before Kasselmann could draw breath to suspend her.

"The bulk of the manpower should go to Nolan," he conceded. "There's a chance we can still get to her before it's too late. Tinks and Elwood should stay on Penny Gray. I'll keep a hand in each."

The captain looked at his watch. "I have to go upstairs and explain this to the chief. Keep me up to the minute on Nolan."

Kasselmann left the room, taking none of the tension with him. Kovac felt like something huge had sunk its talons into his shoulders.

"He'll look worse to more people if we don't drop everything and chase after the missing news girl," Liska said bitterly.

"Brass is brass," Kovac returned. "Now tell me again how you want to go into management."

"I'd rather eat my gun than be like that."

"I'm glad to know it."

Ignoring the office politics, Quinn had gone to the wall to scrutinize the photos from the New Year's Eve scene. Kovac watched him take in the details as if he were looking at a Picasso exhibit, trying to make sense of the lines and the details.

"This was sloppy and careless," he concluded. "If Doc Holiday didn't do this, and the media has been trying to pin it on him, he might have taken Dana Nolan to prove a point."

"And if that's the case?" Kovac asked, dreading the answer because the only reason the media was blaming Doc Holiday was because he had told them to.

John Quinn looked grim. "Then God have mercy on her soul."

"WE FOUND THIS video on YouTube late last night," Elwood said, setting up his laptop.

Kovac had gone to organize the Nolan investigation. Elwood had arrived together with Sonya Porter, who was wearing the same sweater she had had on the night before, Liska noted.

"There are a bunch of them," Porter said. "They all look like they were uploaded from her phone. So there could be more. Do you have her phone?"

"We don't," Liska said. "We don't have her phone or her laptop. But my son, Kyle, says Gray was always shooting video with her phone."

"Her mother told us she keeps everything on her laptop and she keeps her laptop with her," Elwood said. "We found some notebooks with her writing in her room, but those were all a few years old. It's safe to assume the laptop is either in her car, wherever that is, or the killer took it for his or her own reasons."

He clicked the Play icon.

Penny Gray had chosen to shoot herself in profile as she looked down. She shot from the side where her hair was long and hung down like a curtain, hiding half her face. She moved the camera slowly as she spoke, bringing it around from one side of her head to the other, to the side where the hair had been shaved to the scalp and piercings rimmed the shell of her ear with wires and spikes.

The poem was entitled "Help Me."

```
Refuge
Asylum
Safest place to be
Secrets
Hard truths
Soul laid bare to see
Comfort
Guidance
Shoulder. Lean on me
Seduction
Destruction
Help not meant to be
Silence
Shameful
Not to be believed
Don't tell
Go to hell
There's no one here for me
```

"That certainly sounds like abuse to me," Sonya declared. "I say you go arrest the son of a bitch and string him up in public by his balls."

"I told you why we can't just do that," Elwood said gently. "She doesn't spell out what happened to her, let alone name names. And even if she did, we would need some corroborating evidence."

"You should at least be able to drag him in here and scare a confession out of him," she said stubbornly.

"Miss Journalistic Integrity," Elwood said. "Would you write a story about it and present facts not in evidence?"

"No, but there's no law against you lying to him in an interview, right? Tell him you have video of him molesting her."

"I like your style," Liska said. "But if we do that and he calls our bluff, we're screwed. We have to be cagier than that. I want to go to Julia Gray first and plant some doubt. If we attack Michael Warner head-on, he's going to call a lawyer, and he's going to tell her to call one too."

"Do you think she knows he abused her daughter?" Porter asked. "How could a mother know something like that and not do anything about it? And not only not do anything about it but also get engaged to the creep. That's fucked-up!"

Her outrage pushed her out of her chair to pace back and forth with her arms crossed tight beneath her breasts.

"I'm betting the daughter never told her—or if she told her, she wasn't believed," Liska said. "Look what the girl wrote in that other poem—that she's a burden, a liar, no one believes her."

"What's the matter with women like that?" Sonya asked. "It's not the 1950s anymore. Women need to believe each other and stand up for each other in the face of sexist oppression. Men suck! Present company excluded, of course," she added, smiling sweetly at Elwood.

"I understand your sentiment," Elwood said. "Most violence committed against women is perpetrated by men. I once read a quote that the thing a man fears most from a woman is that she'll laugh at him, and the thing a woman most fears from a man is that he'll kill her."

"I think Dr. Warner has more to fear than being laughed at," Sonya said. "His whole existence is based on people trusting him with their kids. And if he molested her, his fiancée's daughter had the ability to destroy him."

"The day the girl's wrist got broken, she was supposedly on her way home from an appointment with him," Liska said. "He made out like he didn't have much knowledge of the event, but Julia Gray gave the impression she included him in the decision making about a doctor.

"So what was Michael Gray doing the evening of the thirtieth?" she asked.

Elwood flipped back through his little notebook. "He and Mrs. Gray went to see the Joffrey Ballet company at the Orpheum, followed by dinner at Solera. He dropped Julia Gray off at her house between twelve and twelve thirty and says he was home when his daughter got in around one."

"And the last we can account for Penny Gray is leaving the Holiday station between nine thirty and ten," Liska said. "She doesn't show up again until she falls out of the trunk of a car on New Year's Eve. That's a big chunk of time to account for. We need to know what Michael Warner, Christina Warner, and Julia Gray were doing all that time."

"I've already spoken to Dr. Warner a few times," Elwood said. "I can reach out to him again on the excuse of tying up loose ends."

"We need to feel him out on the general issue of whether or not Penny Gray may have suffered abuse without him playing the patient confidentiality card. Maybe we can ask him if he thought she might have had someone else she would confide in."

"You'd think the girl would have confided in somebody," Elwood said. "A girlfriend, a counselor."

"I don't think she trusted anyone," Liska said. "Kyle knew her. He said she didn't have friends like most girls have friends. She pretended with one group of acquaintances that she had friends elsewhere, and vice versa."

"She internalized everything," Sonya concluded, looking at the pages of poetry Elwood had taped to the wall. "I get that. Her poetry was her outlet. That's how creative people are. We bottle the feelings up inside until the feelings turn into words or images that have to come out onto a page or a canvas or a—"

"Tattoo," Elwood said.

The two of them exchanged a look.

"If you put out raw emotion, people can reject you directly, personally," Sonya said. "If you form that emotion into something else, then the thing you create can be rejected, but at least it's once removed from you."

"Everyone in this girl's life found her to be an irritation, a problem, something they didn't want to be bothered to deal with," Liska said. "But something happened that night. She pushed somebody's button one time too many."

"Or Dr. Warner bought her silence with that car he gave her for her birthday," Elwood pointed out. "Or she was just in the wrong place at the wrong time."

"Sam is working the wrong place / wrong time angle. We get to take a harder look at the people she knew. The last people we know who interacted with her were the kids at the Rock and Bowl. She said something to Christina Warner that made the Warner girl angry enough to lunge at her. I want to know what it was."

"The Warner girl said Penny Gray attacked *her*," Elwood said.

"She lied. Kyle was there. He saw it go down. I want to know why." She looked at her watch. "PSI is having an assembly today for Penny Gray's classmates and any other students who feel the need to attend. It might be our only chance to talk to any of these kids without a parent or attorney looking over their shoulders."

She pointed a finger at Sonya. "You didn't hear me say that."

"Say what?"

"I'm not looking for anything to use in court. I'm looking for loose threads to pull to unravel the story these kids have woven together. Somebody knows exactly what went down. We have to find a way to make one kid want to tell us."

"What about me?" Sonya asked. "Can I come?"

"Absolutely," Liska said. "You're known to these kids through social media. I want them to feel like they can contact you somehow if they have something to say but don't want to say it to us. Can we make that work?"

"I'm in if the school will have me."

Nikki smiled a nasty smile, thinking how happy Principal Rodgers would be to have Sonya Porter with her tattoos and multiple facial piercings address his students.

"Oh, they'll have you," she said. "I will take great joy in making that happen."

38

"I can't believe they're making us go to this," Jessie Cook said as they walked down the hall toward the assembly theater, Jessie shoulder to shoulder on Christina's left, Brittany on Christina's right. "Like any of us are traumatized because of Gray." She rolled her eyes dramatically. "Please."

Brittany said nothing. She hadn't wanted to come to school at all. Ironically, her mother had made her come because of the assembly. She thought it was important for Brittany to be at school among her friends instead of home alone, brooding, and for them all to listen to the counselors and talk about what had happened and how they should try to deal with their emotions.

"Are you traumatized, XT?" Jessie asked Christina. They shared a knowing look, like it was the funniest joke in the world that they didn't have any human feelings toward a girl they had known for years, a girl who had been killed and dumped in the road like a sack of garbage.

"How about you, Britt?" Jessie asked, leaning forward and looking at her past Christina. "Are you traumatized? You and Gray were *such* good friends."

Brittany wanted to call her a bitch and tell her to go to hell, but none of those words came out of her mouth. The best she could manage was to say, "Yeah, Jessie, I happen to think being murdered by a serial killer is a traumatic event no matter who it happens to."

"Britt's right," Christina said. "What happened to Gray is terrible. If you don't think that's terrible, Jessie, what kind of fucked-up person are you?"

Jessie frowned. "Well, I mean, of course it's terrible, but it's not like it happened to one of *us.*"

Brittany rolled her eyes and heaved a sigh.

Aaron opened the door to the theater and held it for them like he was a gentleman or something. They all went in and were herded down the stairs by a teacher to the lower third of the auditorium. A group of adults had gathered on the stage. Principal Rodgers looked fussy and unhappy as he discussed something with a petite woman with short-cropped blond hair—Kyle's mom, who had come to school a few times for the antidrug program. With her was the big, burly detective who had come to Brittany's room that first night anyone had realized Gray was missing. A younger woman with a sleek dark bob and tattoos peeking out of her sweater stood to one side of the big detective—Sonya Porter.

Emily leaned ahead in her seat on the far side of Jessie, looking down the row at all of them, and said, "That's Sonya Porter from *TeenCities.*"

Behind them, Aaron leaned forward and put his hands on Christina's shoulders and whispered something in her ear. Christina laughed.

Brittany squeezed herself to the far side of her seat, away from them, wanting to slink out and disappear. Christina leaned toward her, all loving concern, and put a hand on her knee. "Are you all right, Britt?"

"I'm fine," Brittany said, avoiding eye contact. "I've got a headache, that's all."

"Do you want something for it?" Christina whispered as Principal Rodgers took the podium and the room began to quiet. "Aaron can get you something."

"No, thanks," she said, thinking there was no drug to help what was bothering her.

Principal Rodgers started droning on in his self-important, condescending way, telling them all what a tragedy had befallen their school and how their school would be here for them in their time of need. He didn't have a clue what went on in his school. He didn't have any idea who his students were. How much help could he possibly be? He had hated Gray, was always angry with her for the way she dressed, for the way she did her hair. Brittany had once seen him stop Gray in the hall and make her take out all but two of her earrings and give them to him right there.

Kyle's mom took the podium next. Brittany had never actually met her, but she had seen her at school a couple of times and had been fascinated with the idea that she was a homicide detective. Kyle didn't like to talk about it. To him, his mom was just his mom, who happened to be a cop, who happened to investigate murders.

"My colleague and I are here today to talk to you about what happened to Penny Gray," she began. "I'm sure you've all seen the reports on the news. I know there are a lot of rumors going around. We're going to be very honest and straightforward with you.

"Penny Gray was murdered. That's upsetting. It's disturbing. I know people would rather not have to hear about things like this, but it's important that you know the truth. This isn't a story about a stranger in some other place. This happened to a girl many of you knew, a girl who walked the halls of this school. Maybe you liked her, maybe you didn't. That doesn't matter. It's important that you know what happened to her. This is real. This is as real as it gets. We want you to know the truth and we need you to tell the truth.

"If any of you have any information at all about Penny Gray, we need you to share it with us. Anything she might have said to you, rumors that you heard about her, anything at all—even if it doesn't seem like it could be important. It's impossible to know what impact even a small, seemingly insignificant detail might have.

"At this point we don't know if Penny was abducted by a stranger or was victimized by someone she knew. We know she was at the Rock and Bowl on the evening of the thirtieth. We know she left that place and made a stop at a nearby convenience store. So far as we know, she was not seen again—except by her killer—until her body was found New Year's Eve.

"We don't know why Penny was killed," she said. "We don't know if she was a random victim or if she provoked someone. We don't know if someone was angry with her or hated her for some reason, or if she knew something that was a threat to someone. This is why we're asking you guys to help.

"I want you all to look around this auditorium this morning. You're all individuals who are part of a community. Look at your friends. Look at the kids you don't know or don't like. Realize that other people are looking at you and thinking the same things. And I want you to imagine, what if you were Penny Gray? What if you found yourself in a terrible situation? You would hope the people who knew you would help. You would hope if someone could do something, they would."

Brittany looked around the room. The seats were filled with students and teachers. One section had been reserved for parents. Some people were listening. Some weren't. Some were on their phones, texting, playing Angry Birds or Words with Friends.

She glanced at the people sitting in her row—Emily, Jessie, Christina—and wondered what they would do. *If I was missing, would they care about me?*

The answer sat like a stone in the pit of her stomach.

Sonya Porter got up next and talked about social media and social consciousness and the obligation young people—and particularly young women—should have to one another.

Brittany watched her, taking in the avant-garde style, the piercings and the tattoos juxtaposed against the sleek haircut and the retro-chic outfit. She listened to Sonya Porter speak with passion and conviction. Gray might have turned out like this, she thought. She might have channeled her anger into passion and honed her self-expression into style. Gray might have grown up to be a Sonya Porter, but she would never have that chance.

"I want to finish by reading you something," Sonya Porter said. She adjusted her cat-eye glasses and began.

```
"Fight
Struggle
Clash
Square peg, round hole
Force to conform
Blend in. Fall in line
Stifle
Smother
Hate each other
You're red
I'm blue
I don't want to be you
You don't want to look at me.
Stop
Shift. Now. Change.
Look
See
Everybody be free
Open hearts
Open minds
```

```
See what's real
Listen
See me
Unique
Special
Unlike another
Be who you are
Live
Acceptance."
```

When she finished, she looked up, her gaze scanning from one side of the silent room to the other.

"That poem was written by Penny Gray," she said. "This is who your school lost. This is who the world lost. Whether you liked her or not, approved of her or didn't, she had a unique voice, and a unique talent, and a unique view of the world. Just like each one of you. You should be angry that someone took her away."

Jessie Cook leaned into Christina, rolled her eyes, and whispered, "I wish someone would take *her* away."

The two of them giggled under their breath.

Brittany gave them both a look of irritation. She wanted to get up and leave, move to another seat in another part of the theater. But she could imagine everyone looking at her, and she could imagine what would be said about her by Jessie and Christina and the rest of them.

Be who you are.

If she only had the courage. If only she could be more like Gray—the girl nobody liked.

The counselors spoke. People asked questions. Business cards were passed out. Phone numbers and e-mail addresses were posted on the projector screen.

Brittany counted the minutes until they were told they could leave. When that moment came, she popped out of her seat and started up the aisle, not even looking to see if Christina and company were behind her. Let them think that she wasn't feeling well, that her headache was making her sick, that she had to go to the bathroom. She just wanted out and to be away from them.

She hurried to her locker, got her coat, grabbed her purse. It was lunchtime. They were allowed to leave the campus. Lots of kids did to go to the nearby restaurants and coffee shops. Brittany had no interest in lunch. As much as her mother thought it was the last thing she should do, she just wanted to go home and be alone and not have to pretend everything was all right.

She didn't care that it was a cold, long walk. In fact, she thought it was all the better to feel cold, to feel the pain of numbing fingertips and tense shoulders hunched against the wind. Head down, she put one foot in front of the other and just kept going, away from school, across the parking lot, heading for the street.

"Britt! Brittany!"

She didn't want to look up or acknowledge the person calling her. She didn't want to be recognized. Of course, it did her no good to ignore him. If she knew one thing about Kyle, it was that he didn't give up.

He caught up to her and fell in step beside her. She glanced at him. His cheeks were red from the cold, but he'd had sense enough to put on a gray watch cap with the letters UFC embroidered in red. He wore an old letterman's jacket from some school in St. Paul over a gray hoodie. It irritated her that she thought he was cute.

"What are you doing here, Kyle?" she asked, annoyed. "I thought you were suspended."

"I am," he said. "But I got the text about the assembly. I wanted to come."

"Your mom is investigating Gray's murder. That must be weird."

"Yeah. What part of any of this *isn't* weird? Someone we knew was murdered. I can't get my head around that, can you?"

"No."

"Where are all your good friends?" he asked sarcastically.

"Don't give me a hard time," she said, annoyed with him for asking, more annoyed with herself for suddenly feeling like crying. She had no "good friends." She was stupid for ever thinking otherwise.

"Want to see what Jessie was tweeting during the assembly?"

"No."

"You get that it's their fault, don't you?" he asked, then corrected himself. "*Our* fault. You got her to go there. I didn't stop her from leaving."

Brittany stopped and faced him. "Yes. I get it, Kyle. It's all I think about. Does that make you happy? I'm sick about it. I wish I'd never moved here. But what do you want me to do?"

He looked back toward the school. She had left. Literally. She had walked away from Christina and the rest of them. What more could he call her on?

"I don't know," he admitted. "I don't know either. I feel like we should do something. Go see her mom or something. Tell her we're sorry."

From the corner of her eye, Brittany saw the car approaching—Aaron Fogelman's midnight-blue Lexus, cruising slowly toward them. The window on the passenger's side ran down as the car came alongside them at the curb.

"Hey, Britt," Christina said. "Need a ride?"

It wasn't a friendly offer. There was accusation in Christina's expression and her voice. It wasn't hard to imagine what she thought—that Brittany had ditched them to meet up with Kyle.

Brittany hesitated. She didn't want a ride. She didn't want to be with those people another minute. And yet, there was a part of her that was afraid to say no. She hated herself for it, and she hated Kyle for putting her in this position.

Aaron put the car in park, got out, and looked at them across the roof. "Jesus, Hatcher, don't you ever take a hint? Leave her alone. She doesn't want to be with a loser like you."

"Fuck you," Kyle said. "I'm looking at the loser. You got your boyfriends in the car with you?"

"You're so funny. You're such a funny little shit," Aaron said without a hint of humor. He came around the hood of the car, moving with a menacing swagger. His leather coat hung open, emphasizing the width of his shoulders and chest. "You're living in quite a fantasy, faggot, drawing pictures like that one you put on Twitter."

"Yeah, I thought you'd like that," Kyle said.

Butterflies swarmed in Brittany's stomach. "Kyle," she said under her breath.

Aaron looked at her as he came forward. "Brittany, get in the car."

Kyle stood his ground with his chin up. "You'll have to come through me."

"I'm gonna like kicking your ass again," Aaron said with a nasty smile.

"You can't do it again if you never did it in the first place," Kyle shot back.

Brittany shrieked and jumped back as Aaron charged toward Kyle, his right arm pulled back, bare hand balled into a fist.

Much shorter, Kyle easily ducked the punch and threw one of his own. Aaron's momentum carried him right into it, and his breath left him in a hard *whooosh!* as his solar plexus met Kyle's fist. He dropped straight to his knees on the sidewalk and made a terrible alien sound as he tried to suck in a breath.

Christina screamed, "Aaron!"

One of the back doors of the Lexus opened and Eric Owen started to get out.

Kyle took a defensive stance, hands raised, knees bent, his gaze going from Eric to Aaron, who was already pushing himself to his feet.

"I'm gonna fucking kill you, Hatcher!" he said, his voice hoarse and thready.

Before anything more could happen, a maroon sedan with a flashing light on the dash pulled to the curb behind Aaron's car, and the big detective, Knutson, got out on the passenger's side and came toward them, an authoritative figure in a leather trench coat and a porkpie hat. Kyle's mother sat behind the wheel of the car but made no move to get out.

"Is there a problem here?" Knutson asked.

Kyle dropped his hands. "No, sir."

Aaron shook his head even as he pressed a hand across his stomach.

The detective gave Aaron a cold look. "Then you'll get back in your car and move along, won't you, son? There's no parking on this street."

Aaron cut Kyle a narrow-eyed, nasty look as he got back in his car. Christina shot Brittany the same look and ran up her window.

Knutson looked at Kyle and Brittany as the Lexus pulled away. "You two kids look like you need a ride somewhere." He hiked a thumb in the direction of the car. "Get in. Let's go."

39

Dana Nolan was the happiest, friendliest, most generous, optimistic, talented, well-adjusted, well-loved person in the Twin Cities. To say nothing of beautiful and kind to human beings and small animals.

Kovac spoke to one after another of the young woman's coworkers. No one had a bad word to say. No one had a story of a jealousy or an office rivalry. She had a sunny smile on the darkest day and never complained about anything, not even driving to work in the dead of winter at three in the morning.

She had been working at the station for nine months, had come to Minneapolis from a small town in Indiana, had aspirations to be a host on the *Today* show someday. Her relationship with her college sweetheart had ended three months past, not strong enough to hold up long distance. The breakup had been amicable, according to Dana. She lived alone—not counting her cat—because of her odd schedule.

She had many male admirers, but friends only, no one special at the moment. To the best knowledge of her many friends at work, there were no angry exes, no disgruntled would-be lovers.

Like many women in broadcasting, she had her share of weirdos who called, wrote, e-mailed the station wanting to convey their affections, but none of them had threatened anything violent. Station management was more than happy to compile a list of names, addresses, and phone numbers for further investigation.

She had voiced no concerns in the last few days about anyone bothering her or following her. She had been wrapped up in her extra assignment, reporting on the disappearance of Penelope Gray—an assignment she had lobbied hard for. She had been one of the first newscasters to report the story, and she saw the opportunity the extra exposure might provide her. According to Roxanne Volkman—the woman who had taken over that morning's broadcast when Dana Nolan had failed to show up for work—Dana had expressed a small sense of guilt that reporting on a tragedy might, in the end, be the break that furthered her career.

The irony hung in the air like a foul odor: that her big break had probably attracted the thing that could end her career in tragedy.

Kovac took it all in with a familiar sense of déjà vu. Tragedy, loss, fear, grief, disbelief, anger. The cycle repeated itself crime after crime. The emotional undercurrent was essentially the same. Only the faces changed.

He learned as much as he could from the people Dana Nolan worked with. He looked over her messy work cubicle, finding nothing of real interest. Snapshots of family and friends. Assorted trinkets and odd keepsakes. The usual.

When he didn't think his head could hold any more detail, he took himself outside into the cold surrealist landscape of a television station under the scrutiny of other television stations. Several competition news vans sat across the street, recording footage of their brethren's misfortune.

Kovac dug a cigarette out of a coat pocket and lit it, taking a deep drag and watching the bitter wind take the smoke on his exhale. *Hell of a world,* he thought. News people reporting on news people missing because they were covering the news so people sitting in the safety of their homes could dig up some sympathy while secretly feeling glad their lives were so mundane they would never make it on the news themselves.

In need of food, he got in the car and drove away from the station. There was bound to be something nearby—fast food, a coffee shop, a convenience store.

A Holiday station.

He saw the sign as he cruised under the freeway. A left instead of a right at the bottom of the exit Dana Nolan would have taken every day to get to work.

The gas pumps and the store were busy with lunchtime customers. Kovac went inside and scoped the place out, looking for the security cameras. There were two clerks working the registers—a tall, bone-thin man who looked like his dour face was carved from ebony, and a short, doughy-looking kid with a shaved head and earrings that looked like miniature walrus tusks had been driven through his earlobes.

Kovac showed them Dana Nolan's picture.

The kid with the earrings didn't recognize her. The other man nodded.

"Oh, yes," he said slowly, his somber expression never changing. "The lovely lady."

"Has she been in here recently?"

"Nearly every day," he said. His speech was heavily accented, some African dialect, but carefully enunciated. "Very early. Not today."

"In the last few days have you noticed anyone with her, bothering her, talking to her when she was in here?"

"She is very friendly," he said. "People know her. They speak to her always. She always has a smile."

Kovac thanked him and stepped away from the counter to let him tend to his customers. He couldn't imagine the place had too much traffic at three in the morning. Then again, there were enough people up at that hour of the day to warrant every TV station in town having an early news program.

God forbid we let any hour of the day go by undocumented, unrecorded, or without scrutiny, he thought. Then again, if not for that conceit and paranoia, there would be no surveillance tapes.

Needing fuel, Kovac got himself a hot dog off the carousel and loaded it up with condiments, ready to settle in front of another bad TV in another cramped back office to look for another predator.

"WE'RE CONCERNED, Mrs. Gray, that Penny might have been victimized by a sexual predator at some point over the past year or so," Nikki said carefully.

It was important to be diplomatic in the wording of these things, though she felt as if she had already used up her quota of diplomacy for the day. Dealing with Principal Rodgers had taken a good share of it. Dealing with Kyle's situation had taken the rest.

She wasn't angry. She understood his desire to attend the assembly. In fact, she was proud of him for going. God knew, most of the kids who had been in attendance would have cheerfully gone off and done something else with that time. She felt sad and frustrated that so few of them seemed to care about what had happened to their schoolmate in any way other than how what had happened might directly affect them.

She was frustrated with Kyle's ongoing problems with the Fogelman kid. She didn't know what to do about it. She didn't know that there was anything she *could* do about it. And for the time being, she couldn't allow herself to be distracted by it.

Now she sat in the living room of the woman who had punched her hard enough that she still had half a headache from it, trying to scrape together the last of her diplomacy reserves. The Christmas tree had dried to a fire hazard, no doubt neglected for the past few days. The festive tree skirt was littered with needles. Julia Gray gripped the arms of the chair she sat in, as if she were afraid it might eject her at any moment.

They had arrived just minutes after calling. A surprise appearance had seemed the way to go, rather than requesting Julia Gray come downtown and allowing her time to get her guard up. As cruel as that seemed, they needed a genuine response from her, whether it was shock or outrage or whatever the emotion that came instantly.

"No," she said emphatically, shaking her head. "That can't be. I don't believe that."

Nikki and Elwood exchanged a glance. They sat side by side on the sofa. Elwood had set his laptop on the coffee table. He lifted the screen and turned it on.

"She didn't give you any indication of something being wrong?" Liska asked.

"Something was *always* wrong," Julia said impatiently. "She was *always* unhappy. She's been like that her entire life, always angry and difficult. Even as a baby. She cried all the time. Then came the temper tantrums. She never got along with other children. She was too shy or too sensitive. It was always something. I don't know why, but it was nothing like *that*. No one ever abused her."

"When she was in therapy with him, Dr. Warner never gave you any indication—"

"No." She put her hands in her lap and turned her engagement ring around and around on her finger.

"And you said she never really spoke to the therapist she saw after him."

"It was a complete waste of money," she said. "Don't you think if she had been abused she would have told one of them? She didn't."

Elwood turned the computer on the table so she could see it. "We found an online video account where your daughter posted videos of herself reciting some of her poetry. This poem in particular caught our attention. She posted this in April."

He clicked the Play icon.

Liska watched Julia's face as her daughter's image came on the screen. She held herself stiffly. Tears misted her eyes, but she turned slightly away, as if it was simply too painful to see her daughter alive, knowing she was dead. Or maybe the emotion was shame. Kovac had said the first time they had come to Julia Gray to ask about her daughter, the woman had shown them a photograph years old because she couldn't stand to look at what the girl had become.

On the computer screen, Penny Gray recited her poem "Help Me," her voice a painful mix of monotone edged in bitterness. A disappointed girl trying to sound too adult to give a shit. Both the words and the visual image spoke to a loss of trust, a transformation from vulnerability to disillusionment.

Julia Gray didn't want to see it. She literally turned away from it.

Nikki leaned over and turned up the volume.

```
Refuge
Asylum
Safest place to be
Secrets
Hard truths
Soul laid bare to see
Comfort
Guidance
Shoulder. Lean on me
Seduction
```

```
Destruction
Help not meant to be
Silence
Shameful
Not to be believed
Don't tell
Go to hell
There's no one here for me
```

"She seems to be talking about the betrayal of an authority fig-ure," Elwood said when the video was done.

Julia shifted restlessly on the chair. "She was angry with her father for leaving. There was never anything abusive between them."

"Your ex-husband's new wife is young, isn't she?"

She gave him a dirty look, offended on her ex-husband's behalf. "Brandi is young; she's not a child, for God's sake! Tim is a rotten philandering bastard, but he's not a pedophile! He never laid a hand on our daughter—even when he probably should have."

"Sometimes when girls Penny's age lose their fathers," Nikki began, choosing her words like footsteps through a minefield, "they're at an age where they're just coming into their sexuality. They're just discovering they have a certain power with the opposite sex. They can confuse the lines between love and sex."

"I can't believe we're having this conversation," Julia muttered.

Her body language screamed that she wanted to get up and leave. She didn't want cops in her house. She didn't want to talk about her daughter's problems. She probably would have been just as happy to pretend she'd never had a daughter at all.

"I know this is hard, Mrs. Gray—"

Julia Gray's head snapped around, her eyes narrowed and hard. "You *know*? What do you *know*? What do you *know*, Detective? You don't know how hard this is. You don't know how hard it's been to be my daughter's mother. You've never lost a child. Have you?"

"No, ma'am. I haven't," Nikki said, without apology this time, out of patience.

"But let me tell you something, Julia," she said, leaning forward, instantly changing the dynamic of the situation with her energy. "If someone hurt one of my boys and the police came to ask me questions about what might have been going on in their lives, I would damn well answer them. I would be in their faces every minute of every day demanding they turn over every possible rock no matter what ugly thing might crawl out from under it. I would not be sitting in my living room, whining and crying about how hard it all is on *me*."

Julia Gray's jaw dropped.

Elwood made a sound of disapproval. "Tinks—"

"No!" she snapped, standing up. "I've had it with this bullshit. Your daughter is dead, Julia. Somebody killed her. Horribly. Brutally. Would you like to see the pictures? Would you like to see what we had to see the night her murdered corpse fell out of the trunk of a moving vehicle?"

"No!"

"No, you wouldn't, because that would take the attention away from you, wouldn't it? Poor you. Poor you. What a burden your daughter was. You should be happy she's dead."

Julia Gray got to her feet. "That's outrageous!"

Nikki looked her hard in the eye. "Yes, it is. Your daughter is lying dead on a slab at the morgue and you haven't even asked to see her. You've just left her there—"

Elwood rose then to put space between them. Nikki walked away with her hands on her hips.

"I apologize for my partner, Mrs. Gray," he said, taking up the mantle of Good Cop. "These cases are very stressful for us as well, especially for those of us with children and those of us who have worked on cases of child sexual abuse."

"Penny was not abused," Julia said staunchly.

"Dr. Warner told us she had become very manipulative toward men, that that was one of the reasons he decided he shouldn't be treating her any longer," Elwood said. "Was there some specific incident that prompted him to make that decision?"

"Michael has done nothing wrong."

"We're not suggesting that he has. We're looking at the changes in your daughter's behavior over the past nine months or so, and we think there might have been something that triggered those changes around the time she broke her wrist."

"You said the accident happened on her way home from Dr. Warner's office—" Liska started.

"What is wrong with you people?" Julia shouted, her anger bursting its seams. "My daughter was taken by some maniac! Some maniac who has already killed eight other girls. Now he's taken another girl—that news girl—and you're wasting time treating me like a criminal and accusing a good man—"

Even as she said it the front door opened and Michael Warner came in looking like a well-tailored superhero, his shoulders broad, his expression serious. Julia Gray went to him, dissolving into tears as she fell against his chest.

"Julia, what's going on?" he asked. He looked to Elwood and Liska. "What do you people want from her?"

"The truth," Nikki said. "Maybe you can help us with that, Dr. Warner."

"We're done dealing with you," Warner said tightly as he put his arms around his weeping fiancée. "If you have any more questions, you can speak to my attorney."

40

"They lawyered up," Liska announced as they walked into the conference room.

Kovac glanced back at them. "Who?"

"Julia Gray and Michael Warner. We tried to broach the subject of Penny possibly having been sexually abused, and they lawyered up."

"She's leaving out the shouting, threats, and accusations," Elwood said, going to the coffeepot.

"They were upset?"

"*I* was upset," Liska admitted. "I can't decide if I should feel badly for Julia Gray or snatch her by the hair and slap the snot out of her."

"If you go for the second option, there should be mud wrestling and bikinis involved," Tippen said. "We can bill it as a grudge match."

She gave him the finger.

Kovac let the banter float past him. He had been staring at the television screen for too long again. He had borrowed a second television and VCR and wedged them side by side on the stand so he could play them at the same time. His vision was beginning to blur around the edges.

"Tinks, come look at this," he said, fussing with the remotes, getting everything set up the way he needed it.

"Is it porn?" Tippen asked hopefully. "It's been a long day."

"We're not at your house, Tip," Liska shot back. She pulled out the chair next to Kovac and sat.

"The screen on the left is the footage from the Holiday station the night Penny Gray went missing. It's a few minutes before she comes into the store. Tell me if anyone looks familiar."

No one said anything as the tape played.

Kovac stopped it as Penny Gray walked out of the shot, backed the tape up, and played it again, freezing it when his person of interest appeared. "This guy," he said, tapping the screen with his finger. "Does he look familiar at all?"

Liska squinted and shrugged. "My uncle Leo on my mother's side?"

"No! Look harder."

"Sam, I'm so tired, I can't see straight as it is. If I look any harder, I'm going to burn my retinas."

Kovac grumbled under his breath and hit Play on the second remote.

"This one is footage from the Holiday station down the road from where Dana Nolan works. This is from yesterday. She stops there regularly on her way in to work.

"That's her," he said, pointing to the girl.

Dana Nolan entered the store, waved to the guy behind the counter, went to the coffee station. A big guy in a parka said something to her. She tipped her head back and appeared to laugh. A minute later another man walked into the store—short, squat, bearded.

"That guy," he said, freezing the frame and tapping the screen. "I think it's the same guy. Don't you think it's the same guy?"

Liska shrugged, looking from one screen to the other. The images were distant and blurry. "Maybe. I don't know. They're both short and have beards and parkas."

"They're both short and have beards and parkas, and they're in Holiday stations with girls who went missing," he said.

"Doc Holiday trolling the Holiday stations?" Tippen said. "His idea of a joke?"

"Dana Nolan picked the store," Kovac said. "If our bad guy was stalking her, then he just followed her there. But I'm sure the irony wasn't lost on him."

"I don't know, Sam," Liska said. "If Doc Holiday took Penny Gray, she was a victim of opportunity, like all his other victims. He had to just happen to be there when she was. But the girl had other people in her life who might have wanted her dead. What are the odds she got nabbed by a serial killer?"

"What are the odds anyway?" Kovac challenged. "And just because people in your personal life hate you doesn't mean you can't become a victim of a random crime.

"That's not even my point," he said. "I looked at this first tape this morning and I thought I should know the guy, but I couldn't put my finger on why. Then I see him on the footage of Dana Nolan."

Liska shook her head. "I'm not convinced it's the same guy."

Kovac ignored her protest. "Think back. A year ago."

"Oh my God," she groaned. "I can't remember last night!"

"Stop being a wiseass," he snapped, irritated no one else seemed to be catching on. "Think back a year ago to Rose Reiser."

"Rose . . . ?"

He watched his partner's face as she processed the thoughts and dug up the memory. He saw the second the seed took hold.

"Oh my God," she murmured. She took the remotes away from him and pointed them at the televisions like a pair of laser guns. She backed the tapes up and played them simultaneously.

"It can't be that guy," she said. "We checked him out six ways to Sunday."

"What guy?" Elwood asked.

"The guy that reported finding Rose Reiser's body last year," she said. "New Year's Doe was called in by a guy driving a box truck full of antiques and junk. But he was completely cooperative. He didn't even complain when we went through his truck with a fine-toothed comb."

"Frank Fitzgerald," Kovac said. "He's from Iowa."

"Drives a box truck," Tippen said. "Travels as part of his business."

"But we checked him out," Liska insisted. "There was nothing. Zip. Nada."

"But there he is," Kovac said, pointing at the screen.

"Or a guy who looks vaguely like him," she argued. "As a single woman, I hate to say it, but there are a lot more guys running around looking like that guy than any Hollywood heartthrob."

"Well, I don't like it," Kovac said stubbornly. "That's three too many coincidences."

"You think a serial killer would just happily hand over his vehicle to crime scene investigators?" Liska asked.

"If he knew he'd cleaned it up well enough."

"Those are some cojones."

"Yeah, Tinks," Tippen said. "You might want to reconsider lowering your standards on the rest of the package if the guy has a set like that."

Liska rolled her eyes. "That's just wishful thinking on your part."

"Frank Fitzgerald. I talked to that guy on the phone yesterday," Elwood said, bringing them back on point. "His name was on the call list for reviewing the old cases. He was sorry to hear we had a new one."

"Where was he?" Liska asked.

"Iowa number."

"Doesn't mean he's in Iowa," Kovac said.

"Doesn't mean he's not," Liska returned. She glanced up at the television sets, her eyes going wide. "What the fuck?!"

She grabbed the remote and hit Pause, freezing the frame on Aaron Fogelman walking away from the counter at the Holiday station near the Rock & Bowl the night of Penny Gray's disappearance. Kovac could feel her shock and braced himself for what would follow it. She turned and punched him hard on the arm.

"Are you fucking kidding me?" she asked, glaring at him. "You watched this all the way through, and you didn't mention this to me?"

"I just watched it this far through this morning. This is like ten minutes after the Gray girl leaves the store."

"And gets in the trunk of that sociopath's car! Goddamnit, Kojak! How could you not bring this to my attention?"

"You know, I got a little distracted by a kidnapping," he said. "Do you think this kid was up at three in the morning snatching Dana Nolan off the street?"

"Don't be stupid!"

"I've got the other guy in two videos related to two victims, and reporting the dead body of a victim a year ago," Kovac said.

"You've got a hunch based on a vague resemblance, and you want to bet it like a trifecta at the racetrack!" Liska argued. "Are you out of your freaking mind?

"Aaron Fogelman hit Penny Gray not twenty minutes before this video," she said. "He *punched* her. The kid has a violent temper. He's a liar. Here he is in this store within minutes of our victim. And you're going off about some poor schmuck from Iowa who probably isn't even in the state? Have you gone senile?"

"I'm not saying we exclude the Fogelman kid as a person of interest on the Gray homicide," Kovac said. "I'm saying there's a bigger possibility here."

"Well, say it to someone else," Liska said, getting up to move away from him. "We've got people in Penny Gray's life who are lying out their asses every time they open their mouths, and that kid is one of them," she said, pointing to the screen. "For Christ's sake, the girl's own mother just lawyered up. I've already got a call in to Aaron Fogelman's father. I'm betting he does the same. I know where my focus is staying."

Kovac spread his hands in surrender. "That's fine," he said. "Stay on it. I hope you're right, Tinks. Because if you're not, we've got a bigger monster on our hands than I want to think about."

41

On the upside of kidnapping a news reporter was the fact that he didn't have to wonder about the investigation. There were no long lapses in coverage of the case, particularly on the station she worked for.

Fitz kept the TV tuned in for all the breaking news—of which there was none, of course. They kept showing the parking lot of Dana Nolan's apartment building, blocked off with fluttering ribbons of yellow crime scene tape and crawling with cops and crime scene investigators swarming around her car like ants on a scrap of food.

He recognized Kovac moving around the scene with his hands jammed in his pockets and his shoulders hunched against the wind. There was no sign of his partner, Liska. That was a bit of a disappointment.

The NewsWatch people kept putting up photographs of their missing news girl and making pleas for information. The level of desperation was very high. He liked that. The adrenaline rush he got from hearing that was something new and intoxicating and probably addicting. He had always been happy with his way of doing things. The balance of risk to reward he maintained had always been just right for him. But this, he admitted, was heady stuff. He had to be careful not to get drunk on it and make a mistake. He had to keep his objective in mind.

He had a point to make.

He couldn't get too excited that the homicide captain, Kasselmann, made a personal appearance not only at the official press conference but in the studio on the *News Watch* set, to say the police department was taking very seriously the idea that they were dealing with a very dangerous predator in Doc Holiday. Giving credit where credit was due.

That was all he really wanted at the heart of it, he thought with a smile as he turned to his latest victim, who was still alive and crying, waiting for him to kill her. He was an artist, and he wanted recognition for his work.

He chose a knife with a fine sharp point and leaned over the terrified girl. She was naked, tied down spread-eagle to the work table. He had removed the duct tape from her mouth and replaced it with a red ball gag. He could smell her fear. The scent was an aphrodisiac like no other. Her eyes widened with panic as he touched the tip of the blade to the center of her chest. Blood bloomed rose red against her pale white skin.

"And you, my love," he said as the excitement stirred within him, "will be my masterpiece."

42

"The address on his DL is one of those mailbox places," Kovac said, pouring another cup of coffee. He figured he had to be on his second gallon of the day. Dinner was pizza someone had left over from lunch. Dessert would be a handful of whatever antacids he could find in his desk drawer. Tinks had gone home to feed her kids. He wished he was one of them.

"We've got a phone number, right?" Kasselmann said, taking a seat at the table, which was littered with paperwork and file folders, coffee cups and food wrappers. He cast a dubious glance at the lone remaining piece of pizza drying out like a piece of roadkill on the abandoned greasy cardboard box. He had spent most of his day dealing with the media. The knot in his tie was still square. His only concession to exhaustion was the removal of his suit jacket.

In contrast, Kovac knew he looked like he had crawled out of bed after sleeping off a three-day bender in his clothes. He needed a shave. He needed a shower. He needed a good night's sleep and a long vacation on a beach someplace where no one had ever heard the words *windchill factor*. He had spent the day either freezing his ass off outdoors or sweating like a horse in this room.

"Elwood spoke to him yesterday. He said the guy was cordial and sympathetic and wished he could do something to help," Kovac said. "I called the number this afternoon and left a message requesting a callback. I haven't heard anything."

"We need his phone records," Kasselmann said. "Find out where that phone is pinging."

"I've got no cause for a warrant." He shrugged. "I talked my way into getting as much as the address. He's got no wants or warrants. I've got nothing but some iffy surveillance video. Tinks isn't convinced it's him on the tape. I can't swear to it, but I've got that feeling in my gut."

"I wouldn't bet against that," Kasselmann said. "You've got good instincts, Sam."

"Right now, that and a dollar will buy you jack shit," he said. " 'Cause other than my hunch we've got nothing to go on here. No witnesses. No fingerprints. No suspects. No leads."

He walked to the wall where he had taped a copy of the missing persons flier with the photo of Penny Gray and the signature of a killer.

HAPPY HOLIDAY

Smug bastard.

"This guy is sitting out there somewhere laughing and giving us the finger," he said.

"We'd better hope that's all he's doing," Kasselmann said, getting to his feet.

Kovac said nothing, but he couldn't help but recall what John Quinn had said that morning. Doc Holiday had taken Dana Nolan for the primary purpose of killing her. He had had her in his control now for seventeen hours.

And there wasn't a damn thing Sam could do about it.

"HE THREW THE FIRST PUNCH, MOM."

"I know," Nikki said, glancing at her son.

He sat at the kitchen island with an ice pack wrapped around his right hand. He looked like less of a little boy to her tonight, more of a young man. Today she had seen him stand up to a bully and protect a young lady. He was growing up. She couldn't decide if she was sad or proud or scared to death. All of the above, she supposed.

It had been so difficult to stay in the car as she had pulled up to the scene of the fight. But she had stayed put and let Elwood step in, knowing she would only have embarrassed Kyle and given his enemies future ammunition to use against him.

"Are you going to want more of this?" she asked, as she replaced the aluminum foil over the pan of lasagna. She had stopped at their favorite Italian restaurant on her way home and picked up dinner. It wasn't homemade, but it was better than nothing.

She hated the thought that the best she could do these days for her sons was "better than nothing."

"Maybe," he said. "Probably."

She slid the pan back into the oven and left the temperature on the lowest setting. "Don't let me forget this and burn the house to the ground."

"Okay."

R.J. came into the kitchen to refill his glass with milk. "Can I have a brownie?"

"Yes."

"Can I watch TV?"

"Is your homework done?"

He nodded, digging a brownie out of the pan Marysue had brought over. *Better than nothing . . .*

"Can we get a dog?"

"No. Thought you would just slip that one by me, did you?" Nikki said.

He made a goofy face. "Can't blame a guy for trying."

Nikki shook her head, glad for the comic relief. But as soon as her youngest had left the room, her mind went back to the matter at hand.

"What's the story with the Fogelman kid?" she asked. "Has he always been a problem for you?"

"That guy's such a jerk."

"The world is full of them," Nikki said. "Some are worse than others."

Some grew up to be criminals. Some grew up to be serial killers. Aaron Fogelman had a temper. He didn't hesitate to use his fists—even against a girl. Where did he draw the line? Nikki wanted to know everything about him. Did he have empathy for other people? Was he cruel to animals? Did he have a history of destroying property?

"Does he make a habit of hurting people?" she asked.

Kyle shrugged. "He's mostly talk. He's a bully. He does what bullies do."

"You said he struck Gray that night at the Rock and Bowl. Had you ever seen him hit a girl before?"

"No, but he calls girls bitches and whores and stuff like that."

It was terrible to imagine a kid Kyle's age doing what had been done to Penny Gray, but Nikki knew it happened. She hoped to God it hadn't happened this time. Because of the complication of her being Kyle's mother, she had passed the responsibility of further investigating Aaron Fogelman to Elwood. He had requested a meeting with the boy's father and had been referred to the Fogelmans' attorney.

"So what's the story with you and this girl Brittany?" she asked, pouring herself a cup of coffee.

He shrugged and blushed and dodged her gaze. "She's a friend."

She was the friend whose photograph Nikki had found in the trash some months ago. Her baby's first girlfriend. "She's very pretty."

"Yeah, I guess so," he said, squirming on his stool.

Nikki took the seat beside him. "She seems very sweet. She was friends with Gray?"

"Yeah. We were all in that writing workshop last summer. Gray and Britt and me. We used to hang out."

"And then?"

"Then Brittany wanted to be with Christina's crowd, and Christina and Gray don't get along."

"She seems to be rethinking that now."

"She's so much better than that," he said with frustration. "I don't get why girls want to be like Christina."

"I vaguely remember being a teenage girl," Nikki said. "It seemed so important to be accepted by the coolest kids."

"Accepted," he muttered with a small ironic twist to his mouth. "Accepted by kids who don't accept anyone different from them."

"People don't always make sense."

"Brittany talked Gray into going to the Rock and Bowl that night," he said. "Now she feels guilty. We both do. I told her maybe we should go see Gray's mom. You know, give her condolences or whatever."

Nikki's heart swelled with pride. She was somehow managing to raise a responsible young man.

"That's a really nice idea, Kyle. I'm sure Gray's mom would be touched by that," she said. "But I'm going to ask you to wait on that. Brittany should go if she wants to, but things are complicated with me investigating this case and you knowing Gray, and all of that. It's best if you stay away from all of those people for now—Gray's mom, Christina, Aaron Fogelman. Can you do that for me? Just lay low for a while until this gets sorted out."

He frowned down at the ice pack on his hand, thinking for a moment. "Can I still text Britt?"

"I don't have a problem with that."

He didn't like being taken out of his role, but in the end, he nodded. "Okay."

"Thank you," Nikki said.

She leaned over and hugged him around his broadening shoulders and kissed his cheek. "Do you know how proud I am of who you're growing up to be?"

He ducked his head and blushed and slipped away, embarrassed in a good way, Nikki thought. She loved him so much she thought her heart would burst.

The doorbell rang, saving him from further humiliation. Nikki excused him to go to his room as she went to the door to find Kovac standing on her porch.

"Is everything okay?" she asked.

"No," he said, his face set in his trademark scowl. "The world is going to hell on a sled and there's not a goddamn thing I can do about it."

"And this is news?"

"No, but I figured if I came over here and said it, you might feed me something that isn't crawling with salmonella."

"You didn't eat that pizza, did you?"

"No!" he said. "Maybe. Just a slice."

"Get in here," she ordered, holding the door open.

He came in with an armload of files and toed off his shoes in the foyer. "Do you think I'll get food poisoning?"

"Oh, for God's sake. You have a stomach like a billy goat."

"As it happens, I smell like one too."

"You can't scare me. I live with boys."

They went into the kitchen and he set his stack of paperwork on the island counter beside the stack of paper she had brought home and took the seat at the island that Kyle had vacated. Nikki pulled the lasagna out of the oven and made him a plate.

"You didn't make this," he said after the first bite.

"Why do you say that with such conviction?"

With food in his stomach he found half a smile. "I'm glad you got to eat with your kids tonight. Who cares where the food came from?"

Nikki took her seat beside him and warmed her hands with her coffee mug. "Any news on our news girl?"

He shook his head. "I've got a call in to my serial killer. Just waiting for him to call me back and confess."

"Do you really think it's Fitzgerald?" she asked. "If that turns out to be true, we're going to look like a bunch of assholes. We could have had him a year ago. He's killed how many girls since then? How could we have missed that, Sam?"

"He's damn good at what he does. He's got it down to a fine science. We already knew that," he said. "I'm trying to find out what I can about Frank Fitzgerald, but I've got nothing to go on. All I know right now is he has no police record and he gets his mail at a storefront in a strip mall in Des Moines. That's probably not even his real name."

"He's been so careful," Nikki said. "We've gone over all of the Doc Holiday cases ten times. He hasn't made a mistake. I just can't buy that he screwed up so badly with Penny Gray. Quinn said these guys make their mistakes when they change their MO. If he snatched the Gray girl, she fit his pattern. Dana Nolan doesn't fit his old pattern, but I believe that's him."

"And I'm waiting for the mistake," Kovac said. "I hope to God he makes it soon. Anything new on your side?"

She filled him in on the situation with the Fogelman boy.

Kovac gave her a careful look, like he thought she might punch him and he had better keep his distance. "You're sure you're being objective about this kid, Tinks? You're not just being a momma tiger?"

"No," she said. "It's two separate things. Do I want to kick his ass for giving Kyle a hard time? Yes. Do I put my detective cap on and look at him and see a narcissistic sociopath with violent and misogynistic tendencies? Yes. You interviewed him. What did you think?"

"That he's a narcissistic sociopath with violent tendencies. And he's a liar. And he needs his ass kicked."

Nikki lifted her hands. "See? Nobody wants to believe kids could do what was done to Penny Gray, but you and I both know they can and do. And we can't rule out Michael Warner yet either. The sex abuse angle is too strong. I'm hoping maybe we get some kind of tip out of the assembly at the school today. Tippen's niece connected well with the kids. I'm hoping she'll hear something through one of the social media outlets.

"I keep coming back to Julia Gray," she went on. "What does she know that she's not telling us, or that she's not admitting to herself? Does she just not want to see it?"

"She's lost her daughter," Kovac said. "Maybe she just wants to hang on to what she has left."

"Even if what she has left is a man who, at best, had sex with her child, or, at worst, killed her? That's insane."

He raised his eyebrows and pointed to the tiny caterpillar line of stitches above her left eyebrow where Julia Gray had struck her.

"Yeah," she conceded, reaching across the island to grab a file folder off the stack. "She's walking a mental tightrope, praying her

fiancé isn't a pedophile and hoping her daughter was taken by a serial killer."

Kovac slid his dinner plate aside. "Yeah. I nominate that one for
Mother of the Year."

"If we could get our hands on the girl's phone or her computer, I
know we'd get some answers," Nikki said. "Kyle says Gray made a
lot of videos on her phone. She posted some of herself reciting her
poetry to her YouTube account, but it's safe to assume there are a
lot more. I wouldn't be surprised if she had a video diary."

"Her mother told us she kept her laptop with her at all times,"
Kovac said. "It could still be in her car, wherever that is. More likely
it's with her killer. If that was someone in her circle, they would have
to know it might contain evidence. They would have to get rid of it.
If Doc Holiday killed her, he would probably keep it for a souvenir."

"We know someone still has her phone," Nikki said.

"And they were nearby when they sent texts to Julia Gray."

"Michael Warner and Aaron Fogelman both live within a mile or
so of the Gray house as the crow flies. And we have no way of
knowing where Doc is. He could live nearby or he could be watching Julia Gray's house for all we know."

"There's a grim notion," Kovac said.

Liska arched a brow. "Do we get to have any other kind?"

43

can't blieve u btrayed me like that Britt. So hurt!

Brittany stared at the text and sighed. There were a dozen like that, at least. She had answered none of them.

It made her angry to read them. Christina made out like she was the wounded party. She hadn't asked for Brittany's side of the story. She hadn't asked why Brittany had left the assembly the way she had, or how she had come to be walking down the street with Kyle Hatcher. Christina was only about Christina. The universe revolved around her, and everything that happened, happened to her or because of her.

She was so selfish. Even when it appeared she was being generous, she was being selfish. Brittany looked now on the reasons she had liked Christina in the first place and saw them in a completely different light. What she had seen as strength, she now saw as arrogance. What she had seen as generosity, she now saw as manipulation. She saw that Christina did nothing without expecting something in return. She was like a fairy-tale queen who pretended to love her subjects but only wanted what they could give her or do for her. And when they didn't meet her expectations, they were punished.

Brittany knew she was being punished even as she sat alone in her bedroom. She had gone on Facebook and Twitter to see what was being said about her and about Kyle by Christina and her minions. Lies, accusations, name-calling.

The flip side of friendship with Christina Warner.

Her phone pinged again.

I wish I understood. Can we meet and talk?

Brittany didn't answer. Christina didn't want to understand. She wanted to ambush her—just like she had Gray that night at the Rock & Bowl.

Gray might have been strange and out there and difficult, but she had always been honest. She called a spade a spade, as Brittany's father liked to say—which was why she had so few friends.

That was the catch, Brittany realized. Now that Gray was gone, she was finally seeing the truth: that Gray would have been a better friend to her than Christina ever could have been.

It was the same with Kyle. Kyle had no time for the bullshit games of Christina's crowd. He said what he meant and meant what he said. And for a while, Brittany hadn't wanted to hear it. His truth had made her angry and resentful. But he only wanted her to see what was real and be the best person she could be, and wasn't that a better friend than the kind of friend Christina was?

She walked around her happy yellow bedroom with her arms wrapped around herself as if she were freezing, wishing life didn't have to be so hard, wondering what she should do next. Something strong, she thought. Something positive.

She thought about the poem Sonya Porter had read at the assembly that morning—Gray's poem about acceptance. And she thought about what Sonya had said after, that they should all be angry someone had taken Gray and her talent and everything she had been and could have become away from them.

I am angry, Brittany thought.

She was angry with Christina; she was angry with the killer; she was angry with herself. The question was: What was she going to do about it? Wallow and cry and pout and wish the world was a different place? Or stand up and make the world a different place by being who she needed to be?

She picked up her iPad from her bed and paged through her pictures from the writer's workshop that summer—herself and Kyle and Gray—and realized that Gray was touching and changing her life even now. More now than when she had been alive. She owed her friend something for that.

She and Kyle had made a plan to go to see Gray's mom, to give her their condolences. They didn't want to wait until there was a funeral or a memorial, when it would be easy to just be one of a bunch of people saying what they were supposed to say. They wanted to do it together, on their own, when it took an effort, and they couldn't just blend in with the crowd. They had decided they owed it to Gray to go tell her mom that they had considered her daughter their friend and that they were sorry she was gone.

They wanted to do it tonight—before they could talk themselves out of it. They had agreed to go after supper. Brittany wanted to go and come back before her mother returned from her pottery class. Kyle would come here and they would walk together the few blocks to Gray's house.

Her phone announced another text message with a bright *ping!* Brittany glanced at it, braced to see Christina's name on the screen, but it was Kyle.

how r u? r u ok?

That was how he always started his texts to her—with concern for her. As many times as she'd been a bitch to him, as many times as she'd told him to leave her alone, his first concern had always been her well-being.

Wish u were here, she typed, then hesitated, thinking she wasn't brave enough to send it. She looked at the picture of Gray on her iPad and drew on the memory of her friend's strength. Gray would have sent the text. Gray would have told her to send the text. Gray would have said, *Fuck yeah! Send it!*

She hit the Send button, and butterflies took wing in her stomach as the message went out into space.

The answer came back right away. *Me 2*

She felt giddy and guilty at the same time. She'd been so mean to him, and he was so nice.

Can't go with u to c Gray's mom cuz of my mom/investigation. Really sorry

Her disappointment was instant. She wanted to see him, to spend time with him without all the tension and BS of school and the people in it. More than that, she realized, she wanted to hide behind his strength when they met with Gray's mom.

Her first excuse was that she was shy by nature. She had met Gray's mom only a couple of times, and her perception of Julia Gray had been colored by the things her daughter had said about her— that she was cold, that she was selfish, that she was a bitch. But that had been Gray's reality with her mother and didn't have anything to do with the here and now, or with what Brittany needed to do to fulfill her obligation to her friend.

The truth was that she didn't want to be strong on her own. She wanted to let Kyle be strong for her.

No.

No worries, she typed. *will txt u when I get back.*

UL go alone? U shouldn't.

It's just a few blocks.

Still wish u wouldn't.

I'll b fine.

B careful.

I will. Thnx.

She sent the message and tucked her phone into the front pocket of her baby-pink cashmere hoodie, feeling like she had him close to her that way. Grabbing the handle of Gray's duffel bag, she went downstairs to pull on her coat and the new Ugg boots she had gotten for Christmas. It would take ten minutes to walk to Gray's house near the lake.

It seemed strange to be carrying the belongings of someone who would never use them again, she thought as she started down the street. Makeup, underwear, sweaters, and socks. A toothbrush, a hairbrush, her laptop computer.

The weirdest thought was that Gray lived on inside her computer. She kept everything on it. Her journal, her poetry. iPhoto contained hundreds of pictures of herself and her friends, and all the places she had been and people she had found interesting. She had always been snapping photos with her phone, making videos on her phone. She recorded everything and everyone—friends, strangers, homeless people, dogs. She was always recording her thoughts and ideas.

In her recordings and in her poetry, Gray would always be alive, telling her story.

Brittany wondered if Gray's mom would let her copy some of what was on the computer. She could keep it like a digital scrapbook. She would end up spending more time with Gray after she was dead than when she had been alive.

Her nerves were vibrating as she walked. The night was pitch-dark. There seemed to be no stars in the sky. She could see people in their homes looking warm and snug on the other side of their picture windows. They didn't notice her. She was alone out in the cold.

She hurried from one pool of white streetlight to the next, suddenly too aware of being the only person on the street. The police thought a serial killer might have gotten Gray. She thought of someone like that haunting dark alleys in bad parts of the city or on isolated roads in industrial parks or out in the country—like they showed in the movies—not in her nice upper-middle-class neighborhood. That was what she thought when she was in the safety of her own home. Now she was on the street, alone, walking to the home of a girl who had been murdered.

Inside her hoodie pocket her phone pinged with another message. Brittany stuck her hand inside her coat and fished it out. Another message from Christina.

I can pick u up. We should talk.

What was there to talk about? The fact that Christina thought she was too stupid to look on Twitter to see the things her friends were saying?

Annoyed, she turned the sound to Vibrate and tucked the phone back in the pocket of her sweater. A bolt of panic went through her as she thought Christina might already be in the neighborhood, expecting Brittany to cave in and agree to meet her somewhere or let Christina pick her up. What if Christina was at Mrs. Gray's house, along with her father?

Dr. Warner was engaged to Gray's mom now, something Gray had been strongly against. She disliked Michael Warner. He had been her therapist for a while. She had probably told him all kinds of things she wouldn't have told her mother. Having him dating her mother was like some kind of breach of patient/doctor trust. Gray and her mother had fought about it, and her mom had kicked her out of the house because of that fight. Maybe Gray had said the same vile thing about Dr. Warner to her mother that she had said to Christina that night at the Rock & Bowl.

Brittany had met Dr. Warner on several occasions, and she had to admit she didn't like him either. There was something vaguely creepy and phony about him. She didn't like the way he was always touching Christina when they were together—putting his hand on her shoulder, on her back, touching her hair. Christina wasn't bothered by it, but it made Brittany uncomfortable. She decided if there were cars in the Gray driveway, she was going to turn around and go home.

She turned onto the block where Gray had lived and squinted against the glare of headlights coming her way. Her heart picked up a beat. The dark car seemed to crawl toward her like a panther stalking, sliding closer and closer to the curb. She thought of Christina and Aaron. Aaron's dark car. She thought of the look on his face that morning as he ordered her to get in his car. She thought of him rushing at Kyle, fists swinging, and the way he had struck Gray that night at the Rock & Bowl . . .

She thought about serial killers . . . and girls turned into zombies . . .

She was all alone.

The car came alongside her, and the passenger's window slid down.

Brittany's heart was in her throat. She should have listened to Kyle and stayed home.

"Excuse me, miss," a middle-aged woman said. "Can you tell us how to get to the freeway?"

Brittany was so relieved her knees went weak. She didn't even think about the fact that these people were strangers and could have been dangerous too. The lady was her mother's age. In the movies and on TV serial killers were all creepy-looking guys with scary eyes, not soccer moms.

She gave the people directions and took a deep breath as they drove away. She was alone again.

The day before, this neighborhood had been all over the news. Brittany had seen some of the coverage on television. News vans had lined the street. Cameramen and photographers and reporters had been camped outside the Gray home. Gray had been a missing person then. Now she was dead, and the news vans were gone. What happened after a person was gone was of no interest to anyone outside that person's life.

The neighborhood was empty now and dark there at the end of the block backing onto the darker, emptier park. A creepy feeling scratched at the back of Brittany's neck as she walked up the driveway to Gray's house. A part of her hoped Julia Gray wasn't home. She wanted to turn around and just go back. She could wait and do this another time, when Kyle could go with her. But then she told herself to stop being a chicken. Lights glowed in the downstairs windows.

Her phone vibrated inside the pocket of her hoodie. She opened her coat and dug it out and checked the screen. Kyle.

RU there yet?

Brittany slipped her gloves off and typed: *Just got here. Will txt you l8r.* She tucked the phone away, rang the doorbell, and waited.

44

The girl looked at him with fear and loathing. Fitz had to give her credit for being feistier than he would have expected.

Victims could be surprising. Sometimes the ones who fought hardest at the outset were the most pathetic in the end, begging for their lives, choking and gagging on tears and snot, peeing and shitting themselves in abject terror of death. While sometimes the meek ones rose to the occasion and defied him with more will the longer he tortured them.

Dana Nolan was one of those. He felt a certain weird kind of pride for her. He couldn't have chosen a better victim for taking his game to the next level.

He struck her once more with the hammer, feeling the energy of the scream that was stifled by the gag. The sexual rush that came with that was more intoxicating than any drug.

Still, he walked away from her. It was important to exercise discipline. It was in succumbing to the seduction of that rush where mistakes could be made. Caution would fall by the wayside. Discipline was the key to success.

He had a schedule. He had a plan. He had to stick to it or risk failure.

Beneath those thoughts, he was well aware that he was already taking more risk than was prudent. But with great risk would come great reward. He was tired of success in anonymity. He wanted recognition for his achievements. He couldn't escape the fact that he had an ego. He just had to be smart enough to control it. Riding that razor's edge was becoming almost as addictive as the rest of it.

He walked away from his worktable to his tool bench, where he had left his beer. He took a long, refreshing drink as he checked his phone for messages. He smiled as he listened, then hit the Return Call button and listened to the phone ring on the other end.

Why not? What the heck?

He took another sip of his beer and walked back to the table to admire his work. His work stared back at him.

On the other end of his call a voice answered. "Kovac."

"Hey, Detective Sam!" he said. "Frank Fitzgerald, returning your call. Hey, I'm sorry to hear about what's going on. You know, I spoke to your colleague the other day. Detective Knutson. Heck of a nice guy."

"Yeah," Kovac said. "We've got a situation going on here. We're reaching out to everyone connected to some of these older cases."

"Yeah, so he said. A serial killer, you think."

"Looks that way. Hey, you don't happen to be in the area, do you, Mr. Fitzgerald? We'd like to have you come in and look at some pictures of possible suspects."

"You know," Fitz said. "As it happens, I am in the area. I've got a big indoor flea market downtown next weekend. I came up from Des Moines early to make some contacts. Let's set something up for tomorrow. Late morning?"

"How's ten?"

"Perfect. See you then."

"Thanks."

"No problem. You have a nice evening. And please say hello to Sergeant Liska for me."

He ended the call, a big smile cutting through his beard.

He looked down at Dana Nolan. Her eyes were barely open, but he thought she was still conscious.

"Appreciate this now, Dana, while you still can," he said. "You have the privilege of being the victim of a genius."

"WHO WAS THAT?" Tinks asked.

"My killer called," Kovac said. "He sends his regards."

"He can't be the guy," Tinks said. "If he's the guy, he's got a set of balls on him that would put an elephant to shame."

"If he's upping his ante, this is a good way to do it," Kovac said. "Admit to being in the area. Come in and talk to the poor dumb cops working the case. Look at the surveillance video and say *Hell, yes, that's me buying doughnuts at the Holiday station.*"

"Then he's either a genius or delusional. Let's hope he just got too big for his britches."

"Pride goeth before the fall," Kovac said. "Let's hope it goeth straight into custody."

He got off his stool and went to the coffeemaker.

"Do you want more?" he asked, refilling his mug.

Nikki glanced over at him. "If I drink one more cup of coffee I'm going to be shaking like I'm riding a jackhammer," she said. "Not that that idea doesn't have great appeal to a single woman."

He groaned. "Please don't tell me about your sex life again."

"Lucky you, I don't have one," she said. "Even my battery-operated devices have broken up with me. The most exciting thing I think about these days when I see my bed is getting more than three hours' sleep."

"You and me both."

45

Brittany debated ringing the bell a second time. The duffel bag hung heavy on her shoulder. She could just leave it by the door. Maybe Mrs. Gray wanted to be left alone.

Even as she tried to talk herself out of it, her finger pressed the button.

Gray's mom opened the door and peered out at her with red, glassy eyes in a pale, drawn face. She looked like a ghost of the woman Brittany remembered.

Brittany swallowed the lump in her throat. "Hi, Mrs. Gray. I'm Brittany Lawler. Gray—your daughter's friend. Remember me?"

Gray's mom stared at her for a moment without saying anything. Brittany wondered if maybe she was on drugs, sedatives for her nerves. Probably, and who could blame her?

"Brittany," she said at last. A fragile smile trembled on her mouth. "Of course I remember."

"I brought Gray's bag over," Brittany said, lifting the duffel on her shoulder. "She left it at my house."

"Oh."

"It's just some clothes and makeup and stuff," she said nervously. "And her computer."

"Her computer? Oh, well, thank you. Thank you for bringing that over."

"But I was wondering," Brittany said. "Would it be okay—if I—um . . . I wanted to talk to you about Gray. Would that be all right? Is this a good time?"

Julia looked surprised. "Of course," she said. "Yes, that's fine. Come in. Please."

Brittany had only ever been in this house a couple of times. Gray usually came to her. She had told Brittany she didn't like to have people over because she felt like this house was her prison and her room was her cell, and she didn't want to subject herself or anyone she cared about to the bad energy here.

"You have a lovely home, Mrs. Gray," Brittany said, looking around the foyer.

"Thank you. Come in. It's been very quiet here. I'll appreciate your company. It's sweet of you to come."

They went into a living room with a dead Christmas tree and a fireplace. An old photo of Gray sat on a side table. Her hair had been long and plain, and she looked sad and small.

"I'm really sorry for your loss, Mrs. Gray," Brittany said. "It's terrible what happened."

Gray's mom motioned for her to sit down. "Thank you, Brittany. It's very kind of you to come by. I know Penny didn't have many friends."

"She had a few," Brittany offered, feeling badly for Gray.

Julia smiled sadly. "You're the only one I've heard from."

"I'm sorry. I guess kids just don't know what to do, considering what happened and all."

"You don't have to make excuses, Brittany. Penny didn't make it easy for people to like her. I know that more than anyone."

"No, I guess she didn't," Brittany conceded. "But sometimes I think the people who are the hardest to get to know sometimes turn out to be the most worth knowing. I think Gray was like that."

Tears came to Julia Gray's eyes as she tried to smile again. She glanced away and took a drink of something that looked like it might have alcohol in it—a pale amber liquid over ice in a heavy crystal tumbler. The glass was almost empty.

"I don't think I knew her very well," she admitted. "She was my child, but that doesn't make it easier. That makes it harder. Are you friends with your mom, Brittany?"

"Yes."

"You're lucky. Your mom is lucky," she said. "I didn't have that with my daughter. We didn't get along at all. I would imagine she didn't have many nice things to say about me."

Brittany didn't say anything at all. She was a terrible liar. And what could she say that wouldn't sound lame, anyway?

"She probably told you about the fight we had that night before she came to stay with you," she said, making an odd motion with her right hand, which was bound up in some kind of a brace, as if the fight she'd had with her daughter had been the cause of that. Or maybe the injury was the result of the fight.

Brittany said nothing. Gray was always fighting with her mother, though she had never said anything about the fights being physical at all. She couldn't even imagine getting in a physical fight with her mother or anyone else.

"Did she tell you about that?" Julia asked.

"Not really."

"She wasn't very happy about me getting engaged to Michael," she said. She took another sip of her drink. "She was always so jealous of anything good happening to me."

Brittany squirmed in her chair, physically uncomfortable with being there and hearing this. It seemed a weird thing for a mother to say about her daughter. She couldn't imagine why Gray would have been jealous of her own mother—especially when it came to creepy Michael Warner. Gray had plainly loathed the man.

Julia's mouth trembled as she tried to smile. "You're a very sweet girl, Brittany. You don't strike me as the kind of girl who would have been friends with Penny. You're so . . . normal. What brought you together?"

"The writer's workshop last summer."

"You're a writer too?"

"Not like Gray. She was really good. But you probably knew that."

"Penny didn't share her writing with me."

"Oh. Well . . ." Brittany brightened as the idea struck her. "You'll have all her poems now. You can watch the videos!"

"Videos?"

She pulled the duffel bag around and unzipped it and dug around inside to pull out Gray's MacBook.

"Everything is on here," she said enthusiastically as she opened the laptop and turned it on. "Gray recorded everything. She was always shooting videos and taking pictures and recording stuff on her phone. I used to give her a hard time about it, but now . . . I guess it was a good thing after all."

The computer came to life with a musical *ta-dah!* and a screen full of purple flowers.

"You're familiar with her computer?" Julia asked.

"Yeah. I have the same one, but I mostly use my iPad now," she said. "I can show you how to get to everything on it. It's not hard."

"I'm afraid I'm not very good with technology."

"This is easy," Brittany said, typing in Gray's password.

"You know her password?"

"We made them up for each other last summer."

And she hadn't changed it, Brittany noted, despite the fact that

Brittany hadn't been a very good friend to her in recent months. Guilt sharpened its claws on her a little bit for that.

"Did she share that with a lot of people?" Julia asked. "That doesn't seem like very good security."

"I don't think she shared it with anybody else," Brittany said, refraining from saying that Gray had no one else to share her password with, unless it was with one of her coffeehouse friends. Britt didn't know any of them.

She swept the cursor around the screen, pointing and clicking until she came to the page she wanted.

"These are all the poems she posted to YouTube," she said, scrolling through the list of videos. She clicked on one at random and turned the sound up.

Suddenly, Gray was looking at them both, and her voice came out of the computer's small speakers like a ghost.

```
I'm not who you see
I'm me
Face is a mask, a shell
You think you know me
You don't
Ink and steel is a suit of armor
A test to sort the worthy
You don't like me?
Good
Close the store, lock the door
I'm saved.
Saved the trouble, saved the pain.
```

The poem said a lot about who Gray had been, and why. It only occurred to Brittany belatedly the impact the words might have on Gray's mother, who had never been able to get past her daughter's defenses—and maybe had never really tried. Gray had said her mother hated everything she had ever done to express herself—her hair, her piercings, her tattoo, the way she dressed.

Julia Gray brushed stray tears from her cheeks, her hands trembling.

"I'm sorry, Mrs. Gray. I didn't mean to upset you," Brittany said. "I just thought that you'd be able to see her again and hear her voice."

And be reminded of every fight they'd ever had and every reason they hadn't gotten along.

"It's okay, Brittany," she said. "It's not your fault my daughter shut me out of her life—especially lately. I don't know what made her so angry, do you? I wish I understood. Did she share things with you? Her feelings, her life. Did she tell you things?"

Brittany shook her head. Gray had never been one to confide. She was too guarded. She best expressed herself through her poetry, and even in that she cloaked her pain and experience in verse. She had always spoken in riddles, alluding to experiences and ideas Brittany knew nothing about. She had always put it off to Gray being Gray, an artist.

But even as she thought that, Gray's words to Christina came back to her from that night at the Rock & Bowl. The thing Christina had made her promise not to tell. It wasn't true, Christina had said. Just a cruel lie from an angry Gray, striking out with her best weapon: her words. Brittany wondered now if that was the truth or if Gray's words had been the truth.

"Brittany?" Julia Gray asked.

How could she say it? It probably wasn't true. Julia Gray wouldn't want to hear it. What purpose would be served in repeating something said in anger, designed just to cut the other person as deeply as possible?

She could see it in her mind's eye, though, like a scene from a movie: Gray almost nose to nose with Christina, her expression as vicious as her words. Christina's eyes going wide in shock, then narrowing to slits like the eyes of a snake.

I fucked your precious father.

Christina's father. Julia Gray's fiancé.

"No," Brittany said, pushing to her feet. She couldn't look at Julia Gray now. "She didn't tell me anything. I should probably go," she said. "I need to get home."

Julia stood and went with her to the foyer.

"Thank you again for coming, Brittany. You're a kind, sweet girl," she said. "I'm glad to know Penny had a friend like you."

She embraced Brittany tightly, with more emotion than seemed appropriate, and a strange chill went through Brittany just before Julia Gray said, "I'm so sorry. I really can't let you go."

46

"I'm sorry I don't have a trunk for you to fall out of," Fitz said as he put Dana Nolan in the back of the van.

She had finally given up and succumbed to the relief of unconsciousness. He went on speaking to her anyway. She was like a doll now, a thing he could play with. She couldn't answer him. She wouldn't scream, didn't move, didn't react, didn't resist. She was more inanimate object than human.

"Then again," he said, "that was really sloppy. That was what really pissed me off—that they would think I would be that careless and that sloppy. That was offensive to me.

"I've been doing this a long time," he told her. "And with great success, I might add. But here's the thing with being that good: No one knows. Genius wants recognition."

He covered her with a blanket, just in case. Couldn't have someone looking in the window while they sat at a stoplight. Those were the kinds of stupid, sloppy mistakes that ended with incarceration.

The key to success was riding that fine edge of the ego.

He had been the tactical master for a long time. Tonight he would take it to the next level: art.

Euphoria filled him as he got behind the wheel of the van and started the engine. Tonight the world would be his stage, Minneapolis would be his canvas, Dana Nolan would be his masterpiece—a living piece of art.

They wanted to credit him with a zombie.

He would give them a zombie.

47

Brittany tried to pull away, but Gray's mother held her, saying over and over, "I'm so sorry. I can't let you go. I'm so sorry."

"Stop it!" Brittany said, struggling. "You're scaring me!"

She tried again to pull away. Julia Gray grabbed her hair in each fist, fingernails digging into her scalp, and gave her a rough shake.

"Be still! I can't let you go!"

"Oh my God."

Brittany started to cry, huge tears slipping from her eyes, but she made no sound. She should have been screaming, she thought, but there was a part of her that couldn't believe what was happening. This couldn't be real. She had to be imagining it or misinterpreting it.

Her brain struggled and scrambled to make some kind of sense of it. Julia didn't want her to go because she was lonely, because she was missing her daughter. *I'm the only one who's come to say they're sorry. I'm the only friend her daughter had.* She was just overreacting to the stress of losing her child.

I'm just overreacting, Brittany thought. *She's not really trying to stop me from leaving.*

She tried to turn toward the door. Julia kept hold of her hair in her left hand and began striking her with the right, despite the fact that she had already injured that hand and wore a brace.

"You can't go!" she snapped. "Stop trying!"

The scent of liquor soured her breath.

"Let me go!" Brittany said. Shouted. Screamed. *"Let me go! Oh my God! Stop it! Let me go!"*

Frantic, she tried to scramble backward, her feet slipping and sliding on the floor. She kicked at her attacker. She slapped at her. She felt like a kitten pawing at a lion.

"Don't fight me!" Julia screamed. "Stop fighting me!"

Brittany twisted and tried to lunge for the door. Julia came with her, suddenly rushing forward instead of pulling back. Their legs tangled and then they were falling, the back of Brittany's head striking the heavy wooden door like a hammer.

Black spiderwebs flashed across her vision; then everything went dark as her phone silently vibrated against her belly in the pouch of her hoodie sweater.

R u home yet?

Kyle typed the words and sent the message and waited impatiently. He didn't like the idea of Brittany walking to Gray's house and back by herself. It wasn't far, and it wasn't a bad neighborhood or anything. He just thought a girl shouldn't go walking around by herself at night, especially with all the talk about serial killers in the news and everything like that.

He would have felt better being there with her. Even if he had just walked her over and back without ever going in to see Mrs. Gray. He wished he had thought of that sooner.

He walked around his room feeling like a tiger in a cage, watched by the life-size cutout of Georges St-Pierre mounted to the back of his bedroom door. St. Pierre in fight shorts, bare-chested, muscles bulging, a serious expression on his face, his hands resting on his hips. A stack of Japanese characters were inked on his left chest, expressing the nature of his character—saying that he has a good side and a dark side but that respect is the most important thing. Respect for self. Respect for others.

Kyle imagined he felt his hero's disapproval. GSP wouldn't have let a woman walk alone in the dark of night. Ultor, the hero Kyle had created, would never have neglected his duty to protect. What had he been thinking letting Brittany go alone?

Gray was dead. Murdered.

His mom and Sam were downstairs talking about a serial killer.

Kyle flashed back to the scene from the morning—the nasty look on Christina's face as she glared at Brittany from the passenger's seat of Aaron Fogelman's car, Fogelman's rage as he had come at Kyle swinging his fists with bad intentions. Christina was angry with Britt. What if she and her henchman decided to do something to her? He could still see Christina lunging at Gray that night at the Rock & Bowl.

His hands were shaking as sent another text.

Where R U? Pls answer!

But she didn't answer.

She was probably still talking with Gray's mom, he reasoned. Kyle wouldn't have had that much to say beyond *I'm sorry for your loss,* but he was a guy. Women liked to go on and on.

He stood by his window and looked out at the dark, seeing only his shadowed reflection looking back at him.

R U OK? He typed and sent and paced some more.

He stared at his phone until his eyes burned.

No message came back.

SHE DIDN'T KNOW how long she lay unconscious. Seconds? Minutes? Longer? She came to with a sense of floating. Or maybe she was dead. No. A hand was wrapped tight around her wrist. Her arm being pulled from her shoulder. She was being dragged, dragged across the floor, down the hall.

Adrenaline burst through her like a bomb exploding. In an instant she was struggling, flailing, scrambling. She yanked her arm free of Julia Gray's grasp and struggled to get her feet under her and get up.

Julia was on her in a heartbeat, grabbing her head, falling down on her, banging her head against the floor, over and over, shouting, *"Stop it! Stop it! Stop it!"*

Black splotches burst before Brittany's eyes with each hard smash of her skull against the floor. She would lose consciousness again if she couldn't get away. She gathered all her strength to roll and push and get the woman off her. Again she scrambled to gain her feet and try to run.

She was running in the wrong direction now, running toward the kitchen and away from the front door.

Julia dove onto her from behind like an animal dragging down prey, knocking her forward, knocking her down, knocking the wind from her. Brittany's chin hit the floor with a horrible, shattering pain in her jaw and inside her mouth as teeth broke. The bright metallic taste of blood flooded her mouth.

She couldn't move. She couldn't struggle. She tried to suck in air and choked on her own blood as Julia Gray kicked her and struck her again and again.

Beneath her, trapped against her stomach in the pouch of her hoodie, her phone vibrated, alerting her to another incoming text. She couldn't answer. She imagined the person on the other end waiting for her reply as she was being killed.

48

They had been sitting at the island in her kitchen for long enough that her butt was starting to go numb, going over notes and reports and interviews until they were bleary-eyed.

Nikki had Penny Gray's cell phone usage details in front of her, looking at the calls and text messages sent the night of her disappearance and the days following. After the night the girl had gone missing there had been only a couple of messages sent and received.

"This doesn't make sense to me," she said. "She went missing the night of the thirtieth. She stopped calling and texting friends. I don't know about the other kids, but I know Kyle continued to text her right up until we ID'd her body. He never got an answer from her. He never heard from her after she left the Rock and Bowl."

"I think she was dead that night," Kovac said. "Dead or incapacitated."

"But if her killer had her phone, why bother to answer the mother's text messages and no one else's? If the idea was to toy with her loved ones or, for whatever reason, try to make it look like she was still alive, why not answer a friend's text? It's not like it's hard just to acknowledge a text. *OK. Not now. Fuck off.* Whatever. Why only answer the mother?"

Kovac pulled his reading glasses off and cleaned them with the tail of his wrinkled shirt. "I don't know."

Nikki paged through the records. Penny Gray's phone use had been covered in a family plan. The service records they had gotten from the carrier included both Gray cell phones, mother and daughter. Nikki turned the page to the usage attributed to Julia Gray's phone.

She thought back to what Sam had said about Julia Gray having left her phone in the car the morning she had made the appeal to the media downtown with Captain Kasselmann. She remembered when he'd said it thinking, *What mother of a missing child forgets their phone someplace?* She had forgotten about it after that. They'd had so much going on, had gotten pulled in so many different directions. This was the kind of investigation they could drown in. Too many details, too many people, too many possibilities. It was too easy for things to slip through the cracks as their attention was pulled one way then the other.

She sighed and twisted her neck against the stiffness setting in. She looked at Julia Gray's phone records now, looked at the dates and times and numbers called and text messages sent, and a sick feeling began to swirl in the pit of her stomach, stirring the gallon of oily coffee she had drunk.

"What?" Kovac asked.

He could feel the change in her energy. She hadn't moved, hadn't said a word. He just felt it. They had been partners for that long.

"Kyle texted this girl over and over after she went missing," she said. She looked at her partner, seeing her concern mirrored in his face. "Why didn't her mother?"

The moment hung between them, a thick tension vibrating with a dark sense of something too close to excitement.

"She wasn't looking for her, Sam," she said, glancing down at the paperwork again. "Even after she knew Penny was missing, Julia Gray wasn't looking for her daughter."

"But the girl's phone went dead or got turned off at some point," Kovac said.

"That doesn't stop her mother's phone from working."

In a flash every conversation Nikki had had with Julia Gray went through her head. She saw her expressions, heard the emotions in her voice. She thought of the mixed messages of guilt and blame and self-absorption. She relived the moment Julia Gray had struck her, hard, with a hand she had already injured somehow. She thought of how she had described Aaron Fogelman earlier in the evening: narcissistic with violent tendencies. The same could be said of Penny Gray's mother.

"Something set this all off," she said. "They were going along, consistently miserable. What changed?"

"The engagement," Kovac said.

"Let's assume the molestation," Nikki said. "Her mother gets engaged to the man who molested her. That's got to be the biggest fuck-you ever."

"There's a confrontation," Sam speculated. "Things get out of hand."

"If what we think is true, Penny had the capacity to ruin Michael Warner."

"Warner is the better suspect of the two. Seriously, Tinks. You're a mother. You think a mother could do that to her own child?"

Nikki frowned. Her head was throbbing. "I don't know. I don't want to think so, but people lose their minds. Her daughter was a burden, a problem, a thorn in her side. She finally gets a shot at wedded bliss with a doctor, no less, and her daughter had the capacity to ruin that for her."

"That's about as fucked-up as it gets," Kovac said. "Maybe she didn't try to reach the girl because she didn't want her to come back.

She could hate the kid and want her gone, but she didn't want to hear you telling her her daughter was dead."

"She was pissed off," Nikki said. "Maybe she didn't want to hear it because she never wanted anybody to find that body. Who knows where Penny Gray would have ended up that night if the DOT had fixed that road. Maybe Julia was one giant pothole away from committing the perfect crime."

"Mom, can I go out?"

Nikki looked at Kyle as he came into the kitchen, her brain shifting gears awkwardly. He was in his coat and putting his watch cap on.

"No," she said. "Of course not. It's late."

He gave her that look of incredulity perfected by teenagers everywhere. "But, Mo-om—"

"Where do you think you have to go all of a sudden?"

His cheeks flushed. He wanted to look away from her, but he didn't. "I can't get Brittany to answer my text messages. I've sent her a million of them. She hasn't answered. I'm worried about her."

"And you're going to track her down?" Nikki said. "That's called stalking. No. Absolutely not."

"You don't understand!" he said. "She said she would text me and she hasn't."

"Kyle—"

"She said she would text me when she got back, and she should have got back by now. But she hasn't texted and she isn't answering. I even *called* her," he said, as if that was the surest sign of desperation. "She's out alone and there's some crazy serial killer running around loose! She shouldn't have gone by herself. I was supposed to go with her."

"Go where?"

"To see Gray's mom."

49

"We can't let her go, Michael!"

"Oh my God, Julia. What have you done?"

"She had Penny's computer. They were friends. She knows every-thing!"

The voices brought Brittany's consciousness rising to the surface like a leaf floating up from the depths of black water. The pain in her face and her head was so terrible, she couldn't even feel the rest of her body. Blood pooled in her mouth. She could feel chips of broken teeth against her tongue. She wanted to cry out, but she couldn't move, couldn't open her mouth, couldn't seem to form sound.

"Oh my God." The man's voice was strained, frightened. "What are we going to do? Look what you've done, Julia!"

"But I had to. Don't you see that? If Penny told her. If she wrote about it on her computer . . . I had to, Michael. To save us."

"Us," the man said, incredulous. "Oh my God."

"You have to help me," she said. She sounded almost childish.

"We can't do this, Julia," he said. "I helped you with Penny. I had to. I know you didn't mean for that to happen. That was— That was a—a tragedy. She was your daughter. She pushed you to it. You snapped. I understand that. I understand why. But this? This is murder."

"And it's your fault," Julia said bitterly. "You know it's your fault. You slept with my daughter!"

"One time! It happened one time!" he said. "I made a mistake. I told her it could never happen again."

"She would have ruined you! She would have ruined *us*! You thought you could buy her off with a car? She would have held that over our heads for the rest of our lives!"

Brittany tried to move—just her fingertips, just her toes. She lay on the floor. She opened her eyes to the narrowest of slits. She could see tile, a piece of a rug, the tip of a shoe.

As she slowly became aware of her body, she became aware of lying on something, something pressing into her stomach. It vibrated against her. Her phone.

She lay with one arm outstretched, the other half beneath her. If she could get to the phone . . .

"Penny was an accident," Michael Warner said. "You acted in the heat of the moment. This is murder, Julia! I can't help you kill an innocent girl!"

"Then what are we supposed to do, Michael? She'll ruin our lives! We can't let her go now!"

There was a long silence. He moved, walked away. Brittany could hear him pacing.

She tried to lift her belly from the floor, to slip her hand into the pouch on her sweater.

"If we take her to the lake house," Dr. Warner said quietly. "We can put her in Penny's car . . . and run the car into the lake. Oh my God, I can't believe I'm saying this! This is insane!"

"We don't have a choice!" Julia whined.

"No," he murmured, "we don't. God help us."

50

"We were going to go together," Kyle said. "To give Mrs. Gray our condolences, you know, tell her we're sorry about what happened to Gray. Then you asked me not to," he said, looking at his mother. "But I should have gone with her anyway. I could have just walked her over there. She had some stuff of Gray's. She wanted to take it back. Clothes and stuff Gray left at her house."

"Clothes and what stuff?" Sam Kovac asked.

Kyle shrugged. "I don't know. Makeup. Her laptop. Stuff."

Kovac swore under his breath and rubbed his hands over his face. "Brittany has had Gray's computer all this time?"

"I guess."

Kovac looked at Kyle's mom. "That first night we talked to her, Brittany told us Gray had stayed a couple of days and then left. We just assumed she took her stuff with her. Her mother said she carried her computer with her everywhere. If she left Brittany's house, why wouldn't she take her stuff with her? We assumed the laptop was with her, in her car or that whoever killed her took it. It never occurred to me—"

"It doesn't matter now," Nikki said.

She was punching a number into her cell phone. Her hands were trembling. Watching her, Kyle felt more nervous and more nervous. She pressed the phone to her ear, avoiding eye contact with him and turning toward Sam.

"She's not answering," she said.

Kovac got off his stool.

"What's wrong?" Kyle asked. "Who's not answering? Britt?"

"Sam and I will drive over and make sure Brittany gets home."

"I'll come with you," Kyle said.

"No. You stay here with R.J."

"He can stay with Marysue. I want to come—"

"I said no," his mother said in a tone of voice that meant he shouldn't ask again.

Kyle followed them into the hall. Sam was shrugging into his coat.

"But, Mom—"

"Stay here with you brother," she said, grabbing her coat from the hall closet. "I'll call you."

51

She should have been dead. After everything he had put her through, she should have died hours before. He had done things to her she could never have imagined, would never have wanted to know one human being could be capable of doing to another. She had tried to resist the overwhelming desire to break down mentally but had learned resistance was rewarded only with pain. The pain had been like nothing in her most terrible nightmares. It had surpassed adjectives and gone into a realm of blinding white light and high-pitched sound. There were no words. She had ceased to fight and had found that in seemingly giving up her life, she was able to keep her life.

Where there is life there is hope.

She couldn't remember where she had heard that. Somewhere long ago. Childhood.

Where there is life there is hope.

Those words had played through her head over and over. They played through her head now as she lay there on the floor of the van. *Where there is life there is hope.*

She was more alive than he knew. In giving up, she had reserved strength. She had stopped him short of rendering her completely incapacitated. She could still move. She could still think.

The cold floor beneath her was numbing the pain. The blanket thrown over her offered a cocoon, a place to be invisible. Her wrists were only loosely bound together in front of her with a red ribbon, her elbows bent, her hands tucked beneath her chin as if in prayer.

Prayer. She had prayed and prayed and prayed.

No one had come to save her. And yet, she should have been dead, but she wasn't.

He was singing in the front seat, happy, elated, proud.

She was his masterpiece.

She was alive.

She moved her hands and felt the ribbon loosen.

Where there is life there is hope. Where there is life there is hope. . . .

The van hit a pothole, jolting her world, rocking her violently side to side. And next to her the collection of tools he had brought bounced and rattled in their open tote.

Where there is life there is hope. . . .

FITZ WAS EUPHORIC. High as a frigging kite. He didn't even bother to curse this wretched pockmarked stretch of road that was going to ruin his wheel alignment by the time they arrived at their destination. It didn't matter. Nothing could spoil his mood. He turned the radio up and sang along.

He had chosen his perfect spot , the perfect stage for his show. Fucking genius, that's what it was. Every major news outlet in the country would be flocking to Minneapolis to cover the story. He would be the subject of a *Dateline NBC* special.

He had chosen the Loring Park sculpture garden for the setting of what would be his most famous tableau. Amid the huge and whimsical works of art he would present his masterpiece, wrapped in a beautiful bow no less.

He smiled and laughed and glanced in his rearview mirror to check on her.

His smile died. His laughter caught in his throat.

His eyes met the eyes of a zombie.

52

Michael Warner picked Brittany up off the floor like she was a rolled-up rug or a corpse already. Better if he thought she was, if he thought she was dead he wouldn't have to kill her.

The pain in her head was like an explosion. Every muscle in her body tightened against it. She pressed her hand hard against her stomach, holding her phone tight against her. If it wasn't broken, if she could see to use it, she could call 911 from the trunk of the car.

She had never imagined being so terrified in her life. She had never imagined what that felt like, what that did to the body. She was trembling all over. She had wet herself. Nausea choked her like a ball in her throat. Dizziness swam her head in circles.

Michael Warner swore as he carried her. Julia Gray kept telling him to hurry. *Who might know the girl had come here?* she said. Someone could come looking for her. They had to hurry. They had to get rid of her quickly. They would say they had been out for the evening, that they had never seen her. She must have been snatched off the street.

Dr. Warner swung sideways and Brittany's feet hit the frame of the door as he carried her into the garage. Julia Gray stood beside the car. *Hurry, hurry, hurry!* He dumped Brittany like a bag of trash into the trunk of the car, threw a blanket over her, and shut the lid.

They were going to kill her. These people who seemed so ordinary. Parents of kids she went to school with. Michael Warner was a doctor. Brittany had come to this house to give Julia Gray her sympathies. It was all so crazy, she wanted to think it wasn't real. She must have been dreaming, having a nightmare. And yet it was all too real.

Her heart was racing wildly. She could hardly see the illuminated screen of her phone through her tears. Her hands were shaking so badly, she couldn't work the keyboard. Fingers on her left hand were broken and useless; only her thumb was functional. Over and over she tried to get the numbers keyboard to come up. Nine-one-one. That was all she needed, but she couldn't do it.

The car dipped as someone got into it and started the engine.

They were going to take her someplace, put her in Gray's car, and run the car into a lake.

Brittany managed to hit the phone icon. Contacts came up. The letters were a blur. She tried to hit a name. Whoever answered could call 911. If she could speak. If they could understand her. She touched the screen again and again, but nothing happened.

Nausea swept over her like a crashing wave, and she had to turn her head and vomit. The pain in her broken jaw was like being hit with a hammer over and over. She cried and retched and choked on her own blood and vomit. Her ribs hurt so badly from being kicked, she could hardly draw breath. Panic followed the nausea, another wave to drown her. She had to fight to keep from dropping the phone. Her hands were shaking so violently she thought she might fling the thing away.

She was too young to die.

She touched the screen again and a list came up. She couldn't read it.

Her fingers shuddered against the glass.

Oh, please, God, please, God, please!

She could hear the garage door opening. The car lurched backward.

She could hear a phone somewhere ringing at the other end of her desperation.

Please answer, please answer, someone, anyone.

The voice that answered was familiar.

"Britt! Where are you?"

Kyle.

She managed the only words she could.

"Help me."

53

The words of Kyle's text message seemed to leap off the screen of Nikki's phone: *MOM HURRY!!!*

Kovac drove. Pedal to the metal, careening around corners, running red lights. They were in his own personal vehicle. They had no dash light. They had no siren. They had no radio.

Nikki used her cell phone to call for backup and braced a hand against the dashboard as they hurtled through the streets. For once, she didn't complain about Kovac's driving. She egged him on.

It wasn't that far to Julia Gray's house as the crow flew. Driving was another matter. One-way streets, stoplights, pedestrians, cars double parked. It would have been faster to fucking run. A child was in danger.

"If she's hurt that girl, I'm gonna fucking shoot her!" she said.

"I'll get rid of the body," Kovac growled as they made a hard left onto Julia Gray's street.

They were going too fast. The car skidded sideways on the rutted, icy pavement and the rear passenger quarter panel pounded hard into the front end of a BMW SUV parked at the curb. It was like hitting a tank.

"Fuck!" Kovac shouted as they came to a hard stop.

Headlights were coming at them from the end of the street.

He gunned the engine and spun his wheels, the cars locked together where wheel met wheel.

Nikki scrambled out the door and ran toward the oncoming vehicle.

Weapon in hand, Kovac planted himself in the middle of the street beside her.

Both of them were shouting at the tops of their lungs.

"Police! Police! Stop the fucking car!"

The car kept coming.

KYLE HAD NEVER run so hard or so fast in his life.

He stayed in the street when he could, avoiding snow banks, cut through yards when he had to, jumped fences when he had no choice.

The cold air burned his throat and lungs. He was freezing cold and sweating all at once. His legs felt huge and heavy with the buildup of lactic acid, but he kept running. He kept running and thinking of Brittany.

He was never going to forgive himself if something bad happened to her. He never should have let her go to Gray's house alone. He didn't know what could have happened to her there. All she had been able to say over the phone was *Help me,* and that was muddled and garbled. If not for her name showing up on the screen, he never would known the caller was her.

What could have happened to her? What was happening to her right that minute as he was running? He couldn't even really know where she was, he realized. He only knew where she had been. If she had been taken, she could be anywhere. In his imagination he saw her getting grabbed off the street by the serial killer they called Doc Holiday.

How crazy would that be? She would be kidnapped by the maniac who had killed Gray, the maniac his mom was trying to catch. And she would be in the clutches of this madman because Kyle hadn't gone with her to and give her condolences to Gray's mother.

It wasn't that far to Gray's house. A mile, maybe. The longest mile he had ever run. If he got there too late, he was never going to forgive himself.

THE DRIVER JERKED the wheel at the last second, trying to shoot between them and the tangle of crashed cars on the side of the street. The Lexus slid sideways on the icy ruts created by the herd of news vans that had clogged the street just the day before.

Metal crashed on metal as Julia Gray's car plowed into Kovac's.

The car alarms were screaming. A horn was blaring. Nikki ran toward the mangle, gun outstretched in front of her.

The passenger's door opened and Julia Gray flung herself from the vehicle looking dazed.

Nikki shouted at her: "Up against the car! Get up against the car, you fucking bitch!"

The woman looked at her with wide, blank eyes. "What's happening?"

"I'll tell you what's happening," Nikki barked. She grabbed Julia Gray by one shoulder and spun her around, shoving her roughly up against the Lexus. "You're under arrest. Where's the girl? Where's Brittany? Answer me!"

"I don't know! I don't know what you're talking about!" she cried.

Michael Warner was sobbing as Kovac hauled him out from behind the wheel of the car. "She's in the trunk! Oh my God! I'm so
sorry! I'm so sorry!"

"Not as sorry as I'd make you if I could," Kovac said. He dragged
the doctor by his coat collar away from the car, shouting, "Get down
on the ground!"

Sirens were wailing as radio cars sped toward them.

A man came running from one of the houses shouting, "I'm a
doctor! Is anyone hurt?"

Nikki had hold of Julia Gray by a handful of blond hair. She
leaned in close and spoke directly into her ear. "If you killed that
girl, I will personally see you in hell."

IT LOOKED LIKE a scene from a *Die Hard* movie, Kyle thought as he
turned onto Gray's block—a chaos of flashing strobe lights and uniformed officers, sirens and voices, and cars clogging the street at odd
angles. Crashed cars and an ambulance.

"Britt!" he shouted, wide-eyed with terror. "Brittany!"

A uniformed cop tried to stop him from running into the middle
of the madness. Kyle feinted right, then ducked left and ran past him.

"Kyle!" his mother called. She caught him by one arm and hung on.

Someone had been put on a stretcher that was being wheeled
toward the ambulance. Kyle didn't recognize the face. It was bloody
and swollen and misshapen. A girl, he guessed by the hair—blond
hair.

"Brittany!"

His mom wrapped her arms around him and held him in place
as he tried to lunge toward the ambulance.

"She's going to be all right," his mom said. She reached up and turned his face toward her and said it again. "She's going to be all right, Kyle. She's alive. She's alive."

Kyle stared at her, not knowing what to do next. He was shaking and sweating, and there were tears in his eyes.

"It's going to be all right," she said again, putting her arms around him.

Kyle hugged his mother as tight as he could, and they stood in the middle of the street and cried.

54

Nikki walked beside her son through the waiting room of the Hennepin County Medical Center ER. Post–New Year's madness, it was a slow night. Assorted drunks and junkies, people who thought the common cold was a medical emergency.

"I can't believe any of this happened," Kyle said as they walked outside, where flurries had begun to fall like crystals in a snow globe. "It's like a crazy nightmare."

"I wish that's all it was," she said, rubbing a hand slowly up and down his back—as much to comfort herself as to comfort him.

Kovac had gone back to the office to get the paperwork started on Julia Gray and Michael Warner, letting her bring Kyle to the ER to see that Brittany would be all right.

Fractures to her chin and jaw would require surgery, and she had a concussion and several broken fingers and fractured ribs, but she would recover physically faster than she would recover from the trauma of what had happened to her. That would be a much longer battle.

With her mother sitting beside her in the exam room, stroking her hair, Brittany had answered what questions she could, barely able to speak, mostly using her uninjured hand to indicate yes or no. With her mother's heart breaking for the girl, Nikki kept her questions to the bare minimum. Yes, Julia Gray had attacked her. Yes, Michael Warner had been a party to it. Yes, they had talked about Julia Gray having killed her daughter.

When she was done asking questions of Brittany, Nikki asked Mrs. Lawler if Kyle might see her daughter for a minute. Standing beside Brittany's bed in the exam room, Kyle had earnestly promised her he would be there for her through her recovery.

Nikki thought she would die of pride and love for him.

Now they stood outside the ER doors. Nikki breathed in the cold night air and wished it would cleanse them both of what had happened that night.

"Gray's mom killed her," Kyle said. "How could that happen? How could she kill her own kid? Over what?"

Nikki didn't know what to tell him. There would be a long explanation made by psychiatric experts at Julia Gray's trial. Explanations of Julia's personality disorders and the stresses of raising a difficult child, of tainted family dynamics and how normal needs and desires could morph and twist into something grotesque. Some expert witness would cast the blame on Penny Gray, painting her as a seductress who had tried to usurp her mother's dominant position by sleeping with her man. They would beg for mercy and understanding for a woman who "just snapped."

And all of it was just a fancy way of saying that people could be selfish and people could be evil, and even if your only real desire in the world was to be accepted, life could fuck you up in the blink of an eye for no reason that made any sense to anyone.

All she could say to her son was "I don't know."

Kyle gave her a long look. So quiet, so internal. She always had to wonder what was going on inside him, but she had never wondered that he didn't have a good heart.

"I love you, Mom," he said.

"I love you too," Nikki said. She looked up at him and reached up and touched his cheek. "I love everything about you. Don't you ever think I don't. Even when you make me mad, I love you so much I can hardly stand it."

A radio car was waiting at the end of the ambulance bay to take them home.

"When this is over, I'm going to take a hot bath and sleep for an entire day," she said as they walked toward the car. "But when I finally come to, we're going to talk about spending some serious family time together. How does that sound?"

"Sounds good," he said. "We miss you, you know. When you work too much. We miss you, me and R.J."

"I know," she said. "I miss you guys too. We're going to fix that. I promise."

But the promise would have to wait.

Kovac stood beside the radio car with a grave expression.

He put a hand on Kyle's shoulder. "The officer is going to give you a lift home, sport. I need your mom."

Nikki didn't ask the question until the squad car had pulled out. And then it wasn't a question, but a statement.

"Dana Nolan."

THE SCENE WAS already awash in artificial light by the time they got there. At a glance it appeared to be a traffic accident. A nondescript panel van had run head-on into a light pole on an otherwise dark stretch of service road leading to the Loring Park sculpture garden. Police vehicles blocked off the scene. Kovac pulled in behind one, and they got out to walk the rest of the way.

A young uniformed officer hustled toward them and filled them in as they walked.

"He told her she was his masterpiece!" he said excitedly. "It's fucking sick. You'll see."

"She's alive?" Kovac asked.

"She's messed up. In and out of consciousness. They're loading her in the bus now. She just keeps saying 'I'm his masterpiece' over and over. Apparently, he decided he wanted to leave a living victim, but she was a little more alive than he realized."

Kovac's breath caught hard in his throat at his first sight of Dana Nolan. The perky morning news girl was unrecognizable, her face battered and cut and misshapen. Her tormentor had drawn a huge red smile around her mouth. She looked like a clown from a macabre nightmare. Her eyes were glassy and flat, like doll's eyes, and she babbled incessantly.

"I'm his masterpiece. I'm his masterpiece."

Kovac swore under his breath. Liska gasped and looked as shocked and shaken as he had ever seen her as the EMT drew back the sheet that covered the girl.

She was naked except for a wide red ribbon tied around one wrist, the long trailing ends fluttering in the cold breeze. The number 9 had been carved into her chest with a knife.

"Quinn was right," Kovac said as they watched the crew load the girl into the ambulance. "He didn't kill Penny Gray, and he didn't want credit for it. There's his ninth girl, right there."

"It's fucking sick. I told you," the uniformed officer said, leading them toward the van. "But you have to see the rest."

They stopped under the pool of white light washing down from the bent light pole and looked into the van from the passenger's side.

"License says his name is Gerald Fitzgerald," the officer said. "The van comes back to a Gerald Fitzpatrick."

Kovac made a sound that was part laughter, part disbelief as he looked at the driver and said, "Frank, we hardly knew you."

The man they had known as Frank Fitzgerald, the man who had reported the body of Rose Reiser a year past, sat slumped over the wheel of the van, his face turned toward them, eyes open, a screwdriver buried in his temple.

"He finally made his mistake," Kovac said. "Happy holiday, motherfucker."

55

"It only happened once," Michael Warner said. He sat with his elbows on his thighs, his head in his hands, ashamed to look up, to see Kovac staring at him, to see his own attorney looking away in embarrassment and disgust. He had spent the last ten hours in a holding cell and looked like he hadn't slept in a week.

"She came to my office upset, heartbroken, sobbing. She'd had a terrible fight with her father. It was always the same thing with Penny. So antagonistic, a tongue like a razor. She would push and push, then be crushed by the outcome. She dared people to love her and then couldn't understand when they didn't."

"So she came to your office . . . ," Kovac said. He sat with one arm resting on the table, looking bored, he suspected. Looking like he'd heard this story a hundred times. He had, in fact. The story of the young girl and the grown man who couldn't help himself. It still made him want to puke. But it didn't serve his purpose to let that show.

The lawyer spoke up for the third time. "Michael, I'm going to advise you again not to do this."

"Shut up, Harold," Warner said.

He was trembling visibly though the room was like a sauna and he had sweat through his shirt.

"That was both infuriating and heartbreaking," he explained. "To see her crushed like that. I have a daughter of my own. I can't stand to see her disappointed."

Did you fuck her too? Kovac wanted to ask, but he said nothing.

"I wanted to comfort her," Warner said. "That's all I meant to do."

And now would come the part of the story where the girl started to move against him, and then they were kissing, and one thing led to another, and he just couldn't help himself . . . with a child.

He started to cry, then fought it back and wiped his face with his hands.

"I told her it could never happen again," he said.

Because, of course, it had been her fault. Blame the victim. He couldn't keep his dick in his pants, but it was the girl's fault. A messed-up sixteen-year-old girl whose father rejected her and mother resented her. She was supposed to be the one in control.

"But . . . ," Kovac prompted.

"I don't mean to make it sound like I'm not taking blame," Warner said, looking up at him. "I know it was wrong."

But . . .

"Penny was a very manipulative girl. She understood power."

And now, the seductive-temptress part of the story. Kovac heaved a sigh.

"What happened the day she broke her wrist?" he asked.

"She threw a tantrum. She came to my office with the intent of us . . ." He didn't want to say "having sex." The idea was disgusting to him now—or so he wanted to pretend.

The man of integrity standing up for what was right.

"She blew up. She started hitting me. I grabbed her arm to stop her. She tried to pull away . . . I was sick about it."

"Did Julia know?" Kovac asked.

He shook his head.

"I didn't want her ever to know. I care about her. I truly do. There was no reason for her know any of it. It was just a terrible mistake. I stopped seeing Penny as a patient . . ."

"And started seeing her mother."

Warner said nothing.

And he bought the girl a car to shut her up. And he had probably kept fucking her on the side because she had probably blackmailed him into it. And that was why she hadn't told anyone else. Kovac could have spun the story on and on into yet another sordid quilt of human perversion.

"What happened the night the girl died?"

The attorney stepped forward. "Michael, please . . ."

Warner turned away from him and looked across the table at Kovac. "You have to understand it happened in the heat of the moment. She just snapped."

"Julia?"

"You have to understand what a struggle she's had with Penny these last few years. Her whole life, really. One defiance after another. She was at the end of her rope."

He stood up to move around, his hands on his head, his hands on his hips, his arms crossed in front of him.

"Why is it so hot in here?" he asked, rubbing the back of his neck. "I feel nauseous."

"I don't think that's the heat," Kovac said. "You need to sit back down, Dr. Warner."

"Penny was upset about our engagement," he said, coming back to the table. "She was at the house when we got back that night. She'd been drinking. She was belligerent."

He paused and looked off at the wall as if he were watching the memory play there like a movie on a screen.

"They were in the kitchen. I was standing at the doorway to the hall . . ."

"SHE SAID, 'How can you marry him when I fucked him first?'"

Julia Gray stared at the table, her eyes vacant and glassy.

Liska sat across from her. She glanced up at the one-way mirror, knowing a prosecutor from the county attorney's office stood on the other side.

"That must have been a terrible shock," she said.

"She had said it before. The night she left. We fought," she said, absently rubbing her injured wrist. "I called her a liar. I told her to get out. Do you have children, Detective?"

"I have two boys."

"Boys are so much easier." She sat for a moment chewing at a thumbnail. "With girls, everything is a fight, a competition; they want to control and manipulate. It's exhausting. She was *relentless*."

She was a child.

"When she said it that night, Michael was behind her," she said. "I could see his face."

"You realized she was telling the truth. What happened then?"

Her eyes darted all around the room as if following the flight of some tiny frantic bird. Her attorney sat quietly, offering nothing. They would go for some kind of insanity defense, Liska imagined. Diminished capacity: the inability to know the difference between right and stabbing your own child to death because your boyfriend molested her.

"I don't know," Julia said, though her eyes filled with tears. "I don't know. I don't remember. It was like a nightmare. I still can't believe any of it happened."

Liska picked up Penny Gray's iPhone and tapped her way to the screen she wanted. The phone had been found in Julia Gray's kitchen. Kyle and Brittany had both said Gray had made videos of everything with her phone—her performances, her poetry, her few friends . . . her own murder.

"Maybe this will jog your memory," she said, touching the Play icon. She put the phone on the table and pushed it toward the woman.

Julia appeared on the screen, angry, her face contorted with rage, screaming, "Shut up! Shut up! You're lying!"

Her daughter's voice behind the camera: "I fucked him first! How do you like that, Mommy? Your precious fiancé. He's nothing but a fucking child molester!"

"I hate you!" Julia screamed, her face nearly purple, her eyes bulging. "I hate you, I hate you, I hate you!"

There was no question at all what happened next. They didn't need Julia Gray's memory or Michael Warner's eyewitness testimony. It was captured there on her daughter's phone: Julia grabbing a short knife off the kitchen counter and lunging at the girl, screaming and slashing.

The picture went topsy-turvy as the phone fell to the floor. The rest of the video was of the ceiling, but the audio went on and on and on. The screams, the pleading, the horrible sounds of a horrible crime. Michael Warner shouting in the background, "Julia! No!"

Across the table, Julia Gray's eyes went wider and wider. Her whole body began to shake violently, as if she were being given jolt after jolt of electricity.

"*Oh my God. Oh my God! OH MY GOD! PENNY!!*"

Scream after scream tore from her throat. Her eyes rolled back in her head and she fell to the floor, convulsing.

"SHE GRABBED A KNIFE and just started stabbing her," Warner said. "It was surreal. I couldn't move. I couldn't believe it was happening. It was all a blur."

"Really?" Kovac said. "She had seventeen stab wounds. It takes a while to stab someone seventeen times."

He raised his fist and brought it down on the tabletop once, twice, three times, four times. Over and over and over. Michael Warner flinched with each blow. Seventeen of them.

Penny Gray would have ruined him. He had thought about it every day, that a bitter, angry, hurt child had but to say something to the right person and his life would unravel like a cheap sweater.

"Why didn't you call the police?"

Warner rubbed a hand across his forehead and shifted on his chair, his agitation growing.

Now came the hard part of the story. How could he explain away what they had done next? A crime of passion happened in the heat of a single moment. Nearly twenty-four hours had passed between the murder of Penny Gray and her body falling from the trunk of Julia Gray's car.

"It was too late," Warner muttered. "The girl was dead. Julia was out of her mind. I had to help her. I felt responsible. What good would it have done to call the police? It happened in the heat of the moment. She just snapped. Julia doesn't deserve to go to prison. She's not a killer."

Kovac said nothing. His silence was a greater condemnation than if he had pointed out the truth. Penny Gray was dead at the hands of her mother. Julia Gray was a murderer. She was a murderer who had then attacked Brittany Lawler.

"I had to help her," Warner said.

"What did you think?" Kovac asked. "That you could just get rid of the body and no one would notice the girl was gone? People would think she just ran away? No one would give a shit?"

All of the above.

The saddest part of that was that he was probably right. Penny Gray had a reputation of running away, of being defiant. Anything could happen to a girl like that.

"You had to help her," Kovac said. "You had to make the girl un-recognizable, so in the event her body was found, she would be just another Jane Doe. Probably a runaway. And take half her clothes off while you're at it, so it would look like a sex crime. She was probably turning tricks and crossed paths with a bad, bad man."

Warner hung his head.

"Turns out, she did," Kovac said. "You know, *Doctor*, she wasn't dead."

He waited for Warner to look up at him, his expression a mix of suspicion, confusion, and panic.

"She may have been almost gone," Kovac said. "I hope so. But she wasn't dead when you poured that acid on her face. The autopsy showed she had both inhaled and ingested it. You need to know that. You need to think about that. Every damn day for the rest of your miserable life."

Warner turned gray. Sweat rolled down his face and he began sucking in gulps of air.

"You watched your girlfriend murder her child," Kovac said. "You took the girl's body into the garage and poured acid on her face while she was still alive.

"Ironic, isn't it?" he said, getting up from his chair. "Doesn't that doctor's oath you take say do no harm? I guess maybe you didn't read that part."

Kovac left the room, closing the door on the sound of Michael Warner vomiting.

Tinks stood in the hall, leaning back against the wall with her arms crossed over her chest. She looked as disgusted as he felt.

"I need some air," he said.

"Me too."

They went out on the steps on the south side of the building. The sun was shining its weak winter glow, too far from the earth to be of any real good to Minnesota in January. Liska shoved her hands in the pockets of her purple wool blazer and hunched her shoulders up to her ears. Kovac flipped the collar of his sport coat up, a token defense against the wind. He dug a cigarette out of his pocket and lit it.

"Does that get rid of the taste?" Liska asked.

He shook his head. "No."

They stood in silence for a moment.

"Why do you think she kept the video on the phone?" she asked.

Kovac shrugged. "She probably didn't realize what she had. The girl never says anything about the camera running. She would have just been standing there holding the phone in her hand . . . Julia said she wasn't very good with gadgets. By the time she picked that phone up after everything that happened, the screen was probably blank. . . ."

They went silent again as both of them played the whole thing through in their heads for the millionth time.

"They'll go away for a long, long time," Tinks said at last.

"How long is long enough?"

"There's no such thing."

Kovac took another long drag on the cigarette and blew a stream of smoke toward the sky. "Gotta hope there's a special place in hell."

"At least we get to say we sent them there."

"That's something."

"Is it enough?" she asked. "I don't know, Sam. I look at this— Julia Gray took the life of the child she brought into the world and threw it away so she could have what she wanted. I look at my boys, and all I want is to spend time with them. We know better than most people, it can all be gone with one bad decision, one wrong turn off the freeway."

Kovac gave her a long look. "Are you gonna leave me, Tinks?"

"I don't know," she admitted. "I don't know what to do. I just know these are years I don't get back with them. There are no do-overs.

"I love what I do," she said. "And I love the people I do it with. But I love my boys more."

"You're gonna do what you need to do," Kovac said, one side of his mouth curving upward. "I might not like it, but what else is new?"

"You'll be miserable without me."

"I'm miserable most of the time with you," he teased.

She squinted her eyes down to mean little slits and punched him on the arm as hard as she could.

"Ouch!"

He pinched out his cigarette and threw it away.

"Before you leave me, let's go have a drink for Penny Gray."

Liska nodded and sighed. "All she ever wanted was to be accepted."

"I guess that's what we all want deep down," Kovac said.

"I accept you, Kojak," she said, mustering a little humor. "In spite of your many flaws."

"That's big of you, Tinker Bell," he said. "I accept you too. I mean, who else would have us?"

They turned and started back inside, mutually frozen.

"Hey, partner," she said. "After we get that drink will you go with me somewhere?"

"Sure. Where?"

"I want to get a tattoo."

Kovac chuckled and put an arm around her. "That's my girl."

Leabharlanna Poibli Chathair Baile Átha Cliath

Dublin City Public Libraries

ACKNOWLEDGMENTS

Every four years I donate a special opportunity to the fundraising auction for the United States Equestrian Team Foundation: the chance to appear as a character in one of my books. Proceeds from the auction go to help fund our Olympic equestrian team.

The winner of the 2012 auction was Ullrich Kasselmann of Performance Sales International. Based in Hagen, Germany, P.S.I. is renowned as one of the largest and most famous auctions of international quality show horses in the world. Mr. Kasselmann himself is a longtime fixture in the horse business as a top rider, trainer, and supporter of the industry. My thanks to Mr. Kasselmann and everyone at P.S.I. for their incredible generosity in supporting the USET Foundation. And to Dr. Ulf Möller, also from P.S.I., happy birthday from Betsy Juliano!

For the purposes of the story, Mr. Kasselmann is playing the part of Minneapolis Homicide Captain Ullrich Kasselmann. Dr. Ulf Möller appears as assistant chief medical examiner of Hennepin county. And P.S.I. has become Performance Scholastic Institute. Sorry there wasn't a horse to be seen in this book!

My cup runneth over with generous people this time around. I also need to thank Mr. Kevin Boyle, who purchased the same privilege for his fiancée, Marysue Zaytoun, with the proceeds going to the American Heart Association. I hope Marysue enjoys her fictitious stint as Nikki Liska's wonderful neighbor!

Author's Note

In *The 9th Girl*, fifteen-year-old Kyle Hatcher both experiences bullying and crusades against it, supporting the acceptance of others regardless of race, religion, interests, or sexual preference. Kyle's hero and role model is real-life hero and role model, Ultimate Fighting Championship mixed martial arts welterweight champion of the world Georges St-Pierre.

GSP, as he is known to fans around the world, is the shining example of what a champion should be: dedicated, driven, hardworking, generous, a gentleman, and, above all, respectful of himself and others.

As a boy growing up in Saint-Isidore, Quebec, Canada, St-Pierre experienced bullying on a daily basis. As one of the most famous mixed martial artists in the world today, he now works through his Georges St-Pierre Foundation to bring awareness and solutions to the epidemic of bullying in contemporary society.

Please visit GSP's website, www.gspofficial.com, for more information on his foundation and for links to other excellent sources of information on fighting the good fight against bullying, such as www.stopbullying.gov, www.bullying.org, and www.stompoutbullying.org.

Blackpepper & Seasalt.

ABOUT THE AUTHOR

Tami Hoag's novels have appeared on national bestseller lists regularly since the publication of her first book in 1988. Her work has been translated into more than thirty languages worldwide. She is a dedicated equestrian in the Olympic discipline of dressage and is an avid fan of mixed martial arts and Brazilian jiu-jitsu. She shares her home with two English cocker spaniels in West Palm Beach, Florida.

Find Tami Hoag on Facebook at www.facebook.com/TamiHoag and on Twitter at www.twitter.com/TamiHoag.

Or at www.tamihoag.com.